Detroit

The Veil: Book One

J.N. Smith

jnsmithcontactme@gmail.com

To E, S, and E. I love you.

Chapter One

Day 1 // 9:44 a.m.

ONE HUNDRED AND twenty miles per hour. How had she never noticed it before?

Who the hell makes a minivan that can go that fast?

Not that she was going *quite* that fast.

Jane pressed the horn, and it blared.

She glanced at the speedometer as the needle climbed—*Oh god.*

"Ninety-two miles an hour," she whispered. *On a surface road.* A belt whined beneath the hood as the hula dancer she bought in Hawaii the previous fall twerked on the dashboard.

She could see the headline now, "Jane Moore, forty, wife of attorney Thomas Moore, was apprehended Tuesday morning…"

Sweat dripped between her breasts, soaking the band of her bra.

Rush hour was over. Why was there so much traffic?

She checked the rearview, pushing her blond hair from her face, wondering where the police were. Shouldn't they be onto her by now? Shouldn't there be a train of flashing lights and wailing sirens?

She peered over the steering wheel into the empty gray sky. Shouldn't there be a helicopter or *something*?

Jane glanced down at the speedometer again as the engine of her Grand Caravan strained.

Ninety-three miles an hour.

It had to be some sort of record, because no woman in her right mind would ever go more than eighty-five in a fucking minivan.

Adrenaline surged as she raced through another red light. That made four total—not that she was counting.

Jane honked as she cut off a car that had started through the intersection. Its tires squealed on the pavement. She dug her nails into the steering wheel as she swerved around the back of a Ford Fiesta. Her heart banged against her ribs, and she pressed a hand briefly to her chest, trying to steady it. It didn't work.

"Come on, get out of the way…" she mumbled to herself, slamming the heel of her hand into the horn again.

Almost every instinct told her to slow down before it was too late. But she didn't because the one driving her on was stronger than the rest combined. She glanced in the rearview, then back to the road. And it urged her to go faster.

Two miles to the freeway, she noted as the sign flew past.

Thank god.

"Get out of the way!" she yelled, as cars continued to crawl in front of her. Her head felt like it was going to explode as she weaved between them.

Robert.

"Get out of the way!" she shouted again through the windshield at a white pickup slowing down in front of her.

Robert had told her she had—she glanced at the clock, quickly calculating the minutes—less than fifteen minutes to escape.

Escape what?

Jane pushed her hair back again. Well, that was unclear at the moment, but there were only three people on earth she trusted implicitly. Her husband, her sister, and Robert. If he told her to get out of the city—Jane slammed on the brakes as a maroon sedan pulled onto the road in front of her—he must have had a good reason.

Her phone slid off her thigh and onto the floor.

"Shit," she hissed.

The van lurched as she punched the gas again. The V-6 engine groaned beneath the strain.

Jane threw her palm into the horn, swerving around more cars. It reminded her of an arcade game she'd played as a kid, only much less fun. She reached down for her phone, brushing her hand across the carpet. The van veered across the yellow line, and her heart skipped as she swerved back into her lane and sat up.

Careful, Jane.

"Mom?" a voice asked from behind her.

Jane adjusted the mirror and glanced back at her son. Tommy was strapped in his car seat behind her. His eyes were wide and blue like his dad's—and he looked like he was about to throw up all over his favorite T. rex T-shirt.

Jane reached down again, trying to keep her eyes on the road, as she felt around for her phone.

"Everything's okay bud." It wasn't okay. Not even close.

There! Her fingers finally found it and the screen lit up in her hand, revealing Thomas's handsome face. It was a photo she had snapped last summer at the Tiger's game they had taken Tommy to. She had bought the boys matching jerseys. It had been a rare, fun day as a family.

Jane pressed the green call button again. It went straight to voicemail.

Was he in court? He wasn't supposed to be.

"Damn it." She dropped the phone in her lap, and tugged at the front of her sweatshirt, trying to release some of the heat as a familiar, terrifying sensation swept through her body.

Jane checked the rearview. The pupils of her brown eyes were saucers.

Not good.

Her head felt too light.

You cannot have a panic attack now.

Her vision began to swim, and she gripped the steering wheel tighter. Unfortunately, her daily dose of Xanax was at home, sitting on the counter beside her uneaten bowl of oatmeal.

Jane reached between the seats for her purse and her emergency supply, but her leather handbag was not there. Had she forgotten it? She chanced a look back and saw that it had rolled back between the seats. Then she remembered.

Thumping the steering wheel, she blinked back tears. "Damn it," she whispered again.

She had forgotten to fill the emergency pill box *again.*

Jane wiped her eyes and tried to remember how to breathe.

Fight it, Jane.

"Mom?" Tommy whimpered.

She clutched the steering wheel, trying to remember the mantra her therapist, Dr. Sanchez, had told her to repeat when she was first diagnosed with panic disorder almost twenty years ago.

"Let go of thought." The van swerved onto the on-ramp, and Jane shook her head. This was never going to work.

Find your stillness.

If she could breathe, she would have laughed. Except in an airplane, this was the least 'still' she'd ever been in her *life*. The seat belt tightened across her chest as they sailed around the giant loop that led to the freeway.

And let it pass.

The lane straightened out and air whooshed out of her lungs as she merged into the northbound traffic.

Jane blinked in disbelief. They were on the freeway.

Inhaling deeply, she flexed her fingers on the wheel. "Breathe, Jane," she whispered to herself.

In. Out.

In. Out.

Slowly, her lungs found their rhythm again as they headed north in the light mid-morning traffic.

Jane mopped her feverish forehead with her sleeve and flipped on the air-conditioning as she searched the rearview mirror. Unbelievably, there were still no police.

"Holy shit," she said under her breath.

Her phone buzzed in her lap. Jane glanced down hopefully, but it wasn't Thomas.

It was Maggy McCarthy, her neighbor, and tennis partner at the gym. She was late for their weekly match. Jane's finger hovered over the green button.

What would you even say?

She'd tell her the truth. She couldn't make it to tennis today because her old thesis advisor and long-time friend had called her this morning, frantic, saying her family would die if she didn't get them out of the city immediately.

Then, no.

Jane hit the red 'ignore' button.

Keeping one hand on the steering wheel, she anxiously tried Thomas again, praying he would pick up. She ground her teeth, and her head throbbed as the call went straight to voicemail.

She tried again.

Voicemail.

She sighed and dropped the phone into her lap.

The highway stretched out in a blessedly straight line as they headed north, and it didn't take long for the suburbs to give way to flat, green fields. Thick groves of maple and birch dotted the landscape the further they went. Jane relaxed her fingers a little on the wheel—thankful and surprised that the freeway was nearly empty.

A familiar red barn zoomed past her window. It had been there since she was a little girl. As a child, that barn had marked the transition from city to country in her mind. Had she made it?

Jane rolled the window down and inhaled deeply. It certainly didn't smell like the city.

As the wind whipped through her window, the adrenaline quickly wore off. Jane blinked as if waking from a dream only—

It wasn't a dream.

The stark reality of everything she had done hit her at once.

"Oh, god." She fought off another wave of panic as she adjusted the rearview mirror and met the eyes of her red-headed seventeen-year-old niece in the back seat. Maddy was gripping the back of Tommy's car seat as if her life hung in the balance. For a few minutes there, perhaps it had.

Jane cringed as the sound of squealing brakes echoed in her head. "Oh, no." How many accidents had she just caused?

She met her own reflection again. Had she just committed every moving violation known to man in a van full of *kids*? "Shit."

Jane glanced back at Tommy, his skin pale against his adorable, six-year-old freckled face. The kids. *That* was the instinct that had driven her. The fierce need to protect them. The terrifying fear of something bad happening to them if she didn't act quickly. It outweighed everything else, including the voice of reason, which had taken the back seat with Maddy as Jane had barreled through each intersection.

She turned back to the road and tapped her thumbs nervously against the steering wheel. But now that they were safe, the question was, protect them from what? What could possibly be back there that would kill her children if she didn't flee? An escaped lion from the zoo? A meteor? World War Three?

Nothing? That possibility was like an ax against her skull, blinding Jane for a moment. Instinctively, she hit the brakes. The van and her stomach lurched simultaneously, as everyone was flung forward against their seatbelts. In the passenger's seat, her nephew Austin cried out and threw his hands up against the dashboard.

She jerked her foot back. "Sorry," she wheezed. "Are you okay?"

"Aunt Jane?" His blue eyes begged for answers to questions he looked too afraid to ask. *Why did you take us from school? Where are we going?* Despite being only twelve, he acted more like a grown-up than most adults she knew. But right now, he looked exactly like Tommy—wide-eyed and terrified.

Vomit lurched up her throat. *Oh god.*

Jane quickly signaled and crossed onto the shoulder. The van rolled to a stop on the side of the highway. She unbuckled her seatbelt and threw the door open just in time to bend over and spew her morning non-fat latte all over the ground.

"Mommy?" Tommy whispered again. "Are you okay?" He hadn't called her that since he started kindergarten last year.

Jane squeezed her eyes closed at the approaching sound of wailing sirens. *Ah, there they are.* She wiped her mouth with the back of her hand as she clung to the door. No. She wasn't okay. This was it. Mommy was either going to prison or a mental health facility for a very long time.

Her eyes flew open in disbelief as three state troopers went barreling past them on the southbound side of the road. They weren't after her? Jane was so relieved she almost laughed.

"Sorry about that." Jane forced her voice to steady as she sat up and adjusted her seatbelt.

She gagged on the taste of sour milk and tried to cover it with a cough. "The milk in my coffee must have been bad." She glanced at her niece in the mirror again. "Maddy, try your mom again, will you? I… I need to talk to her."

Jane turned and gave Tommy's leg a comforting squeeze. It did nothing to change his fearful expression. She took in the mess on the floor.

Her purse had spilled as it rolled. Two pacifiers, breath mints, several pens, and about two dollars in loose change covered the floor. She reached for the breath mints. Her hand shook as she popped one into her mouth. The diaper bag had overturned too, and Bria's bottle was dripping onto the carpet. Jane glanced at her infant daughter—thankful she was still asleep. One chunky little leg hung out of her llama pajamas. Jane pulled the blanket out of the diaper bag, spilling a container of Cheerios as she draped it over her baby. Then she picked up the bottle, turned back around, and placed it in the cupholder.

Calm down, Mama.

Jane took a deep, minty breath and pushed her hair back out of her face again. Yes. "Calm down," she mumbled.

She grabbed her phone from between her legs and dialed Thomas again. She was in a *lot* of trouble. But he was the best defense lawyer in Detroit. He would know what to do.

"Hello, you've reached the personal voicemail of Thomas Moore…"

Jane hung up and buried her head in her hands for a moment.

Stay calm.

She took another deep breath—she was trying to—then put the van in drive. Glancing over her shoulder at the nearly empty freeway, Jane merged back into the slow lane.

"She's still not answering," Maddy called from the back.

Jane met her niece's eyes in the mirror.

"Look up the number to her yoga studio. Call them. Tell them it's an emergency."

"Emergency?" Maddy's voice shook as she continued to cling to Tommy's seat.

"Just do it." Jane snapped.

Tommy whimpered quietly behind her. Jane rubbed her eyes, then glanced at Austin, who was braced for the next impact.

Stop scaring them.

She winced. "Hey, are you guys hungry?" she asked, knowing how insane she sounded after everything that had just happened. At least she sounded how she felt.

Is that what this is? Have you finally lost your mind?

Jane's breath stuck in her throat. Had she imagined Robert's call? She had *thought* she was crazy before, but it turned out her medication…

There is always a first time.

With one eye on the road, she scrolled frantically through her call log.

She exhaled in relief when she found it. Nope. Not delusional.

Robert had called at 9:26 a.m. Their conversation had lasted twenty-two seconds.

At least there was that. When the police finally caught up to her, at least she could point to her phone, and say '*He* started it.'.

Jane checked the rearview mirror again. Strangely, there were no cars behind her at all—not one. The freeway was completely empty.

She called Thomas's office again. No one answered, which was odd, because at the very least, his secretary should be there. She tried his cell again, and—

"Watch out!" Austin cried.

She dropped her phone as a car appeared in front of them out of nowhere, driving about thirty miles an hour. Jane slammed on the brakes and swerved. The man in the other car was staring at his phone. She honked as they sped by.

"Jesus Christ," she breathed as her anger surged.

This was all Robert's fault! Had *he* suffered a mental break? He seemed totally sane the last time she saw him, but that was six months ago at Christmas. That was plenty of time for him to lose his damn mind.

"Shit." She thumped the steering wheel. Why hadn't she thought to call him back until now?

She checked the rearview mirror again and dialed his number.

An emotionless woman's voice spoke. "I'm sorry, but the number you have reached has been disconnect—"

"Aunt Jane!" Austin cried as the tires crossed the rumble strips. Adrenaline surged again, making her hot and cold all at once.

Jane jerked the van back on the road and glanced at her phone, to make sure she'd dialed the right number. A picture of Robert in his typical khaki pants and sports coat, with his arm around her shoulder, smiling, filled the screen. How could his phone be disconnected when they had spoken less than an hour ago?

"Aunt Jane?" Maddy's voice pierced her thoughts.

"Did you get your mom?"

"She's not there."

Jane looked down at the clock, then rolled her eyes skyward.

What was with the world today? It was Sarah's regular yoga time. "What do you mean, she's not there?"

"The lady that answered said she didn't know anyone named Sarah McIntyre…" Maddy said, shaking her head.

That wasn't possible. "Downward Dog. That's the one you called? It's on Woodward."

Maddy nodded.

Jane pinched the bridge of her nose, trying to control her frustration. "Was she new?" Sarah had been going there every Tuesday for the past… well, since before Austin was born. How could they not know who she was?

"I–I don't know."

"Try her cell again," Jane ordered.

"Mommy?" Tommy asked.

"What?" she snapped.

"I'm scared."

She briefly squeezed her eyes closed.

Come on, Jane. You are better than this.

"I know, bud," she said, checking her tone. "I'm a little scared too, but we're okay. Just take care of Bria for me, okay? Does she have her paci?"

"She's sleeping. Where are we going? Where is daddy?" His voice wobbled, and Jane could tell he was trying not to cry. So was she.

Calm down.

Jane inhaled deeply through her nose. "I don't know. I just…" She blinked back tears and tried Thomas again.

Voicemail. Jane wished she had a wall to bang her head on.

She waited. "Thomas," she whispered. "Please. Drop whatever you are doing and meet me at the cabin. Either something bad is about to happen, or…" Jane lowered her voice. "I've just really fucked up. Either way… It's important. I need you." She ended the call.

"What's happened?" Austin asked. "Is my mom going to be okay?"

"I'm sure it's just a… misunderstanding," Jane shook her head. "We'll figure it out. We're going to go to the cabin to wait for your mom and Uncle Tom. Okay?"

Chapter Two

Day 1 // 10:03 a.m

MATT AND EVERYONE else in the small diner on the outskirts of Detroit stared at the tiny TV that hung in the corner next to the 2-for-1 Coney Island hot dog sign. The volume was low, but in the absolute silence of the restaurant, every word the news anchor said was loud and clear.

"This footage is from only moments ago. Some kind of electric barrier has appeared out of nowhere, surrounding the city of Atlanta. It has cut Atlantans off from the rest of the country. The sudden appearance of this mysterious 'veil' is causing massive traffic accidents city-wide…"

"What the fuck?" Matt said to himself. He rubbed his hands over his tired, brown eyes, and frowned as he met the glare of the old woman sitting at the booth across from him.

He grabbed his wallet out of his jacket pocket and pulled out a twenty. His breakfast hadn't even arrived yet, but he threw it on the table anyway as he downed his coffee. The bitter liquid burned his mouth and throat. "Shit." he choked, coughing. The old lady gave him another disapproving look.

His chair screeched against the tile floor as he stood up. No one else moved as he grabbed his jacket off the back of the chair and slid his arms into the sleeves.

Matt pulled out his phone, zigzagging between the dozen tables, as he scrolled for the number of the local recruiting office. There was no way the Army would turn him away again. Not with a terrorist attack, or whatever this was. He found the number and dialed it. Matt held the phone to his ear and pushed the door open, as he stepped out into the cool June morning.

The line rang busy as he rounded the corner of the building onto his street.

He stopped cold.

"Holy fuck." Matt stared up at it, forgetting about the call. *There is one here too?*

It sparkled like sunshine through raindrops, tiny iridescent flashes dancing and popping as it stretched across the road. And it was enormous. He looked to the left and right, trying to see where it was coming from, but buildings, which it passed right through, blocked the view.

He dropped the phone in his pocket.

The shimmering curtain cut across the street, blocking access back to his apartment, which was half a block away.

There was a charge in the air. He could feel it through his coat. The static tugged at the hair on his arms. The alarming smell of burned flesh wafted in the breeze—bringing back painful memories of Afghanistan and Tony and—*This is not the time.* No. It wasn't. It never was.

Hesitantly, Matt stepped closer. He held out his hand, and his palm tingled. The news lady was right, it was some kind of high-tech, electric fence.

"What the fuck?"

He had seen some things during his time in the military, even some top-secret stuff, but none of it came close to whatever this was. He looked up, trying to see to the top. It was several hundred feet high.

He rubbed his scruffy chin, feeling like he'd stumbled onto the set of a sci-fi movie.

A squirrel darted across the street, ran directly into the "veil" or whatever it was, and disappeared. The sound it made on contact was a quick buzz, like a moth hitting a bug zapper, and the scent of char in the air intensified for just a moment before evaporating.

Matt jumped back, and his jaw fell open.

"What the hell? Where did it…"

Then he noticed the trees. Where the branches met the shimmering beam, it looked like they had been sheared with a giant chainsaw.

Matt stared, trying to understand what he was looking at. How could something so massive be constructed so quickly, without someone noticing? The veil stretched as far as he could see in both directions.

A flock of sparrows swooped overhead and caught his eye. Several of the birds disappeared with a faint buzz as they collided with the veil. He took another step back, heart-thumping, as dozens of feathers and bird bits dropped to the ground.

He scrunched his nose as he leaned down for a closer look.

A bird brain lay half-enclosed in its skull—looking like a mushy walnut in a shell.

Matt recoiled as he looked back up at the veil. Was he hallucinating? It was possible. He hadn't had a good night of sleep in over two years. He rubbed his eyes and looked again.

Nope. It was still there.

A car turned the corner with a squeal. Matt spun around and met the terrified eyes of an old woman through the windshield. Her bony white knuckles gripped the steering wheel as she drove past him.

Before he could even raise his hand in warning, she drove through the veil and vanished from the front seat. Matt stumbled back in horror and covered his ears as her car slammed into the sign in front of his apartment complex.

"What the—"

This can't be happening.

He took a step closer, then stopped as his skin prickled again. Matt ran his hands through his damp brown hair. He looked back up the street, trying to figure out what to do. His eyes ached in their sockets, and his head throbbed. One cup of coffee had definitely not been enough to deal with whatever this was.

Another car turned the corner, and Matt found his legs just in time.

"Stop!" he yelled, racing into the street. He slammed his fists on the hood of the black Impala and shook his head at the terrified woman behind the wheel. She looked about his age, late twenties. Her hair was covered in tinfoil—like she had rushed from the salon. "You can't go through it!" he yelled through the windshield, gesturing toward the deadly partition.

She yelled back, but he couldn't hear through the glass. Matt pointed to the smoking car that had just crashed on the other side.

She rolled down her window. "I have to! My–my mom is babysitting my son and they're saying there's some kind of attack—"

"You can't go through it." He shook his head.

A blue station wagon rolled up on the other side of the veil and stopped. A man in his seventies, and nicely dressed, exited the car. His brows scrunched together as his neck arched back to take in the veil.

He stared, as if mesmerized, then took a step toward it.

"Stay back!" Matt warned as his eyes fell again to the smoking car in front of his apartment. He should have stopped her. "Fuck," he growled to himself, kicking the ground in regret.

The old man's mouth hung open in disbelief as he took another step.

Matt waved his arms, coming as close to the veil as he dared. "Hey! Get back!" he ordered.

The old man met his eyes. "What in god's name is this thing?" he asked, his voice carrying perfectly through it.

Matt shook his head as a black pickup truck pulled up behind the old man. A man in his early twenties, with a sleeve of tattoos and a backward ball cap, stumbled from the cab. He pulled his phone out and held it out in front of him like he was taking a video. "Holy shit," he repeated over and over.

"Stay back. Everyone just… Stay back," Matt ordered again. "You!" he called to the tattooed man. "Go check on the woman in that car."

Was it like this everywhere? Matt retrieved his phone from his pocket. The screen was filled with alerts. His eyes landed on the list of cities. Dallas, D.C.… *Beijing.*

Every hair on his body stood on end.

It was happening all over the *world*?

This isn't terrorists.

He shook his head. No, it wasn't. It was something else.

The young man jogged back to the car and leaned down to look inside. "There's no one in here!" he called.

That was what Matt was afraid of. He ran his hands over his face. It also wasn't possible.

An engine revved, and Matt spun as the Impala sped past him.

"No!" he shouted, lunging for the trunk of the woman's car.

It passed easily through the veil, then quickly veered to the right and crashed into an enormous oak tree.

Matt froze as the echo of the impact and the crumpling sound of metal reverberated through his body. Images of Tony flashed in his mind again, and he tried desperately to keep them at bay. The men raced toward the car to help. "Goddamn it!" Matt bellowed, wishing he could punch something.

"She's gone!" the younger man shouted incredulously. "What the *fuck*? Where–where in the hell did she *go*?" His voice cracked with incredulity.

"Get back!" Matt shouted as the hood burst into flames.

The men ducked back, shielding their faces.

"She fuckin' disappeared!" The younger man shouted again, sounding like a teenage girl. "Holy fuck." He grabbed his head in disbelief. "What the fuck…"

"Damn it!" Matt yelled again. He met the eyes of the older

driver, who was once again staring at the shimmering curtain. "Do you live around here?" he demanded.

"On Elmwood."

"Just go home."

The older man nodded and headed quickly back to his car. He turned it around and left.

"What the hell is this thing?" The younger man asked, walking toward Matt.

Matt shook his head. "I don't know, but it's dangerous. Stay away from it. Go home."

"Fuck yeah, I'm goin' home," the other man nodded as he rushed back to his truck. His tires squealed as he made a U-turn and followed the old man down the street.

Matt spotted two Adirondack chairs on a front porch and ran to retrieve them. He placed them in the middle of the street in front of the veil, hoping it would deter anyone who might be stupid enough to drive through it. His hands shook as he pulled out his phone again and dialed 9-1-1.

He looked up as another bird disappeared with a zap. He had no idea what it was, but rule number one was pretty clear. *Don't fucking touch it.*

"Copy that," he mumbled to himself.

Chapter Three

Day 1 // 10:12 a.m

JANE SAW the sign for the local supermarket and took the exit.

They were definitely out of the city and she needed something for the kids for lunch and probably dinner, too. There would certainly be nothing at the cabin.

"You guys wait here. I'm going to go get something for us to eat," Jane said slowly, trying to sound calm.

On wobbly legs, she made her way into the store. She shivered as the cool, sterile air found its way under her shirt and across her sweat-soaked skin.

Picking up a basket, she went to the deli, trying to imagine how her conversation with Thomas would go when he showed up and demanded an explanation for why she had pulled the kids out of school and taken off like a damn psychopath.

She dropped a package of chicken breast and some cheddar cheese into her basket. Her eyes darted between the regular and whole wheat pita wraps. A familiar country song she hadn't heard in ages played softly from somewhere above her.

Regular? Whole wheat? Why couldn't she decide?

Jane pinched the bridge of her nose, attempting to ward off the massive headache forming behind her eyes, and took one of each.

"Aunt Jane?"

She spun around and her heart stopped. Maddy's face was pale and her lips were almost translucent as she stood under the fluorescent lights. Had the police finally shown up?

"Where are the kids?" Jane choked.

"In the van. They're fine," Maddy replied, her voice eerily flat.

"Then what—"

"It's this." Maddy held up her phone and Jane squinted at the screen.

It was an amateur video, taken through a window high above a freeway somewhere. Tall buildings from a downtown metropolitan area stood in the distance.

Jane watched as a car driving toward the city approached what looked like a transparent curtain that was somehow hanging across the road. The camera zoomed in as the compact sedan passed through it, untouched. A moment later, the car veered out of its lane and crashed head-on into the concrete median. The explosion that followed lit the screen like fireworks.

Jane's brows came together as she leaned closer.

Three more vehicles approached the sparkly barrier on the opposite side of the median, heading toward the camera and out of town.

"What am I looking..." Her voice trailed off as one car after another sped through. Each emerged on the other side intact, then veered off uncontrollably. "Oh, shit," said a man's voice through the speaker. Jane cocked her head to the side, noticing something odd.

"Did the people in that car just disapp—"

Her question was interrupted as the cars crashed one by one. Everyone on the busy highway began slamming on their brakes. Everything on the side of the road heading into the city came to a stop... Except for a semi-truck.

"Oh no," Jane said, pressing her fingers to her temples. *That is not good.* She resisted the urge to cover her eyes.

The eighteen-wheeler lost control, overturned, and slid sideways across the highway.

"Oh. Shit! Oh, shit!" The voice from the phone filled the quiet deli section.

Jane placed her hand over Maddy's icy fingers to steady the small screen and watched as the truck slammed into several cars, shoving them through the curtain. One car exploded as it slid to a stop in the pile-up on the other side. Seconds later, the rest were ignited. It was like the Fourth of July.

Just when she thought the worst was over, the camera panned to an SUV that had pulled onto the shoulder. A woman jumped out, ran toward the shimmery wall, and disappeared.

"Where did she go?" the video guy repeated as the camera darted around. It made Jane dizzy, but she could not look away. There was no sign of the woman. She was just gone.

"Where the fuck did she go? Did you see that? She just *disappeared*!" The cameraman shrieked as he zoomed back out.

Several other vehicles had stopped on either side of the roadway. A tow truck and a school bus pulled over dangerously close to the strange partition. A man jumped out of the tow truck and ran into the center of the road, waving for cars to stop.

It only took moments for the busy highway to become a parking lot. Hundreds of people got out of their cars and started toward the deadly *thing*. The tow truck driver and a woman began shouting and warning people back. The video ended abruptly.

Jane's hand fell across her mouth as her heart pounded in her ears. "Oh, my god."

She grabbed the phone and replayed the last ten seconds. White, hot fear raced through her veins as the woman from the SUV vanished a second time. That couldn't happen, could it?

"Where–Is this here?"

"I-75. Outside Atlanta." Maddy's voice trembled.

Jane's head snapped up at the wail of a siren. The basket and the wraps clattered to the ground as they rushed back to the entrance of the store. Several emergency vehicles race down the freeway past the store, back toward the city.

Both their phones buzzed.

Jane hoped it might be Thomas. Instead, it was a news alert.

"Fifteen U.S. cities under attack…" Maddy read the words

aloud as she thumbed the screen. "Washington D.C., Philadelphia…"

Jane scrolled down the list of notifications. There it was. *Detroit.*

Her vision swam as she fell onto the handle of the shopping cart beside her. So, it was true? And it was a *terrorist* attack? How?

"My mom…" Maddy whispered, looking up from her phone. Her eyes finally reflected the fear Jane had felt all along.

More emergency vehicles flew southbound down the freeway.

How could Robert be involved in something like this? It didn't make any sense.

Jane remembered one of his undergraduate biology lectures on human survival. "What if zombies took over the world?" he had asked, as she and the other students laughed. But he was serious. That had been their actual assignment. "I want to know how you would survive the end of the world. I want to know how you would save humanity from a biological invasion."

Jane had taken the assignment seriously, as she did everything else back then, and compiled data on diseases that spread via saliva —the same way zombies would presumably infect people. Then she analyzed it and made a detailed list of hypothetical procedures to combat the crisis and survive. Robert had been so impressed by her analysis it had prompted him to offer her a scholarship for grad school, and a research grant to further explore the spread of infectious—

Focus, Jane.

She blinked. Is that what this was? An invasion? By whom?

Hurry.

"Right." Food, water, and distance from the epicenter. That was step one. "Maddy, grab a cart. I need you to get as many gallons of water as you can, bleach, dish soap, hand soap, and toilet paper. Then get milk, the shelf-stable kind. Almond, coconut–I don't care. Grab anything along the way that comes in a box or a can. I need you to fill the cart. Do you understand? Then meet me in the front. You have ten minutes."

"Aunt Jane—"

"Please, Maddy. I'll explain later."

The girl grabbed a cart and took off running. Jane watched Maddy's red hair bounce as her sneakers smacked against the linoleum floor.

More sirens wailed as Jane gripped the handle of her own cart and headed into the store. For the most part, the surrounding shoppers appeared calm. Some had looked up curiously as more emergency vehicles passed, but most appeared unhurried as they browsed. They had no idea what had happened.

Jane squeezed her eyes closed in a momentary prayer to the universe.

"Please don't let it be zombies," she whispered as she raced toward the Rx sign on the far wall of the store.

Five minutes later, she had enough cough medicine and pain relievers to last a year.

Her phone buzzed again as she headed back the other way. Jane read the update while she steered her cart toward the pantry items. The noise in the store grew, and she knew other people were catching on. She grabbed a dozen boxes of mac and cheese, then pushed an entire row of soups off the shelf directly into her cart. The crash echoed through the store. She moved on, tumbling things into her cart—ramen, beans, rice… anything that would last.

She met the wide, fearful eyes of a woman holding a bag of mashed potatoes in one hand and her phone in the other. Jane glanced behind her, toward another younger woman. She wore the same expression.

All three of their phones dinged simultaneously, and Jane looked down. Paris and London had also been attacked.

Jane's head felt like it might float away as she quickened her pace. She veered her cart past the woman with potatoes, grabbing several bags as she rounded the corner and headed down the next aisle.

Her phone buzzed again in her hand. Her eyes caught the word, *'Beijing.'*

She grabbed cereal, peanut butter, and granola bars.

The phones around her dinged again.

Rome.

Jane grabbed boxes, jars, bottles and cans—moving too quickly to even read the labels.

A woman abandoned her cart and broke into a run for the door, and Jane knew she was out of time.

Delhi.

She tried to think—but the adrenaline surging through her blood made it impossible. So she blindly continued to shovel things into her basket.

"Watch where you're going." An older woman snapped as their carts collided. Jane stared as the woman pushed her glasses up on her nose, casually consulted her list, and headed down the aisle. Like Thomas and Sarah, the old woman's phone must be off, or maybe she didn't have one. God, how Jane wished she were that woman right now.

She almost laughed, but her phone buzzed again. *Istanbul, Moscow…*

Her smile faded.

…Dubai.

Jane broke into a run.

Maddy was already at the register, throwing cans onto the belt. Jane barely pulled her cart to a stop before it crashed into her niece. Then she remembered.

She smacked her forehead as sweat dripped down her back. "Shit."

"What?" Maddy asked.

"Keep going." Jane pulled her credit card from her wallet, spilling dollar bills onto the floor. Frantically, she scooped them up.

Handing Maddy the pile of bills and the card, she said, "I'll be right back."

Jane ran for a new cart, then down the aisles of the store, searching for the baby section. She had forgotten diapers. It was a gross oversight.

Diapers weren't in your zombie survival plan.

No, but it was rule number two of being a parent. Rule number one was never leave the house without the diaper bag. Rule number *two* was never go anywhere without checking to make sure there were diapers in it. The more the better.

She found the baby aisle.

Gasping, Jane ran to the middle and stared. How many boxes did one need to survive an invasion?

"All of them," she whispered under her breath.

She unloaded the entire shelf of size four and five diapers. Then she grabbed all the wipes she could fit in her cart and raced back to Maddy.

The other shoppers were making their way up to the front or abandoning their carts altogether and heading for the door. Thankfully, no one had gotten in line behind them.

It took three times as long to get through the line as it had to shop, and Jane almost lost her mind as the cashier swiped a can of cream of chicken soup five times.

"Forget it!" She snatched the can out of the woman's hand and threw it on the empty register behind her.

Not amused, the cashier pursed her lips in obvious annoyance, then looked at the total on the computer screen in front of her. "That will be 2465.98. Do you have any coupons or bottle slip—"

Jane swiped her card several times before it finally went through. The machine beeped its approval.

"Come on," she hissed, pulling Maddy by the elbow.

Jane pushed one cart awkwardly in front of her while pulling the other behind her. Maddy followed closely as they made their way to the automatic doors.

A woman in a blue vest ran past them, looking positively terrified. "Carole!" she shouted to the cashier. "They're closing the store. Something's happened in the city. I don't know what… We're all supposed to go home. Right now."

The blood drained from Jane's head, and she gripped the cart to keep herself upright. A voice came over the intercom to announce the store was closing, and everyone looked up.

As they shoved the carts through the doors into the parking lot, Jane fumbled with the keys. She finally found the button to open the trunk.

Austin's eyes were wide as they began to throw bags into the back.

People rushed to their cars.

"What is going on?" he asked, as he jumped out and ran around to help. "What is all this stuff for?"

A bag ripped and Jane swore as its contents spilled, and a can landed on her toe.

Engines roared to life around them.

Austin dropped to the ground and grabbed at the cans of peaches rolling under the van as Jane and Maddy continued tossing bags, one on top of each other.

Frantic shoppers cranked their cars into gear and sped away.

Tommy twisted in his car seat. "I wanna help—"

"No!" Maddy and Jane shouted at the same time.

As soon as the bags were in and the kids were buckled, Jane threw the van into reverse. There was a loud crash as she backed into the shopping cart she hadn't bothered to put away. No one said a word as she jammed it into drive and squealed out of the parking lot.

She was about to turn onto the ramp for the freeway when she noticed the gas gauge.

"You've got to be kidding me," she groaned, slamming her fist against the steering wheel.

Jane gripped the wheel and made a U-turn in the middle of the road. Everyone in the van let out a cry. Austin's head thumped against the side window, and she winced.

"Sorry. Are you okay?" she asked, splitting her attention between him and the road.

Austin nodded as he rubbed his head, and his eyes filled with tears.

"I'm sorry, buddy." She ruffled his hair as she headed back to the gas station she had just passed.

Jane heard a faint scream from the back seat and looked up. Maddy was once again glued to her phone. Swearing and the distinct sound of crumpling metal filled the van.

"Maddy, turn that down please," she asked as patiently as she could muster.

From her car seat, Bria *finally* began to cry.

Jane pulled up to the nearest pump, and the van jerked as she threw it into park and jumped out.

All the other drivers at the station were staring in disbelief at their phones. She would look later—once she knew the kids were safe.

"Austin, give Bria her bottle," she yelled through the open door as she fumbled in her pocket for her credit card.

A moment later, the crying stopped.

With shaking hands, Jane jammed her card into the reader, then shoved the nozzle into the gas tank.

More sirens flew by. Now she knew where all the police were.

She rose on her tiptoes to see if she could spot anything. Part of her expected to see the curtain, an explosion or… something. But there was nothing. Nothing but gray, Michigan skies. She tapped her foot against the concrete nervously while the dollar amount slowly climbed.

The van door on the opposite side opened, and Maddy crawled out and came around the side. "Aunt Jane, I'm scared."

Jane spotted a stack of red portable gas containers.

"Maddy, go buy one–No, two of those gas containers."

"But, my mom…"

"I don't know! I don't know what's going on. Just do it." Jane thrust a handful of cash into the girl's hand.

Maddy returned a moment later with the containers.

"Open them," Jane snapped.

The clerk came over the speaker, sounding thoroughly dazed. In a robotic voice, he announced the closing of the gas station.

Jane was halfway through the second container when the gas stopped and the lights at the station went out. She yanked the nozzle out of the tank, and Maddy opened the rear door and pushed several bags aside to make room. They shoved the containers in, then quickly closed the trunk. "Come on," Jane said, running around the van. "We have to hurry."

Once they were back on the freeway, Jane glanced in the rearview as the containers in the back sloshed—filling the van with the uncomfortable smell of gasoline.

There were still almost no cars on the northbound side, and now she knew why. Her throat constricted, cutting off her air supply. What if she'd been just a few minutes longer? What if she had taken the time to get Bria dressed properly and pack their bags? The edges of her vision darkened again.

Breathe.

"They're everywhere," Maddy whispered from the back seat.

Austin turned toward his sister. "What is?"

Jane sucked in a desperate breath. "Nothing." She gave Maddy a hard look. "It's going to be okay."

But it wasn't. Thomas was back there. Her sister was back there. All those innocent kids at Tommy and Austin's school were back there. She should have warned them. She wanted to, but… there just hadn't been time.

No one would have believed you, anyway.

Guilt stabbed at her stomach. Still, she should have tried. Right?

They would have ignored you or detained you, and you never would have made it out.

More emergency vehicles came into view on the southbound side, tempting her to speed again.

Jane's palms bounced against the steering wheel as she fought off another panic attack.

Breathe, Jane. Just get to the cabin.

Chapter Four

Day 1 // 11:55 a.m

"AUNT JANE?" Austin's hand gripped her shoulder, gently shaking it.

Jane blinked and realized she hadn't been paying attention to the road.

"Shit!" She jammed her foot on the brake and braced for an impact that never came.

Then she realized why.

They were parked. She released the brake, and her eyes darted around.

"Are we going to get out?" Austin looked at her like she had lost her mind.

For the second time, she wondered if she might have.

Jane blinked, recognizing the familiar brown log-siding and green-trimmed windows of their cabin.

She looked behind her at the yellow cottage across the street. They were already there? Where had the last hour and a half gone?

"How?" Jane stared back at the house in confusion, pulling the keys from the ignition.

She looked at Austin.

Bria began to fuss in the back seat, and Jane turned around to see the worried faces looking back at her.

Had she blacked out while driving a van full of kids?

"I have to pee," Tommy whined, straining against his car seat.

Jane unbuckled, then the kids followed suit. The side door

opened and Maddy climbed out. Her mouth was pressed together in a thin, worried line.

"Did you get a hold of…" Jane began.

Had she already asked Maddy that question? She couldn't remember. Her niece just shook her head.

Jane's legs wobbled as she stepped onto the grass. She had never held off a panic attack like this before. The cocktail of chemicals swirling in her blood made it feel like she might drop dead at any second. Maybe that's why she didn't remember the last ninety minutes. She unbuckled Tommy.

The hood of the van burned her palm as she leaned against it and made her way around the passenger side.

She held out the keys for Austin. They jingled in her shaky hand. "C–can you open the door? It's the butterfly one. Find Tommy's old playpen and set it up? Do you remember how? It's in the closet in the bedroom."

Austin nodded and headed for the door.

Jane paused before opening the van's side door. She stared at her reflection in the tinted window. Was this all a dream? Had she just imagined the last few hours? Who was this terrified-looking woman staring—

Bria cried out from her car seat.

Not a dream, Jane.

Jane yanked the door open and unbuckled her baby girl. She put Bria's leg in her jammies and zipped her up.

Carefully, she lifted the chubby ten-month-old into her arms. Bria's warmth seeped into her skin as her dark, little head rested against Jane's shoulder.

You made it.

Yeah, she'd made it, but… "Now what?" she asked herself.

The clouds had parted, and the sun danced between the branches of the sugar maple that towered over their property. The wind rustled the trees and somewhere nearby a robin sang. Its sweet melody reminded her, as it always did, of being a little girl and playing here with her sister.

Bria lifted her head and stared at her mom, as if she were contemplating the answer, then broke into a toothless smile.

Jane instinctively smiled back. But when she looked past the backyard, southward, toward the city, it faded.

What was happening down there?

What did the terrorists want?

She clutched Bria to her chest.

Were they safe there?

Chapter Five

Day 1 // 12:25 p.m

MATT HAD BEEN STANDING guard for over two hours, but the police still hadn't showed up.

They needed to barricade the roads before anyone else died. And he couldn't leave until they did.

He had also tried to call the recruiting office several times, but the lines were busy.

He paced the road.

Another car turned the corner, and he issued his spiel once again. "You need to turn around. You can't go through it," he said to the older couple after they had rolled down the window.

"But we live on—"

He shook his head. *Not anymore.* "You can't go through it. Do you know anyone on this side of it?"

"We were at church." the woman said.

Matt nodded. "Then you should probably go back there."

"What's going on?" the man asked.

Matt took a deep breath and sighed. "I don't know. But you can't touch that thing. Do you understand?"

The couple nodded, backed up, and drove away.

Matt's phone buzzed in his pocket. He pulled it out and pressed it to his ear.

"Mom?"

"Matty? Are you alright?" she asked, her voice filled with motherly worry.

"Yeah. I'm fine."

Another car turned onto the street and he raised his hand and signaled it to turn around. "How are you and dad?" he asked.

"We're on our way to you, actually."

Matt frowned. "What? No, Mom. Stay home. This thing is—"

"We are already in the city," she said. "We will be at your place shortly."

"What?" Matt stopped pacing and looked through the veil.

"Your father had a doctor's appointment this morning in Warren."

"Oh, god."

"It's okay for us to come, right? You don't have company?"

Matt rolled his eyes. "Fuck."

"If you do, we can—"

"No, mom. I don't have company but I'm… I'm on the other side of it."

"You're not ho—?"

Her voice was cut off. Matt pulled the phone away from his ear. The call had been dropped.

A few minutes later, his dad's rusty pickup turned onto the street and signaled to turn into his complex.

Matt waved his arms and yelled. His father finally spotted him and pulled up to the veil.

Only his mother got out.

"Don't get too close," Matt warned.

She just shook her head and looked like she might cry.

"Hey, mom. It's okay. I…" He pulled his hands through his hair.

She wiped her eyes. "I know." She smiled. "I'm just so glad you are out there."

Matt got his keys from his pocket and tossed them through. They landed at his mom's feet on the other side.

She bent down and picked them up.

"You guys can stay at my place until…" Matt glanced at his dad, still sitting in the truck. "As long as you need."

They stared awkwardly at each other.

"What was the doctor's appointment for?" he asked.

"Your father had a colonoscopy. I just came along for the ride." Her voice faltered. "To do a little shopping."

"I'm sorry, mom." His helplessness to do anything churned in his gut.

Another silence followed.

"So anyway, now that we have a minute, what have you been up to?" she asked with a small shrug.

Matt smiled. Everyone said he got his sense of humor from his mom, and it had to be true because his dad didn't have an ounce of humor in him.

"Oh, you know. Same old stuff." he said, playing along. They should have been having this conversation over a cup of coffee, not through—He looked up at the veil again, hardly believing it was really there. "I finished physical therapy last month. I've been working out, trying to get back into shape."

"You still want to go back? To the Army?" she asked.

"Yeah, I do. It's where I belong."

His mom nodded. "If anybody can do it, Matty, you can." She looked up as another bird flew into the sparkling veil and disappeared. "And they are going to need you now."

He hoped so. It would drive him crazy if he had to sit this out. His parents, however, just needed to sit tight. A thought occurred to him. "Hey, mom. I don't have much to eat at my place. There's a market two blocks down. Maybe you'd better go grab some stuff. You know, ah, coffee and whatever. Just—"

She looked like she might cry again. "I think I'd just rather stay here with you for as long as—"

The blast of a police siren pierced the air.

"Fuck," Matt ducked and spun around, blinking back tears of his own.

The officer rolled down the window of his cruiser. "You need to go home." He glanced at Matt's mom. "You too," he said. "It's not safe here, and the mayor has issued an immediate curfew."

"I live over there," Matt said, pointing through the wall.

"Well, you've got to find somewhere else to go. You can't stay here."

Matt looked at his mom. "Go ahead, Mom. Do what I told you. I'll call you later."

She hesitated. "I love you, Matthew."

"I love you too, Mom. I'll talk to you soon."

He met his father's eyes, and the old man immediately looked away and pretended to wipe a spot off the dashboard.

Once she was back in the truck, and they had turned around, Matt turned to the police officer. "What in the hell is going on? I called you guys like two hours ago."

The officer shook his head. "No one fucking knows. This thing is huge, though. It's like this everywhere. And it's completely surrounded the city. I have orders to clear out everyone within a mile of it. So, you've got to go."

"But those were my parents. I've got to—"

"Man, my *wife* is in there, and…" The officer's eyes got watery. "Fuck. Everybody's got someone in there. I'm sorry, but you need to clear out. I can give you a ride if you want."

Matt shook his head. "No thanks. I'll walk."

Matt headed up the street with no idea where to go. The farther he walked, the more cars appeared on the road. They were all headed in the same direction. Away from whatever the hell that thing was behind them.

He'd just found a bench and sat down when his mom called to inform him she was appalled by the lack of food in his house.

"Mom, I'm a single guy. I don't cook. I eat out. That's why I told you to go to the—"

"And those magazines in your bedroom? Matthew Albert—"

Matt winced. His best friend, Max, had got him a porn subscription for Christmas last year as a joke after he'd confessed he was having a bit of a 'problem' in the bedroom area. He had totally forgotten those were even in his nightstand. "What? I'm a guy. And I wasn't expecting guests. I'm sorry, Mom." He didn't even know why he kept them. Those girls had not helped anything, anyway. He changed the subject. "Were you able to get some stuff from the store?"

"Yes. A few things."

"Are you guys okay, then?"

"Yes. For now. Your father has the news on. They are telling everyone to stay inside. What about you? Where are you?"

"I had to clear out. I'm headed to the recruiting office now."

"I'm sure they'll take you back, but if you change your mind, you know you can always go home."

Yeah, no thanks. "Okay. Thanks, Mom. I'll talk to you soon."

Matt hung up and stared at the ground. There was no way in hell he was going back home.

The Army had to take him back. He had done everything they'd asked. He was in better shape than ninety percent of the recruits, and he had passed the physical. They *had* to take him back.

Chapter Six

Day 1 // 12:37 p.m

JANE SENT the older kids to bring the groceries in, while Tommy collected branches for the firepit in the backyard. She put Bria in her playpen in the bedroom, then sank into the worn beige recliner that had once belonged to her father.

She tried Thomas again, but he didn't answer. The lines had to be jammed, because not even he would ignore twenty missed calls and not call her back. Maddy couldn't get through to Sarah either, and she was in absolute hysterics about not receiving any communication from her boyfriend—not that Jane cared about him at all.

She looked around the room. Unlike her home, everything at the cabin was worn and mismatched. Dark wood cabinets hung in the kitchen. A light oak dining table and four random chairs sat between the kitchen and the side door. Wood paneling lined the walls, making it feel like a cave, and brown shag carpeting that had been there since Jane was fourteen covered the floor in the living room and bedroom. A couple mismatched crocheted blankets hung over the back of the couch, and a rather bad painting of the Edmund Fitzgerald, a freighter that had sunk in the Great Lakes, hung over the TV.

Jane sighed and tried Robert's number again. It was still disconnected. She tried to email him, but the internet on her phone wasn't working. Absolutely nothing would load. Finally, she gave up.

A small flat-screen television sat on an old TV stand she and Sarah had carved their names into when they were five and seven.

Hesitantly, she turned it on. She hadn't started up the cable subscription, so she had to settle for what the decrepit TV antenna on the top of the house could provide. Jane flipped through the stations. The only one she could get was from Canada.

She turned up the volume.

"... ***Among the U.S. cities that have been imprisoned are New York, Washington DC, Chicago, Detroit, Dallas, Houston, San Antonio***..."

She sat in utter disbelief as the news anchor, in his navy-blue suit and red tie, revealed the state of the world.

Jane heard the drop of grocery bags on the kitchen floor.

"... ***Miami, Los Angeles, San Diego, San Jose, and Philadelphia. Major U.S. cities that have been spared include Pittsburgh, Denver, and Seattle. In Canada, just Toronto and Vancouver have been attacked. For unknown reasons, Montreal has been spared."***

"This is crazy," she whispered. Maddy sat beside her and intertwined their fingers together as the anchor continued.

"Overseas, the terrorized cities include Paris, Dubai, Barcelona, Rome, Moscow, London, and Beijing..."

Jane leaned forward as flashes of videos and images from around the world crossed the screen.

The news anchor went on to explain that some kind of "electric veil" had been erected around each city. His voice wavered as he spoke, ***"A translucent, laser-like barrier has blocked anyone from entering or exiting the areas. The veil is connected via towers that have appeared on the outskirts of each metropolitan area. Reports —"*** The man paused, shaking his head. ***"—Eyewitness reports indicate the towers rose from the ground out of nowhere. The walls do not appear to follow any particular path. In some places, they run along roads, but in other places they cut across them, passing through houses, stores***..." The anchorman pressed his hand to his ear and his eyes widened.

An aerial view of Detroit showed several dozen towers isolating the high-density city and suburbs from the surrounding area. A ripple of light rolled over the city every second or two—revealing that the other-worldly structure had some sort of low, flat… ceiling that completely closed off the city not only from the surrounding area, but from the sky above as well.

"This just in, a Euro Air aircraft, landing at Charles de Gaulle in Paris, passed through the translucent 'ceiling' that caps each veiled city only moments ago… with devastating results."

A video that looked like it was taken with a phone showed the plane coming in to land. At first, the ceiling wasn't visible, but then a shimmer rippled through it, exposing the flat, smooth surface just as the plane crossed it. A moment later, the enormous plane crashed onto the runway and collided with a maintenance hangar. ***"All 244 passengers and crew are presumed dead. Jesus."*** The anchorman paused a moment before remembering he was live. He coughed. ***"I apologize,"*** he said. ***"The Federal Aviation Administration…"***

The feed changed again. Jane swallowed the lump in her throat as a video from the ground showed a news helicopter rising into the air.

"Shit," Maddy whispered.

It passed easily through the ceiling, that shimmered from the underside like plastic wrap stretched tightly over a tray, then veered wildly for a few seconds. A moment later, it plummeted back through it toward the ground. The helicopter exploded on the airfield below.

The anchor covered his mouth. ***"Oh my god. That was Rick and Denise… Oh my god. I-I can't do this…"***

Another news anchor stepped in as the man pushed his seat back and hurried off-camera. Her face was pale, but she was calm as she adjusted the tiny microphone on her blouse, tucked her shoulder-length black hair behind her ear, and began to speak, ***"The Federal Aviation Administration has grounded all air traffic, effective immediately. Those flights en route to the affected cities have been notified and rerouted to surrounding airports and airfields. The***

walls, or 'Veil' as it is being called by some, are all tied together in one massive structure—completely closing off each population hub from its surroundings. The cities, it seems, are being held hostage."

Jane dialed Thomas again and held the phone up to her ear. It rang busy. She didn't know if that was better or worse than going straight to voicemail. She ended the call, dropped the phone back into her lap, and continued to listen.

The video feed switched to footage from a freeway cam. Jane cringed as a veil appeared across the road.

Her heart thumped in her ears as each vehicle drove through it. Just like she'd seen before, a split second later, they flew out of control on the other side. In each instance, the driver was no longer visible behind the wheel.

Her vision blurred, and she placed her head between her knees. That could have easily been them.

"Oh my god," Maddy whispered, obviously thinking the same thing.

Jane's head flew up. What if that was why Thomas wasn't answering? Had he been trying to get out and gotten caught in the veil? She sank back into the chair, shaking her head. Was he already dead?

"This just in. This footage is from less than an hour ago. A mob in Beijing tried to take down one of the towers."

Jane sat back up. Someone had recorded a huge crowd of people that had gathered in the dark, inside the veil, under yellow street-lights. They were shouting, waving their arms and cheering as they followed behind several pieces of heavy machinery.

She looked over her shoulder at Austin, who was standing next to the kitchen table staring at the TV.

"Maddy?" She nudged her niece. "Can you help your brother finish up with the bags?"

The girl got up, took her brother by the shoulders, and led him back outside. Jane turned back to the TV.

One of the bulldozers broke away from the rest and headed for the nearest tower. The crowd went wild as the edge of the bucket pressed against the steel. The camera zoomed up and down the tower, which looked like a tall, hexagonal telephone pole. It began to lean and then…

The lights went out, and the veil vanished at the same time.

It happened so quickly Jane just stared in confusion. She could just barely make out the bulldozer as it continued to roll forward, pushing the tower. It fell onto a building—revealing a wide metal base and a hollow interior. A moment later, it exploded, illuminating the area surrounding it.

She covered her mouth, aghast.

Everyone was gone. The entire mob of people had just… disappeared.

She got up and stepped closer to the television. "No…" she whispered in disbelief.

The camera panned around. Not a *single* person remained.

"They were unsuccessful. A whole section of Beijing, with an estimated population of… 1.2 million people… Oh my god… everyone in the southeast quarter of the city has—" The anchor's voice faltered ***"—disappeared."***

Disappeared? Jane frowned. *What the hell? How?*

"Authorities are urging that under no circumstances should anyone try to destroy the towers. Destroying one of the towers apparently only causes the wall to shift as it reestablishes connection with the next closest one. Oh my god…" The scene cut to an aerial view. Explosions ripped through the freed section of the city.

Jane continued to watch the coverage as video after unbelievable video aired. A similar scene unfolded in Moscow ten minutes later—with the same devastating effect. A whole section of the city was wiped clean of its inhabitants. Moments later, the abandoned streets burst into flames as vehicles, relieved of their drivers, crashed and exploded everywhere.

The news anchor announced that the President of the United

States was going to address the nation at six p.m. eastern-standard time.

Jane checked her watch. That would not be for another several hours.

Maddy dropped the last bag on the floor and announced they were done.

Jane turned off the TV.

The entire kitchen floor was covered in bags. It would have been laughable, except it appeared their splurge at the grocery store might be the difference between life and death for them. At least for now.

Tommy pushed the door open. "You get the yard cleaned up?" she asked, struggling to keep her voice even.

Tommy shook his head. "Nope. But I found a ladybug!" he said excitedly.

Jane glanced at Austin. "Would you mind helping your cousin collect wood?" she asked as cheerfully as she could manage. "We can have a bonfire tonight before bed. Won't that be fun?"

"I want to wait until Dad gets here," Tommy said.

Jane's heart dropped. "Um… I–I don't think your dad is gonna make it up here tonight, buddy."

Maybe he made it out.

"But dad always does the fire."

Tears welled in her eyes. "Well, I'm going to do it tonight, just–just like dad does, okay?"

She clapped her hands and forced a smile, not feeling even half as determined as she sounded. "You know what? The yard can wait. First, we have to clear a path through the kitchen. How about we empty all the bags onto the table and then sort everything out?"

They all stared at the pile.

"Yikes," she said, making a face. Tommy and Austin laughed.

"After this, we need to see if Mommy left any clothes up here last summer." Jane's smile wobbled as she tousled Tommy's hair.

"Do you know I forgot to bring your jammies?" She shook her head. "What was I thinking?"

You were thinking you were saving the kids. And now, it was starting to look like she actually had.

"But, mom…" Tommy complained.

"No 'buts,' mister. Come on. If we all help, it will go fast. Then you can go back outside." She blinked back her tears and picked up one of the bags, and the kids reluctantly followed her lead. The voice of Dr. Sanchez sounded in her head. *Only worry about what you can control, Jane. Let the rest go.*

While the kids emptied the bags, she organized the groceries into the old wooden cabinets, and tried to do just that.

Chapter Seven

Day 1 // 6:00 p.m

JANE SAT on the edge of the bed and turned on the television she had dragged in from the living room. She gasped as President Rodriguez appeared on the screen. He was sitting in the Oval Office, which meant—

He is inside the veil.

She held her breath as he began to speak.

"My fellow Americans, here are the facts as we know them. Contrary to the news reports, this is not, I repeat, not, a terrorist attack. But it is just as grave. On May twenty-ninth, the Center for Disease Control was informed of an outbreak of a mysterious virus in lower Manhattan. Six people were admitted across two hospitals with symptoms of high fever and sudden blindness. By June first, all six were dead." He looked up for a brief pause and then continued to read. ***"The CDC immediately put out an alert to all health care facilities nationwide. On that same day, the first symptoms were reported by the treating hospital staff. On the second of June, an astonishing ninety-six more cases were reported in New York. The CDC was made aware of similar cases through the National Notifiable Disease Surveillance System, or NNDSS, in Dallas, Atlanta, Los Angeles, and Baltimore. Internationally, Paris, Rome, Moscow, and Jakarta reported similar cases. All of these patients were immediately quarantined, and all died within twenty-four hours of each other."***

He paused and consulted the paper in front of him again before continuing.

"On the second of June, over two-thirds of the treating hospitals, and their families were infected, initiating a complete shutdown of the facilities, and more than nine-hundred New Yorkers were reporting similar or related symptoms. CDC protocols were implemented immediately. New cases were reported in St. Petersburg and Beijing."

The President sighed heavily.

"Twelve hours later, the CDC had accumulated evidence of over two thousand cases worldwide. Even with the CDC's strictest and fastest protocols, the virus had resulted in over eight hundred American deaths, and all, I repeat all the health care workers—including those not even in direct contact with the patients—who had been in exposed Emergency Departments, and their families were either dead or dying."

President Rodriguez rubbed his forehead. He looked as incredulous as she felt.

"We are currently calling it the X-virus. And to be frank, this is something the likes of which we have never seen. All we know at this point is that it is incredibly contagious, and it spreads ruthlessly fast."

He cleared his throat and continued. ***"On the morning of June third, the leaders of the free world, myself included, along with other members of the International Coalition for Preservation of Humanity, met in accordance with a treaty conscripted over fifty years ago by our forefathers, to decide whether or not to enact the Global Protection Protocol. This protocol was constructed decades ago in response to the possibility of biological warfare. Over the years as technology has developed, and our understanding of biological systems has grown, the protocol has been modified by the best biologists, virologists, immunologists, engineers, statisticians, and mathematicians from around the world, keeping it both current and relevant."***

He paused, sliding his glasses back up the bridge of his nose. ***"Hundreds of men and women from different countries around the world are employed by the ICPH to monitor all known infectious diseases and study ways to improve this protocol. Each year, the GPP is updated and ratified by the ICPH. Because of this, a team is already hard at work to neutralize the virus as quickly as possible."***

He set the paper he had been reading aside, looking much older than his sixty-two years. His normally healthy, brown skin was pale, and Jane was reminded he was just a man—like she was just a woman. He was probably worried about his family, the same as everyone else, and just wanted to be with them. Instead, he was on international television, trying to comfort the entire world.

The President went on. ***"The goal of the ICPH has always been to save as many lives as possible—and please believe me when I say, every life matters to us. Even the ones already lost."***

Jane thought about all the people she'd seen die before her very eyes on TV and knew it was only the tip of the iceberg. It was devastating.

"If there was any way they could have been spared, they would have been. There was not."

The President's expression was pained, his eyes sad as he went on.

"Here is what we know about the X-virus so far. Like other viruses, for example, the pneumonic plague or, more recently, COVID-19, the X-virus is transmissible through the air. I repeat, it is airborne. Unlike those other viruses, however, it does not favor a particular age or demographic." He looked right at the camera. ***"At present, the mortality rate of the X-virus is an unheard-of one hundred percent, which means everyone we know that had been infected has now died. The virus affects us all equally—adults and children alike."***

Jane shook her head as a chill raced down her spine.

"Therefore, until the origin is revealed, and a cure is discov-

ered, the quarantine of the affected cities is not only the best but also the only solution we have." He removed his glasses again and met Jane's eyes through the screen. ***"The problem we face, my fellow Americans, and citizens of the world, is not another typhoid or Covid scare. It is much, much worse. It is the annihilation of our species."*** His chest rose and fell heavily, and Jane felt hers do the same. ***"Our very existence hangs in the balance."***

Another chill raced down her spine as he shook his head.

"Believe me when I say, I wish it were anything else." He pinched his nose. ***"I honestly would have chosen aliens over this,"*** he said under his breath.

President Rodriguez looked off screen for a moment, then back at the pages in front of him. ***"It appears ground-zero was the May twenty-seventh taping of 'Mornin' Manhattan.' This local talk show was filmed on the lower east-side of Manhattan, in a studio off Broadway. Whether the virus was introduced purposefully or accidentally remains unclear at this point."***

He flipped to the next page in the pile of papers on his desk.

"As I stated earlier, in response to this incident, the ICPH initiated the Global Protection Protocol, which activated the Veil. Again, those of us in the ICPH are deeply sorry for the loss of lives the Veil has taken. We simply did not have a choice. We had to move quickly."

Jane calculated the days from the initial outbreak to quarantine. Seven days. She winced. It was already too late if the infection rate was nearly a hundred percent.

"The Veil was initiated in the affected cities, which are defined as any city with a known case of the disease."

He put his glasses back on and glanced at his notes. ***"We have also quarantined any city where any member of the audience or crew of the May twenty-seventh taping of 'Mornin' Manhattan' was said to have traveled through—whether or not a case was yet reported."***

Jane inhaled sharply. But what about those living in smaller towns? Or in the suburbs? The infection rate would be lower, but still—

"It is essential that everyone, especially those of you living in the affected cities, quarantine. Law enforcement has been given instructions from the CDC and the ICPH. Now that we know a little bit about this deadly virus and its rate and method of transmissibility, we have developed a series of guidelines that must be followed to the letter if there is to be any hope for the quarantined cities."

"I have issued several executive orders based on the recommendations of the CDC and the ICPH. They are as follows."

He sat up in his seat. ***"As with other pandemics, maintaining social distance is the greatest tool you possess to protect yourself and your family."***

Jane shook her head and pressed her fingers to her mouth, still hung up on how long it had taken the government to take action. She remembered the simulations she'd run back in grad school. Seven days was definitely too long. There was no way they'd contained the virus. The President had to know that. She wondered how he was dealing with the outliers. If there were only a few, maybe he'd been able to quarantine them in time?

"I cannot stress this enough. This is why we have had to move so quickly to contain it and why the Veils were activated without warning."

He cleared his throat.

"Any physical contact outside of your household is strictly prohibited. Since the X-Virus is airborne and extremely contagious, all businesses are to remain closed until further notice. There will be a zero-tolerance for gatherings of any kind. Only essential workers will be allowed to leave their homes, and they will be required to wear PAPRs or a higher-grade mask when out in public. These masks are already en route to the cities. Anyone on the streets without authorization or proper protection will be arrested. I cannot emphasize enough how crucial it is to follow

this order. This is not a joke. You cannot bend these rules. Your lives depend on it. Your children's lives depend on it."

Jane stared at the television, struggling to wrap her mind around what these mandates meant for Thomas and Sarah if they were still alive—and the world.

"The federal government is teaming up with local authorities, per ICPH guidelines, to provide and maintain necessary living conditions for citizens residing in the affected cities. The greatest effort will be made to keep all essential services, water, electricity, and waste pickup, up and running. Effective immediately, all of these services will be fully subsidized by the federal government. Food and water services are being organized as we speak. And local authorities will be providing that information as it becomes available."

The President took a sip of water from the glass on his desk, then continued. ***"For those of you on the outside, things will be a little simpler. A two-week quarantine is in effect for persons living outside the Veil. Stay home. If you need something, food, medical attention, call your local emergency services, they will assist you. If you experience symptoms of the virus, call your local 9-1-1 dispatcher. Do not leave your residence. Effective immediately gas will be regulated by the federal government, dispensed only for official business, and local necessary travel. Travel across county lines will be by permit only, and will be issued through the state police working in conjunction with the Coast Guard. Travel across state lines is strictly prohibited until further notice. If the virus has escaped, this is our only means of containing it. When the fourteen days have expired, and assuming no outbreaks have occurred, there will be a set of new preventative guidelines issued, and certain businesses will be allowed to reopen."***

Tommy knocked on the door, but Jane distractedly shooed him away.

"I know many of you in the cities must be feeling abandoned right now. But know you are not alone. I am with you, and I have

been assured by the highest authorities on the matter, if—if we can come together, there is hope. If we follow the rules and wait it out, we have a chance. All is not lost."

Jane stared at the TV, unable to do anything but shake her head.

"I am sure that by now you are aware of the devastation in Beijing and Moscow, and why it occurred. Once activated, the Veil system cannot be brought down. If any attempt is made, the walls will realign with the next-nearest tower and anyone and anything within the exposed segment will be incinerated. This is to protect everyone, and necessary to keep the virus isolated."

Incinerated? How?

Jane stared as the President went on to explain that the walls were designed and constructed by an undisclosed third party of independent bio-engineers and physicists working closely with the ICPH and that until more was known about the virus, it was unknown how long they would remain active. He warned that while the Veil did not block frequencies, or affect non-organic matter, it was biologically active and designed to destroy all *living* organic matter on contact. That included humans, animals, plants, fungi, and bacteria. Could the Veil detect cell division? Jane shook her head. How else would it distinguish between living and nonliving? *Robert would know.*

Tommy pushed open the door. "I'm hungry, Mom. Can I have some cereal?"

Jane turned off the television. The President was still talking, but her brain couldn't take any more. Besides, if the simulations she had run all those years ago were right, she already knew what would most likely happen next, and it wasn't good. Her arms tingled in response to the panic seeping into her veins.

She followed Tommy into the kitchen. The President's words played on a loop in her head. *One-hundred percent mortality rate?* That wasn't possible, was it? Jane didn't think so. But it could be close. Either way, it was a worst-case scenario, and the President was right. They would have better odds with an alien invasion.

An ominous cloud of foreboding hung over Jane as she made dinner, then tried and failed to start a bonfire in the backyard. Eventually, she gave up and got the kids ready for bed. They had to sleep in their clothes except for Bria, and brush their teeth with their fingers, and toothpaste, but they made due. At least they were together. At least they were *alive*.

Bria went down immediately, while Maddy helped the boys make a bed in the living room.

Jane could wrap her mind around the idea that *she* might die, but she could not bear the thought of the kids dying. But what could she do? There was nothing to do but sit there in the cabin and wait, was there?

Her mind kept going back to her research in college. The more she thought about it, the guiltier she felt—as if she had accidentally written the virus into existence.

"What's the matter, Aunt Jane?" Maddy whispered from the couch. The quilt was tucked around her shoulders, and her head rested on a throw pillow. The boys were asleep on the floor, back-to-back, and snuggled under the blanket from the bed. Jane realized she was standing in the middle of the dark room, staring at nothing.

"Nothing," she lied. "I'm just tired."

The matter was, she had seen this virus before. The matter was....

You practically invented it.

Chapter Eight

Day 2 // 2:12 a.m

JANE'S PHONE vibrated in her hand, and Thomas's face flashed on the screen. She bolted out of bed and jabbed the green button—praying Bria wouldn't wake up.

"Thomas! Thank god," she whispered, hurrying into the living room.

She tiptoed past the boys asleep on the floor. Moths fluttered around the yellow light that illuminated the porch as Jane slipped out the door.

"Jane?"

"Are you okay? Did you get my messages?" She started down the walk, toward the van. "Did you make it out of—"

"What the hell, Jane?" he interrupted. There was an edge to his voice that she recognized immediately.

She stopped. "Wh–what?"

"Where in the hell are you?"

"You didn't get my—"

"Yeah, I got them. So, you really made it out? You took the kids, and you left?"

"I—"

"You took our kids and fucking left *us* here?" he asked bitterly. "How did you even know?"

Us? Us who? Was he accusing her of something? "I… Did you make it—" she began.

"No. We didn't make it."

Jane fell back against the van, overwhelmed by the confirmation that her husband was trapped. What did that mean? Would he die now? Would Tommy never see his dad again? She found her voice. "We?"

"Sarah is here at the house. She came straight here as soon as the news broke. Jane, she is beside herself."

Oh god—Sarah too?

"Thomas, I tried to call you! I didn't–There wasn't enough time. I had to go. Why didn't you answer? We called Sarah too. Maddy tried a hundred times. Were you in court? Why was your phone off?"

"You're putting this on me?" he snapped.

"No, of course—" Jane shook her head, running her fingers through her hair.

"How did you know, Jane?" he asked, making it sound like she was somehow responsible for the whole thing.

"It was Robert," she whispered.

"Robert? You've got to be—How in the hell would *he* know?" Thomas sounded as incredulous as she felt.

"I–I don't know." She pulled her sweatshirt tight across her chest as the breeze tugged at her hair.

"He told you this was going to happen?"

"Yes. Well, no. Not exactly. He told me we had to leave. He said to get you and the kids and get out of town." Jane paced back and forth down the walk as she spoke.

"And you believed him?"

She shrugged in the darkness. "No. Of course, not. But he sounded so… scared."

"How did he know?"

"I don't know!" she cried, throwing her hands up in frustration. She had asked herself that a million times in the last several hours, and she could not think of a single plausible reason.

"Why did he tell *you*?"

"You know we are close…" Jane had always sensed Thomas's

dislike for Robert, although she couldn't figure out why. To be fair, Robert had never particularly liked Thomas either. He had voiced a fatherly concern over her husband on more than one occasion.

"Are you having an affair with him?"

Jane stopped pacing, not quite believing the question she had just been asked. Robert was like a father to her. *How dare Thomas even suggest—*

"What is wrong with you?" she hissed. "You know I'm not. He's Tommy's Godfather for Christ's sake! He's... seventy-two years old!"

"So, what now?" Thomas asked, like it was her job to know.

"Thomas," she said, pulling the hair out of her eyes and taking a deep breath. "Please, you have to know I didn't mean for any of this to happen. I didn't mean to take the kids. Ours or Sarah's. It all happened so fast—"

"Yeah. Your sister wants to talk to you."

Jane sighed and listened to the shuffle as Thomas handed the phone to Sarah.

"How dare you take my children, *my children...*"

"Sarah—"

The door behind her opened and Tommy stepped out, letting in a dozen moths in the process. "Shut the door!" she whispered, pulling him outside.

"Is that daddy?" he asked hopefully.

"Sarah, can you put Thomas back on? Tommy wants to talk to him."

Her sister didn't answer, but Jane heard her hand the phone over. Jane crouched down and pressed her phone to Tommy's ear and listened.

"Hi dad!"

"Hey, bud! I sure miss you! How was the ride up to the cabin?"

"Scary." Tommy looked at his mom apologetically.

"Yeah, I bet, but you're okay, right?"

"I guess. Mom is not as good as you at building fires. Will you be here soon?"

There was a pause. "Not tonight. Maybe–maybe tomorrow. We'll see."

It pained Jane to hear Thomas lie, not because it was untrue, but because she felt like it was her fault he had to.

"Are you okay?" Tommy asked.

"Sure am, bud. I'm here with Aunt Sarah. We are just fine, pal."

"I'm scared, Dad," Tommy confessed. Jane pulled him into her arms.

"I know. But you are safe and sound with Mom. You know she'll take good care of you. And what do we always say?"

"You guys will never let anything bad happen to us?"

"That's right! Now put your mom back on and go to bed. I love you."

"I love you too," Tommy whispered. He reluctantly handed the phone back to Jane.

"Hurry inside," she said. "And don't let the bugs in."

Tommy disappeared inside, and Jane lifted the phone back to her ear. "Thomas—"

"You heard what your son said." The fury in his voice returned. "You decided to take him. So, you had better damn well be ready to protect him."

"Why are you so angry? I thought you'd be relieved that I got the kids—"

"How would you feel if I had taken them and left you?" Thomas demanded.

Was he implying she had done it on purpose? Nothing could be farther from the truth.

"I didn't *want* to. I... There just wasn't time to wait. What would you have had me do? Are you suggesting I should have stayed?" Jane's breath caught in her throat. For the first time since it all happened, she realized that choice had always been there. She could have stayed. They could have been together at home right now. They could have faced all of this together as a family. "I—"

"At least then we would be together. At least Sarah could hold her kids."

Jane sank down on the step. "But Robert said… We would have been trapped."

The line went quiet for a moment. "I know things have been tough between us lately, but I never thought…" Thomas let the sentence hang.

It took her a moment to realize what he was implying. "Thomas. It has nothing to do with that. This is not revenge for you deciding to… to leave me or anything else. I was just trying to protect the kids. I swear. I wasn't thinking about anything beyond that."

"Don't get me wrong…" his voice softened. "I'm glad they are safe. I just–Damn it, Jane. They are my kids, too."

"I know," Jane sighed, swatting at a bug. "I'm sorry."

"I am too," he said, sounding defeated.

She heard Sarah's angry voice in the background.

"They're safe," Thomas said to her sister. "That's the main thing, right? And according to the news, it's better out there than in here."

Jane couldn't make out Sarah's reply.

"Listen," he said into the receiver. "We are all tired. Let's talk again tomorrow morning. Maybe, by then, someone will know what the hell is going on. Maybe we will wake up and find this has all been just a nightmare."

"Okay," Jane whispered, not wanting to hang up.

"Get some rest," he said.

"You too."

Thomas hung up and Jane sat on the step and stared at her phone. He hadn't said 'I love you.'

Neither had she. The truth was, they hadn't said those words to each other in a very long time.

The clouds had thinned, and Jane looked up at the stars that peeked out between them. Once again, her conversation with Thomas had left her feeling confused and guilty. All their conversations lately seemed to end the same way, with him trying to pick a fight, and her feeling like the harder she tried to smooth things over, the more he resented her.

It hadn't always been like that, had it?

Jane thought back to their life together—trying to remember a time when they hadn't been at odds, but she couldn't.

The piece of bread she had eaten for dinner lurched up her esophagus. She turned to the lawn just in time to throw up. Her knees sunk into the cool grass, and her arms shook as she struggled to inhale.

Maybe she really was as awful as he thought. Look what she'd done to their family.

She gagged again, fighting for air as her heart pounded in her ears. The helplessness was like a tornado, dragging her up higher and higher as she clawed for control.

She shouldn't have taken the kids.

You had to.

How would she ever survive without Thomas? The answer came to her as a sliver of moon slipped out from behind a cloud. *The same way you survived living with him*—one lonely day at a time.

Chapter Nine

Day 3 // 10:17 a.m

MATT COULDN'T BELIEVE IT. The world was ending, and the Army *still* didn't want him back.

He shifted gears as the truck bounced over the pothole-filled gravel road he wasn't supposed to be on.

The police were doing their best to keep people from traveling, but 'lucky' for him, there was no way they had the manpower to patrol every back road in the state.

God, he was so angry he could—Matt slammed his palm into the steering wheel.

The truck swung to the left, toward the ditch.

"Shit—" He jerked the wheel, guiding it back onto the road as a cloud of dust billowed behind him.

He looked out over the fields, with a clenched jaw. He hated this place. Nothing but giant, fucking fields everywhere.

Then why are you here? Because he had nowhere else to go! Everyone he knew outside of the military, which didn't amount to many people, was either inside the damn Veil or too afraid of getting sick to let him stay with them. Because even if he could get to his car, it apparently couldn't go through Veil without the computer getting fried, which was why he was driving this piece of shit—

In an exquisite twist of fate, a tie-rod ripped through the hood of the truck with a bang. The ear-shattering noise was immediately followed by the smell of burning oil. Tony flashed before his eyes and he shoved the image away. *Not now.* Smoke billowed out from under the hood as the truck slowed.

"Are you serious?" Matt yelled. "Are you fucking *serious*?"

It coasted to a stop in the middle of a bleak intersection, because… of course, it would stop there.

"Goddamned piece of shit," he cursed, smacking the wheel again.

He got out and didn't even bother to lift the hood. He knew he couldn't fix it, and it wasn't like he could call a tow truck. The world was in lockdown.

He gripped the inside of the door with a grunt and pushed the truck to the side of the road. He pulled his bag out of the back—to make themselves feel better, the Army had given him some clean clothes and a toothbrush—and rolled the truck into the ditch.

He looked through the bright sunlight to the north. He could just make out the top of his dad's silo. God, he hated that silo.

"Fuck," he said, kicking the dirt.

With a sigh, he hoisted his bag over his shoulder and began to walk.

He had gone about half a mile when his phone rang. How the phones were still working, he hadn't a clue. It was a damn miracle.

He dropped his bag and fished it out of his pocket. He looked at the name on the screen and his mood improved immediately.

"Maxi-dress," Matt said with a smile.

"You're such a dick, and the only man I know who actually knows what the fuck that means," Max replied.

Matt owed at least that much to Katie. If nothing else, she'd improved his fashion vocabulary. "You okay? Are you stuck inside or—"

"Denver," Max said. "There's no wall here. Thank god."

Matt was pretty sure god had nothing to do with it.

"Carlos, Bingo, and I are being sent to Dallas. I was just wondering if you were—"

Matt's throat constricted with anger. "They don't want me back."

There was a pause on the line. "*Still?* Are you fucking kidding me?" Max sounded truly surprised.

"Nope." Matt picked up his bag and heaved it over his shoulder.

"Cock-suckers. Can you call Marty, or—"

"I did call Marty, but there's nothing he can do. I'm damaged goods." Matt looked down at his feet as sweat dripped down his back.

"That's bullshit."

It was bullshit, and his beloved Army was acting like a spoiled kid. They'd broken their toy, and now they didn't want to play with him anymore. But Matt held his tongue.

He continued down the road, pressing the phone against his ear. "Anyway, have you heard from Diggs or Gates?"

"Gates is stuck in LA. I don't know where Diggs is."

The sun beat down on Matt's head and he wished he'd thought to get a haircut before the world went to hell. It was only a little over an inch, but his hair hadn't been this long since high school, and it was fucking hot. He brushed it away from his forehead and squinted. He also wished he had a pair of sunglasses.

Max continued, "We need you, Farmer. You're the fuckin' glue that keeps us from killing each other. Can't you call—Who's the guy you talked to in rehab?"

Matt rolled his eyes. Of all the nicknames that could have stuck, fucking *Farmer* was the one that had. "I'm not gonna beg to come back. That's not how it's supposed to work."

"Yeah, well. Maybe you just need to convince them."

"I'm in better shape than I ever was, and they still won't…" He swatted at an insect that took a couple of turns around him.

"Well, they are fucking stupid. I'd take you in a fistfight with both your goddamn hands tied behind your back. They are wrong about you, Farm. They are fucking—"

Matt pulled the phone away from his ear. "Okay. Thanks brother…"

He glanced behind him, to make sure the road was still clear since he was in the middle of it, and continued walking. The fields were so flat he could see for a mile in every direction. In his head, he went over the names of the farmers who owned them. *The Carters, the Lawsons, the Hamiltons.*

"I got your back, man. Always, and for goddamn ever," Max said vehemently.

Matt sighed and pushed his hair back again, grateful for the vote of confidence from his best friend.

"They'll come around," Max said. "You'll see. With all this shit that's happened, it won't take long for the Brass to figure out how much they need you. Just sit tight until they do."

The wind picked up, blowing dust in his eyes.

"Yeah." He would be sitting plenty because there was literally nothing else to do out here but sit on your ass and twiddle your thumbs. That's why he left. He switched the bag and his phone, absently looking at the seedlings sprouting in neat rows beside him. He knew every crop too, even now when they were still young. He cataloged them as he walked. Corn back there. Sugar beets. Soybeans and hay up ahead. It was all the same.

"… in touch man, okay?" Max said.

Matt's thoughts drifted back, and he realized he hadn't been paying attention. "Yeah. Keep me posted."

He hung up as a gust of wind shoved the putrid scent of chicken-shit fertilizer up his nose. He covered his mouth with the hem of his shirt and gagged.

Welcome home, soldier.

"Goddamn it," he choked.

Chapter Ten

Day 4 // 11:13 a.m

JANE HAD JUST WRESTLED Tommy out of his wet clothes and into a T-shirt when Thomas called. "Go take that rock outside," she ordered, pointing to the sharp piece of granite he'd collected from the beach. She checked on Bria, who was napping, then followed her son outside.

"Hey," she said.

"How'd the kids sleep?"

"Good. Better. We went to the lake this morning. And guess what? Tommy caught a minnow and—"

"Did you hear?" Thomas interrupted.

"No. What?"

Maddy came back outside, looking worried. Her ear was pressed to her phone as she started down the street barefoot.

Jane shouted after her. "Get your shoes on!"

Maddy ignored her and kept walking. The last thing Jane needed was to have to take her in for a tetanus shot. She didn't even know where the nearest hospital was. Port Huron, maybe?

"It's bad, Jane," Thomas said.

She wasn't sure she'd want to head back toward the city. Wasn't there another town with a hospital farther up north—Jane frowned as his words finally sunk in. *Bad?* "What is?"

"The virus, or whatever it is."

"Has there been an outbreak by you?"

"No. New York."

"How are you…?"

"I feel fine."

"How about Sarah?"

"We're both fine."

"Have you heard of any cases in Detroit yet? Do you think—"

"How in the hell should I know? Why don't you ask Robert?" Thomas spat.

She had tried many times to call him. "His number is disconnected."

Thomas sighed. "I'm sorry. I don't want to fight."

The hair on the back of Jane's neck stood up. She followed the feeling until they landed on a huge thirty-something man with a beard. He was standing on the front porch of the house three doors down, smoking a cigarette. The porch and the yard were covered in trash bags, half of which had been ripped open by animals. There was a dishwasher and an old dresser sitting in the flowerbed on the side of the house.

As Maddy walked by, he said something Jane couldn't make out. Unwisely, the girl stopped long enough for him to approach her. A moment later, Maddy stepped back and shook her head, clearly uncomfortable.

"Damn it," Jane whispered under her breath. "Hey, I have to call you back." She ended the call before Thomas could respond.

She started across the neighboring yard. "Hey, Maddy"—Jane frowned at the very inappropriate way the man was staring at her niece's chest—"go check on Bria."

Maddy passed her a grateful look—mouthing the words 'thank you' as she quickly made her way back to the house.

"I was wonderin' who owned that place." The man held out his hand, and Jane noticed he was missing a tooth. His white t-shirt was filthy. "We haven't been properly introduced. I'm Jake. I'm your neighbor." He smiled.

Make that 'teeth.' He was certainly missing more than one. Jane did not take his hand.

He shoved his dark, greasy hair back. "And you are?" He prompted with a raised brow.

The cinnamon liquor on his breath was strong as he leaned forward. Jane backed away. She glanced at her watch. It was not even eleven-thirty in the morning.

"Hey, now. No need to be shy." He leaned forward, putting his large hand on her shoulder.

Jane took another step back, breaking the contact. Her heart thumped nervously in her chest.

Jake held up his hand and frowned. "What's the matter? I'm just askin' your name. You look a little…"

Her instinct was to act dumb, smile, and retreat. Let Thomas deal—*Thomas is not here.*

Jake's watery blue eyes flashed, then narrowed. He lunged for Jane as she continued to back away.

He laughed. "Whatcha scared of?" he asked with a grin.

"Don't touch me. And I'm not scared," she said, squaring her shoulders and meeting his eyes. "There is a quarantine in case you haven't heard—"

His expression darkened. "I can see where your daughter gets her attitude from," he said. "What's her name? Maddy? Seems to me you both need—"

What would Thomas do if he were here?

"What we need is for you to leave us alone. Stay away from her. Stay away from me, and don't talk to my kids." Jane blurted, realizing there was probably nothing she could do if he decided not to.

"Stay away?" He laughed. "How? We live two hundred feet apart! I can see everything that goes on in your house from my fucking couch."

An icy feeling raced down her spine. *He's been watching you.*

"Just leave us alone." Jane turned away before he could see the fear in her eyes.

"See ya' round, neighbor!" Jake called with a laugh that made her stomach churn.

Jane hurried back to the house, kicking herself.

She had done what Thomas would have, but Thomas was a six-foot-five, two-hundred-and-forty-pound man. She was a five-foot-seven, one-hundred-and-seventy-pound woman. There was a difference. She should not have pissed him off. She should have just—Jane looked behind her. He was still there, watching her. She should have just told him her name and shook his damn hand.

"That guy was disgusting," Maddy said as Jane's eyes adjusted to the dim interior of the cabin.

Jane walked over to the living room window that faced his house, and drew the curtains together, making it even darker.

"What did he say to you?" she asked.

"He asked me how old I was," Maddy scoffed. "As if I'd—"

"From now on, we go in and out of the side door." Jane interrupted, locking the front one. She stared at the ancient knob that separated them from the outside.

"What's the matter, Aunt Jane?" Maddy asked, sounding worried.

What if he tries to break in when you are sleeping?

"Nothing," she said, trying her best to sound like she believed it. "That guy is just a drunk, and…" Jane rubbed her eyes, again wishing Thomas was—*He's not*. She sighed. "I would just rather we avoid him."

She jiggled the doorknob again. A man Jake's size could easily break it open.

She pulled out her phone and tried to do a search, but the internet still wasn't working.

"Is your internet working?" she asked.

Maddy shook her head. "Nope. It sucks. I'm just getting texts randomly."

She fished the old phone book out of the drawer in the kitchen, found the number for the hardware store, but no one answered. The recording said the store was closed until further notice. She tried four different locksmiths, but no one would come out because of the quarantine.

That night, as the kids slept, Jane sat up in her dad's old recliner, with a cup of coffee, and watched the doors.

Chapter Eleven

Day 5 // 5:45 p.m

MATT WAS HOME.

After the long walk from the truck the other day, he had wearily climbed the front steps and found the key under the pot next to the front door where it always was. Wondering how his parents hadn't been robbed and murdered in their sleep, he pushed the key into the lock. And just like that, he was right back where he started.

Now, he was sitting on the couch in his father's den, staring at his phone. He had just endured a five-minute rant by his dad, via his mom, about the lack of cable television and the uncomfortable furniture in his apartment. His dad had also demanded Matt mow the lawn—which he absolutely was not going to do. The world was practically ending. Who gave a shit about the yard?

Instead of working from dawn till dusk like his dad would have, Matt slept. A lot. And watched a lot of television. Weirdly, his parents had spared no expense with the premium cable package, and he had over six hundred channels at hand to hear every expert's opinion of the radical action the President and the ICPH had taken trying to control the virus. It was insane what they'd done, and he still couldn't figure out how. They still weren't saying who'd actually developed the technology to build the walls, or how they'd managed to assemble them so quickly.

His phone buzzed beside him on the couch, but he let it go to voicemail. It was the fourth time Katie called him since the Veil went up, and a part of him felt like he should answer because of their history, but he didn't. They weren't together anymore.

Matt went into the kitchen. It had looked the same since he was born. He opened one of the brown painted cabinets and set a bowl on the worn yellow countertop. He got the cereal out, sniffing the milk before pouring it in. Then he put it back in the ancient avocado green refrigerator that somehow still worked. He wondered how long it would be before milk was hard to come by? According to his mom, all the stores in the city were closed, and they were receiving rations. But at least they had power and water.

Unlike him, his mom had plenty of food. He would be fine for a couple of weeks, more than that. After, he would just have to figure it out.

He flipped off the light in the kitchen and headed back to the den. Luckily, the power remained on there too. And four days in, despite the dropped calls, his phone still worked. To be honest, he was amazed that anything was still up and running. Matt took a bite of his cereal and went back to the couch.

On the one hand, it made sense. People on the outside weren't stuck in their homes, and essential workers in Detroit were exempt from the quarantine, so really the only difference was some people could no longer make their commute and had to be replaced. He read the headline plastered on the screen. Oh, and gas had practically become non-existent.

Matt looked out to the empty driveway. Not a problem for him, though. As far as he knew, his car was still parked out in front of his apartment, and the shitty truck he had bought for two hundred dollars was still in a ditch where it belonged.

Chapter Twelve

Day 5 // 8:27 p.m

JANE CHECKED the lock on the front door again. Then she checked on Bria before heading out back to try a second round of fire-making with the boys.

It was cool and breezy, and Jane shivered as she pulled her sweatshirt tighter around her. She could hear the waves hitting the beach at the end of the street.

It took half a box of matches to get the fire lit, and when she did, it provided no warmth and barely burned. They stood as close as they could to the pathetic flames. Each time she thought the fire was starting to catch, it would blow out again.

Jane coughed and poked at it with a stick, not understanding why it was so smoky. It never did this when Thomas was there. She pushed a big branch over, sending a billowing cloud into the sky.

Tears stung the back of her eyes. She didn't even want to have a fire, but the last few days had been so hard on the kids, she had finally given in.

"Maybe the wood is wet?" she suggested. "What if we throw some of these leaves on it?" She scooped up a handful of leaves and tossed them in.

That only made it worse. Jane sighed and added fires to the list of things she had made worse over the last several days. Things like her anxiety, her relationships with Thomas and Sarah, and her relationship with Maddy. *Bria's diaper rash.* Her poor baby.

"I think that's what's making the smoke," Austin observed.

"Leaves were a bad idea," she admitted as the boys coughed and stepped back, waving the smoke away. The wind blew, and she shivered again. It was so much warmer in the city.

"I'm sorry, guys, but maybe we should call it a—"

"Y'all look like you guys could use some help," a voice slurred from behind them.

They all jumped as Jake appeared out of the darkness. Despite the cool temperature, he wore a baggy pair of shorts and a stained tank-top, over a pair of cheap flip-flops. He had some sticks in one hand and a bottle of malt liquor in the other. He staggered toward them.

Instinctively, Jane placed herself between him and the boys.

If he scared her before, he positively terrified her now. In the dark, his eyes were so sunk into the shadows of his skull they were just two black voids. She only hoped the porch light made her look just as frightening.

"No, thanks. We've decided to call it a night," she said, trying to keep her voice neutral. After her mishap the other day, she didn't want to sound friendly, but she definitely didn't want to piss him off either.

Jake tossed the branches on the fire and shook his head. "Don't give up yet. I'll help you get her going. You got any dry wood round here?" His words ran together as he glanced around in the dark.

"Really, we're done." Jane insisted, nudging the boys toward the house.

"Hey, I'm just tryin' to be a good neighbor." He took a step around the fire pit toward them.

"Go inside and lock the door," she whispered to the boys. They turned and ran.

"Come on," Jake said with a laugh. "I'm not gonna do nothin'." He took a swig of his drink. The door to the house slammed shut. "I'm a nice guy…"

He took another step, and Jane backed away. A dark thought

crossed her mind. What would happen to the kids if this man killed her…

Jane pulled her phone from her back pocket. "Get off my property or I'll call the police," she threatened, dialing the first two numbers.

Jake's friendly demeanor evaporated. He jabbed a finger in the air toward her. "What is your fuckin' problem? You think you're better than me, 'cause you come from the city?" He took a sip from his bottle. "You think I'm stupid, don't you?"

Jane's jaw was tight. "I told you we are done."

"Somebody needs to put you in your fuckin' place," he sneered.

Jane backed away. "I asked you to leave."

Jake held up his hands in mock defeat, and the cheap liquor sloshed out of his bottle. A gust of wind swept between them, covering her in his stench. Her stomach churned, and she fought the urge to gag at the sour mix of booze and body odor.

"Fine," he conceded. He turned to go, mumbling to himself. "Fucking cun—" He stopped, swaying a little as he turned back. "Come on. Last chance. Let's be friends?" He held out his hand, waiting for her to shake it. Jane stared at him. Hell would freeze over before she took that man's hand voluntarily. "You realize I have nothing better to do than make your life a living hell, right?" he asked, like she was stupid.

Her jaw hurt from clenching it, and her eyes burned from the smoke, but she continued to stare.

"Suit yourself." Jake dropped his hand, took a drink of the bottle he was carrying, and continued back down the driveway. He raised his eyes skyward. "Why does *everyone* underestimate me?" he asked the clouds.

As he neared the edge of the darkness, he held up his bottle and called back. "See ya round, bitch!"

Jane raced to the door, pounding on it frantically. It was only a second before it opened. Maddy stood on the other side, wide-eyed.

Jane pushed her aside, slamming the door behind them. At the sound of the lock, she breathed a shaky sigh of relief. That could have gone much worse. Lesson learned.

No more going outside unprotected.

No more going outside at all.

Chapter Thirteen

Day 6 // 3:14 a.m

JANE STARED AT THE CEILING, watching a tiny spider weave a web between the blades of the ceiling fan. To say she was ill-equipped to protect the kids was a gross understatement. She made them all frighteningly vulnerable. And the worst of it was, she didn't know what to do about it.

It had come so naturally to Thomas to be their protector. He was quite literally built for it. Although, to be fair, she couldn't remember anything as dramatic as tonight ever happening when he was there. But maybe that was the point. Men like Jake didn't bother families who had men like Thomas around.

How do single mothers do it? They had to be on edge all the time.

The encounter with Jake had left her terrified enough to never want to leave the house again. How was she supposed to keep the kids safe when she couldn't even defend *herself* if he came back?

Jane grabbed the phone off the nightstand, tip-toed into the bathroom, and shut the door. She dialed Thomas.

It rang busy three times before he picked up. She wiped her eyes as she turned away from the door—hoping it would be enough to muffle the sound of her voice and not wake the kids.

"Is everything alright?" Thomas's sleep-filled voice asked, sounding worried.

She looked at her watch and winced. It was after three.

"Fine. We are all fine," she said in a low voice, trying not to cry. "I just... There is a new neighbor down the street, a real ass—"

"What happened?"

She explained.

"And you are still there? Get them the fuck out of there, Jane," Thomas demanded. He sounded more annoyed than concerned. He sounded like he was more worried about what would have happened to the kids if she was gone, not if *she* was gone.

"And go where? Everything we have is here..."

"Well, then call the damn police. Fuck. You've got to–Christ, Jane. Did you at least get a photo of him, so you can—"

She winced again. Why hadn't she thought of that?

"No... I—"

"Goddamn it!" he roared. "You're married to a lawyer for Christ's sake. How many times have you heard me say—"

She pulled the phone away from her ear and dropped her head in her hands.

"A picture is worth a thousand words," she whispered.

Calling Thomas had been a mistake. She waited until he stopped yelling, and pulled the phone back to her ear.

"No. I know. I was just... He came out of nowhere and–It's over now. We're okay. I just wanted to hear your voice. I am so overwhelmed, Thomas. I am so—"

"No. Don't even start. Don't you dare fucking start," Thomas seethed, as tears spilled down her cheeks. "You lost the right to complain to me the moment you took off with the kids."

"I'm sorry." She wiped her eyes with the back of her hand.

"Stop crying, damn it."

"I know. I just need you to listen—"

He laughed bitterly. "I am done listening, Jane. That's all I've been doing for twenty-fucking years is listening to you cry about every goddamned—"

"I'd better go. I–I don't want to wake the kids," Jane whispered, trying to keep her voice even.

"You're gonna have to suck it up. Whatever happens next, you have to protect the kids. You have to keep them safe until this is over. I don't care how hard it is or how overwhelmed you feel."

"I know."

"And make sure the doors are locked."

"I will. Good night, Thomas."

He snorted and then ended the call.

She let herself cry for a minute, his little 'pep-talk' ringing in her head.

She honestly hadn't realized what a drain she had been on him. But she could hear it now in his voice. She'd been a burden to Thomas for a long time, and he had finally reached the end of his rope, which was probably why he was planning to leave her in the first place. He was done carrying her. She also saw the extent to which she had put the responsibility of their family on him, and it was almost completely. Besides feeding and caring for the kids, Thomas had done… Everything. So how could she blame him?

Jane got up and looked at herself in the mirror. She hadn't always been this way.

At one time she'd been ambitious, adventurous and… brave. But after the accident–She sighed, not recognizing the woman staring at her. Not that it was an excuse, but they had made everything so easy for her, her parents, Sarah, and especially Thomas. And somewhere along the way, Jane had started to believe she was as helpless and fragile as they all thought. And now she really was.

Jane went to check the doors again, then went to get a glass of water.

She peered out the kitchen window, and her breath stuck in her throat.

She leaped back into the shadows, pressing a hand to her wildly beating heart.

Jake was in the backyard—exposed and peeing on the remains of their fire.

Blood hammered in her ears.

It took every bit of courage she had to take another look.

He was still there. The fire steamed as he took a swig from the clear bottle of alcohol in his hand. Where was he getting all the alcohol from?

Jane quickly dropped to the floor and crawled back to the bathroom to retrieve her phone from the sink. She dialed 9-1-1.

"There is a man outside my house," she whispered into the receiver.

She gave the dispatcher the details, and the woman promised they would send a cruiser over.

Jane crawled back into the kitchen. She was determined to take a photo, but Jake was gone.

A shadow moved past the dining room window and she dropped back to the ground. He couldn't see her through the closed drapes, but her terror forced her down, anyway. He went past the living room window, behind the couch where Maddy was asleep, toward the front of the house.

Her eyes widened when the front door handle shook.

He's going to kill you.

Jane pulled the drawer above her open and felt around for the paring knife, and glanced up at the kitchen window. If he came back around to the back of the house and looked in, he'd see—

She jumped up and closed the drape. Falling back to the floor, Jane clutched the tiny knife in her shaking hand—trying not to imagine how pathetic she looked.

By the time she saw flashing lights, Jake had gone. To where, she didn't know.

She stepped outside, hoping the kids wouldn't wake up.

The heavily masked officer had the audacity to laugh when she explained Jake had urinated on her fire.

Jane crossed her arms. "This is not funny," she said angrily.

The officer held up his hands and apologized.

"Everyone around here has had at least on run-in with Jake. He drinks a lot. He's a nuisance and a hell of a shit-talker, but nothing else. I would just ignore him."

Jane was incredulous.

"There is not much we can do unless you have proof. We can serve him a 'no trespass' that says he *has* to stay off your land." The officer shrugged. "But we can't arrest him for sitting on his porch looking in the direction of your house."

"But he was in my yard! He tried to open the door!"

"Well, that's your word against his."

Jane rolled her eyes. "You can't be serious—"

"Listen, the truth is, with everything that's happened in the last few days, we just don't have the resources or manpower to deal with this petty stuff."

"It's not petty! He threatened my kids. I—"

"I got three guys in a holding cell right now back at the station that were armed with hand grenades and headed down to the city to take out that goddamned wall. *They* are a threat. I have a man who stabbed the owner of the Harborview Liquor Store on his front porch this morning because he wouldn't open it to sell him a twelve-pack of shitty beer. *That* man is a threat. I had a lady try to drive her car full of kids into the lake this morning because she thinks the damn apocalypse is coming. *She* is a threat."

"But—"

The officer held up his hand. "The world has lost its goddamn mind. And I'm sorry, but Jake Reynolds pissing on your bonfire is just not a priority right now." He pulled his glasses off, rubbed his tired eyes, and shook his head.

"So that's it?"

The officer slid his glasses back on, then adjusted his mask. "If you get something on him besides putting out your fire, give us a call and we'll pick him up. But you want my advice?"

She didn't answer, but she was sure he was going to tell her, anyway.

"Just ignore him. He's harmless."

"But he threatened me."

"Trust me, in a couple of days, this will blow over. He'll find someone else to annoy."

Jane watched Officer Beale take off, unable to believe the police were going to do nothing. She went inside, locked the door. Thomas would have threatened to sue the police department, which is probably what she should have done. How did they expect her to protect the kids? There wasn't even a decent knife in the cabin—not that she would ever have the guts to stab anyone, anyway. She was a suburban housewife, for crying out loud.

Jane didn't know how they did things out here in bum-fuck Michigan, but if Officer Beale was any indication, she had been fortunate to spend her life in the city. The people up there were crazy.

Jane shook her head and wondered again at her decision to take the kids and flee.

She laid back down in bed and tried to sleep, but every creak sent her heart pounding. She kept trying to pretend she was at home. She tried to imagine Thomas was asleep downstairs in the den, and they were all safe, but it was useless.

Every unfamiliar sound in the darkness dragged her back to the cabin and made sleep impossible.

At five-thirty, she tip-toed into the kitchen and turned on the coffee pot. She pulled her sweatshirt tighter around her body while it gurgled.

Today will be better.

After all, how could it possibly get worse?

Chapter Fourteen

Day 6 // 10:23 a.m

MATT SAT on the couch in his underwear, despite the fact that his mom had kept a closet full of his old clothes. He could not quite believe what he was seeing. Rubbing his eyes, he looked back up. Video footage of thousands of people being systematically vaporized in the Veil filled the screen. Thank god they are dead already, but still...

The aerial coverage showed trucks going down the streets of Manhattan, Queens, and Brooklyn. City workers in hazmat suits picked up bodies, tossing them into the back of garbage trucks like trash. Once the trucks were full, they found the nearest access point to the Veil, and with lights flashing, backed into it. As the rear of the truck passed through the shimmery barrier, the bodies disappeared. The truck rolled forward again, heading out to collect more.

The news anchor's voice was thick with emotion as she spoke. ***"The incredible state of New York today as bodies continue to accumulate. Medical personnel and law enforcement officials have become overwhelmed. The interim mayor gave a brief statement today confirming the city has reached its breaking point."***

The video switched. The new mayor stood behind the podium; speaking through his full-face mask. ***"We continue to do all we can, but the truth is, there simply are not enough of us left to manage this crisis. May God help us."***

The video switched back to the news anchor. ***"His message is***

simple. Do not leave your homes under any circumstances and pray."

The anchor, who looked like she hadn't slept in a week, rested her elbow on the desk and rubbed her forehead for a few seconds before continuing. There were tears in her eyes when she looked into the camera again.

"Due to the massive death tolls, emergency supplies and medical support are no longer being offered to those in need. Bodies are to be placed on the curb for pickup..."

Matt watched as the news anchor tried to regain her composure again.

The video clip switched to a close-up of one of the trucks. People of all ages and ethnicities were unceremoniously dumped into the grimy bins where bags of trash and recycling belonged. Then one of the men activated the compression mechanism, and the bodies were shoved into the bowels of the truck, to make room for more. It didn't look real, and Matt couldn't even begin to imagine the stench emanating from all those rotting corpses.

"The origin of the virus is still unclear, and White House officials..."

Matt turned down the volume. Since the virus had exploded in New York, the debate continued over whether it was a result of biological warfare or a natural-born illness. Some thought it was purposefully being released into the population. Many argued that there was no other explanation for how quickly it was taking over the cities. But Matt wasn't so sure. The terrorist groups that had tried to take credit for the outbreak were ones he knew, and no. No way. They simply did not have the organization, skills, or money to pull something like this off.

He watched in horror as city workers threw the body of a frail, elderly woman in the back of a pickup. Her glasses fell from her open eyes onto the ground and her head bounced lifelessly as the truck rolled through a pothole to collect its next victim.

One thing was for sure, if whatever was in New York got out—

Matt got up and looked out the window at the fields surrounding the house—it wouldn't be long before it was everywhere. Even here, in the middle of nowhere. Maybe the President had been right to do what he had.

He rubbed his aching leg and swallowed two ibuprofen with the cold remains of his coffee. He watched the next segment detailing the outbreak in Toronto.

Then it switched to Dallas. Video feed, taken from a cell phone inside the Veil, showed a high-density area of the city where bodies were being removed from apartment complexes by the dozen. He turned the volume back up. ***"… despite the executive order, people in many sections of the city are refusing to quarantine."***

The next report was on LA, where a small section of the city near Santa Monica had erupted with the virus, but, miraculously, so far it had not spread to any of the neighboring communities.

Matt watched over his shoulder and slowly made his way into the kitchen to find something to eat as the segment switched again. ***"In Rome, despite warnings from both the President and Pope, people continued to gather by the thousands in St. Peter's Square to pray…"***

He leaned against the kitchen counter and looked out the window over his dad's fields of sugar beets.

Was it just a matter of time before it hit Detroit? And what would happen to his parents then? His mom said they were okay. But for how long? Would he be sitting here next week watching their bodies being dumped into the back of a garbage truck on national television? The thought made him sick.

He pulled his hand through his hair. "Fuck."

Matt glanced over his shoulder. His phone was waiting on the table in the den.

Maybe it was time to talk to his dad.

Chapter Fifteen

Day 7 // 4:15 p.m

BRIA FUSSED in her car seat, frustrated by her restraints and overdue for her nap, while Jane shook her head in amazement.

If there was one thing she thought she could count on from backward country folk, it was easy access to firearms. Much to her disappointment, that had turned out to be untrue. They had only been able to find one pharmacy and one liquor store, both illegally open. Unsurprisingly, neither carried guns. And unfortunately, for Jane, a gun was the only thing she could think of to protect her family from Jake.

Everything else in Port Huron was either closed, boarded up, or —in a few instances—vandalized. She didn't know if it was like that everywhere or not, but she imagined it was. What was she going to do when they ran out of the supplies she had purchased? What if the quarantine wasn't lifted by then? How would she feed the kids? Where would they find food?

Police were out patrolling. Twice they had stopped Jane to ask where she was going. She'd promised to go straight home both times. Thank god, they hadn't arrested her.

They passed several vacant, lake-side homes on their way back up to Harborview that looked a lot like the home she had left behind. She imagined there would be lots of stocked pantries in those houses.

That had to be what Jake was doing when she had seen him loitering around a neighboring house earlier that morning. He had been stealing. Just another reason to have a gun. Clearly, the man had no problem breaking and entering.

She would do it if it came down to it, but it had only been seven days. They had enough food to make it a couple of weeks. Maybe more, if she rationed.

Who knew? Maybe by then, the Veil would be disabled if there were no outbreaks in Detroit, and everything would be back to normal.

She noticed flashing red and blue lights ahead and slowed. There was a pickup truck in front of her, and as they came to a stop, an officer detoured them down a dirt road. Jane followed the truck slowly around the accident and down the country road.

Having no idea where she was going, Jane turned and headed north at the first forlorn intersection. Then headed back east at the first opportunity. None of the streets were marked, making her wonder how anyone knew where they were going.

"Turn left at the old tree-stump and right at the broken-down pickup truck," she muttered to herself. Or maybe all five people that lived out there just knew, she thought sarcastically.

The countryside was beautiful, though. Most of the fields were sprouted and green—with what crops, she had no idea. They went on for miles in every direction, punctuated by little clusters of trees. The sky was incredible. Ten times bigger than it seemed in the city, blue, with a bank of clouds to the east that looked like mountains hanging over the lake.

They passed a quaint house with a barn and pond. Two girls ran around the vibrant green lawn. They were chased by a golden retriever. Hanging baskets of purple impatiens lined the porch of the farmhouse where a man and woman sat, watching the kids. On a homemade sign planted in the middle of the lawn was a warning: **Private Property**. **Trespassers will be shot on sight**.

The scene was enviable.

Jane brought her eyes back to the road. Life at that farmhouse looked like heaven compared to the little slice of hell they were returning to.

Another big, red barn came into view, followed by a nondescript, two-story, white farmhouse with black shutters. The main house was surrounded by several smaller buildings.

Jane slowed down. One of the shutters on the upstairs windows hung at an odd angle. The grass was tall and the yard unkempt. The whole place looked like it had been abandoned. It was exactly the kind of house that would have a gun in the back closet.

The kids seemed to be enjoying the outing, so Jane took the long way through the surrounding lakeside neighborhood, hoping to find a For-Rent sign in one of the windows. The more she thought about it, the more she realized Thomas was right. She needed to get away from Jake, if for nothing more than her peace of mind. She found a single cottage with a rental sign in the window. It was in a similar neighborhood a mile to the south. She pulled over, dialed the number, and left a message. Then she headed back to the cabin.

While Bria slept, Jane took a quick shower. It was one of the few luxuries from her former life that she still possessed. She would have to put back on the same clothes she had been wearing for a week, but at least she would be clean. She lathered the wildflower-scented dish soap on her arms and shoulders and let the hot water run over her head and down her back as she inspected her body. The upside to all of this was her jeans were fitting looser. It had to be the stress. *Or maybe it was the fact that you're surviving on coffee and the kids' leftovers.*

Jane got out, quickly dressed, and flipped her wet hair in a towel before heading into the living room.

"I'm going to watch the news," she told Maddy. "Keep an eye on Bria."

Her niece nodded, and glanced at her little cousin, snoozing in her playpen in the middle of the kitchen.

Jane took the TV back into the bedroom, flipped it on, and found the news.

Ever since the President had explained what they knew about the virus, a worrisome thought had been festering in the back of her mind. It had been decades since she'd thought about grad school and her work, but everything that was happening… Well, it was all coming back to her now. And it almost seemed like…

She turned the volume down so the kids couldn't hear it.

The first bit was about what was happening in Canada, which made sense. She still hadn't been able to get anything but a Canadian station.

Then they replayed President Rodriguez's statement that she had missed the night before.

"In light of the events in New York City," he began, ***"I have been forced to declare martial law for the entire country."*** He sighed and pinched his nose, clearly frustrated. ***"Despite clear warnings, and mandates demanding everyone on the outside quarantine, people continue to pour out of the unwalled-cities…"***

The hair on Jane's arms stood on end.

Well, that sounds eerily familiar, doesn't it?

Jane nodded to herself, remembering. She had written almost those exact words.

"… faster than the roads can accommodate them. As of this very moment, there are over a hundred-thousand Americans trapped in their cars along our nation's highways. Not only are they at risk of contracting the virus, they are cutting off important routes necessary for the transportation of supplies."

"Roads will become impassable," she quoted from memory. "The virus will become concentrated along the thoroughfares like tentacles infecting…" Her voice drifted off.

"… like tentacles infecting the entire country." Jane's eyes widened and her ears began to ring as the President repeated her almost verbatim.

"Let me be clear, and I am speaking to those of you thinking to flee. If the virus has escaped, it will be concentrated along these thoroughfares…"

She pressed her fingers to her temples, trying to ignore the terrifying and very bizarre possibility taking shape in her head.

"... cannot do that with everyone running around in a panic." He shook his head sadly. ***"We need to come together, and we need to stay put. We need to assist law enforcement, not..."***

"... overwhelm them." Jane choked. She pressed her palm to her forehead. "Order must be maintained. Without it there..."

"... is no hope of containing the virus." The President finished.

Jane couldn't swallow. She could barely breathe. Her arms shook as she continued to press her hand to her forehead. Why was he reading excerpts from her master's thesis?

The President flipped to the next page.

"Shit..." Jane swayed with dizziness. *Is this how Robert knew?*

The President continued. ***"To assist in the growing crisis, I have activated all branches of the military. All active-duty members who are state-side have been called up. The Coast Guard and Red Cross have been deployed full-force to help with the ensuing panic, and help people return to their homes until a tracking system can be set up or the quarantine is over."***

Is this why he called to warn you?

"Shit," she whispered again. She really hoped not.

Jane hugged her knees against her chest. It had literally been decades since she had even thought about her research.

Her project had been to model a hypothetical highly transmissible super-virus and then find a way to contain it. It had been her second year of grad school and she, with the help of Robert, had created a series of simulations. They had been painstakingly constructed using several million data points that she had cataloged and collected—some of which spanned back hundreds of years. Jane ran her virus through them. Unsurprisingly, none of the CDC protocols at the time even came close to containing it.

She spent months tweaking every variable she could think of, to see what effect it had on the final death tolls. Once she weeded out the ones that had little or no effect and found the ones with the greatest impact, she adjusted them, combined them, trying to alter the outcome and bring the numbers down, but nothing worked. She ran the simulations over and over, trying to find a way out, that *one* thing that would give them a chance. But there was nothing.

Jane stared at the television as the President continued to speak.

She spent weeks sitting at her desk in Robert's office watching the scenarios play out, and they all ended the same. Complete annihilation of the species. It was terrifying. And then one late evening she'd had a stroke of genius. Instead of running the simulations forward, she put in the result she wanted and then ran them *backward.* Most of the resulting variables and input ranges weren't viable. They just weren't plausible in the real world. Four days was not enough time to create and test a vaccine. But just when she thought there was no hope left, she finally found *one* that they just might be able to bring into the range the simulation demanded. And if they could, according to the model anyway, it would successfully stop the spread of the virus.

Jane rubbed the goosebumps on her arms and remembered sitting at her desk staring at the screen. She had been elated, as her mind raced through the possible ways to achieve the target range. She had been horrified when she could only think of one that would get the job done. She confided in Robert that her conclusion upset her. But he had just shrugged. 'It's only make-believe, Jane. And the numbers don't lie,' he said. He told her to write up her findings. So, with a great deal of discomfort, she did.

It didn't take long for people to find out what that one way was, and it made her wildly unpopular, both in the department and around campus. All but one of her classmates stopped speaking to her. The school paper even featured an unflattering article about her. Even though none of it was her opinion, even though it was founded on solid math and science, they had labeled her as an extremist. One of the professors teaching a course on human rights had called her "paranoid" and a "danger to society." She was called other names as well. On top of that and everything else, she was sick all the time and barely sleeping.

She had been in the middle of trying to decide if she should scrap her project for something less controversial when the accident happened.

Jane never stepped foot in the department again. She never finished her thesis, and as far as she knew it was still buried in the hard drive of her old laptop. No—wait, that wasn't true. *Robert has a copy.*

"Shit," she said again.

Jane dropped her feet to the floor and her knees bounced nervously as she continued to listen. If the President was using her paper as a template, he would know the only variable that affected the outcome of the outbreak in any meaningful way was time. In the event that it had escaped, and she was almost sure it had, being able to track the spread of the virus in real-time was their best chance at moving quickly enough to eradicate it before it spread out of control. It was the only thing that gave them even a small bit of hope. If he had read her paper, he would also know if it had escaped, and again, she was almost positive it had, it was barely worth implementing. Still, a five percent chance was better than nothing.

"… we speak wrist bands are being distributed to the communities adjacent to the walled cities. Everyone in every household is required to have one, even children and infants. These wristbands will allow us to follow the trail, should the virus…"

Jane's knee stopped bouncing, and sweat popped out on her forehead. She turned off the TV, and the all-too-familiar pressure on the back of her throat forced her off the bed. Stumbling into the bathroom, she slammed the door shut and dropped to her knees on the cracked vinyl floor. She lifted the lid of the toilet.

Was she really responsible for all of this? *The Veil certainly was not your idea.* But everything else? Jane's stomach lurched and her eyes watered as she pressed her hands against the toilet seat and threw up. She wasn't in the right mental space to deal with the possibility that she might be the fifth horseman of the apocalypse. What name would they give her? *Destruction?*

"Oh god." she moaned, resting her head on her arm.

"Mommy?" Tommy's worried voice called through the door.

Her stomach lurched again, and she squeezed her eyes shut as she emptied its contents into the bowl.

"Mommy? What's that noise?"

She wiped her mouth. "I'm okay bud. I'll be out in a minute."

Jane got to her feet, then rinsed her mouth with shaky hands. She stared at herself in the mirror. She had to be imagining things.

Focus on what you can control.

She closed her eyes shut and took several deep breaths. When her heart finally steadied, she pulled the door open. Tommy looked up at her from the floor and she tried to smile.

Jane checked on Bria, then put the TV back in the living room. She found a cartoon for Tommy, then made her way into the kitchen. On the off chance the President *had* gotten a hold of her paper, all she could do was pray he had not read it to the end.

Jane tied her apron around her waist, then got to making dinner.

The familiar routine calmed her and it wasn't long until she was hovering over the stove, humming along to one of her favorite tunes from her jazz playlist. For a moment, life almost felt normal. Jane was relieved that she was no longer a scientist. Cooking was more her speed now. It was much less stressful.

Jane stirred the pasta sauce, recalling her last dinner party. Even though they sat at opposite ends of the table, those were her best times with Thomas. When she could almost believe he felt something for her other than contempt. Maybe that's why she loved hosting so much? Because standing next to him, welcoming their guests was as close as he ever got to being her husband. When she was lucky, he would even get drunk enough to make love to her afterward.

She looked at Bria laying on her back in the playpen. She was the byproduct of their yearly holiday party and a little too much mulled wine. Their daughter was the best Christmas gift Thomas had ever given her.

Jane's phone rang. She made her way around the playpen and picked it up off the sill. It was Thomas.

"Hey! I've been trying to get—" she said, pressing the phone to her ear as she headed back to the stove.

"Something's happened, Jane." Thomas choked.

The blood drained from her head. "What?"

"Do you have the TV on?"

She shook her head. "No. The kids are…"

"Oh my god. If… if I go… just tell the kids"—his voice broke—"I love them. I can't believe this is… Tell them I love them, Janie. Tell Tommy that I was so proud to be his dad. Remind Bria when she's older how much I loved her and I used to sing her to…"

Loved? Used to? "What? What's hap—Hold on," she said as she picked up the remote. "Maddy, take the boys in the bedroom. Now."

For once, her niece didn't argue. "Come on," Maddy whispered to the other kids as she moved them off the couch. "Let's play one of grandpa's board games from the closet." The boys followed her and Jane shut the door behind them.

She sat on the coffee table in front of the TV and turned the volume down as low as she could without muting it.

"Thomas…" she began, then stopped. There was something wrong with the TV. The ticker at the bottom said New York City, but the screen was gray. "Thomas? I don't see—" The color shifted, and she stared, realizing it was smoke. The camera zoomed out and a gigantic, gray haze filled the screen. But what caught her eye was the tiny, very familiar silhouette in front of it. Jane stood, and without blinking, leaned into the screen.

Is that…?

She gasped.

It was the Statue of Liberty.

Her eyes returned to the mountain of smoke billowing behind it.

Jane backed away, feeling for the arm of the recliner, and hoping she found it before her knees gave out. She dropped into the cushions.

She pulled her hand through her hair in disbelief. "No, no. This cannot be…" She squeezed her eyes shut, then opened them again. The infamous skyline was still missing.

"Oh my god."

Thomas started talking again, but she couldn't hear his words over the pounding of her heart.

The whole city was just gone?

Her phone slipped from her fingers. "No."

Again, she tried to convince herself none of this had anything to do with her paper.

"Jane!" Thomas yelled from her lap. She picked up the phone and held it to her ear.

It had to be a coincidence. It *had* to be. There was no way the U.S. Government—No, the ICPH—would base their pandemic protocols on a decades-old research paper written by a twenty-three-year-old grad student. She stared at the screen. It sure did look like it, though.

Jane bit her lip.

Suddenly, Maddy was standing in the doorway. "Aunt Jane, the stove?"

Jane jumped up. "Shit." Smoke billowed from the pan as the smell of burned sauce hit her nose.

"Jane? Are you listening to me?" Thomas demanded.

No, she wasn't. "Hold on…"

She turned off the stove and threw the pan in the sink, then headed back to the chair. Maddy was on the couch, looking as shell-shocked as she felt.

"Jane!"

"Thomas," she whispered into the receiver. "I—"

"I need to talk to my mom." Maddy interrupted in a wobbly voice. The fear in her eyes reflected Jane's own.

"Is Sarah there?" she asked into the phone.

"Yeah. Hold on." Jane could barely hear him above the ringing in her ears.

New York doesn't exist anymore.

Jane handed the phone to Maddy and buried her head in her hands. Bria started to cry. She switched it back to the movie the boys had been watching, afraid to see more, definitely not wanting to know what came next. The room spun dangerously as she stumbled to the bedroom door and pushed it open. Tommy and Austin were sitting on the edge of the bed, holding hands, looking scared. The game *Sorry* was spilled out on the bed behind them. She pulled them in for a quick hug.

"Come on, you guys can finish your movie, and then we'll have dinner." Her voice sounded far away—like it belonged to someone else.

How many people even lived in New York? She pinched the bridge of her nose. They were dead? All of them?

She picked up Bria and kissed her softly, savoring her sweet, baby smell. How would she feel if she were Thomas right now? He might never hold his kids again. She blinked back tears. Jane couldn't imagine not being there to watch her baby girl grow up. How could the President kill millions of people? *Because you told him to.* She squeezed her eyes shut. That wasn't true.

"Your daddy loves you so much," she whispered, unable to keep her voice steady.

"Aunt Jane." Maddy handed Jane the phone, then fled to the bathroom, slamming the door behind her.

"Thomas?" Jane asked, shifting Bria to her hip and heading back to the living room.

"Thank you." It wasn't Thomas. It was her sister.

"Sarah, I…"

"Thank you for getting them out. I… oh my god. I can't believe this is happening. It's so surreal, you know? I–I don't know how to say everything"—Sarah's voice broke—"I'm so sorry. I am so sorry I wasn't there when you called."

Jane heard Thomas. "Hey, it's okay. Come here," he said. There was a tenderness in his voice that Jane hadn't heard in a long time, and she was glad. She was glad he was there for her sister when she couldn't be.

"I don't understand," Jane said, trying to explain. "We tried to call you… We called the yoga studio, but the girl there said—"

"I know. It doesn't matter now. Just promise me you'll keep my kids safe, take care of them as if they were your own"—Sarah's voice cracked—"Oh god… I can't believe this is happening. Remind them every day"—Sarah inhaled shakily—"of how much I loved… love them…"

"Sarah…"

"Thank you, Janie, for saving my kids. Really. I love you. And I'm sorry I wasn't a better sister to you." Her voice was heavy with regret.

What in the world is she talking about?

"Sarah? What are you —"

Her sister's sob cut her off.

Except for a couple of years in college, they had been as close as two sisters could be. She struggled to breathe as she wiped the tears spilling down her cheeks with the back of her hand.

"Just promise me."

"Of course, I will," she whispered. "I love the kids. I love you too, little sis. Maybe this will all—"

"Does Austin know?" Sarah asked.

"Not yet. Not really," Jane whispered. "I didn't know if I should tell him or not… I didn't know what you'd want me to say."

"I think… I think it's time. Can you put him on the line?"

"Sure." Jane wiped her eyes again and tried to relax her devastated expression. "Austin! Your mom…" She couldn't get the rest out and turned away when he reached for the phone.

Austin spoke to his mom for a couple of minutes before he told

Tommy his dad wanted to talk to him. Before Tommy could even speak, Austin rushed into the bedroom and threw himself on the bed. Jane heard him crying quietly into the quilt.

Tommy grabbed the phone, happy it was finally his turn to talk. "Hey, Dad! When are you gonna get here?" The question sent Jane over the edge. The pain was so raw, so acute, she could not contain it. She rushed into the corner of the kitchen beside the refrigerator and pressed a towel to her mouth. She faced the dark corner, trying to keep the kids from hearing her sobs.

Her shoulders shook and her head felt like it was going to explode. The accident, and then the day she found out her parents had died, flashed through her mind like gunshots. The sadness had been so overwhelming it had almost destroyed her. It was the same now. She squeezed the towel in her fist. No, this was worse, because those other things had been accidents. But this awful farewell? This was *her* fault. Thomas was saying goodbye to his son because of *her*. How could she do that to him? To Sarah?

A small hand on her arm forced her bitter thoughts aside. Jane swiped furiously at her eyes, arranging the magnets on the side of the fridge, pretending that was what she had been doing.

"Hey, mommy," Tommy said. His smile faded when he saw her face. "What are you doing?"

"Just, got a little… soap in my eye. What's up, bud?"

"Dad wants to see the picture of me with the minnow."

Jane forced the corners of her mouth up and smacked her forehead, somehow managing to find her voice. "That's right! I forgot to send it."

Tommy's smile returned. Then he rolled his eyes. "You always forget. And he wants to know if we have any more fish food for Sir Spaghetti, and I told him we do, but he can't find it."

She did her best to smile. The truth was, she hadn't been able to get the picture to go through.

Jane looked up at the ceiling and wiped her eyes one last time. She willed her game-face into place. "I just bought some food for

Sir Spaghetti. It's in the pantry, on the shelf just above the filters." That grocery shopping trip felt like a lifetime ago, and she supposed it kind of was. This was a different world they were living in now. "Here, give me that. Go find Austin and finish your movie."

"Can we have popcorn?" The boy asked, raising his eyebrows hopefully.

Jane turned to the cabinets as she balanced the phone between her shoulder and her ear. "I'll look. Go watch."

Tommy turned and shouted, "Austin! My mom is making popcorn. Come on! Let's watch."

Jane stayed on the phone while she made popcorn, and through the evening. Every time they got disconnected, she feared the worst as she frantically called them back.

Chapter Sixteen

Day 8 // 3:07 a.m

MATT WOKE up in a cold sweat. The explosion in his head gave way to the rumble of thunder in the distance. He looked at the clock, appalled by the fact that his mom still had the old, digital one he had used in high school.

The nightmare had pulled him from sleep again.

He rubbed his eyes. How was a man supposed to recover when he couldn't fucking sleep? It was a miracle he hadn't lost his mind already, although to be fair, he felt close. Everything about being home was stirring things better left buried in his subconscious.

It was hard enough getting up every morning in his old bed, without the memory of burned flesh in his nose and the depressing fog of exhaustion that shrouded him.

His foot ached, and he tried to ignore it. 'It's all in your head,' his therapist had said.

Matt pushed the blanket back and sat up. That same doctor had gone on to suggest electric shock and seizures as a cure for his PTSD. After which, Matt got up, flipped him off, and stormed out of his office. He had never bothered to return.

The good news was his brain was shock-free, the bad news was he still had nightmares.

Matt scratched his itchy chin. He couldn't remember the last time he had shaved. It took him a moment, but he got out of bed.

He slowly made his way to the bathroom and flipped on the light. He blinked, then stared at his reflection, not recognizing the man staring back at him. That happened a lot lately. Yes, he had the same wavy, sandy-brown hair and beard, but the body that had once been a friend, despite being stronger than it had ever been, was now his enemy. He studied his hard-earned physique in the mirror. His considerable biceps, his defined abs, all of that work for nothing. All the time and energy he'd put in and still it stood in the way of everything he wanted and everything he had been before.

Matt opened the drawer and found the shaving cream and shook his head at the cheap razors his dad still used. He sprayed the thick white foam that smelled like his father, onto his hand. Then he dabbed it on his face. He knew he should just resign himself to the fact that he was someone else now. *Everyone else has.* But he just couldn't, which was probably why he was so fucking miserable.

He spread the cream onto his neck. How else should he feel, knowing no matter how hard he worked, he would never be good enough? Knowing he would never again have the only thing he wanted. The Army had made that abundantly clear. His career was over, which meant his *life* was over.

Then why do you keep trying?

He met his tired eyes in the mirror and pulled the blade across his cheek.

Because he didn't know how to be anyone else.

Chapter Seventeen

Day 8 // 4:31 a.m

JANE SAT UP, rubbing her eyes. She had fallen asleep on the bathroom floor with her head resting against the tub. Her neck ached and her head throbbed.

"They tried to destroy the wall?" she repeated, not sure she'd heard Thomas correctly. She looked toward the door, hoping the kids stayed asleep.

"Shh…" he whispered. She heard a shuffling, and he turned up the volume so she could hear too.

Jane could just make out the voice of the news anchor. ***"Reports are coming in that a coordinated effort was made by the members of the UAW to destroy the Veil. The group of over two hundred tradesmen outnumbered law enforcement. Their plan, which sought to take down all the towers at once, has been carried out—clearly with devastating effect. Witnesses across the river reported a huge explosion…"***

"Oh, my god…"

"What?" Jane asked, wishing she could see, but also glad she couldn't.

"There is a… crater. Where Midtown used to be," Thomas whispered. She heard Sarah gasp. "It's filling with water…" he continued, "Jesus Christ. It's huge."

The anchor continued, ***"The Coast Guard is on-site now, but so far, they have found no survivors. Not a single one. Seven days***

ago, over a million people were living in Manhattan. Now they are gone. New York City is… gone."

"Jesus…" Thomas said. "They are showing the satellite view. There is ash raining down over half of New Jersey." His voice was filled with morbid awe.

Jane pulled her hair back. "Wait. That's good news!"

Her worry over her thesis had been festering since she saw the explosion, but knowing the cause was just desperate citizens, and not the result of—*an executive order*—meant that maybe, just maybe, it didn't have anything to do with her paper after all.

"What is the matter with—" Thomas sounded appalled.

"Thomas," she said in a hurried hush, "It means the people inside did this, not the government—"

"The government? What are you talking about? Why the hell would—"

"Just listen. If that's true, then you will be fine. Everyone will be fine as long as you don't touch the Veil or try to take it down. I–I don't think anything else is going to happen! I think you guys will be—"

Thomas exhaled heavily, catching her point. "God, I hope so."

Jane heard sirens over the phone. "What's happening?"

She heard him get up, probably off the couch, and she could imagine him walking to the front window and looking out over their beautifully manicured lawn. "I'm guessing the cops just had the same idea you did. They are headed toward the Veil."

Bria began to cry, and Austin opened the bathroom door. His blue eyes were red and puffy. "I tried to hold her. I don't know what she needs…" he apologized.

Jane pushed herself to her knees. She leaned against the tub and stood. "Thomas, I have to go. The kids… But I really think everything will be okay."

"Go," he said, sounding relieved—almost like he was smiling.

"I want to talk to my mom again." Maddy appeared behind her brother and held out her hand.

"Thomas, wait! Maddy wants to talk to Sarah."

Jane handed her the phone, and they traded places. She went into the bedroom to get her own daughter as Sarah talked to hers. Hopefully, if Jane was right, it would not be for the last time.

Chapter Eighteen

Day 9 // 11:03 a.m

THE QUARANTINE WAS STILL in effect, but Jane needed formula for Bria, and she couldn't very well leave the kids at home with Jake lurking around. So, she loaded them all in the van and headed out with the promise of a walk at the harbor afterward so long as no one else was there.

Harborview was a quaint, sleepy community just off the water that boasted three churches, two fudge shops, one stoplight, and a handful of other mom and pop businesses. The first store on the south end of town was boarded up. A sign on the door read 'Closed until further notice.'

"Damn," Jane whispered to herself. She knew it was a long shot, but she was still disappointed.

American flags hung from the lampposts that dotted the sidewalk in even intervals as she drove on to the next store. The street down to the water was empty of cars, and she saw only one person walking. Surprisingly, the store was open but unfortunately, they had nothing left to sell except pet food, and she wasn't that desperate… yet.

"Try the one in Mariette," they said.

Jane made the five-mile trip inland, away from the lake, eyeing the gas gauge nervously. None of the gas stations in Harborview had been open, and she had less than a half-tank. Even with the extra gas at the cottage, they wouldn't get too far if, for some reason, they had to flee again.

Don't worry about things you can't change.

Right. Mariette was a little less picturesque than Harborview, but clean and charming in its own way. A typical midwestern town, with sturdy yellow brick buildings along the main street and a rusty grain silo perched next to two neat rows of train tracks. Instead of fudge and souvenirs, the storefronts advertised practical things like insurance and vacuums. She pulled into the parking lot of the small grocery store. There was nothing she could do about the gas situation, but maybe there was still something she could do about the food one. She tied a cloth over her mouth and then secured one over Tommy's. Maddy and Austin decided to stay in the car with Bria.

Like the previous store, the shelves were almost empty, and there was no formula. A knot formed in her stomach as she realized she had no choice but to transition Bria to solid food whether she was ready or not. She hadn't even cut her first tooth yet.

As she made her way down the aisles, she overheard a man arguing with the cashier. She peered around the corner. Beside her and Tommy, he was the only one in the store wearing a face covering.

"Please," he begged. "She is in so much pain. You've got to have something–anything! I can't bear to see her—"

"I know, and I'm so sorry, Ed. You know we love Ruthie. But we just don't have anything left. Not even aspirin. It's just all gone. You've seen the shelves. We haven't had a truck come in since the Veil went up. I don't know if we will ever get another one. If we do, I promise to call you. But that's all I can do."

"Do you know of anywhere else I can go?"

The cashier shook her head. "It's like this everywhere. Most of our suppliers were in the city, and since the government has taken over all transport–Did you try the hospital?"

"They are on some kind of lockdown." He dropped his gnarled hands on the counter. "I can't just leave her suffering!" The old man turned to go and then stopped. "Do you have anything at home you could give me? We planted a garden this spring. You can come and take whatever you want in exchange. The whole damn plants if you—"

"It's not that, Ed." There was real emotion in the woman's voice. "Of course, I would give you whatever we had, whatever *I* had. There just isn't–There's nothing in the back. I'll take you to see if you want."

"What am I going to do? I gotta help her, Diane."

The cashier just shook her head. "I know. I am sorry."

He sighed hopelessly and headed for the door. The helplessness in his voice tugged at Jane's heartstrings, and she thought about the four bottles of ibuprofen under the sink back at the cottage. If she'd had them with her, she would have gladly given him one.

Jane caught her reflection in the security mirror as she turned away. If it weren't for Tommy beside her, she wouldn't have even recognized herself. She looked down at her chipped, red nail polish and the clothes she'd been wearing since they arrived. If she had the energy, Jane would have been humiliated to be seen like this—which was saying a lot among these work boot, plaid shirt-wearing women.

She called Tommy back when she noticed he had struck up a conversation with a thirty-something woman covered in tattoos. She had brown wavy hair pulled back in a messy ponytail and wore combat boots and a t-shirt that said 'I'm The Bitch' on the front.

"I'm sorry," the woman said, smiling. "I didn't mean to—"

"No, it's fine," Jane said, not waiting for the woman to finish. She wheeled Tommy away.

"What did I tell you about talking to strangers?" she hissed in his ear. "Especially these people—"

Jane glanced at a young braless mother, sporting a tank-top over pajama bottoms. She was pushing a cart full of half-naked kids—Dear god, it was a modern-day 'Deliverance.'

Jane kept her voice low. "We have to be careful—"

"She was just asking me what grade I was in and what size—"

Jane rolled her eyes. *Well, that isn't creepy at all.* She probably ran a child trafficking ring.

Jane pushed Tommy down the aisle, past an old woman that smelled like an ashtray. "How many times have your dad and I talked to you about this?" she demanded, taking his hand.

"A million…" he reluctantly admitted before falling into step beside her.

The man coming toward her looked like he could be Jake's cousin. He was even missing his two front teeth. She squeezed Tommy's hand in hers and hurried past him.

The laundry aisle was empty. Jane stared at the shelves. How was she going to wash their clothes? She blanched. What were they going to wear while they dried? The thought of her and the kids wandering around the house for days in towels and sheets seemed both pathetic and funny at the same time.

She sighed. It was looking more and more inevitable that some breaking-and-entering would be happening soon.

Jane paid for her meager purchases, using the emergency cash in her purse, and they headed back toward Harborview.

She quickly came up behind an old pickup and recognized the red cap of the old man from the grocery store. When he slowed his truck and turned down a dirt road, she did too—not knowing why.

"Hey!" Austin called from the back seat. "This isn't the way to the harbor."

"I know. We're just taking a little detour."

She followed him down yet another nondescript country road until he pulled into the driveway of an old farmhouse. Jane continued east and passed the abandoned farm she'd seen before and realized where she was. They were only a mile or so from the cottage. She hopped back on the highway and headed north again toward Harborview.

AS THE BOYS climbed over the rocks that lined the harbor, Jane walked on the concrete sidewalk that topped it, promising herself after the days they'd spent cooped up, she would give them the freedom to explore. It's what Thomas would have done. And they all needed an outlet, a way to cope with what was happening. They were the only ones there except for a man on one of the docks checking on his boat.

"Just be careful!" she shouted as they hopped precariously from rock to rock.

She wished she could do this with them every day, take them out, let them play, and maybe she should. But it was too far to walk, and she was trying to conserve the gas in the van. Still, it was tempting.

Jane walked to the end of the rocks and sat on the largest one while the boys played and the sun sparkled on the water. Across from them, the sea gulls squawked from the docks. It was early in the summer, so only a few boats were moored. Two swans took to the water with four fuzzy gray cygnets.

The wind off the lake was cool but refreshing. She ran her fingers through her hair, then let the wind have it.

Austin shouted and clapped as Tommy jumped from one rock to the other.

Tommy shouted, "Mom, look!" He did it again and Jane clapped too.

"Woohoo!" she shouted back as the boys scampered up the next rock.

The boy's laughter was like medicine for her soul, and she realized she couldn't remember the last time she'd truly laughed. *It's been years.*

She breathed in again, and pushed the sad thought away. The sun was wonderful, and she felt lighter than she had in days. The kids needed to be outside. They needed to be able to play in the fresh air, not be cooped up in that cabin. Things were hard enough as it was. But how could she do that with Jake there, watching them? She really needed to do something about him. But what? Jane tucked her fingers into the soiled sleeves of her sweatshirt and sighed. She needed to do something about their clothes, too.

You need to do a lot of things, about a lot of things.

Jane pulled her fingers through her hair. But for right now, she was just going to sit in the sun and pretend she didn't.

Chapter Nineteen

Day 9 // 12:17 p.m

MATT SIGHED as he checked the rope to make sure it was secure. Why his dad seemed more concerned about his fishing boat being okay than his son, he didn't quite understand. But at least they'd talked. His conscience was clear.

It had been a long walk, almost two miles, and his leg was sore, but he had to admit the fresh air had done him good. He leaned against the boat for a moment as the sun warmed his face.

He had talked to his mom again briefly while he was walking. She said the police had blocked off the entire square mile a little to the south of his apartment, but they were not saying why. They had also received ration packages as promised. She said the first two had contained fresh produce, but the last one had only contained instant oatmeal and canned soup. Three packages for almost two weeks did not seem near enough.

"Well, it's not what we're used to, but it's okay. We are fine, Matty." She went on to assure him it was plenty. "Finally, a diet I can stick to." She laughed. His father had grunted in the background. But her attempt at humor did nothing to alleviate his worry. She reminded him of her pantry in the basement. "Your father always said I had enough food down there to ride out the end of the world. I guess we'll see, won't we?" His dad grunted again, and then they'd said their goodbyes.

Every veiled city in the country had some sort of stay-at-home order in effect. The severity of the order depended on whether they'd had an outbreak yet. For the most part, people were abiding by it. They were too busy sitting in their living rooms, watching the current outbreak in Delhi unfold, to do anything else. The estimated death toll from the virus was already in the millions. Every time Matt turned on the news, the numbers had increased by thousands. It was shocking. And it had only been ten days.

Ten days.

A pair of swans and their babies swam by the dock. One of the adults hissed at him. Matt shooed them away.

True to what the President had said, by the time the symptoms presented, death was already imminent. In other words, by the time you realized you were sick, it was too late to do anything about it. And according to the CDC, the symptoms were all over the place. Muscle spasms, arrhythmia, paralysis. Psychotic behavior was turning up more and more.

Matt had watched in horror as a video filmed in Paris showed a man opening fire on an abandoned street, emptying rounds of bullets into the sky before blindly falling down the steps that led into the underground Metro. In Los Angeles, a woman had supposedly drowned her roommate in the toilet before realizing what she had done and calling the police. By the time they arrived, she was dead, too. A few things were consistent, though. Death was always preceded by an extremely high fever and sudden blindness.

The wind tugged at his hair, and Matt readjusted the ball cap on his head.

But not here. Here...

He looked out past the stone sanctuary of the harbor, over the 23,000 square-mile lake he had grown up beside. Here, things were okay. Predictable. Out here, the thing he hated most, was the thing that seemed to be saving them now—the isolation and the fact that almost nothing here ever changed.

Matt sniffed. *Not even the air.*

He kneeled and checked the second rope, looping it over the cleat a couple more times and knotting it, just to be safe.

It was the same air that he spent all of high school despising. It was the same air he had told his dad he hoped he never smelled again. Matt could still hear the fury in his father's voice when he called from boot camp to let them know that he had enlisted and was not going to be home to help with the harvest. That was almost ten years ago.

It was also the last time they had spoken, before yesterday.

Matt pressed his hand against the side of the boat and pushed himself to his feet.

One of the buttons holding the canvas cover on the boat had popped off. He leaned over and secured it back in place.

According to his mom, the boat was his dad's only joy. Otherwise, all he did was work and sleep. He remembered his dad taking him fishing when he was a boy. It was supposed to be father-son-bonding time, but really, it was just his dad doing what he wanted while Matt impatiently waited to go home. He shook his head as he thought about his dad. *What a waste of a life,* he thought. That was *exactly* what Matt didn't want to happen to him. That was the reason he left. Unlike his father's, Matt wanted his life to *mean* something when it was over.

A flock of gulls squawked and brought his attention back to the present. He blinked in the sun and sighed. So, it was depressingly ironic that after all he'd been through, he was right fucking back where he started.

He heard shouting and looked up to see two boys crawling like spiders across the rocks, while a woman followed behind them. It only took one look to know she was definitely not from around there. Something in the way she walked, in the way she wore her hair down instead of in a ponytail, in the way her jeans narrowed over sneakers instead of widened over boots. Even the way she carried her purse screamed city.

Matt looked back toward town. His mom had told him more people were moving up from Detroit. They were buying the lakeshore property, building expensive houses, and working from home. This woman seemed like one of them. She looked like a lawyer type. From here, she looked like *his* type.

Matt had never dated any of the local high school girls. He had been too afraid of turning out like his parents to take the chance. It also explained why he had been so attracted to Katie when they met. As a social influencer, she was quite literally the opposite of everything his parents stood for. For a time, that had been all he needed until…

Matt kicked at a splinter of wood sticking up from the dock. *Until it wasn't.*

He hadn't been with anyone since her, partly because he no longer knew what he wanted, but partly because… He kicked the dock again and sighed. Partly because he *couldn't.*

The woman walked to the end of the harbor and then sat on a rock while her kids played. She appeared not to have a care in the world. He almost felt like going out there and asking her if she knew the world was in a crisis. From the way she stared out over the water, with her hair flying behind her, she looked like she had no idea.

He stood, watching her for much longer than he should have, because something about her made him forget too. For a moment, the world returned to its normal state, where men checked on their boats and women went for walks with their children.

Chapter Twenty

Day 10 // 8:23 a.m

JANE MADE a single cup of coffee instead of a pot. She had been stupid to make a whole pot every morning—even if she did drink it all. She had been stupid in so many ways, it was getting hard to see past her mistakes to anything she had actually done right. *You are surviving.* Yes, she was.

Jane read the headline again. Things were getting worse in Dallas, and Atlanta had become a hotspot for the sickness. Thousands had died over the last several days. The President had been addressing the country, but he was being held under quarantine too—as was the Vice President, most members of Congress, and dozens of other world leaders. There were no reporters present to ask the questions everyone wanted answers to.

His message was three-fold—stay calm, leave the Veil alone, and pray. That was it. Meanwhile, death tolls in Atlanta and Dallas climbed.

Thankfully, there was no trace of the sickness in Miami, Chicago, or Detroit. Vancouver had also been spared so far. But what that meant, no one knew. Had it not spread to those places? How long would the people in those cities have to wait before they knew if they were safe? If they were virus-free, how long until the Veil came down?

Her research paper continued to nag at her, but she pushed it aside as she had done every time it cropped up in her mind over the last several days. The only thing more preposterous than the Veils themselves would be thinking that it had anything to do with her thesis.

You keep telling yourself that.

She would keep telling herself—and while she was at it—she would remind herself, *again*, that even if they had somehow gotten a hold of her paper, there was nothing she could do about it now. This wasn't her fault.

Keep telling yourself that too.

She had talked to Sarah the night before. A small section on the west side of the city had been closed off. Otherwise, things were quiet. She said the city streets were a ghost town, but intact. There was very little looting and very little violence. To the surprise of the rest of the country and contrary to its bad-boy reputation, Detroit was turning out to be one of the most peaceful, cooperative of the veiled cities. The communities were coming together and staying apart.

After breakfast, Jane went into the bathroom and got an unopened bottle of Ibuprofen from under the sink. She had spent half the night thinking about that old man and his poor wife. What kind of person would she be if she didn't at least try to help?

She could spare one bottle.

Jane loaded the kids into the van and backtracked to the old man's house. She placed the pills on the doorstep, rang the doorbell, then hurried back to the van, hoping to make a quick escape.

"Hello there!" a voice called before she was able to reach the door handle.

Her cheeks burned at being caught red-handed.

She wheeled around and shoved her hands in the back pocket of her jeans. "Hi. Um… I'm Jane. I just overheard you at the store yesterday, and I… had an extra bottle of…"

The old man slowly bent down and picked up the bottle, reading the label.

She cringed and hoped he didn't ask how she knew he needed medicine, or knew where he lived, because she didn't want to explain that she had eavesdropped and then followed him home like a stalker.

His eyes filled with tears. "Let me get my wallet, I can pay you for—"

There was no way she was taking advantage of this poor old man. "Oh god. No, no. It's fine." She held her hands up. "It's no big deal. I—"

"Are you sure?"

"Very."

"Thank you so much…" The man stepped out onto the porch and the door swung shut with a thwack. He lowered his voice. "My wife, Ruth, has stage-four breast cancer and… Well, the treatment center was in Detroit."

"Oh, no…" Jane knew ibuprofen wasn't going to help with that kind of pain.

"Yeah. We knew it wasn't gonna cure her, but it was… holding it off." His voice shook as he spoke. "Anyway, we are nearing the end now, and… she's just in so much pain."

Jane winced. She probably needed morphine. She thought of Thomas's mother, who had died of lung cancer a little over a year ago. "Do you know anyone who has access to marijuana? I've heard sometimes the oil helps…" Her mother-in-law had preferred to smoke it, infuriating Thomas.

The old man shook his head.

"I'm so sorry." Jane stared at him a moment. Then awkwardly turned to go.

"Wait! Can I offer you strawberries from our garden? It's the only thing that's ready now. Or do you need eggs? Our hens lay way more eggs than we know what to do with…"

It would be the first fresh food they had eaten in over a week. "I would love some eggs," she said, gratefully.

The presence of the non-threatening man-made Jane painfully aware of how lonely she was for another adult to talk to. She had been on her own with the kids for ten days, and the comfort of not being the only grown-up was suddenly overwhelming. "Only if you have extra," she choked, embarrassed by the tears that threatened her eyes.

"Lord, that we do. At least till the feed runs out. Come on in. I will get you a couple dozen."

Jane followed him into the house, looking behind her to make sure the kids were still in the van. The screen door closed with another smack.

Her eyes adjusted to the dim interior as she waited by the door. To her surprise, the living room was beautifully appointed. Gleaming cherry wood floors and white leather couches, accented by a gorgeous stone fireplace that disappeared into the ceiling. It was only a moment before the friendly old man was back with a carton of eggs, a plastic bag filled with tiny strawberries, and a grocery bag to put everything in.

"You ever eat farm-fresh eggs?" he asked, looking her over.

Self-consciously she looked down at what was left of her gel manicured nails and filthy designer ripped jeans. Jane winced as she shook her head.

"Well, they'll keep on the counter for a couple of weeks, just as they are. No need to refrigerate. Just wash 'em up before you use 'em, as sometimes they get a little… soiled."

She accepted the carton, wondering what 'soiled' meant. She was tempted to open the carton and see but refrained.

"You got kids?"

Jane nodded. "Two." *Nope.* "Four," she corrected. It was frightening how fast life could change. The accident surfaced in her mind and she pushed it back down. It was the same then, too. The feeling that she had awakened in someone else's life.

The old man nodded. "Come out to the barn with me. Let's see if the girls got another dozen I can send home with you."

"This is plenty," Jane said. "And my kids, they're in the car so I'd better—"

"It will only take a minute," he insisted, brushing past her and heading down the steps.

Jane held up her finger as they passed the van, indicating to the kids to stay put. She followed him out to a big barn, and then he went into a giant, wire-covered pen beside it.

The chickens clucked nervously as he made his way across the pen toward the coop.

Jane hesitated to follow him inside. She had not spent much time around chickens. *Not live ones anyway.* In the hot June sun, the pen didn't smell so wonderful either. She also didn't want to ruin her sneakers. She stood just inside the door, holding the empty carton he had given her.

"You not from around here then?" he asked, looking back at her feet.

"No."

"I see." He lifted a door, and she heard squawking as he rummaged around inside.

"My husband and I own a cabin up here by the lake. We live in the city. Well, we did before…" Jane's voice trailed off.

"I'm Ed Hamilton, by the way. What's your name again?"

There was more squawking as he dumped a chicken onto the dirt beside him. It flapped wildly and hurried away.

"Jane Moore."

"Nice to meet you, Jane." Ed waved her over with a handful of eggs.

Jane carefully picked her way through the seeds and poop. "Likewise. Have you lived here long?"

"Most of my life, which at my age, is a substantial amount of time." Ed smiled as he placed the eggs in the carton. Again, Jane's heart surged in gratitude for his company, and she suppressed the urge to hug him.

He handed her more eggs. They were still warm, which Jane tried not to think too hard about. The soiling was as she suspected. A few of the eggs had little brown skid marks with the occasional downy feather stuck on them. She tried not to gag as she placed them in their slots. If she let the kids see them, they would never eat them.

Ed grabbed a few more and placed them into the carton. Finally, they headed back to the house.

"I really should go. My kids are…"

"I am so grateful to you," he said sadly.

Jane shook her head. "It was nothing. I wish I had something… better to offer you. Hopefully, things will get back to normal soon, and…"

"Your kindness will be repaid, Jane Moore. I am a firm believer in that. The good Lord will make sure of it. Come back for eggs anytime. And if this thing lasts…" Ed waved his bony arm in the direction of Detroit and the Veil, "… produce in the garden will be comin' at the end of July or August. You come help yourself."

Jane nodded. If the Good Lord was real, he had some serious explaining to do.

"It was nice to meet you, Ed. I hope…" Jane stopped, realizing it was only going to get worse. "I am so sorry about your wife."

"Yeah, me too. We've been together fifty-four years and, believe it or not, it hasn't been long enough." His tired blue eyes filled with tears. "I know I should be grateful. But, damn it, I want another fifty-four," he confided. "What am I gonna do without her?"

Jane couldn't imagine wanting to spend a century with anyone, except maybe her kids. Certainly not with Thomas, as sad as that fact was.

"Do you have any family here?" she asked, her own tears stinging the back of her eyeballs.

"Nope, just Ruth and me."

She suddenly didn't want to leave. "Would it be okay if I come out to visit again? Maybe in a couple of days?"

"Sure. We'll have a couple dozen more eggs—"

"No. I'd like to help if I can, be here for… anything you might need."

"There's nothing you can do. Nothing anyone can do," he said, shaking his head.

"Maybe not for her, but… you."

His eyes misted again, and he scratched the back of his head—looking embarrassed.

"I'm not offering out of pity," she said, wondering why she was about to confide in this stranger. "You see, my husband, he didn't actually make it out of the city. So… It's just me and the kids and… I could really use a friend, too."

His eyes softened. "I'm so sorry to hear that." He nodded his head. "Of course. Please, come by anytime."

Jane set the eggs gently on the passenger seat, buckled her seat-belt, and headed for home.

Chapter Twenty-One

Day 10 // 3:01 p.m

AS IF THE eggs weren't good enough news, Jane *finally* heard back from the rental house. Yes, it was for rent, but it would be two-thousand dollars a week.

Eight thousand dollars a month was more than the mortgage on their giant Grosse Pointe home, but it was worth it just to be away from Jake, and she didn't argue. She called Thomas immediately, thankfully got through, and he verified the funds through the bank. The hold the President had placed on all financial transactions would not be lifted for another five days, but the owners gave her the combination to the lock-box anyway. Jane supposed it was one of the benefits of having a famous husband lawyer.

She pulled the van up to the wood-slatted fence that enclosed the backyard, and parked.

And now, she was drenched in sweat, but they were officially moved into their new home.

The cottage was very similar to the one they'd just left—as most were in the area. They had all been built by the same construction company in the 1950s. This one had dark-blue siding and there was a ship's wheel hanging on the front door and white shutters on the windows. On the inside, it had the same small kitchen-living room combination and bedroom layout. But where her cabin was old and dated, this one was more updated, with matching furniture, oak cabinets and freshly painted baby-blue walls. There was one other notable difference.

Jane looked out the window to the east and smiled at the row of vacant houses.

"No neighbors," she whispered in relief.

She turned to the kids. "Go on inside. I forgot the box of DVDs, so I'm going to go get them. I'll be right back."

The boys piled out as Maddy unbuckled Bria and carried her inside.

Jane drove the mile back up the highway, then drove down the dirt road and pulled into the driveway. She was relieved that it would be the last time, hopefully for a while. She made sure all the windows were latched, and took one more quick look around. She juggled the box of DVDs in one arm and locked the door behind her with the other.

"You're leaving?"

She jumped, almost dropping the box, and whipped around toward the voice.

Jake stood between her and the van, a deep frown spread across his face. A cigarette dangled between his lips.

She edged her way to the van.

"We're, uh, headed back down south. Decided to stay with some friends, closer to the city," she lied, wondering why she was bothering answering him at all.

Jake frowned, pulling the cigarette out of his mouth. Ash fell onto his beard.

Jane hurried to the driver's side, pulled the door open, and shoved the box in. The DVDs spilled onto the floor between the seats. She jumped in, shut the door, and locked it. Her heart pounded as she shoved the key in the ignition and the van turned over.

Jake stood in the grass as she backed out of the driveway.

Jane took a deep breath as she drove away. *One problem solved. Now on to the hundreds of others.*

Chapter Twenty-Two

Day 11 // 1:58 a.m

JANE WOKE UP WITH A START.

She glanced at the nightstand and saw Thomas's face light up the screen of her phone.

She scrambled to grab it. "Hello?"

"It's here."

She sat up and rubbed her eyes. "What?"

"The virus. It's here in Detroit."

Her heart sank. "What…"

"They just announced it. We weren't sure when they blocked off that neighborhood. We hoped it was something else, but it's here. The news says it was a single house on the west side. A family of six. So far it seems… isolated, but…"

Jane heard a noise and looked toward the window.

"Just stay inside. Stay away from everyone," she advised, getting up and peeking through the blinds.

"Yeah, I know. Go back to bed. I'll talk to you tomorrow. I just… I wanted to let you know."

Jane pulled her hair off her face. "Yeah. Okay. Thanks."

She heard the sound again and turned. It had come from across the street, maybe? Or next door? She quietly ran to the living room, to the window by the front door and peered out. The porch light illuminated most of the front yard, but she saw nothing.

It had been a weird… cracking noise. *Maybe a tree branch?* She squinted to see if she could make out anything in the yard behind the house.

Jane listened, but heard nothing else. She looked at her watch. Two a.m. It was kind of late for anyone to be out.

She pulled the knife out of the kitchen drawer and set it on the table. Then she pulled out the dining room chair and sat down beside it. Nervously, she waited, staring at the window until light peeked around the edges of the blinds and the kids began to stir. She could not go on like this. Again, she thought of the abandoned farmhouse. She needed something better than a bread knife to protect the kids, and her best bet for finding something was there. It was time to add breaking and entering to her resume.

Chapter Twenty-Three

Day 12 // 11:15 a.m

JANE MADE the kids an early lunch, then put Bria down for her nap and told Maddy she was going to take a quick trip to check on Mrs. Hamilton. She didn't want to tell them the truth—that she was going to break into the farmhouse with the broken shutters.

It only took five minutes, and as Jane pulled up to the old house, she almost lost her nerve. *For the kids*, she told herself as she cut the engine.

She got out of the van and stared up at the old house. Except for the dangling shutter, it actually didn't look so bad up close. But the lawn still hadn't been mowed and there were huge branches sprawled in the grass and on the steps, indicating no one had been there since the last storm, which was before she'd arrived almost two weeks ago.

"I can do this," she breathed, pushing her shoulders back.

Dead geraniums hung limply over the sides of the pots on the front porch, adding weight to her theory of abandonment as Jane glanced over her shoulder and climbed the creaky, wooden stairs.

She stared at the door. It looked sturdy. Hopefully, there was a key—

"Help! Help me!" A man's voice screamed from somewhere above her, tearing her from her thoughts.

Jane froze as his cry set her every hair on end.

"Help!" His voice cracked with fear.

"Shit," she whispered, bolting down the stairs.

"Hold on, man. Please! Somebody. Oh, god." He screamed as if he'd been struck, and the helplessness in his voice brought her to a stop in the middle of the driveway. She skidded on the gravel and almost fell. Was someone holding him hostage? Or… murdering him? She thought of Jake.

"Help me! Get us out of here!" he screamed again. She looked up. It was coming from the open window upstairs, but she couldn't see anything beyond the white curtains.

"Help!"

Jane took a step back toward the house. *No. You have no idea what is happening up there.* She turned back toward the van.

"Help me, please!" he begged.

She paused and looked back again. *Don't do it. This is not your fight.* She didn't *want* to do it, but how could she turn her back on someone screaming for—

"Help!"

You are not a hero. No, she wasn't, but—"Damn it." Jane ran back up the steps and looked around for something she could use as a weapon. There was nothing on the porch. She couldn't just run away when someone was screaming for help any more than she could keep medicine from a dying woman.

This is a bad idea.

Jane's heart thudded in her chest as she ran back down the steps and around the side of the house.

But there was no weapon. No shovel, baseball bat, or machete. *Because this is not a movie.*

She spotted a branch on the ground as she ran back toward the front of the house and scooped it up. It would have to do.

You are definitely going to die—

Jane took the front steps again, two at a time, and tried the knob, but it was locked.

"Help!" the voice called again.

Was he *actually* crying?

She lunged into the door with her shoulder.

The man screamed again.

The Jane Moore that drank lattes, was head of the PTA, and went to Bikram yoga on Monday and Wednesday mornings floated away. An entirely new—surprisingly strong—woman took over her body and, on only her fourth try, busted down the door. It flew open and smacked against the wall.

Jane blinked in shock. "Holy shit."

"Someone. Oh god. Oh god…" he wailed, spurring her back into action.

She raced up the old wooden staircase to the right of the door, as he cried out again.

Whatever she was running into, it was bad. Men didn't cry like that for no reason.

Which is why you shouldn't—

Jane rushed toward the closed door at the end of the hall, clutching the branch in her hand. Bracing herself, she threw it open with a wild, terrified scream and started swinging.

A switch in her brain flipped, and she was reminded of the one time she'd done acid in high school. Time slowed almost to a stop, and she stared in wonder as the most unexpected series of events unfolded.

White sheets fluttered into the air like the wings of a dove as an unthinkably handsome, ridiculously muscular, half-naked man materialized beneath them, landing on his feet beside the bed.

Foot, Jane corrected. His left one was missing just above the ankle.

She blinked again as his wild, cider-colored eyes bore into hers, and he stared at her like a cat ready to pounce. She stood, paralyzed as his slick chest heaved, pushing long breaths out of his mouth in mesmerizing whooshes.

"What the—" Jane blinked once more, and time returned to its normal speed in an earth-shattering instant, shoving her backward. *I told you this was a mis—*

Her heel hit something that felt suspiciously like a body, and she fell back.

"Shit." The man lunged for her.

He caught her arm, but not before she fell backward over what turned out to be a camo-printed duffle bag. Pain ricocheted through her head as she smacked against something hard and her vision went black.

"HEY."

His warm hand tapped her cheek. She swatted it away as her eyes fluttered open. Thomas could be so annoying when—Her eyes focused on the man in front of her. *That is not Thomas.* She threw herself backward, hitting her head again on the sharp corner of the dresser.

"Hey," he said, "Just take it easy. You bumped your head… Again."

"You're naked," she whispered, before she could stop herself.

Technically, he was wearing tighty-whities, but the way he was sitting on his knees in front of her… Well, he might as well have been. There was literally nothing left for her imagination to do.

With tremendous effort, she dragged her eyes up, across his chest, and back to his face. She thought she might die of embarrassment, as Latte-Jane flitted back into her body.

The corners of his eyes wrinkled as he tried not to smile.

"Does that bother you?" he asked with a raised eyebrow.

He actually has the V. Her eyes fell back to his hips, as they descended into his briefs. "Holy shit." He did. She had never seen it in real life before. She wondered—Jane reached out to touch him, then realizing what she was doing, pulled her hand back.

He coughed.

He asked you a question.

"What?" She couldn't concentrate.

"I said, does that bother—"

She finally remembered. "Yes, it bothers me," she rushed.

Where is the other person?

She glanced around the room, and the movement made her want to puke. She had absolutely no idea. The man in front of her seemed to be the only one there.

His brow arched higher. "Well then, maybe you shouldn't have barged into my bedroom."

Jane's eyes widened. Barged in? No, that's not what happened. He'd called *her* for help… only… he looked fine.

More than fine. She touched the back of her head. *Ouch.* That stung. She noticed a bit of blood on her fingers.

"You're lucky it was cool last night. Because I usually sleep naked," he said, winking at her.

Jane's jaw dropped open, and the man's smile widened. It sent a jolt of electricity straight to her…

She reached up and touched the soft fabric covering her breasts. *Put your hands down.* She yanked them away in confusion. Was she hallucinating?

The corners of his eyes crinkled more, as he tried not to laugh.

Jane scooched herself back toward the door, blinking. She must have hit her head harder than she thought because—she looked around the small room again—where was the other person?

He put his hand on her arm, and she jerked it away. His face lost all traces of humor.

"Hey. I'm sorry. I'm not going to hurt you." He looked at the stick lying beside her, and his brow went up again. "And I don't think you meant to hurt me with that?" He asked the question slowly—like she was a toddler, just learning to communicate.

He actually has a six-pack of abs. Yes, he did. Jane realized she was nodding, and shook her head vigorously. She swallowed the urge to throw up again, but could not look away.

Stop staring, Janie.

But he was so naked. So handsome and naked, she corrected,

then rolled her eyes. So *young* and handsome and naked, she corrected again.

"I am curious… what exactly it was you were trying to accomplish?" he asked.

Jane tried to focus on what he was saying, but she was so damn confused. *And nervous.* That too.

The man pressed his hands to the floorboards, easily hopped up onto his foot, and sat back on the bed. He covered his lower half with a blanket. "Is this better?" he asked.

Not really.

"What? I–I don't understand," she stammered, rubbing the back of her head again.

"What part?" He cocked his head to the side. His brow went up *again*.

Jane lost her train of thought and watched breathlessly as he ran his fingers through his unkempt sandy-brown hair. Somehow, it was the sexiest thing she'd ever seen, which was weird, because the gesture itself wasn't really—His eyes crinkled in the corners again and she swore under her breath.

You've lost it.

Yep. But was it before or after she hit her head? Either way, this was easily the most embarrassing moment of her life. And now that she knew no one was being murdered—

You need to get the hell out of here. Jane got to her knees and pressed her palms to her forehead.

"I thought you were calling for… help," she said, shaking her head. Her nausea returned immediately.

Well, then stop doing that.

"I'm so sorry." She immediately forgot and shook her head again.

Damn it.

Jane's stomach rolled as she pulled her knee up and planted her foot on the floor. She looked up at him. "I thought you said someone was dying—I don't know what I thought—" she finished helplessly.

He inhaled sharply and his jaw was tight as understanding dawned in his eyes. “Shit.”

She was glad one of them seemed to know what was happening.

“I’m sorry I scared you,” he apologized. “I have nightmares. I was… It was a dream—”

She grabbed the dresser and pulled herself to her feet.

Dream?

He jumped up and gently pushed her into a chair that was beside the door. “Woah, take it easy. You hit your head pretty hard.”

He hovered over her while she blinked the blurriness away. Her eyes cleared, and she realized she was staring directly at his crotch.

Sweet baby Jesus. “Shit,” she hissed, whipping her head to the side and covering her eyes. Her cheeks burst into flames as she heard him hop back to the bed.

Jane pressed her palms to her cheeks and confirmed they were on fire. In fact, her whole body was. She had stood on *volcanoes* that were cooler than this room.

What is wrong with you?

What was wrong, was this was her first time seeing anyone but Thomas this naked. And this man—*Underwear god*—Sure, was making her feel incredibly nervous and… tingly, and she didn’t know how to make it stop.

She met his smiling eyes, certain he was reading her mind. “Oh my god. I’ve got to get—”

She reached for the top of the dresser again.

“Hey. I’m sorry, just give it a minute. Please. You’re gonna knock yourself out again.”

She averted her gaze, looking anywhere but at him. “Can you please put some clothes on, then?” she asked desperately.

When he didn’t answer, she peeked at him.

The way he was looking at her ignited places in her body she didn’t even know she had, and she squirmed in her seat uncomfortably.

"Sure. Can you hand me those?" he asked casually, pointing to the back of the chair.

She tossed him the gray sweatpants and stared at the floor while he pulled them on. "So, there's no… injured person, then?" she asked.

"Not anymore." His voice was tight.

She waited for him to explain, unsure what that meant.

"There, you can look. I'm decent now." The laughter had returned.

She turned. He was barely decent and smiling.

"So, you…" He scratched his head again and looked toward the window. "You heard me from the road?"

"No, I—"

"Wait a minute." His head whipped around, and his eyes found the branch lying on the floor. "Are you telling me you came up here to rescue me"—he met her gaze—"with a *stick*?"

Jane dropped her head in her hands. When he said it like that, she sounded like an idiot. *You are an idiot.*

"Well, there wasn't a lot of time to—I mean… I wasn't expecting—" Jane fumbled, but the more she tried to explain the dumber she felt.

"No. I'm not knocking it. I just. Huh. Wow."

Her cheeks continued to burn as she sat on the chair. *What are you doing in this man's bedroom?* "Oh, god." She didn't know.

"Hey?" he said gently.

She met his eyes again, and he was looking at her, like… She didn't know what. No one had ever looked at her that way before.

"Thanks. That's pretty fucking ballsy," he said—sounding truly impressed.

Ballsy? Jane almost laughed out loud. She was pretty sure her person and "ballsy" had never been uttered in the same sentence before.

He reached for the prosthetic foot that was propped against the nightstand. It had a flat metal plate that connected to a complicated looking joint that was attached to a cup for his ankle to slide into. She watched the muscles in his back contract like waves on an ocean as he rolled on a sock, then adjusted the cuff over his calf and tightened it. She rubbed her shoulders absently and her eyes dropped to the floor when she realized he was watching her.

"Sorry," she apologized again.

He stood, and she glanced up at his outstretched hand. "Matt Patterson. Thanks for rescuing helpless little old me."

Helpless? She wasn't sure of much in this life, but she was sure of at least one thing. There was nothing old or helpless about the man standing in front of her.

Hesitantly, Jane took his warm hand, and he slowly pulled her to her feet.

"I'm Jane Moore. And I am so embarrassed."

She should say something else, or at least remove her hand from his, but she didn't. And she didn't know why.

He still didn't have a shirt on… Why that was the nail her attention decided to hang itself on, she didn't know. But it was suddenly all she could think about.

He is at least ten years younger than you.

At least.

"Don't be. That was really brave of you," he said with admiration.

She had no idea what he was talking about.

And he had the longest lashes she had ever seen on a man.

You're married for Christ's sake.

Yes. That too. She blinked. Wait, what?

You have—

"The kids," she whispered, jerking her hand away. Her eyes widened in panic. How had she forgotten about the kids? What the hell was wrong with her? She looked down at her watch, having lost all sense of time, but she couldn't focus on the numbers.

"How long was I out?" she choked.

"What?"

She pulled her phone out of her back pocket. No missed calls—at least there was that. "I need to go," she said stumbling toward the door.

"It was only a minute. Wait," Matt appeared beside her. His hand slid under her elbow, and her body lit up like a Christmas tree. "Let me help you down the—"

She pulled her arm away in shame and shook her head.

She was a terrible mother. She was a terrible person.

"No, it's okay I'm—"

"I'm helping you down the stairs." He took her arm more firmly. It wasn't a request.

She gripped the railing as he helped her down the narrow, wooden staircase. He smelled like soap and cheap aftershave, and somehow the combination was amazing. She was grateful for his steady arm as she swayed with dizziness. Hopefully, she didn't have a concussion.

When they got to the bottom, he left her leaning against the back of the couch and walked over to the door, running his fingers across the broken jam.

"You busted down the *door*?" he asked incredulously.

She shrugged helplessly.

"Hot damn." He turned back toward the road. "So, you heard me…?"

His voice trailed off, and he turned to her, frowning. She followed his gaze back to the van.

It took her a second, but then she noticed it, too. All the windows were closed. Her face fell.

"Through a closed window?"

She sucked in a sharp breath. His questioning eyes met her wide-open guilty ones. *He knows.*

"I'm so sorry!" she blurted. "I… know I shouldn't have been trespassing." Her voice went up a couple of octaves. "It's the *one* time, literally, the *one—" It's the second time.*

Jane groaned and clenched her fists, pressing them to her forehead. "Okay, fine. Technically, the second time but—Please don't call the police… my kids…"

Her knees buckled at the thought of going to jail, and the kids being put in the protective custody of Ms. *'I'm The Bitch'* from the grocery store, and having to explain to Thomas…

She slid to the floor, burying her head in her hands.

"I didn't know anyone lived here!" she cried. "I thought it was abandoned, and I was looking for—" Her mouth went dry. If she confessed she was planning to steal a gun, he'd call the cops for sure.

This was exactly why Thomas handled everything. Because she couldn't handle tough choices, because she made mistakes. First, taking the kids. Then confronting Jake. Now, this. She was just going from one disaster to another.

"God. I'm really sorry. I'll pay for the door, just please don't—"

"Relax, Jane Moore. It's okay." Matt's voice was kind as he slid down to the floor beside her. Their shoulders touched.

"You're not the only one who shouldn't be here," he confessed.

Her head came up. "What?"

"This is not my place either—at least it hasn't been for a long time."

She waited.

"This is my parent's house," he said, propping his arms up on his knees. "They're stuck in the city. Bad timing on a routine colonoscopy appointment—if you can believe that."

She winced. "You're kidding."

He shook his head.

"Ouch."

He laughed.

"Sorry. I wasn't trying to make a joke. I didn't mean to be—"

"Relax, Jane Moore."

She stared at him for a moment. So, he was separated from his family too? In her little bubble, she had forgotten that there were other people equally affected by the disaster. There had to be millions of people like her and the kids, displaced from their homes and families.

"I'm sorry, but if it's your parents' house, then surely you are welcome here?"

"I haven't talked to my dad in ten years. Well, I talked to him yesterday, but…" His jaw was tight.

Jane sensed that the conversation hadn't gone well. "Went that well, huh?"

He laughed. "Well, let's just say he was more worried about his boat than…"

"It must be a *really* nice boat then."

Why did you say that? Shaking her head, she pressed her palm to her forehead and groaned.

Matt burst out laughing and her stomach did somersaults as his shoulder shook against hers.

"Sorry. I don't know what's wrong with me—" Jane began.

"What are you looking for?" he asked, turning abruptly and breaking the contact between them.

"What?"

She already missed the warmth of his arm against hers.

You are an idiot.

Yes. That had already been established.

And he's still not wearing a shirt.

Yes, she was aware of that, too.

"You came here looking for something. What were you planning on stealing?"

The gravity of her situation returned. If he called the police, and she went to jail… Jane jumped up. Her vision darkened, and she grasped at the air, searching for the couch. She squeezed her eyes shut as two warm hands closed over her arms and held her in place until everything stopped moving. "Woah, there."

God. How hard had she hit her head?

I don't think that's the problem.

"I'm sorry! I just—Please, I have kids and I can't—"

"Jane," Matt said gently. She felt his breath on her face and her eyes flew open. She tried to back up, but he held her firmly in place. His eyes searched hers, then his gaze dropped to her lips and her nervousness exploded into full-blown panic. For a split second, she thought he might kiss her. He released her instead. She exhaled heavily, trying to interpret the weird energy she was picking up from him. Or was it her?

"That was a terrible joke, and I'm an asshole. I'm sorry." He shook his head, eyeing her warily. "For some reason, you bring out a side of me I haven't seen in quite a…"

He ran his hand through his hair again and gave her a sideways smile. She stumbled back against the couch.

He grabbed her arm again. "You've got to stop that, Jane Moore."

The way he said it left her wondering if he meant falling or staring. She sat on the back of the couch. She wasn't even dizzy anymore. She was just very hot. She tugged at her sweatshirt. "I'm so sorry," she whispered helplessly.

"I'm not going to call the police," he said gently. All the teasing was gone from his voice. "You rescued me, remember? No crime has been committed here."

"I just—" Her eyes filled with tears, and she blinked them back. He had no idea how wrong he was. She had already broken a dozen traffic laws, stolen her children from their father, and kidnaped her sister's kids. She had been about to rob his parent's house for god's sake.

His palms were warm against the back of her hands, and the temperature in the room went up a hundred degrees. Lightning tore through her body, and Jane stared at the floor, half in terror, half in awe as it coursed through her. If she didn't get arrested by the local police, she definitely deserved to be imprisoned by the moral ones for what she was feeling right—

"Tell me, what were you looking for? Maybe I can help. If we have it here, I'll give it to you." His voice dragged her from her bitter thoughts.

She stared at his hand over hers and tried not to cry. If he was Thomas, she would be a sobbing, blubbering mess by now. Again, she realized how pathetic a partner she had become in her marriage. No wonder he couldn't stand her.

She forced the tears back. Unfortunately, she no longer had the luxury of being a woman who took a pill and hid in bed when she was overwhelmed.

Get it together, Jane.

She sighed and pulled her hands back. "Clothes for my kids and I…"

"Out with it."

"A-a gun," she whispered.

"A what?"

"A gun," she said louder.

"What do you need a gun for?" There was a sudden edge to his voice.

She turned away, making sure to keep one hand on the couch as she wiped her eyes. For some reason, like with Ed Hamilton, she wanted to unburden herself to him. But she reminded herself, he wasn't her husband.

"It's nothing, really. Just problems with a neighbor." She tried not to sound as scared as she was. "My husband thinks we should get one, just to be safe. So, I'm out…. looking." The lie came out on its own.

Matt looked at her ring, then back at her. "And where is your husband?" he asked carefully.

Jane realized that while he might be infinitely better-looking than Jake, that didn't mean he was a better person. "At home with the kids. We have a place on the lake."

The fewer people that knew she was alone, the better.

"I see. And you have a neighbor who is…?"

"Well, he's drunk all the time, and… he has trespassed on our property." She looked down at her feet, realizing technically she was no better. Although, to be fair, at least she hadn't peed on his lawn.

"Trespassed?"

"Well, mostly… I called, *we* called the police, but they said they have more important things to worry about. But… um… he scares the kids, and we thought having a gun might make them feel safer."

"I see," Matt said again, slowly.

"My husband, Thomas, I mean, he would never actually kill the guy, but he just thought… maybe it would scare him off, you know?" She glanced at him to see if he was buying it. His expression was hard to read, and he looked much older than he had a few moments earlier.

"Does your husband know how to use a gun?"

She stared at her shoes again. She remembered how easily Thomas could tell when she was lying. Her head throbbed.

"Jane?"

She reluctantly met his eyes.

"Does he know how to use a gun?" His playful expression was gone.

She shook her head.

He was silent for a moment.

"Wait here."

He left and Jane pulled her fingers through her hair. She resisted the urge to run, praying he was actually getting what she hoped he was.

She glanced at the pictures on the wall. There was one of Matt's parents, and an older couple that looked like his mom.

Jane took her first normal breath in twenty minutes, as she smiled at a picture of Matt at about Tommy's age. Why did all little boys look the same at six? And why were their smiles so comforting? She rubbed the back of her head, feeling a small lump. Her head ached, but thankfully the dizziness seemed to be passing.

Matt returned with a rifle of some kind, a box of bullets, and a shirt.

"I'm going to give you a quick lesson, and then you can show your husband when you get home, okay?"

Her heart soared, and happy tears of relief sprang to her eyes. "Really?"

Matt bit his lip as he nodded, making her heart race.

"Yeah," he replied. Just a bit of the humor returned to his eyes.

She followed him carefully through the house, noting the doilies on the couch and the pheasant hunting wallpaper in the den. It was just as terrifying as she expected an old farmhouse to be. They finally emerged onto the back porch.

First, he showed her how to disarm the safety. Then he demonstrated how to load and cock the gun, and how to brace it against her shoulder. He handed it to her and pointed to the fence post that stood about fifty feet away. "Give it a shot."

The gun was heavy as she pressed it to her shoulder.

"Aim a little lower than your target, because until you get used to it, the rifle will kick back, and your shot will go high."

Jane gripped the rifle and could not believe what she was doing. She had never held a gun before. In fact, she hated them. In college, she had even gone to anti-firearms rallies.

Jane shook her head. Two weeks into her first big crisis she had folded like a deck of cards.

The kids. Yes. To keep them safe.

"Take a deep breath. Exhale as you pull the trigger."

He stood beside her, and she did as she was told. The shot rang out, and her right shoulder jerked back much harder than she expected.

"Try it again, but this time… Can I—?"

"Um, sure."

He stepped closer until his chest lightly touched her back. She inhaled sharply as butterflies took flight in her stomach. He put his hands over hers and adjusted her position, pulling the butt of the rifle closer to her neck, and sliding her hand back along the barrel further from her body. "Keep it right there," he whispered in her ear as he released her.

She fired—and missed.

"Again."

She lined up, and again his arms encircled her as he made small adjustments.

Holy Mother of God. How was she supposed to concentrate when he was this close—

"Breathe, Jane Moore." His husky voice created a pulsing sensation between her legs. Then to her utter surprise she felt *him* against the side of her hip. She inhaled sharply and fired. The bullet hit the top of the fence post and she wheeled around. She stepped back, putting distance between them.

"I'm sorry," Matt apologized. He turned away looking mortified. "I didn't mean for that—"

"Oh, um, that's…" She stared at his damn-near-perfect profile. Had she just given him a hard-on? *Her?*

"Will you stop looking at me like that?" he snapped, glancing at her over his shoulder.

Jane blinked in confusion. *Like what?*

"Fuck. What is wrong with me?" Matt mumbled as he ran his fingers through his hair again. The disgust in his voice was palpable.

Janes breath froze in her lungs. She looked down at her filthy sweatshirt, picturing the forty-year-old body she knew lay underneath, as the weird little fantasy her brain had created came crashing down around her.

Humiliation spread across her cheeks. She was making a fool of herself, swooning over him like a teenager, thinking he was purposely flirting with her. Whatever had possessed her to—She set the gun on the rail of the porch and hurried past him down the steps.

"Wait," Matt called. "That came out wrong—"

"I'm *so* sorry," she apologized without looking back.

Jane ran for the van. She was such an idiot. He must think she was delusional or mentally unstable. *You are not*—She never should have come here.

"Jane! Wait!" Matt called. The metal pad from his prosthetic bang against the wooden steps, as he started down after her.

She went faster, and tears flooded her eyes as she reached for the door handle.

Matt caught up to her just as she went to pull the door open. His cologne surrounded her as he pressed his hand against it, holding it closed.

"Wait," he said again, but she ducked under his arm and shoved it open, just enough to squeeze in.

She tried to pull it closed, but he held it open.

"I'm sorry. I didn't mean for it to come out like—"

"I know what you meant." Jane's embarrassment forced unwanted tears from her eyes, as she looked anywhere but at him.

"Jane—"

"Please," she shook her head, swiping at the tears. The pain behind her temples increased and her head felt like it was going to explode. "I need to go—"

"Take the gun at least," he slid it in the gap of the door.

She paused.

Take it, Jane. The reasonable side of her brain urged.

"Take it, Jane," he repeated.

She let go of the handle, took the gun and the box of shells, briefly met his apologetic eyes, then slammed the door. Jane fumbled with the key, as Matt apologized again through the window.

As soon as the engine turned over, she threw the van into drive, and punched the gas. The tires spun on the gravel and Matt stepped back.

Jane's hands shook as she clutched the steering wheel and stared at his retreating form in the rearview. He was watching her too.

She wiped her eyes and found them in the mirror. "What in the actual *fuck*?" she demanded of her disheveled reflection. It just stared back at her with flushed cheeks and a blank expression.

Jane turned onto the dry, dusty road and looked down at her jittery hands. She glanced over her shoulder back at his house. What in god's name had happened back there? She never got flustered around men, never even noticed them, certainly not ones *his* age. Maybe it was because she'd gotten caught trying to rob him? She wiped her eyes again and looked down at the rifle lying beside her. At least she had that.

She could protect the kids now. Jane sat up straighter. Nothing else mattered. Not her pride or her ego—whatever tattered remains were left of it. The humiliation was worth it. She'd finally done something right.

Jane took a couple of deep breaths, and her confidence surged. A long-forgotten song from her college days popped into her head. As she drove back to the rental house, she hummed along with the tune. Between the bump on her head, the shit-show that had just transpired and the lack of sleep, she was a mess. But… *Janie's got a gun.*

"Yes," She met her gaze again in the rearview mirror, and winked at herself. "*And* I know how to use it."

Chapter Twenty-Four

Day 13 // 12:12 a.m

MATT ROLLED over and looked at the clock. It was after midnight.

He rolled left, then right, in an attempt to get comfortable, but his foot ached—despite the fact it was no longer there.

After more than an hour of restlessness, he finally gave up and threw off the blankets. He hung his legs over the side of the bed. He couldn't sleep, but it wasn't for the usual reason.

Matt ran his fingers through his hair. It was because of *her*. As cliché as it was, every time he closed his eyes, Jane's were there, staring back at him. Surprised, when he had leaped out of bed barely dressed. Lustful as she perused his body. Confused as she searched the room for the ghost of his best friend. Fearful when she thought he was going to call the police. *So* embarrassed when—

Matt sighed and shook his head. That last one was the reason he couldn't sleep.

He had never felt like such a jerk in his life, which was saying a lot, because he'd done some pretty shitty things when he was in high school. It was a terrible feeling, and he didn't know how to make it stop without apologizing, which he obviously couldn't do.

He honestly would have been less surprised if a unicorn had busted down the door. But no, instead it was Jane Moore… brave enough to barge into a gunfight with only a stick, yet adorably terrified of a man in his underwear.

You would be too.

Matt frowned. That was true. Either way, he'd been so damn unprepared for meeting her that he'd—

"Gah!" He buried his head in his hands.

It was the most confusing twenty minutes he had ever spent with a woman, and he'd like to think it was because for the first ten he wasn't sure if he was dreaming, but really it was because in a matter of seconds, *she* had somehow managed to light a fire in him that he thought had been extinguished forever. It had been like honest-to-god lightning when she met his eyes. Which was why it was so fucked up that she thought—

Matt rubbed his tired eyes, remembering the mortification in hers on the back porch. He had absolutely *not* meant what he said the way she took it. What he meant was—

What the hell is wrong with you for being attracted to a married woman with kids?

Matt rubbed his temples. Yeah, that.

She was clearly confused and scared and desperate, and instead of empathy, he'd flirted with her upstairs, and then—Well, there was no need to remind himself of what an ass he'd been after she'd risked her life to help him.

Risking their lives was something his men had done for Matt on many occasions, but this was totally different. She was a civilian, a lone *woman*. Yet, she heard him screaming, and she came to help—with a goddamn tree branch no less. Who the hell did that for someone they didn't know? And how had he repaid her?

Matt rubbed his eyes again. He should not have let her go. He knew it as soon as she had started down the driveway. By then, of course, it was too late, and he would have been a moron to try to hobble after her.

He rubbed his calf again, wishing he could forget how good it felt to run.

Somewhere outside, a coyote howled. The lonesome cry was soon joined by several more. Matt hopped to the window and looked out.

The nearest house was the Hamiltons, just over a mile away. He couldn't see the actual house, but he could just make out the light that hung over the barn door. The Gordon Farm was another half-mile up the road, accounting for the only other point of light in the black hole that was this god-forsaken countryside at night.

He caught his reflection in the mirror. His beard was already growing back, and the frown lines on his forehead made him look… old. How could all of this stay exactly the same for twenty years when he had changed so much? It confirmed the theory he had back when he was a teenager. *Out in the country, time stands still.*

Chapter Twenty-Five

Day 13 // 2:27 p.m

"I THOUGHT IT WOULD BE BIGGER," Austin commented, and Jane couldn't help but agree.

Still the hair on her arms stood on end when she got her first real-life view of the Veil in the distance.

Jane followed the signs to the meeting area, and the van passed over a set of rumble strips.

The closer they got, however, the higher it seemed to climb into the sky. Jane slowed and leaned forward, craning her neck to gaze up at it.

"It kinda looks like that fountain at the mall," Maddy said beside her. "You know the one outside the movie theater that spills over that giant piece of glass and you can see through it?"

Jane agreed with that, too. It was actually kind of beautiful, like shimmery gossamer fabric. Then she realized what she was thinking and frowned. "Whatever you do, do *not* get close to it. It may look like a fountain, but it's not. Do you understand me?" Jane reminded the kids for the hundredth time, as she slowed, approaching the checkpoint that was marked by two camo-painted trucks parked longways across the road.

"We know, Aunt Jane," Maddy sighed, rolling her eyes.

"I just…" Jane was worried. Thomas said the Coast Guard was setting up meeting stations along the Veil for separated families to see each other. It seemed like a risky thing to do for those on the inside, but Thomas had said as long as there were no outbreaks, they would be allowed to meet once a month. She got why he and Sarah wanted to see the kids. That's why she didn't say no, but still, it felt dangerous. Especially after the incident on the west side. Thankfully, so far no other cases had been reported, which was why they were allowed to meet at all.

She rolled down the window as a fatigue-clad man in a mask stepped up to the van. "How many in the vehicle?" he asked.

"Four and a baby," she answered, and he handed her four masks.

"Name and meeting time?" he asked as she passed the surgical masks back to the kids and fit hers over her nose and ears.

"Jane Moore, 2:30." She handed him her driver's license.

He consulted his clipboard.

"Name and age of everyone in the vehicle."

She rattled them off as she glanced across the Veil. The list of rules was a mile long for the Insiders—as the news now called all the people trapped in the cities. It included being gloved upon exit of their vehicle and wearing an air-purifying respirator mask—which Jane noted looked like something out of a horror movie—for the duration of the visit. They were also required to pass through ultraviolet tents, which supposedly helped sanitize them, before and after taking their position at one of four meeting stations.

For the Outsiders, the process was much simpler. They were required to wear a mask past the checkpoint, and each of them had to be fitted with a tracking device that looked like a watch with no face on a wire band, before approaching the Veil.

Jane and the kids got out and stood in a row as the device was attached to each of their wrists. The man went around to Bria's seat and put one on her chubby arm, too.

They all climbed back in the van and Jane drove in slowly as a soldier with an orange vest motioned for her to turn and park in the grassy median.

She was surprised at how many cars were parked nearby. Guilt ached in her stomach again as Jane looked at the severed families around them. She squeezed her eyes shut, and prayed again that this wasn't all because of her stupid paper.

It wasn't stupid.

Jane unbuckled Bria as the kids got out. They walked across the empty highway to another checkpoint, where their bracelets were scanned and they gave their names again, then huddled together as they stood beside the orange cone that marked their waiting spot. There were three groups in front of them spaced about twenty feet apart. Everyone, excluding infants, was masked.

Jane looked ahead toward the four stations. Each one was sectioned off by temporary fencing and connected to the one on the other side by something that looked like a dog run with a wagon in it, and two gates on either end. Except for the stations, where more temporary fencing lined the Veil, a ten-foot-tall, barbed-wire fence ran the length of the wall in both directions. It stretched on, as far as Jane could see.

"Why are they wearing those scary masks?" Tommy asked nervously.

Jane watched as a man and a little boy entered the gated area and approached the Veil. On the other side, a woman with long blond hair stepped into her designated area. She could just make out the sound of the woman's voice as it came through a speaker on the full-face mask she wore. The little boy hid behind his father, and the woman tried to wipe her eyes, bumping her hand against the mask.

"It's to protect everyone from bad germs," Jane said. "So, nobody gets sick."

"How come we don't have to wear them?"

"Because the sickness is in there and we are just being careful."

"Well, then why don't they come over here with us?"

"I wish they could, bud," Jane said, switching Bria to her other hip and pressing his head to her side.

Jane strained to find Thomas and Sarah through the shimmery light. It was like Maddy said, sort of like looking through a thin film of glittery water. While everything was visible, you still had to squint to make out the details.

She perused the faces of each person in the line on the other side. They all looked alike with those masks on, but finally, she spotted Thomas's worn Michigan sweatshirt. Then she recognized her sister's slim physique beside him and waved.

"Look, Tommy," she said, bending toward him and pointing at Thomas. "Do you see daddy over there? He is wearing his blue Michigan sweatshirt. And see Aunt Sarah there?"

Tommy stood up on his tiptoes. "Daddy!" he shouted.

Thomas heard him and all their hands went up as they waved.

Finally, it was their turn. Before they could go in, there was one more checkpoint. Jane gave her name to the surly officer sitting at a plastic folding table with a clipboard. The soldier radioed to someone on the other side. A few seconds later, she heard Thomas's and Sarah's names.

Jane nodded nervously when the officer looked at her to confirm.

He flipped the page and then began to read. "Okay. Here's how this works. You have fifteen minutes per visit. Stay on your side of the fence. Do not touch the Veil. Do not toss anything through the Veil. Only pass items through via the designated wagons. Organic matter, electronics, firearms, and weapons of any kind are prohibited."

"Organic?"

"Anything biological will be vaporized as it passes through the wall," the soldier said, sounding tired. Jane's heart raced.

"Anything?"

"Yep. That thing sterilizes whatever passes through it."

Jane shook her head. "How is that possible?"

"With all due respect, ma'am, if I knew that, I wouldn't be sitting here holding a clipboard."

Fair enough.

"But seriously," he continued, "I saw it myself this morning. A thirteen-year-old kid jumped the fence and stuck his hand in it. That thing fried his fingers right off." He nodded toward the medical tent. "Kid screamed bloody murder, and it stunk like hell in there when they wrapped him up."

Jane glanced at Tommy, whose eyes were wide and solemn as he stared at his hand.

"When you are finished, go directly to the inspection station, and then straight to your vehicle. Upon exit, you will be issued gasoline in accordance with necessity. Do you have anything to be inspected before you enter?"

Jane shook her head. She hadn't even realized they were allowed to move things through it.

"Station Four, you'll be up as soon as the people ahead of you clear out. Keep the kids under control."

"Thank you," she said, hoisting Bria up on her hip. She wished she had known, so she could ask Thomas to bring her carrier.

Again, Jane wondered how it had been done? The engineering, the scale. Who had the technology to do this? How in the hell did it even work? Was it somehow able to distinguish cellular function, as she'd initially thought? Or did it just detect water? Robert would know. She rolled her eyes. He probably *did* know.

The more she knew about this, the more up his alley it seemed.

Jane shifted Bria to her other hip.

Thomas and Sarah stood on the other side, waiting. They were up next.

Jane glanced up at the Veil. If that technology had existed back when she'd done her research, it would have totally changed the game. Time had been the limiting factor, and there just hadn't been a way around it. Not a good one, anyway.

Jane bit her lip. Was that what the Veil was for? To buy time that she hadn't been able to find in her sim? She knew the chances of being able to move fast enough to contain the virus were almost *zero* unless you moved quickly and decisively. That was why her solution had been so… abrupt because there was no time to figure out exactly who had it or where it had spread. At the time, the act-now-think-later mindset was the only one that kept the time in the right range to produce a positive outcome. But the Veil changed all that.

She switched Bria to her other hip as the baby drooled and shoved her slimy fist into her mouth. Jane's mind raced at the implications. One thing after another slid into place. It made too much sense. She had to be right. Didn't she?

The Veil created time. It was genius. It allowed those in charge to be less hasty, gave them time to figure out who did and didn't have it. Maybe they had initiated the Veil around too many cities by accident, but they probably had to. In her simulations, in order to have a favorable outcome, the base rate of error had to be over twenty percent. That meant, in order to contain the virus, the models required that a fifth be mistakenly… diagnosed. Anything lower, and the risk of a breach was too high. Twenty percent didn't sound so bad, but when it turned out to be around a billion people, well, people tended to notice. That was why so many people had ended up hating her. A billion people was too many casualties for the average person, even if the alternative was six billion.

The hair on her arms stood on end. Someone had solved her problem. But who?

She took a step forward with the kids and pulled her hair out of Bria's hands.

Jane shivered in the seventy-five-degree sunshine.

Who cares? It's working. Just as you predicted.

But that would still mean that all of this—the father with the child that had been ahead of them hurried past, his eyes red and full of fear—all of this was still her fault. A thirteen-year-old boy lost his hand this morning because of something *she* had written.

For the fiftieth time, she reminded herself that it was very, very unlikely that this had anything to do with her, but her stomach twisted itself into a knot anyway, and her heart thumped nervously in her chest, making her arms tingle with warning.

No panic attacks now, please.

She gripped Tommy's hand and dragged herself from her ludicrous thoughts. Jane pushed the creaky gate open and ushered everyone inside. Thomas and Sarah sanitized their gloves, entered on their side, then sanitized their gloves again. They looked like they were scrubbing in for surgery. She couldn't imagine what it felt like to be on the inside.

She took a deep breath, trying to slow the adrenaline that had seeped into her blood. It was exhausting, the back and forth between thinking the Veil was her fault, then convincing herself it couldn't be. It was absurd. There was no way. This was not her fault. She was just stressed and tired, and… *stressed.*

They all stared at each other for a moment. Austin leaned against her arm, and Tommy sunk his little fingernails into her thigh as he wrapped his arms around her leg.

Thomas was the first to speak. "Hey, bud!" he said cheerfully, through his mask. He sounded like he was on speakerphone. They were less than twenty feet apart, and the sound carried perfectly through the Veil.

"Hi, Daddy." Tommy took a step toward his dad.

Jane grabbed his shoulder as all the adults shouted, "No!"

He jumped back and gripped her leg again. "I wasn't gonna…" he blubbered, then burst into tears and buried his head against her hip.

"I'm sorry," Jane apologized. "We didn't mean to scare you—"

"Tommy!" Thomas said, regaining his composure. "Look what I brought you!" He headed over to the chain-linked tunnel and the wagon that was on their side, dropping Tommy's camping backpack into it. "Can you help me out, bud? Can you use your super strength to pull this over to your side?"

Maddy opened the latch of the gate and Tommy stepped up as Jane's heart practically beat out of her chest. If he ran into that chute…

Don't think about it.

"Ready, bud?"

Tommy wiped his eyes with the back of his hand and nodded at his dad. Jane met Sarah's eyes through her mask and she knew the look. It was the same one she knew she must be wearing. They were both trying not to cry.

Thomas's eyes smiled and although she couldn't see it, she knew his mouth was doing the same. For a moment, he looked just like the man he had been in college when Jane had fallen for him. She shook the memory away. It had been a long time since they'd been those people.

"Grab that rope," Thomas said. Tommy leaned down to pick up the thick cord. "Yeah, that's it. Now pull in through. Go slow, so it doesn't tip over."

Tommy did as his dad instructed, and the wagon rolled through the wall, unharmed.

"Keep going, bud," Thomas shouted with false enthusiasm.

Tommy pulled it the rest of the way through, and everyone cheered as he pulled the backpack out of the wagon and peered inside.

"I put all your LEGOs in there and your monster trucks, and some of your favorite books," Thomas's voice wavered as Tommy burst into tears again.

Jane handed Bria to Maddy and crouched down beside her son.

"What's wrong, buddy?" she asked.

"I miss Daddy. I just want to go home. I want to go with Daddy."

Jane choked back her tears as Thomas pulled the wagon back toward their side. She shut the gate and latched it. "Me too, bud. But we can't. Not right now. But at least we get to see each other."

She glanced up and caught Thomas's eyes.

"Tommy, look at me," he said.

Tommy looked up.

"I love you. Everything is gonna be okay. I'm right here. And your mom's right there. And we are all going to be okay. I promise."

Jane bit her lip, hoping it was true.

The fifteen minutes went by quickly. Thomas made a game out of the wagon for Tommy as Sarah passed care packages through for Austin and Maddy. The kids talked with their parents, while everyone tried their best not to cry. Jane surprised herself by asking Thomas to bring her old biology folder the next time they met.

The next thing she knew, they were on the freeway again.

Her phone dinged, and she saw Thomas's text.

The kids looked good. Thanks for making the trip down.

They hadn't had time to talk, but what could they have said in front of the kids, anyway?

Her phone dinged again.

I wish you would have stayed.

She blinked back the tears. Yeah, a part of her wished she had, too. Who knew, maybe under these conditions, they would have reconciled? Maybe being forced together, Thomas would have realized she wasn't so… terrible after all. But the other part of her, that had seen the bodies in the back of garbage trucks, was glad she hadn't.

The virus was there now. Thankfully, so far it had not spread, but only time would tell if this would be another New York. She glanced at the kids riding quietly in the back. She had done the right thing, even though it didn't feel that way.

The ride back up north was solemn. Everything was closed. There was more looting, she noticed, as she passed several businesses with boarded-up windows. Fear crept over her spine as she looked out the window. And more cars than there should be on the road. Were people finally heading out to their sanctuary?

Chapter Twenty-Six

Day 13 // 4:47 p.m

MATT FORCED himself back to his feet with a hop and then dropped down to the ground again, pressing his hands into the gravel and dropping into another push-up.

He jumped up and did it again, as sweat dripped from his back in rivulets. His remorse over the episode with Jane had festered into anger, and he was so pissed at himself he didn't know what else to do but take it out on his body.

Why had he let her drive away? What the fuck was the matter with him?

And now, even if he had a working vehicle, which he didn't—he dropped down and jumped up again—he had no idea where to find her. There were at least a thousand houses that lined the lake for twenty miles in either direction… His only hope was that she might come back.

Why in the hell would she do that? His elbow buckled, and the gravel dug into his forearms as he collapsed in the cloud of dust.

"Damn it." Matt pounded his fist into the gravel beneath him. She wouldn't.

He pushed himself up to his feet and wiped the sweat from his brow with a gritty hand, playing it over in his mind *again,* trying to sort out his crazy feelings for a woman he barely knew.

One second, she was waving a stick, screaming like a banshee, scaring the shit out of him. The next she was looking at him like—Matt looked down at the gleaming metal plate where his foot used to be and sighed. He didn't know exactly how Jane had looked at him, all he knew was for the first time in two years, he had felt *seen*.

For a moment, Matt had been himself again, the cocky, confident bastard he used to be. It had been amazing. Like breathing air again, after being suffocated. And when he touched her—the bolt of lightning and the way his insides felt like they were being pricked by tiny needles—It haunted him day and night. Especially at night. He'd never experienced anything like it. And he wanted it all back.

Matt wiped his brow and squinted down the road toward the sound of an approaching vehicle. He watched, hoping—

It was a red pickup.

He kicked the dirt and headed back to the house.

He should have never let her go, he told himself for the millionths time. He should have at least offered to confront her neighbor. He should have *insisted* on explaining what he meant on the back porch.

Would you really have explained?

Matt wiped his brow again. Probably not about his tingly insides, but he should have at least clarified that his disgust had nothing to do with her. She was beautiful. He was the—"Fucking asshole," he growled.

Another vehicle barreled down the road, and he turned in the shade of the back porch, squinting.

Gray pickup.

His shoulders sagged. And now she was gone, never to return, and he didn't blame her.

Matt wheeled around, heading for the door. "Jesus Christ." Why couldn't he stop thinking about what an ass he had been?

She's married too.

Yeah. And then there was *that.* He didn't have a problem with one-night-stands so long as they were both on the same page, but he drew a hard line at messing around with women who had families and kids.

Then why are you thinking about her?

He flung the door open, and it slammed against the siding.

Because she was alone, and her husband wasn't there, and she needed help.

And?

Matt sighed. Fine. *And* because of what he felt when their fingers touched, and her big brown eyes met his. But that wasn't why he was so desperate to find her now—He glanced down in surprise as a twitch in his pants called his bluff.

"Come on! I wasn't even–*Again?*" He threw his hands in the air, storming in through the kitchen. "You've got to be *fucking* kidding me," he muttered in disgust.

Matt went straight upstairs and took a cold shower. He pressed his head to the cool tile wall, letting the water cascade off his back.

Jane Moore.

Why couldn't he get her out of his head?

You know why.

Matt banged his head gently against the wall. "Damn it."

His phone rang, and he turned off the water. He grabbed it off the counter, frowning at the 'unknown caller,' and swiped the button to answer.

"Hello?"

"Matt?" He rolled his eyes. If there was an opposite of Jane Moore, it was her.

"Katie?"

"Oh, thank god. Are you okay? Are you—"

He pulled the phone away from his ear and looked at the number again, the area code was from somewhere down south.

"—parents doing?"

"I'm home. In Harborview."

"What, really?" she said, then laughed. "Well, isn't that a little ironic?"

"Yeah."

She went on talking, but he wasn't listening. He had stopped listening to her the moment he had let her see his vulnerability, and she informed him with a smile, that she 'knew a guy who could make a prosthetic that was so good, no one would ever know there was *something wrong with him.'*

Something wrong. How those words haunted him.

It was funny, he thought. Katie was gorgeous. There was no denying it. Yet, in all the time he had been engaged to her, he had never once felt anything like what sparked in his veins yesterday with—

Jane Moore.

Yes. Jane, with her big brown eyes and freckled nose.

"I was headed back up north, but after Atlanta—Well, they've got half the state closed down—"

That got his attention. "Wait, what? What happened in Atlanta?"

"Didn't you hear?" she asked, sounding surprised.

Matt wrapped a towel around his waist, secured his prosthetic, and headed downstairs. He turned on the TV.

"—the crater, where only hours ago, the Atlanta skyline still stood. The Coast Guard has confirmed, just as it was in New York, there are no survivors. Atlanta and all her inhabitants are… gone."

Katie was talking again, but Matt cut her off. "I have to go." He hung up and dialed his mom. But of course, the lines were all busy.

Matt sat long into the night, watching as the horrific story continued to unfold.

Even through the panic erupting around the country, she called to him.

Jane Moore.

Chapter Twenty-Seven

Day 14 // 4:56 p.m

TWO WEEKS. Fourteen days since her world—and everyone else's—had become unrecognizable. 336 hours of fear and chaos in every corner of the globe. 20,160 minutes since Jane had been on her own.

The good news was, the kids were still fine, and there were no new cases of the virus in Detroit. It looked like they might be spared after all. And much to her surprise, her anxiety was abating. Maybe it was because she had no choice anymore but to deal with it, or because they had moved, but she could feel the change in her brain. The control. Her fear no longer threatened to consume her every second, as it had in the beginning, and that felt good. She could barely believe it, but she was surviving.

Jane multiplied the total on her phone by sixty, as Bria made a grab for it, and wondered why she was calculating the seconds. She read the screen. Roughly 1.2 million. Finally, a number that matched the way she felt about the distance between her old life and this one.

Jane shook her head and set her phone down. As crazy as it sounded, they were all getting used to it. The Veil, the X-virus. She and the kids were adapting. If she was being honest, it kind of terrified her how quickly they had settled into their new normal. It made it easier that she was here with the kids, and Detroit seemed to be one of the more stable cities.

That wasn't the case for everyone, and she knew as difficult as this had been for her, they were some of the "lucky" ones. Whole families had been wiped out, or reduced to a single member, in the wake of New York and Atlanta. And conspiracy-spouting militia groups were quickly gaining momentum. According to the Canadian news, an alarming number of Americans actually believed the President had released the virus into the cities, as some kind of political move, and there were even some calling for civil war.

That morning, Jane had watched a man accuse President Rodriguez of being a 'false prophet' and trying to destroy the world. Most people couldn't wrap their minds around the fact that the Antichrist was something so small it made a red blood cell look like a life-raft.

There were also reports of a group calling themselves Army For Freedom, that was threatening to take down the walls if the President did not, which made no sense at all. Because of the unrest, Outsiders had been "strongly advised" to stay home despite the quarantine lift, and military patrols of the Veil were becoming more frequent.

Elsewhere in the world, things were hardly better. Jane read the headline on the muted TV. Dubai had reached critical food supply shortages despite being able to transfer dried goods through the Veil, because two of its main import countries, the US and India, were experiencing their own crises. Beijing was in the middle of a political revolt. Delhi was falling at an exponential rate. Several of the towers had been destroyed by psychotic mobs, obliterating huge triangular swaths of the city's inhabitants in seconds.

There was no word yet on the source of the virus or an explanation of exactly what it was. All they knew was killing people in droves in Dallas, and seemed to be taking hold in Los Angeles. But, Jane noted, there *still,* there was not a single reported case of anyone outside the wall being infected. As she turned the volume back on and listened to the news for the third time that day, she knew if the Veil succeeded in keeping the virus isolated, it would go down as possibly the greatest achievement in human history.

Thankfully, Thomas had thought to tuck Bria's baby carrier in

Tommy's bag, so Jane's hands were free as she bounced the teething baby dangling from her chest. In addition to Tommy's toys, Thomas had also tossed in some of the kids' clothes and the diaper rash cream. Sarah had sent a few clothing items for her kids, too.

Jane twisted her hair behind her at the base of her neck.

Neither of them had sent anything for her. Thomas hadn't even sent her pills. Whether on purpose or not, Jane wasn't sure. Again, she knew it was partly her fault for leaning on him so much, but at least she'd tried to make things work. He, on the other hand, had gone out looking for apartments behind her back.

Despite the President swearing that the federal government would do everything in its power to keep families connected, the cell signals were becoming more and more jammed, and it was harder to get through. She hadn't talked to Thomas for two days now, but even that she was getting used to. She was growing accustomed to not talking to him, not consulting him.

It wasn't easy, but as long as she kept her focus on the kids and didn't think too much about everything else, she was getting by. They were taking the days as they came, one at a time.

Jane flipped off the TV and turned her attention to the mostly empty cupboard.

The food she'd bought was being consumed shockingly fast. Even with rationing herself to only eating what the kids didn't finish, it was still going down much too quickly. She had gone to check on Ed and his wife—taking the long way to avoid the Patterson Farm. Thanks to Ed's generosity, they collected a couple dozen more eggs and ten unripe strawberries that were sitting on the windowsill, but it wasn't enough to feed a family of five for more than a couple of days. They would need fresh produce, eventually.

The problem was, there wasn't any. The government had stepped in to manage the transport of goods, but efforts were focused on the Veiled cities and high-density, urban areas. There wasn't enough manpower or gasoline to keep all of President Rodriguez's promises. Those in charge had begun to pick and choose. There just wasn't enough incentive to send trucks out to places like Harborview, where the population was barely twenty-one hundred in the height of summer. Except for Jane, most families lived on farmland, anyway.

Could they go another two months without vegetables and fruit? What were they going to do in the winter? She couldn't imagine being here then.

Jane pulled her hair out of Bria's tiny hands.

A truck drove by, its tires grinding on the gravel outside, and she glanced at the gun resting on top of the kitchen cabinets. Then her eyes dropped to the sign she had hung in the front window.

Private Property. Trespassers will be shot.

The truck moved on and Jane turned back to the cupboard and pulled out a box of macaroni and a can of evaporated milk and set them on the counter.

Bria grabbed another handful of hair and Jane wrestled it from her as she turned and studied the kids. Maddy was on the couch, and Tommy was on the floor playing LEGOs with Austin.

So far, despite the lack of fruits and veggies, they all looked fine. Physically, anyway. Mentally… she didn't know. It was hard on all of them, especially the older kids, who had the capacity to understand what was happening. Since they had talked to their mom, Jane had stopped hiding the news from them. She had also voiced her certainty to Maddy and Austin, that Sarah would be fine as long as Detroit continued to adhere to the quarantine. It seemed to her they had been sleeping better since.

Jane dropped Bria in her playpen and stretched her aching back, then pulled the pot for the mac and cheese out of the drying rack and filled it with water.

Mentally, it was tough on her too, even though she was doing much better than she would have ever expected. Five people in a one-bedroom cottage, coupled with only sleeping a handful of restless hours a night, was draining. Jane certainly yelled and became more frustrated than she ever had before. She hated being short with the kids, but she couldn't help it. Thankfully, they seemed to know she was doing her best and didn't react too strongly to her outbursts.

She closed her eyes, remembering her marble bathroom with heated floors. If they had stayed, she would be soaking in her jetted tub right now, while Thomas did what he did best and protected his family.

She opened her eyes, and the small cabin pulled her from the fantasy.

But she hadn't stayed. She was here.

The corner of her mouth raised at the irony. A month ago, if someone would have told her *she* would be the one to leave, and Thomas would be the one left at the house, she never would have believed them.

Never say never.

Jane sighed. That seemed to be the motto of her life lately.

Chapter Twenty-Eight

Day 15 // 10:00 a.m

IT WAS A GLOOMY, gray morning, and Jane sensed a storm was on the way. She finished her precious cup of coffee and stared into the empty mug. The wind had howled all night. The scraping of branches against the roof had kept her on edge and awake. She was truly exhausted.

"Can we watch a movie?" Tommy asked.

Jane looked at her watch. It was ten o'clock in the morning. Usually, she didn't let him watch until after lunch, but…

"Sure. Why not?"

She rubbed her eyes. She needed to go get eggs and see if she could scrounge up anything else for the kids to eat.

"I'm going to go see Mr. Ed, get some eggs and see how his wife is doing while Bria is sleeping," she told Maddy. "I'll only be gone for half an hour. Stay inside with the kids."

Maddy rolled her eyes. "I know the drill, Aunt Jane."

Jane grabbed her keys and made the quick drive down the dusty road, speeding past the Patterson Farm.

She pulled down Ed and Ruth's long, gravel driveway and parked beside the house.

She climbed the steps of the front porch, pulled the screen open, and rapped on the door.

No one answered.

She tried again, looking over her shoulder to the north, where the sky seemed darker. She needed to get home before the storm hit.

Finally, she heard the lock turn. Ed looked as exhausted as she felt when he opened the door.

"Jane!" His face was weary, but his red-rimmed eyes brightened a little at the sight of her.

She tucked her hair behind her ear. "Hey, Ed. How are things? How is…"

His face fell, and tears filled his eyes.

"Oh, no…" Jane said, knowing immediately the worst had happened.

"She passed away yesterday evening…" He took a shaky breath and ran his fingers through his thin hair. He pushed the screen open. "The good news is… I took your advice and got a little of that marijuana oil for her. Son of a friend of mine, dabbles in… that. She… she died peacefully, with a smile on her—" his voice broke.

Jane grabbed the door. "Ed, I'm so sorry. Is there anything I can do—"

He shook his head. "The funeral home is closed, and the only place that will take her is the morgue up on Sandusky, but… They said they don't have the personnel to drive the ambulance to come—"

"She's still upstairs?" Jane asked incredulously.

He nodded, wiping his eyes with the back of his hands. "I'd take her up there myself, but…"

"You can't get her down the stairs," she finished.

He nodded.

"Well, maybe I can help you—"

He shook his head. "No. Even as slight as she is now, she's heavier than she looks. I couldn't have you fallin' and breaking your neck. You got kids—"

"Well, when did they say they would come?" Thunder rumbled in the distance and the sky dimmed further. Jane smelled rain. "I could stay here with you for… a while, anyway."

"Could take a couple of days… They didn't know. They said they'd take her now if I could get there but…"

"A couple of days?" Jane was no coroner, but she was pretty sure leaving his wife's corpse upstairs for two days was a terrible idea.

"Can we call the fire department, or the police, or someone?"

"I called the Harborview PD last night. Benny said he'd come out when he could find someone to help him move her, but they are short-staffed and he's still not here."

Good luck with that, Jane thought. She was pretty sure Officer What's-His-Name wouldn't be able to carry Ruth down the stairs, anyway.

Then *he* popped into her head.

"Matt," Jane whispered, thinking fast. The last thing she wanted to do was see him again, but… she couldn't put her pride before Ed's *dead* wife.

Ed looked up. "What?"

"Matt Patterson. He lives just down—"

"Carol and Al's boy?"

She had no idea who Carol and Al were, but she was sure Matt was strong enough to get Ruthie down to the car, and then…

He wiped his eyes. "He's home? Do you think…"

"There's only one way to find out," Jane said, turning for the door. "I'll be back in a minute."

Chapter Twenty-Nine

Day 15 // 10:20 a.m

THE WIND HAD PICKED up substantially, and blew against Jane's neck, making her shiver.

"Matt!" she called, wanting to make sure he knew she wasn't trying to enter unannounced again. "Matt!" Jane pounded on the door. "It's Jane Moore. I met you the other day in… well, in your—"

The door flew open, and there he stood, in jeans and a khaki t-shirt, looking just as incredibly handsome as before. His eyes snagged on her chest and his brow went up slightly before he met her eyes.

"My bedroom, yes, I remember. Listen, about that—"

She held up her hand. "It doesn't matter. I–I need your help."

Matt frowned. "With what?"

"Moving a body."

His eyes widened.

Jane shook her head. "Not that body, a different one. It's for Ed… Hamilton," she pointed back up the road.

"You know Mr. Hamilton? Wait. *He* killed somebody?"

Thunder rumbled again, sounding closer than it had before.

"No. His wife passed away yesterday, and the coroner can't come for…" she threw her arms up. "I don't know how long and he can't take her up to… wherever, because he can't get her down the stairs." Jane didn't know why she was talking so fast. *Because you are still embarrassed about the other day, and even if he is appalled by you, you still find him breathtakingly handsome.* "I'm not strong enough to carry her down either, but you are. And we just can't… We can't leave her corpse up there to rot! He is devastated enough —" she finished breathlessly.

"Of course not." Matt shoved his bare foot into a boot beside the door, grabbed a red and black plaid jacket from somewhere close by, then pushed past her. "Let's go."

Jane realized she was going to take much longer than she'd told Maddy and needed to check on the kids first. She pulled her phone out and dialed. "Wait!" she called after him. It went directly to voicemail.

He stopped and looked back at her and time slowed as it had in his room. He was so beautiful, it was painful. She dropped the phone from her ear. The wind blew his hair across his eyes, and he pushed it back, staring at her with such intense—

Not now, Jane.

Not ever. She blinked and looked away. A cool, humid gust whipped between them, and she felt tiny drops of water on her cheeks. Thunder growled in the sky. The storm was here. "I have to check on my kids," she said hesitantly. "I wasn't expecting to be gone—" She pulled her wild hair back out of her face.

"Sure, whatever," he said, pulling the passenger door open.

"I–I…" If he came with her, he would know where she lived. He would know Thomas wasn't—

"Are you coming?" Matt called, climbing in the van.

Fat drops of rain began to fall. She paused a moment longer, unable to tell if she was making a mistake or not. He watched her from the front seat. His expression was unreadable.

You can trust him. You just can't fall for him.

"Fuck it." She ran for the driver's side.

Jane buckled her seat belt and tore out of the driveway onto the road. She'd check on the kids, make sure they were okay, and then drop Matt off, and then get the hell out of there before she embarrassed herself again. She glanced at him out of the corner of her eye.

Well, this isn't awkward at all.

She tried not to think about the way she looked. Thank god she at least had deodorant on. Not that it mattered—

As if reading her mind again, he said, "Nice sweatshirt."

She looked down at the eagle, wolf and American flag that blazed across her chest, and almost laughed. She had found it at the new cabin and was wearing it while her other one dried. It was ugly, but it was clean. "Thanks."

"So, are you a race car driver in your other life?" he asked. She followed his eyes to the dash.

Jane read the speedometer and almost laughed again. Seventy-three miles an hour was nothing. "Sorry. I'm just—"

Rain splashed on the windshield, and she turned the wipers on.

"Where is your husband?" Matt blurted.

Her smile faded, and she tightened her grip on the steering wheel as they hit a bump in the road.

"Jane, I know he's not with you."

"How do you know that?" she asked, trying to sound amused. It didn't work. She turned onto the highway.

"Because you're a terrible liar, because you look like you have the weight of the world resting on your shoulders, and because something tells me you haven't had a decent night of sleep since the Veil went up."

Her smile fell as her suspicion about her appearance was confirmed. She glanced at herself in the rearview, tucking the loose strands behind her ears. She must look like all kinds of shit—

"I can see how terrified you are," he said softly.

Jane inhaled sharply. Should she tell him? Should she not? Was she just being blinded by her attraction to him? *Wasn't Ted Bundy a handsome man too?*

"Where is your—"

"He didn't make it out of the city," she blurted.

Before he could ask her any more questions, they were at the cabin. She pulled into the grass driveway, threw the van in park, and met his eyes. "Thomas is stuck behind the Veil. Wait here. I'll be back in a minute."

Chapter Thirty

Day 15 // 10:28 a.m

HE KNEW IT! Matt knew her husband wasn't there. And he understood why she didn't want him to know. It was safer for her and the kids if everyone thought he was.

The door opened, and she came out of the cottage carrying a baby. Jane covered its head and ran to the side door, yanking it open.

"Sorry," she breathed, buckling the child in the seat behind him. "Change of plans."

Before he could ask, two boys ran out of the cabin and around the other side of the van, pulling the door open.

"Hi," Matt said awkwardly as they climbed in. Both kids eyed him in surprise.

"Get in your car seat, and get buckled," Jane said, sounding frustrated. A teenage girl, with shoulder length red hair climbed in behind the boys. Her brows rose at the sight of him then she frowned as she squeezed past the boy in the car seat and dropped into the bench in the back. The younger boy kicked a button on the door with his foot and it closed.

Jane pulled the door on his side shut and ran back into the house. She reemerged with a large bag and hurried back toward the driver's side. She threw the bag between the seats and half of the contents spilled onto the floor as she hopped in.

She backed up, and gunned it down the dirt road, hanging a sharp right onto the highway.

Matt wondered why she was in such a hurry since Mrs. Hamilton was already dead, but kept his mouth shut. The road was virtually empty.

They were almost at their turn when Jane muttered a slew of curses under her breath. Her fingers dug into the steering wheel as a golf cart came into view on the shoulder—heading in the opposite direction.

The rain was coming down hard, but Matt was able to make out a heavy, shirtless man with a scraggly beard in the driver's seat. He was smoking a cigarette.

The neighbor.

"Is that him?" he asked quietly, as she accelerated.

She nodded, her jaw tight.

As they passed, the man stared blatantly at Matt, not even bothering to be discreet. *Yep, she is definitely right to be worried about that guy,* he thought. That dude gave off all kinds of bad vibes.

"Who in the hell are you?" The girl behind him asked.

"Maddy!" Jane gasped.

He turned. All the kids were staring at him. He turned a little further in his seat. Even the baby. He counted her chins. She had three. It seemed like a lot of chins for one kid.

"I'm Matt. I'm a friend of your mom."

Maddy folded her arms across her chest. "She's not my mom."

Matt frowned and looked at Jane.

"She's my niece. Austin, back there, is my nephew. Tommy and Bria are mine."

"Are we *really* going to see a dead lady?" Austin asked, sounding excited.

"Her name is Mrs. Hamilton, and yes, we are. She passed away last night," Jane said.

"I don't want to see a dead person," Tommy said, sounding far less so.

"Yeah, me either." Maddy chimed in.

"Well, then you shouldn't have cried about staying home in the storm. You didn't have to come." Jane countered, glancing in the back at the boy.

Ah, that explained it. Matt shoved the stuff that had fallen out of the bag back in and sat back in his seat. The rain was coming down in sheets. He could barely see out the front window.

"But mom—"

"Don't 'but mom' me. It's too late now." Jane pulled her wet hair back off her face, and he had the ridiculous desire to reach out and tuck it behind her ear. "You don't have to look at her if you don't want to," she continued, glancing in the rear-view mirror. "You can just go… somewhere else when Matt brings her down."

"You're going to *touch* her?" Tommy gasped in horror.

"Tommy," Jane warned.

Matt watched her as she barreled back down the road. So, this was the real Jane Moore? Minivan-driving mom with a car full of kids?

He almost laughed. That had definitely not been the impression he had received when she had come bursting into his bedroom. Then she looked like—*What is the woman's name in Terminator?* He frowned. Jessica? Jane flipped the control, and the wipers swept faster across the windshield.

"What?" She glanced at him, then the road, then back at him.

"Nothing."

He turned to the boys. "Either of you guys knows the name of the lady in Terminator?"

Tommy looked confused, which Matt realized made sense because he was like four.

Austin piped up. "Sarah Connor?"

Matt slapped his knee. "Yeah. That's it!"

Matt looked at Jane again. *Yeah.* If Sarah Connor had a bunch of kids and drove a minivan, this would be her. Something inside him, that had been still for a long time, stirred.

Jane frowned, continuing to divide her attention between him and the road. "*What* are you looking at?"

Matt smiled. "You."

Her frown deepened, and he laughed. Did she really not know how attractive she was?

She shook her head, as they bounced back down the straight country road to the Hamilton farm.

Much sooner than he would have thought possible, Jane parked in front of the house, and they all began to unbuckle.

"Can you bring the diaper bag?" she asked, jumping out.

"Help!" called Tommy.

Matt turned and saw him wrestling with the buckles of his seat belt. Matt unfastened his own, then leaned back and unhooked the boy. Then he grabbed the oversized bag squished between the seats and pushed his door open.

The other kids followed Tommy out, and they headed out into the deluge.

It was only ten steps to the porch, but by the time they were all up there, everyone was a little damp. The girl Maddy shivered in her short tank top while the boys stared at his foot, like there was a raccoon hanging on it, hissing at them, their expression half fascination, half horror. Matt slid out of his jacket and draped it over Maddy's shoulders as Jane knocked on the door. The girl looked about to say no thanks, then changed her mind and pulled it around her body.

Jane knocked.

"Hey, where is your foot?" Tommy asked.

"In Afghani—"

Jane cut him off. "Tommy!" she scolded. "Shush."

Matt leaned over and whispered. "In Afghanistan."

Tommy's eyes widened. "Why did you leave it there?" he whispered back.

"Tommy." Jane's voice was sharp.

She knocked again, and Ed opened the door. His eyes grew wide as he took in the—Matt counted quickly in his head. There were six of them. He imagined what they must look like—him,

Jane, and the kids all dripping wet on the front porch. He was reminded of the Sound of Music, which was his mom's favorite movie.

A regular Von Trapp family.

For some reason, it made him smile to be a part of their motley little crew.

"I'm so sorry, I couldn't leave the kids," Jane apologized to Ed. She did that a lot, apologize. "But I brought Matt and we're going to help you—"

"No point," Ed interrupted.

Jane's shoulders slumped. "What? Did someone finally come?" she asked, adjusting Bria on her hip.

The baby was slobbering like a bulldog. She kind of looked like one too. Matt's nose wrinkled at the big string of drool that hung like a suspension bridge between the infant's glistening lips and her mom's shirt.

His brows came together as it got longer and sagged.

Jane swatted it down, and he gagged a little, as she absently wiped her hand on her pants.

He coughed to cover it up as Jane cast her eyes in his direction, frowning.

"No," Ed said. "All's I got is the pickup and our Prius. I can't put her…"

Jane stared at the old man for a moment, as Matt imagined stuffing poor Mrs. Hamilton into the trunk of the Prius. "Take my van," she said. "We can–I'll pull the seats out in the back a-and… I think I have enough gas. How far is it?" she asked Ed.

"Thirty-four miles each way, but I can't use your gas. How will you get back down to the Veil to meet up with your husb—"

She turned toward Matt. Her brown eyes worried. "Do you think you can help me get the seats out? I actually don't know how—"

"Sure," he said, puffing his chest a little. "I was a First Sergeant in the United States Army. I'm pretty sure I can handle pulling seats out of a minivan."

Jane didn't look impressed. "Okay, you guys go inside. Maddy, take Bria."

"But—" Tommy began, sounding terrified. He was still staring at Matt's foot.

"She's upstairs, Tommy," Jane whispered, reading her son's mind. "It's okay. Go in the living room with Austin and Maddy."

Once Jane had handed the baby over, she turned to Matt, the worry in her eyes replaced by determination. "Ready?" she asked. Once again, he admired her steeliness in the face of a crisis. It was a rare woman who could keep their shit together the way she did.

He nodded "Ready." They hurried back out into the rain, which was coming down even harder than before.

Jane unbuckled Tommy's car seat and ran it to the porch while he wrestled with the bench in the back.

Getting it out turned out to be a little more complicated than he thought, but he and Jane managed to heave it out and onto the porch.

He went around the side for the one bucket seat, which would provide them enough room to lay Mrs. Hamilton out comfortably, but he couldn't figure out how to release it. He swore as the rain soaked his back and jeans. He hated wearing wet jeans.

Instead of helping, Jane stood beside him, laughing quietly.

He jiggled, pulled, then shoved the seat. The damn thing wouldn't budge.

He glanced at her over his shoulder.

She was leaning against the van, sopping wet, hands folded across her chest, brow raised. She was trying and failing miserably to hide her smile.

He stood up, sighed dramatically, and slicked his wet hair back. He deserved that. "Go ahead. Say it."

Jane broke into a grin, and his heart practically galloped out of his chest. "You almost done there, Army Ranger?" she asked, as drops of water fell from her eyelashes.

An intense desire to kiss her surfaced hard and fast, and it was all he could do to keep himself from acting on it. "First sergeant," he muttered, turning back to the seat, determined to get it out or die trying.

Finally, he figured out the rather simple mechanism, and with a soft click, it released. Jane was still smiling as she helped him haul it onto the front porch, and it more than made up for his wounded pride. They were both soaked to the bone. Jane twisted the front of her ridiculous sweatshirt, releasing the water, then went to check on her kids while he followed Mr. Hamilton upstairs.

"Are you sure you can…" Mr. Hamilton paused in the middle of the stairs, looked down at his foot, and let the sentence hang.

"Yes," Matt said, trying to keep the annoyance out of his voice.

Mr. Hamilton continued up the narrow staircase. "I didn't mean—"

Matt sighed. It was like that with everyone who knew him before. "I know, Mr. Hamilton." He looked back down the steps and heard Jane talking to her son. But it was not like that with her. With her, he felt whole. "I've got it."

They entered the bedroom, and there was Mrs. Hamilton, tucked under the covers. She was much thinner and far paler than he remembered, but otherwise, she looked like she might just be taking a nap. Oddly, the whole room smelled a little like weed. He spotted the bottle of CBD oil, and his brows went up.

Ed followed his gaze. "Jane suggested it, and Bobby Turner's boy, you know, Marcus—"

Matt nodded. They had gone to high school together.

"Yeah, he was always getting into trouble with this stuff, so I figured… He gave it to me right away when I told him why. It helped her. The last three days we were able to talk and…"

"I think we should get a blanket to wrap her in," Matt suggested quietly.

"Yes. I… think that would be nice. There is a quilt in the guest room."

Matt turned. Jane stood in the doorway, staring at Mrs. Hamilton, looking about the same shade of white as the dead woman.

"Do you have an–an outfit for her?" she asked, putting a hand on Mr. Hamilton's arm.

Mr. Hamilton shook his head. "I don't–I don't know what she'd—"

Jane's eyes remained glued to the dead woman. "Don't worry. I'll take care of it." Her voice sounded both hollow and far away. "She'll be… beautiful." The way she spoke the words sent a shiver down Matt's spine. Mr. Hamilton thanked her and left to go find the blanket.

Jane crossed the room to the closet. Her hands shook as she reached for the knob and turned it.

"Are you okay?"

She didn't answer as she disappeared behind the door.

"Is this the first time you've seen a dead person?" he asked, stepping to the side and bringing her back into view.

Her head was pressed against the inside of the door—She looked like she was trying to breathe.

Matt crossed the two steps between them quickly and put a hand on her shoulder. "What's wrong?"

Jane broke the contact and held up a hand before dropping it back to her side. "I need a—" She continued to press her head to the door, opening and closing her hands, mumbling to herself. He heard the words 'let go' and 'pass.'

Finally, she turned and met his eyes. Her lips were pale. "Second," she said, her voice thick.

He'd lost track of the conversation. "What?"

"This is the second time." Her knuckles were white too as they clung to the edge of the door.

"Go downstairs," Matt said, afraid she might pass out. "I'll help Mr. Hamilton–You don't have to do this."

She pushed away from the door, wiping her eyes with the sleeve of her wet sweatshirt. “Yes, I do,” she said, pushing the hangers back and inspecting Mrs. Hamilton’s wardrobe.

“Why?”

She turned. “Because someone did it for me.”

He recognized the pain in her eyes. He’d seen it enough times in the mirror to know.

Mr. Hamilton returned with the quilt before Matt could ask who had died. Clearly, it wasn’t her husband. Had there been someone else before him?

Maybe a first lover?

His heart thumped with jealousy.

She’s married, he reminded himself again.

Unfortunately, it was becoming very clear to him that he didn’t care.

He helped Mr. Hamilton arrange his wife in the blanket, and Jane chose a blue suit with a pink satin blouse and pearl earrings. Matt bent down and scooped Mrs. Hamilton into his arms.

There was something about cradling the dead that always tore him in half. It just felt wrong, he thought as he struggled to balance her body in his arms. The tug of war inside, between wanting to hold them forever and run away at the same time. He turned and followed Jane as she led the way out of the room, trying not to look down.

Matt carefully made his way downstairs, feeling for each step as he went.

Halfway down, the blanket slipped—exposing Mrs. Hamilton’s pallid face and slightly opened mouth. His jaw tightened as the memory exploded.

Matt swayed as another face swam before his eyes, mouth agape in exactly the same…

“Shit,” he breathed. His heart thudded in his ears.

It’s not him.

“Matt?”

His chest heaved as Jane appeared in front of him, gently covering the late woman's face again.

"Are you okay?" she asked. Her fingers were tentative and warm, on his arm.

He nodded as Tony's face faded back into his memory.

"Come on," she said softly. "It's just a little further."

Focus on her—

Gladly.

Matt blinked to clear his head as he took the remaining steps.

She gently touched his shoulder as he passed through the screen door she held open. He felt her breath against his neck.

"This isn't your first either," she whispered. It wasn't a question.

He shook his head. No, this was not his first time holding a body. Then he hurried as quickly as possible out to the van.

He placed Mrs. Hamilton as gently as he could in the back, then closed the rear door and hurried back up the steps.

Jane grabbed his arm again and pulled him aside before they reentered the house. The heat from her body brushed past him in the cool air. "I'm sorry," she said. "You're a Vet and I wasn't thinking. I shouldn't have—"

"It's okay."

She was so close. She smelled like lilacs or lilies and soap. And all he wanted to do was–*Kiss her.*

If anything could drive his pain away, it would be that. It would be her. He was sure of it.

"No. I shouldn't have–I didn't think." She insisted.

"Really. It's fine. I'm fine," he assured her, but her eyes continued to worry. "How are you?" he asked. Matt did not understand the ache he felt for her. It was almost overwhelming. He found himself desperately wanting to touch her cheek, to be wrapped in the warmth of her embrace. He was dangerously close to begging for either one.

Jane studied him for a moment. "I'm as good as you are."

Explain about the other day.

"Listen, about the other—"

Mr. Hamilton opened the door. He mumbled something unintelligible, and then turned and went back inside.

Jane's warm hand pulled Matt even farther away from the door. She whispered close to his ear, "I can't go with him. I can't leave the kids."

"I can keep an eye on them." Jane flooded his senses, and he felt like he was drowning. He clenched his fists and dug his nails into his palms against the desire to pull her into his arms and hold on for dear life. He had only known her a couple of days, but he knew with certainty he had never wanted anyone in his life more than the woman standing in front of him. Jesus, he could barely breathe.

She shook her head. "I'm sorry, I just... I don't know you well enough."

He stared at her.

Tell her how you feel.

"You could if you wanted to..." he whispered. A storm of goddamn butterflies stampeded through his stomach. He hadn't been this bold with a woman since before his injury, and he'd *never* been this terrified she would turn him down.

She's married, his conscience repeated.

He knew that! Damn it. But... he was beginning to think it was to the wrong person. And he just needed to know...

She tried to step back, but he caught her arm. The heat from her skin through the wet sweatshirt found his palm, and electricity shot up his arm. "I want to know you," he confessed, certain if he didn't do it now, he probably never would.

Part of him knew what he was doing was wrong, especially under the circumstances, but... to the rest of him, she felt right. Righter than anything had in a long time. "I desperately want to know you, Jane," he said, meeting her eyes and letting her see everything he felt, but didn't know how to say. The last time he'd done this, it had blown up in his face.

She's not Katie.

Jane made a breathy, gasping noise that was both the most adorable and sexy thing he had ever heard, and it took every ounce of willpower not to throw her up against the side of the house and kiss her senseless. The way she was staring at him did not help. In fact, if anything, it egged him on, begged him to do what he was trying so hard not to.

Jane bit her lip, looking as confused as he felt.

He held his breath and watched in amazement as his palm slid against her jaw. It was just like in his dreams. Wait, was he still imagining or—he pressed his thumb to her lips and her mouth dropped open slightly—*not imagining*—but she didn't pull away.

Lightning arced through his body again. It was like when they touched the other day. He felt… fireworks. Lust. *Everything.*

He stepped closer, inhaling her scent and gently placed his hand on her hip. "I cannot stop thinking about you," he whispered, dipping his head closer to hers.

She didn't move.

He cupped her flushed cheek in his hand and tilted her chin up. Her shallow breath brushed his lips as he leaned forward and—

"Mom! Bria's crying," her son called from inside.

Jane jumped back and blinked—as if coming out of a trance—and her gaze dropped to the floor. Her hand flew to her chest as her breath became shallow and fast. "Oh, god. I'm sorry!"

Why was she apologizing? "Jane?" He put his hand on her shoulder.

She shook her head, staring at the ground.

He gently pushed her chin up. Her wild eyes met his, and his insides throbbed. His breath stuck in his throat again when he realized she was just as disappointed as he was. Jane struggled to inhale, and he released her as her lustful glace turned to a look of pure terror.

Matt's body screamed in protest and he felt like his body and mind were being ripped in half. It was his turn to be terrified.

What was that?

He didn't know.

Why did you let her go again?

He looked away, over the storm-soaked fields. Fuck. He had no idea. He had only known her for thirty seconds—and yes, she was married. But damn it all, he didn't care.

He turned, and she was still rooted to the spot, staring at him. Her sweatshirt clung to her shoulders and the blond hair that hung in long ropes swayed with the gusts of wind that were now rushing over the fields. Her face was wet and flushed. Her nose was covered in freckles, and he had never seen a more honest-to-god beautiful woman in his life.

Then try again.

Matt found her wide, brown eyes, and tried unsuccessfully to stop himself from reacting to what he saw in them.

Thunder rumbled, shaking the panes of glass in the windows. A bolt of lightning shot across the sky.

She wanted him too.

Kiss her.

Matt clenched his jaw. He knew he should walk away, because she wasn't the sort of woman to have lurid affairs. He wasn't that kind of man, either. But if the last four torturous days had taught him anything, it was that letting her go a second time was not an option if he ever wanted to live with himself again.

Go for it.

Matt squared his shoulders and took a step toward her. "Jane…"

"I've got all her papers." Mr. Hamilton said, pushing the door open.

Matt backed away, clenching his fists. "Damn it," he whispered, grinding his teeth together.

Jane dragged her guilty eyes away from his and stared at her shoes, shaking her head, and he raked his hands through his wet hair. He wanted to tell her it was okay. That he was feeling the same way, and was just as disappointed and afraid. But he didn't. Instead, he stared at her like an idiot while Mr. Hamilton looked back and forth between them.

"Er- Are you ready, then?" he asked Jane.

"Ed, I can't—" she began.

"I'll go with you, Mr. Hamilton," Matt said.

"But—" Ed looked at Jane. "Your van…?"

She cast Matt a grateful look, then turned back to Ed. "Yes. You and Matt go. If it's okay with you, I'll wait here with the kids. I'd go, but it's just… with the little ones… Bria needs a nap and–I'm so sorry." Jane apologized *again*.

Ed took her hand. "You've already done more than enough, Jane. Help yourself to anything you find in the house. The dryer is in the closet by the back door." Ed's smile was sad as he turned away. Matt followed the old man's slumped shoulders, down the steps, through the rain, toward the van.

"Matt, wait!" Jane called. The desperation in her voice made his heart skip.

Mr. Hamilton caught his arm and pulled his head down. "Don't wait," he said quietly. "Life is too… damn short." His voice broke as his watery blue eyes met Matt's. "You understand me, son?" he asked.

Matt nodded slowly, wondering if he did.

"You must be bold in your desires or they will slip through your fingers." Mr. Hamilton released him, pulled the van door open, and climbed in.

"Matt!" Jane called again.

Matt turned and slowly climbed back up the stairs. He met her at the top step, knowing Mr. Hamilton was right, but… He searched her eyes, looking for a clue. What did *she* want? Did she want to kiss him as badly as he wanted to kiss her? Or—

"The keys," she whispered, pressing them into his hand.

He stared at her, then looked down at the keys in his hand, and exhaled the breath he was holding.

He turned away so she wouldn't see his disappointment and

started back down the stairs.

Her hand closed over his, pulling him to a stop. "Don't. Wait! Matt..."

Matt slowly turned to face her.

Jane opened her mouth, then closed it. Her eyes fell to their hands, and she released him, but her fingers lingered over his palm. Matt's heart drummed in his ears.

She went to speak again, but the words just wouldn't come. He knew the feeling. It was the same one he'd had all day.

"I–I... Never mind," she said finally, shaking her head in embarrassment.

She turned to go, but it was his turn to hold on. He could do this.

"Wait." Matt's fingers closed over hers. *Don't wait*—Right.

Matt spun her around and cupped her surprised face in his hands. He met Jane's eyes, giving her a chance to pull away if she wanted to. She closed them instead. He took that as a yes, bent his head and kissed her hard.

She gasped against his mouth and pressed her hand against his chest. But then her lips answered his, as her fingers curled, and she clutched his shirt. Her breath was shallow against his mouth as it moved over hers. Matt's knees almost buckled. His brow went up as he grabbed her shoulder to steady himself. That was new. *Don't stop.* He had no intention of stopping. He tilted her head back and deepened the kiss, pressing her teeth apart and dipping his tongue between them. His knees wobbled again. She moaned as she slid her hand from his chest to his jaw. It nearly undid him —*Dear god.* Kissing women had only made him feel things in one place before, but now—Matt felt her *everywhere.* Every cell in his body ached with pleasure and pulsed in time with his heart. He didn't know what was going on, but whatever it was, he never wanted it to end.

She gasped against his lips, and electricity shot through his veins all the way to his fingertips.

"Jane," he whispered against her lips.

Thunder boomed, and they both jumped bringing the kiss to a grinding halt.

It took every ounce of self-control he had, to pull away. He didn't want to, but Mr. Hamilton was waiting and—

Matt set his hands on her shoulders and gently pushed her back. Jane's expression was even wilder than before, and her chest heaved as she gasped through her bruised lips, like she had been running a race.

Her eyes were dark as she met his. He searched them. Was she angry or—All he saw was confusion and desire. No regret. Did she feel like he did then? Did she want more? Because instead of satisfying him, the kiss had lit the gaping hole in his heart on fire. And he had the sinking feeling that the only way to put it out was more of *her*. It was a terrifying, helpless, wonderful feeling.

"Ask me anything, Jane Moore," he whispered, taking her hand. He knew all the terrible things he should be feeling and felt *none* of them. He touched her cheek. "I'll tell you whatever you want to know."

She stepped back and unconsciously pressed her fingers to her lips. "I just…" She swallowed hard. "Wh–what time will you be back?" she whispered hoarsely.

Matt gave her his most dashing smile, because fuck it—it was too late to turn back now. He looked down at his watch. "A few hours. Four–maybe? Will you miss me?"

She met his eyes briefly. Her guilt was palpable, and he felt bad for that. But not for the rest of it. She ignored his question. "Okay. Thank you. Drive safe."

Then she turned and fled into the house.

The door slammed, and Matt stared at it for a minute. *Well, that just happened.* He took a deep breath. "Yep." He'd kissed Jane Moore. He shook his head before heading down the stairs and back out into the rain. And it was even better than he'd imagined.

Chapter Thirty-One

Day 16 // 12:06 a.m

PER EXECUTIVE ORDER from the President, the mortuary was closed, and all bodies were to be cremated immediately. Mr. Hamilton hadn't been prepared for that, so the coroner gave them the empty hall and a few minutes to say goodbye. Matt had dragged the only chair to the far end of the short hall and waited. His chest ached in the place that Jane had illuminated only hours ago, as Mr. Hamilton touched his wife's cheek and held her hand. Matt had repeatedly wiped his eyes as he stared at Mrs. Hamilton's unneeded clothes in his lap, trying not to listen as Mr. Hamilton spoke intimately, and lovingly to her for the last time. It was excruciating.

Then, like something straight out of a horror movie, men in hazmat suits came and wheeled her away, and left poor Mr. Hamilton standing there. Knowing they wouldn't have enough gas to go back up and get her remains, they had sat cold and shivering in the waiting room for four hours waiting for them.

While Ed Hamilton mourned quietly beside him, Matt had a lot of time to think. And think he did. In the harsh, fluorescent glare of the crematorium, he found way more clarity than the daylight had ever afforded him. There was more to life than the Army taking him back. A lot more. He could see it so clearly now. He had been stupid to think there wasn't.

IT WAS midnight before they got back to the farm.

The good news was they had been able to find a priest to do a small service over Mrs. Hamilton's ashes. Matt looked down. The bad news was, she was in a plastic sandwich container in his hands. Mr. Hamilton was too distraught to hold it, so he did.

Strangely, or perhaps not, even as dust, she still felt heavy. *Rest in peace, Mrs. Hamilton,* he thought as he followed Ed through the front door. In the soft lamplight, Jane was asleep on the floor, her back propped up against the couch. The baby was on a blanket, butt in the air, sleeping beside her. Tommy was on her other side with his head on her lap.

The smell of… something delicious filled the house—reminding him of his grandma. Matt smiled at the vase of tiger lilies on the mantle beside a photo of the Hamiltons. The sweet scent lingered and smelled like Jane. The other kids were gone, maybe sleeping upstairs in the guest room.

Matt took Ruth's remains and set them by the flowers.

"Should we let them sleep?" Ed asked quietly, looking down at Jane.

Matt scratched at his forehead. "I don't know. I don't think she gets a lot of sleep, but with her head like that…" Matt mimicked her and immediately felt the strain on his neck. "She'll be sore tomorrow."

Matt crouched down beside her, careful not to bump the baby. "Jane?" he whispered.

She didn't move.

"Jane," he said a little louder.

She snored softly, and Matt smiled, finding it strangely adorable.

Neither mother nor children budged. He looked down at Tommy, then at the couch. Carefully, he picked the little boy up.

"Come on, bud," he whispered as Tommy threw his arms around his neck. Matt held him for just a second, savoring the warmth of his shallow breath against his neck, then laid him on one end of the couch. It was a completely new feeling for him, and he marveled at how comforting it was. Matt realized he had never hugged a child before. How was that possible? Mr. Hamilton pulled a blanket out of the closet and draped it over him.

Then Matt picked Jane up, incredibly relieved to feel the thumping of her heart against his arm, and laid her on the other end. She curled up in a ball and sighed. He tucked her hair behind her ear and smiled again. It was just as satisfying as he had imagined. He glanced at the baby, still asleep on the floor. After he ate, he'd sit by her until Jane woke.

He stood up and turned to Ed. "Come on. I smell food in the kitchen. You haven't eaten all day. A little something in your stomach will help you sleep."

"And maybe a shot of whiskey," the old man said sadly.

Matt put a comforting hand on his shoulder. "Maybe two."

Chapter Thirty-Two

Day 16 // 3:00 a.m

MATT WAS JUST BARELY BUZZED and sitting on the floor next to the baby, with his back against Mr. Hamilton's recliner. He stared at Jane while she slept, trying to understand what it was that welled up inside him every time he looked at her. It felt damn good, whatever it was. And he craved it even more after the afternoon he'd had.

He could not get the image out of his head. Mr. Hamilton's gentle kiss on Mrs. Hamilton's unanswering lips. The agonizing cry that had torn itself from the old man's mouth and the regret in his eyes as they carted her away, for having let her go. Hell, Matt had felt like running after her himself, and he didn't even know her. But that too-late kiss was seared into his brain. The whole drive to the morgue, Matt had been unsure if he had made a mistake by kissing Jane. But on the drive back, he was sure he had not, because all he could think about was her warm lips answering his. He knew he would do it all over again if he had the chance.

The baby made a noise and Jane whispered 'shh' in her sleep.

He wished he could kiss her now.

The baby made another sound, stuck her hand in her tiny mouth, and started sucking on it. Jane didn't move.

Mr. Hamilton was right. Life was too short. Especially if you were lucky enough to find the kind of love that he and Mrs. Hamilton seemed to have shared. Matt looked back at Jane, curled up in her ripped jeans and redneck sweatshirt, and felt it again. That jolt of… something. Was what he felt for her the beginning of love?

He'd never been in love before. Was that how it started? With tingly insides and undeniable feelings that just wouldn't leave you alone? Were he and Mr. Hamilton at opposite ends of the same journey?

The baby started rolling around and crying. He sat up and tried to corral it—*Her.* Right, her. But beyond making sure *she* didn't escape, he was at a loss—

"She needs a bottle." Maddy's tired voice came from the stairs.

Matt turned. "A bottle?"

Maddy passed behind the chair. "Yeah, it's what babies drink out of." She went into the kitchen and flipped the light on.

Matt patted the baby, and she began to wail.

"Shit. Shit. Shit," he whispered to himself, glancing at Jane. Miraculously, neither she nor Tommy moved an inch.

Maddy returned with the bottle and gave him a look. "You want me to feed her?"

Yes.

"No. I got it." He reached for the bottle.

"Baby first."

For the first time in his life, Matt picked up a baby.

"Jesus." It was like lifting a wiggly bag of cement. He raised his knees and placed her in his lap, facing him as she squirmed and fussed. Maddy handed him the bottle, and he shoved it in her mouth. Bria grabbed the bottle like a little gremlin. Her silence was immediate. And by silence, he meant a slobbery-sucking sound, similar to removing octopus tentacles from a pane of glass.

"Don't forget to burp her," Maddy said, turning for the stairs.

"Yeah. Thanks."

While Bria shot-gunned her bottle like a college freshman, Matt's mind wandered back to Jane.

He felt something for her. He really did. Something weird, and real, and very, *very* powerful. He would understand if she didn't feel the same, even though he was sure she did, but *he* couldn't close the door, even if she was married. People made mistakes all the time. He'd almost married Katie.

He looked down. The bottle was empty, and the baby was sleeping.

"Shit." He hadn't burped her.

He slowly lifted her up and hung her over his shoulder. He inhaled the scent of warm milk and maple syrup and wondered if it was some kind of baby perfume, or if that was just the way she smelled. Either way, it was nice.

She turned her head toward his neck, and he felt her warm breath as she rested against his shoulder. He patted her back gently. Nothing happened.

He patted her a little harder.

She began to snore, her little belly pressing into his chest with every inhale. It was strangely super fucking adorable, and he couldn't believe it, but he was really enjoying it. Burping would have to wait.

He looked at Jane and felt it again.

Don't let her go.

He didn't want to, but… Matt sighed. It had only been a couple of days. Maybe he was jumping the gun. Maybe it was too soon to think like that. Maybe he should—

Mr. Hamilton's words rang in his head again.

Don't wait.

Chapter Thirty-Three

Day 16 // 2:03 p.m

JANE SAT UP, not recognizing the couch she was lying on. Her brain felt like mush as she dragged herself from the black hole of deep sleep. Sunlight streamed through the windows.

She looked down at the floor, and the empty blanket sprawled on it and was gripped by terror.

"Bria?"

She launched herself from the couch. "Bria!" she called with a strangled cry. "Bria! Tommy!" she screamed, stumbling past the recliner into the kitchen "Mad—"

The word died in her throat, and she blinked. Bria sat on Matt's knee at the kitchen table. She was drooling all over him. They both turned in surprise.

"Good morning, Sunshine," he said, trying not to smile. Even with clothes *on* and covered in baby spit, he was perfection. The memory of him kissing her felt like a dream in her foggy head.

Jane's hands flew to her hair, and she pushed it back off her face, absolutely certain she did not want to know what kind of hot mess she looked like right now. It fell back forward. "What—"

"The kids are outside. There's coffee in the thermos." He inclined his head toward the white thermos on Mrs. Hamilton's gorgeous granite countertop. "And this little thing…" he held Bria up. "Well," he shrugged. "She leaks."

Jane looked at her watch. *Two o'clock*—she glanced at the sunshine-filled window—*in the afternoon?*

She pushed her hair back again. "What the—"

He turned Bria from side to side as if inspecting her while she cooed. "I don't know if she just needs a tune-up or some—"

"Oh god," she said, stepping toward him. "I'm so sorry." She reached for the baby.

He set Bria back on his lap and shooed her away with a gooey hand. "I'm just kidding, Jane Moore. Ms. Bria and I have finally made friends. Haven't we?" he said in a sing-song voice, wiping his hand on his pants. "It took a while because this little girl is skittish and complicated"—he glanced at Jane with a meaningful smile, and then back at the baby—"just like her mom. Isn't she?"

Jane's mouth curled up as Matt bopped Bria's little nose. The baby gurgled and laughed as more drool dripped down her chin. Matt wiped his hand on his pant leg again. "I'm surprised you haven't dried out and turned into a little raisin." He sing-songed to the baby again. Jane's grin widened as a warm, fuzzy feeling filled her heart. Matt bopped Bria's nose a second time, and she laughed out loud.

"Seriously though, how often does your mommy have to fill you up?"

Jane's smile faded as she realized how hungry Bria must be. "You should have woken me up earlier. Where is the diaper bag? She is probably starv—"

Matt laughed. "Relax Jane, Maddy fed her… twice–I think."

"She did?"

"Yeah. And you seemed like you needed a little extra rest." His expression sobered. "Austin informed me you stay up all night 'watching for strangers'. So, I figured, with all of us here to keep an eye out…"

"Austin said—?" What else had the kids told him while she was unconscious? She rubbed her neck.

"Have a cup of coffee." His gaze swept her from head to toe. "Maybe two," he joked.

Jane tried to tame her hair again. Her fingers got caught in the tangles. A drowned rat, that's what she was. And a horrible mother. She twisted her hair and tied it in a knot at the back of her head. "God, you must think I'm—"

"That was a joke. And I don't think anything." But his eyes said otherwise. He was definitely thinking *something.* And whatever it was, it made her insides hum.

She looked away as the scene on the front porch yesterday rolled through her mind again. It had played on a loop all last night.

Jane glanced over her shoulder and met Matt's eyes. He was remembering too. She felt it like a current in the air between them. She pulled her fingers away from her lips and turned, catching her reflection in the window.

But just like she had told herself all day yesterday and reminded herself repeatedly after the kids had fallen asleep, as she stared at her reflection in Ed's bathroom mirror, it was impossible. Whatever she thought he felt… it just wasn't possible. There was nothing left of her body that a twenty-something-year-old man would desire… unless it was a quick roll in the hay, and she didn't want to be an easy fuck, damn it. She'd spent most of her adult life trying to be just that for Thomas, and look where it had gotten her.

"What's the matter?" Matt asked.

The matter was, she was a forty-year-old mother with crow's feet and stretch marks, who'd wasted her youth married to a man who had never once looked at her the way Matt had yesterday. And now it was too late. *It's never too late.* Yes, it was. Matt couldn't possibly desire her the way she thought he did, and believing he did would just break her heart. And she was tired of being broken-hearted. And she was embarrassed by her quickly developing feelings for him when all he probably wanted was casual sex. Jane's jaw tightened as she blinked back tears and reminded herself he wasn't *trying* to hurt her feelings.

"Jane?"

The worst part was, despite all of that, she wished he'd kiss her again. She shook her head. *Don't go down that rabbit hole.* She swiped her eye. It didn't matter anyway, because kiss or no, she wasn't about to have an affair with a man practically half her age. "Nothing." Jane dabbed her other eye, poured herself a cup of coffee, and sat down at the table, exhaling heavily. It was just a kiss.

Then let it go.

Matt watched her for a moment, but didn't say anything.

Jane sat up straighter. Let it go. Avoiding Matt's eyes, she admired the Hamilton's kitchen for the first time, despite having spent hours in it the night before. It was spacious, with white shaker cabinets, a custom countertop and stainless-steel appliances. The décor was sort of a wine-themed shabby-chic. "So, what else did I miss?" She took a sip from her mug and traced the grapes and wine glasses that covered the tablecloth. The coffee was surprisingly good.

"You sure you're, okay?" Matt bounced Bria on his knee and Jane turned as a big, stringy drop of drool dripped onto the hand he had around her fat little belly. He switched it out with his other one and wiped it on his shirt. Jane smiled slightly. "Yeah."

"We finished your egg dish—" he started.

"Quiche Lorraine."

"Sure, we finished *that* for breakfast. It was delicious, by the way. I had some last night too. Thank you."

He had kissed her. And now he was just acting like…

"Let it go," she whispered under her breath.

"What?"

"Nothing." She took a sip of coffee.

"Ed took the boys out to get eggs. And I think Maddy is out on the back porch trying to call her boyfriend. And–uh…"

He scratched the back of his head, looking uncomfortable.

Jane swallowed her coffee and set the mug down. "What?"

He opened his mouth, then closed it, then opened it again.

"What?" she demanded.

"I may have–Your husband called."

Jane's stomach dropped, and her guilt returned. She had tried calling him last night before she fell asleep, but the lines were busy.

"I wouldn't have answered, but he called four times, and I didn't want to wake you up, but then I thought maybe he was worried—"

She sighed. "What did he say?"

"Well, there isn't much of our brief conversation that I'd be comfortable saying in front of the baby," Matt said, lowering his voice. "But the gist of it was, he wanted to know who the hell I was, and if his kids were okay. Oh, and he wants you to call him back at your 'earliest fucking convenience.' That is a direct quote. His words, not mine." He frowned at Bria and pointed a finger at her. "Don't repeat that." She grabbed his finger and tried to shove it in her mouth. Matt wrestled it away. "Ew. No. That's mine."

Bria giggled as Jane buried her face in her hands. She knew exactly what Thomas was going to say. She could already hear him yelling. She should just save herself the phone call. "Great."

"I'm sorry," Matt said quietly.

"No, I am. It's my fault. I shouldn't have slept."

"You have to sleep. You didn't do anything wrong, Jane," he said slowly.

"Yes, I did. I left the kids—"

"You didn't *leave* the kids. You were tired, and they were safe, so you slept. That's all."

"He's not going to see it—"

"Who the hell cares what he thinks?" Matt's voice became defensive. He squeezed his eyes shut and sighed. "I'm sorry, but he sounds like a prick."

"I took his kids. *Our* kids." Jane blurted.

Matt's knee stopped bouncing. "What?"

"I shouldn't have, but I did. I thought I was doing the right thing, but the truth is… I don't know anymore. Maybe I wanted to hurt him as much as he hurt me. Maybe I was tired of being a coward, a…" Jane propped her elbows on the table and buried her head in her hands with a short laugh. "… a glass doormat," she said bitterly. "Fragile and so damn easy to walk—" She stopped herself. Why was she telling him all of this? "Anyway, Thomas has always been the anchor in our family and he's just worried for the kids that I'll mess things up, and he won't be here to—"

Bria started fussing, and Jane reached for her before getting up and turning toward the kitchen window. Her ears burned as she wiped her eyes. She watched Austin and Tommy running back and forth, laughing, trying to catch a chicken that had escaped the coop. She huffed a laugh, then her face fell again, and she wondered how she'd let her life become such a pathetic mess. "I took his kids, Matt. And the reason is—"

"You don't owe me an explanation, Jane. I'm sorry."

"I know. But I want you to understand. That's why he is angry. He's a good father."

"Was he a good husband?"

She didn't answer, not even sure she knew what that meant. He had financially supported her for most of her life. He never hit her. In fact, he jerked away every time *she* touched him. He was wonderful to his kids. He bought her beautiful jewelry and took her on fancy vacations. He found her so repulsive he couldn't sleep beside her anymore, leaving her alone in their king-sized bed while he slept in the den. Did that make him a good husband or a bad one?

Matt came and stood by her at the window. "The only thing that matters is you got away. And you're not alone, Jane. You have Ed," —he paused—"And me."

He was doing it again. Making her feel things that couldn't possibly be true. And it hurt so much she thought she might be sick. He had kissed her. And worse than that, she wanted him to do it again. So badly she could think of nothing else. *Then let him.* She shook her head. The last time she let a man kiss her when she knew better—*He's not Thomas.*

"I need to go," Jane said abruptly.

Give him a chance. No! Oh god. She was an adulterer.

"Jane, come on," Matt said as Maddy pushed the screen door open. They both turned.

"Ugh. The phones are jammed again," Maddy interrupted. "How am I supposed to have a conversation when my calls get dropped every five minutes? Oh, and Uncle Tom wants you to call him back. He sounded pretty pissed off."

Jane turned to her. "We need to go. Hold Bria."

Maddy eyed her drooling cousin. "Yuck. No. Where's her bib?"

"I'll take her." Matt offered, reaching for her baby.

"No, that's—" Jane's voice wobbled, and her head felt light as she stepped back. *Let him in.* She pressed the heel of her free palm to her temple. No. She *couldn't*. "No, no," she whispered to herself.

Matt put a hand on her arm, and lightning shot through her body. "Let me help you, Jane."

She jerked her arm away, before she did something stupid, like fall into his arms. *You're not an adulterer.* She would be if she didn't get the hell out of there! The thought filled her with shame. Panic rushed up her spine and seeped into her voice. "You did. You have, but we need to go."

Thomas never loved you.

Matt plucked Bria out of her arms. "Jane," he said, his eyes worried. "What's the matter?"

But maybe Matt—

She stumbled back, clenching her fists and then releasing them. The beginnings of a panic attack swirled in her blood. She turned to Maddy. "Go get the boys."

"What's the rush to go back to our prison?" Maddy said, opening the refrigerator obliviously. "The boys love it here. I love—"

"Maddy! Get out of there." Jane's voice was shrill. Maddy sighed and shut the door.

"Jane—" Matt tried again.

"And the rush is because I said so." She hurried into the living room to find the diaper bag, feeling like she was losing control, feeling like if she didn't leave *right now*, her body would betray her.

"But—"

"Go, Maddy!" Jane cried as she gathered up Bria's blanket and grabbed Austin's book off the end table. She had to get out of there before—*Before what?*

"Jane," Matt said softly from the doorway. "Talk to me."

She shook her head and tried to scoot past him. She had to leave before anything else happened. He placed a hand across the doorway and stopped her.

What might happen?

Jane met Matt's eyes, and she couldn't breathe. "Oh god."

Everything.

Chapter Thirty-Four

Day 18 // 4:43 p.m

MATT PACED the house all morning, and well into the afternoon. His leg ached in protest. He had spent the entire day trying to decide whether he should walk to Ed's and ask to borrow his truck or not.

After the fiasco with Jane the other day, he had become obsessed with fixing his mistake, with helping her, with easing the agony that had burned in her eyes as she dragged the kids out of Ed's house and drove off.

Not that he regretted kissing her, he didn't. But *she* did, and now he felt responsible. He felt like he'd taken advantage of her. He'd just gotten so caught up in the moment.

Matt imagined her and the kids stuck in that little cabin for the last three days. He imagined her sitting up in the dark while they slept, listening for her terrible neighbor. If he would have kept it friendly, he was sure he'd be there now, keeping an eye out for things, letting her sleep soundly once in a while. He pulled his hands through his hair. He actually missed the baby, for Christ's sake.

But he hadn't kept it friendly. He had crossed a line and now she couldn't accept his help without… She was a decent human being, and he'd kissed her. How did he expect her to feel afterward?

"Fuck."

She wanted you to. That was beside the point. She was scared and confused. *And attracted to you.* Also, not the point. He should have realized how fragile she would be…

She's not fragile. He sighed and buried his head in his hands. No, she wasn't. She was *vulnerable*, especially if that neighbor decided to make a nuisance of himself, but she wasn't fragile. Whatever made her dick husband think that he was mistaken.

Matt rubbed his temples. And him, Thomas, what a piece of work he was. Pissing all over their brief conversation like a dog marking his territory. He never once asked if Jane was okay or why she was so tired.

When he'd recounted their conversation to Jane, Matt had left out the part where Thomas had accused him of having an affair with her, sneering, "Don't even deny it, asshole. You can't bullshit a bull-shitter."

Matt's blood had turned to ice at those words.

Yep, Thomas was having an affair.

The question he had been mulling over was, did Jane know? His gut and her guilt told him no, because she'd defended him. But then she confessed to wanting to hurt him and taking the kids. So, maybe she suspected, but didn't know for sure? It irked him that she was probably wallowing in shame while her husband sat at home fucking another woman.

He punched the wall, and a picture of him in the first grade rattled in its frame. The whole thing was a mess.

What are you going to do?

Matt stared at his six-year-old self. He had looked like a fucking beaver in first grade, but man, he had confidence. Unlike now. The photo of his innocent younger self, smiling like a lunatic, stared back at him. *Come on. Grow a pair,* it seemed to say. Matt frowned. Cocky bastard.

But Beaver-Face was right about one thing, he was acting like a coward. *And Matthew Patterson is not a coward. At least he didn't use to be.*

Matt stared at his younger self and hammered out a really great apology in his head. Then grabbed his dad's ball cap and headed for the door.

He stopped briefly to run his fingers over the splintered wood where Jane had forced the door open, before storming out. He was going to do what he should have done in the first place—try to be her *friend*, which was what she actually needed, and offer to help. She'd broken down a door for him. The least he could do was knock on hers, apologize, and help her with the kids until this was all over.

THE WALK down the road toward the Hamilton farm didn't seem as bad, or as long as the one from the truck to his parents had been. For one thing, the rain had beaten the dust from the fields down, for another… Well, sitting with Mr. Hamilton in those miserable chairs while his wife was reduced to dust in an oven had given him some much-needed perspective, and ever since, Matt couldn't help but feel like he'd been given a very precious chance to do something different with his life. Actually—Bria's fat little face popped into his head, then Austin's shy smile followed by Jane's stormy eyes—he had the sneaking suspicion his *life* had just begun, and he suddenly wanted to go wherever it took him, even if it meant staying right here. He thought of his dad. Is that how he'd felt all these years? If so, Matt owed him an apology.

He quickened his pace. For the first time in years, he felt needed, worthy, like he was *enough.* He turned onto Ed's driveway. Enough what, he didn't know, but it felt good.

Matt watched a doe with two little fawns eye him nervously from the edge of the woods behind Mr. Hamilton's barn. She was like Jane, he thought, wary, nervous, but somehow beautiful and totally capable too. *Are you enough for her?* He desperately wanted to find out, but… he had to stop thinking like that. *For now.* Forever, unless she told him otherwise.

Fifteen minutes later, Matt found himself parked behind her van in Mr. Hamilton's green Ford, staring at her house. He hesitated, going over his speech one more time. Finally, he got out and, with a hopeful sigh, rapped his knuckles against the hollow wooden door.

A moment later, Tommy opened it. He squinted up at Matt and broke into a goofy grin that warmed his heart. "Matt!" Tommy said, hugging his leg excitedly.

Tommy was yanked back inside, and Matt heard Jane's hushed scolding. The boy's indignant voice whined, "But it's Matt!"

Matt pushed the door open. "Jane, listen—" He started as she stood up, blocking his entrance.

"You need to go," she said, putting her hands on her hips and avoiding his eyes.

"Just—"

She went to close the door, but he held it open.

"Wait. Come on. I came here to apologize. I—" He forgot his speech. *Damn it.*

"You have nothing to apologize for," she said, staring at his feet. "*You* didn't do anything wrong."

"No, it was *my* fault. Come on—"

"We both know it wasn't. Please, just go."

"I want to help you. Can't we just be friends?"

She met his eyes, and he inhaled sharply at the regret in them. She looked like she was about to cry. "No," she said vehemently.

He pressed his foot into the door as she tried again to push it closed. This was not going the way he had hoped. "Why not?" he begged, not caring how desperate he sounded. "Please?"

"You know why," she said, shaking her head guiltily.

"Listen," he said. "It didn't mean anything—"

She laughed and shook her head. "Thanks."

He winced. "Shit. No, what I mean is—"

She cut him off. "It did to *me,* Matt," she said, like he was an idiot. She slammed the door, and he heard the lock turn.

He stood on the stoop, staring at the door. "Damn it."

He'd thoroughly fucked that up. *She likes you.* He shook his head. What she needed right now was a friend.

He knocked on the door. "Jane? Please, just let me help you."

She didn't answer.

"Please?" he asked as he eyed Austin peeking at him through the blinds. The boy shook his head sadly.

Matt stared at him a moment, then headed toward the truck in defeat. He didn't turn the engine over right away. Instead, he sat, trying to decide what the right thing to do was. *Give her a couple of days.* Then what? *Try again.*

Matt put the key in the ignition and hesitated. Was that the right thing? Back off, respect her wishes, and try again another day? He flipped the key, and the engine turned over, then he backed out of the driveway and headed for the highway.

He was eyeing the clouds rolling in from the west, thinking they were in for another storm, when he recognized the familiar face of Jane's neighbor cruising on his golf cart. It was loaded down with odds and ends, a fan, an ottoman, no doubt stolen from a nearby cottage. A laundry basket was balanced on the front seat and filled to the top.

Matt rolled to a stop in the middle of the road and his anger flared as he cranked the window down. At least he could take care of this problem.

The golf cart slowed to a stop and the other man frowned as he stared, unafraid.

"You leave her the fuck alone," Matt growled.

The neighbor looked down the road in confusion and scratched his head. "Um. Who exactly—"

"I mean it," Matt warned. "Stay away from Jane and the kids."

The other man's eyes flicked to his and an icy chill raced down Matt's spine. The neighbor held up his hands and smiled innocently. "Hey, man. I don't know what—"

"I'll be watching you." Matt threatened before Jake could finish. "And I swear to god—"

"Pff. Whatever, man." The neighbor waved his hand nonchalantly, but his eyes were filled with venom as he punched the gas and the golf cart took off.

Matt thumped his hand on the steering wheel as he watched him retreat in the rearview. Dread pooled in his gut. And he knew better than to ignore it. He did a U-turn in the middle of the road and headed back to Jane's, feeling like he'd just made a big mistake, but not sure how.

He pulled back in her driveway and hurried to the door, glancing over his shoulder, and pounded on it. "Jane! Open up—"

The door swung open. "What do you want?" she asked, the rims of her eyes red from crying.

"I saw your neighbor. He's—" The fear that crossed her face made his hair stand on end.

"Where?" she asked anxiously.

"About a mile up the road. I—"

She exhaled, and her expression relaxed a little. She pointed to the sign on the window. "I can handle him if he comes around."

Matt looked at her homemade, no trespassing sign. "Jane, be reasonable. Let me stay here with you guys, just for tonight. I've got a bad feeling and you need—"

Jane shot him an accusing look he didn't quite understand. "If the Veil has taught me anything, it's that I don't need anyone. You, Thomas, or anyone. So, leave me alone, Matt."

She shut the door in his face again and he balled his fists at his sides, as he talked himself down from beating the door in and demanding she listen to reason. But if he did that, he wouldn't be any better than her shitty neighbor—would he?

"Damn it."

With a frustrated sigh, he climbed back into Mr. Hamilton's truck and headed home.

Chapter Thirty-Five

Day 20 // 9:59 p.m

JANE'S PHONE clattered to the coffee table. She pulled her feet up onto the seat of the recliner and sighed. She had finally gotten through to Thomas, and it had gone exactly how she expected, which was him putting intentions in her mouth that were never there, accusing her of endangering the kids, and making her feel like she was trying to purposely ruin his life. He was more worried about the gas that had been 'wasted' driving Mrs. Hamilton up to Sandusky than he was about her and how she was coping.

"Hope you're having fun with *Matt,*" was the last thing he said before hanging up on her. The funny thing was, there was no jealousy in his voice, just… anger.

She turned the volume up on the TV, just loud enough so she could hear it. Jane had seen the pretty dark-haired Canadian news anchor so often over the past three weeks, she felt as familiar as a member of the family. The anchor adjusted her microphone and got ready to deliver the ten o'clock news.

Every day it was the same, always about the Veil, never about anything else. And it made sense. What could be more interesting or terrifying than millions of people trapped in impenetrable cages, losing their minds and dying? It practically *was* a zombie apocalypse. One thing was for sure, every day the world was changing. Every forty-eight hours it became unrecognizable all over again.

Twenty days in and some cities like Detroit were still fine. While others were much worse off. Dallas was looking bad. At least everyone seemed in agreement now that the virus was serious. At first, that hadn't been the case. The question on everyone's mind now was, if it was man-made or not. The other question that had recently popped up again was, who in the *hell* had invented the Veil in the first place? Jane heard a noise and muted the TV, looking over the kids as they slept. She heard it again. Then she saw it. The knob on the front door jiggled again, catching her eye.

Jane grabbed her phone and dialed 9-1-1, then crept around the boys, into the kitchen and pulled the rifle down from the cabinet. She stood with her back to the refrigerator. It was the only place in the cabin that offered a clear view of all three doors.

Fifteen minutes later, Officer Beale knocked and announced himself.

Jane sighed in relief, shelved the gun, and hurried to answer it as Tommy rolled over and called to her.

"Go back to sleep, bud," she whispered before slipping out the door in her socks.

She blinked in the harsh light of the porch, swatting at whatever had buzzed by her ear.

"Mrs. Moore." He nodded, and she noticed he wasn't wearing a mask like he had last time. She was surprised by his bushy gray mustache.

"Officer Beale," she said curtly.

"I see you've… moved," he said dryly.

"Yes, to get away from him, but he found us. Jake was *here*. I told you he's—" she tried to steady her shaking voice.

"Calm down. So, he tried to break in?"

"Yes, he tried to open the front door. And, no. I will not calm down!"

"Okay, what was he wearing?"

Jane frowned. "W–what?"

His eyes narrowed. "Did you actually see him?"

"That man tried to break into my house," she hissed. "I have *children* in there, sleeping. I moved to get away from him. You have to do something. You want proof, take his damn fingerprints off my door and put him in jail!"

Officer Beale tried his best to look like he cared, which wasn't very convincing at all. He sighed, making Jane furious. "I think we can hold off on lifting prints. And if you didn't see him, how do you know…?"

"I just do and—"

Officer Beale held up his hand. "Unfortunately, 'I just do' is not admissible in court."

"I know that. My husband is a lawyer! But I am telling you, it was Jake. And I swear to god, if anything happens to my kids, we will sue the entire Harborview—"

Officer Beale looked up from his notepad. "Are you threatening me?"

Great. Now you pissed him off.

Jane let out a frustrated sigh. "No. I'm asking you to help me protect my kids. Can you please just… do that?"

Officer Beale scratched his sagging chin. "I can't arrest him without proof. If you get a video of him, I'll take him down and lock him up. Otherwise…"

Jane just shook her head and blinked back her tears. "You know what? I'm sorry I called. Just… have a good night, Officer." She went inside, not even waiting for his reply. She shut the door behind her. Seconds later, the police lights faded from the curtains.

She paced the small kitchen for several minutes, then put a dining room chair in front of the refrigerator, grabbed the rifle off the cabinet again, and sat down. She glanced at her watch and sighed. 10:41 p.m. It was going to be a long night.

A few minutes later, the lights reappeared. Jane frowned. Officer Beale was back? Had he caught Jake? Jane placed the gun by the door as she stepped outside again.

"What is it?" she asked anxiously.

He shrugged, looking like he hadn't slept in days. "It wasn't him."

She frowned. "What? How do you know?"

"I went over to have a talk with him, and his wife confirmed he's been home all evening."

He's married?

"Are you sure?" That didn't make any sense. There was no one else around here… was there?

"Well, based on the facts that you didn't actually see him, and he has an alibi, I'd have to say, I'm sure."

Jane frowned. If it wasn't him, then who was it?

"People have been making their way up from the city. It could have been anyone."

"He's married?" she asked wearily, feeling immediately sorry for whoever she was.

"Yeah, her name's Nikki. Anyway, when I told him to leave y'all alone. He said he thought you'd left."

Jane's heart sank. *Now he knows you didn't.*

"Keep your doors locked in the meantime," he glanced at her sign in the window, and his brow went up. "And if you need me, don't hesitate to call." He handed Jane his card, and she slipped it into her back pocket.

Jane locked the door behind her as, once again, the red and blue lights faded away.

She leaned against the door and buried her head in her hands.

What had she just done?

Chapter Thirty-Six

Day 21 // 9:52 p.m

THUNDER RUMBLED as Jane put the last dish away and wiped down the counter. Between Tommy's meltdown earlier, and Bria's diaper blowout in the playpen, she couldn't wait to put the day behind her. Quietly, she made her way past the sleeping kids, to the bedroom, pulling the ponytail out of her hair. Her scalp ached as she massaged it. She went to plug in her phone, but her charger was not on the nightstand where she'd left it.

Damn it. Maddy had taken it out in the van again to call her boyfriend 'in private' and forgotten to bring it back in. This was the third time, and they couldn't afford to waste the gas.

Jane went into the living room and peeked out the rainy window, then down at the eight percent battery she had left on her phone. Lightning flashed, illuminating the van. A second clap of thunder rattled the pictures on the wall. She sighed heavily.

She couldn't go without her phone, even for a night. If something happened and Sarah or Thomas needed to get a hold of her, she had to be available.

As quietly as possible, she unlocked the door, bent her head into the rain, and hurried through the darkness to the van. Jane pressed the key and pulled the door open.

She wiggled the charger from the socket and realized Maddy had left the driver's side window cracked. Half the driver's seat was soaking wet.

"Damn it." Jane ran around the other side, put the keys in the ignition, and rolled it up. She pulled the keys out. Rain pelted her back as she pushed herself back and slammed the door. Lightning flashed, followed by a terrific boom.

She caught his reflection in the window at the same time the scent of a wet ashtray hit her nose. Before she could react, his gigantic hand closed over her arm like a vise, and Jake spun her around. Her eyes snagged on the white hood of his golf cart parked in front of the house. Her mouth fell open in disbelief. Jake's wet hair stuck to his head and his black eyes glittered in the dim porch light.

He leaned in with a sly smile as she tried to back away. He squeezed her arm, holding her in place. "I thought you left town?" His breath was hot and foul, making her stomach turn. He tilted his head and his smile widened as he raised his eyebrow. "Did you lie to me, Jane?" He was very drunk.

She yanked her arm free and stepped back. The side-view mirror dug into her back as she collided with it. "Get your hands off me." She met his eyes, pulling her phone out of her back pocket. "And get off my property or I'll call the—"

He slapped the phone out of her hand, and it clattered against the door of the van and fell to the ground.

She stared in disbelief at Tommy's sweet smile beneath the cracked screen as it illuminated the ground at their feet.

"Are you crazy?" she cried. "What's the matter with—"

There was a crack against her skull, and her head flew to the right. Fire lit up her cheek as she pressed her fingers to it. Jane turned back and stared at him. The shock of being struck stung more than the physical pain.

Jake shoved her back against the van. Lightning flashed again as his rough hands pinned her arms to her sides. He crushed her with the weight of his body and the scent of body odor and bourbon made her gag. She turned her head away and took a deep breath, ready to scream, when he growled in her ear. "Go ahead. Who do you think will come out to help you? Your daughter? Your little boy?"

Her breath caught in her throat. He was right. If she screamed, it would only make things worse. He pressed into her again, and his weight forced the air out of her lungs. She clamped her mouth shut as the terror of what was probably about to happen flooded her body with adrenaline.

Jake nuzzled her neck, and she did the only thing she could—she slammed her forehead into his face.

"Goddamned bitch!" Jake stepped back, grabbing his nose. But before she could run, the full weight of his fist met the left side of her head. Sparks flew in the darkness and she doubled over as thunder rumbled overhead.

He hit her again, and she fell to the soggy ground, unable to see.

"Now you're gonna pay for being a snooty little cunt, and for bringin' the cops to my house." He kicked her hip with the heel of his shoe and the pain was so sharp she almost blacked out as she fell back into the wet grass. She wanted to let the darkness take her, sure she wouldn't want to remember anything about what happened next, but…

The kids.

It took every ounce of will she had not to scream as he straddled her and dropped to the ground.

You should have stayed inside.

It was all happening so fast. Tears didn't even have time to form in her eyes.

"Now you're gonna lay there and be quiet until I'm done. You understand?" he said, yanking down the waistband of his shorts. "Or I swear to god, I'll kill your kids."

She nodded and closed her eyes as he shoved her shirt up. Icy drops of rain splattered on her face and stomach as squeezed her breast through her bra.

You shouldn't have sent Matt away.

His breath was heavy against her neck as she turned her face away. The button of her jeans popped at the same time she felt the rock beneath her palm in the grass beside her. She knew exactly which one it was because she'd tripped over it a dozen times. It was the one Tommy had brought up from the beach. The one he insisted on bringing to the new house, then dumped unceremoniously on the ground and forgot about. Her hand closed around it.

Jane pictured the rough edges and the point that looked like a Swiss mountain top. Jake grunted and pulled her pants down past her hips. She knew if she did this, only one of them was coming out alive. She tightened her grip on the slick rock as he fumbled with her panties and prayed it was her.

Then, with every ounce of strength she had, Jane swung.

Chapter Thirty-Seven

Day 21 // 10:47 p.m

MATT WAS ASLEEP, so it took longer than it should have for him to realize she was actually calling for him and he wasn't dreaming.

"Matt!"

He sat up and looked at the rain-drenched window and then at his watch. It was after ten at night—

"Matt! Matt!" she screamed.

Dread launched him out of bed as she pounded on the door downstairs.

Not even bothering with his prosthetic, he skidded down the stairs as she continued to scream his name.

He fumbled with the lock, and threw the door open, gripping the jamb to balance. She stood in the porch light, soaking wet, her face and her neck and her shirt covered in… *Blood?*

His eyes widened. *Jesus Christ.*

He pushed the screen open. "What happened?"

"I–I…" she held her hand out as if warning him back. Her whole body trembled. She backed away another step and dropped to the ground, clutching her stomach and crying.

He fell to the floor beside her. "Jane! What–what's happened? Are you hurt?" He pushed her head up and ran his fingers gently over her face and neck, trying to figure out where all the blood was coming from. She tried to push him away.

She pulled at her hair. "Oh god. Oh god. Help me! Help—" she cried pitifully. He recognized the desperation in her voice. He knew the helplessness that came with it. It was like being swallowed by a darkness a thousand times your size and finding nothing to hold on to as you fell.

Matt grabbed her icy fingers and squeezed them in his. "I've got you, Jane. Hold on to me. I've got you." Then he cupped her face, smearing the blood. "Do you feel my hands? I'm right here, and I won't let you go. I promise." Her bloody hands covered his, and her nails dug into his wrists as she held on for dear life.

The memories of the last time he had spoken those words stabbed at his heart. He pushed them away.

"You need to calm down. Tell me what—"

Jane jerked away and turned in time to vomit on the front steps.

He crawled over to her and pulled her back into his arms. "Help me. Help—" She curled into a ball as he rocked her, trying to ignore the tangy scent of blood that surrounded them.

"Where are your kids?" he asked.

She didn't answer, and his fear grew.

Matt pushed her back, gently shoving the hair out of her face. "Jane. Where are your kids?"

She looked up at him, her eyes wild with fear. "Safe," she whispered.

"Are you sure?"

She nodded.

"Are you okay? Are you hurt?"

She just stared at him a moment, then shook her head again and began to cry. Big, wracking sobs shook her shoulders as Matt looked down at his shirt. It was soaked in blood.

That's not good. His heart thumped in his chest.

"Let's go inside," he said, but she didn't move. Instead, she just cowered against him, like she was trying to hide.

"Jane, I need you to get up," he said, rubbing her back.

She didn't answer.

He looked at the door. There was no way he could carry her

without his prosthetic. He made a quick decision. "I'll be right back."

He scrambled up the stairs and crawled to his room. Forgoing the sock and wrap, he strapped the prosthetic straight onto his leg and banged back downstairs.

Matt threw the screen open and scooped her off the porch. She threw her frozen arms around him. Her breath was shallow and fast against his neck as he carried her inside.

Jane shook as he set her on the couch. Matt quickly got a towel and a glass of water from the kitchen, then sat across from her on the coffee table.

He pushed the glass in her hand and she took a shaky sip, staring unblinkingly at his knees.

Shock. He'd seen it enough times to know.

He took the water and then took her hands in his, rubbing them together between his palms.

"Jane."

She continued to stare.

"Jane?"

Finally, she looked up. Her eyes widened, and she looked surprised to see him sitting there.

"I need you to tell me what happened. Where are your kids? Can you do that?"

She nodded and opened her mouth, but no words came out. Instead, she started hyperventilating again.

He gently took her face in his hands and pressed his forehead to hers. "It's okay. As long as your kids are okay…"

She nodded.

"… it can wait. Just close your eyes and breath with me. I've got you. You are okay now."

She grabbed his wrists again and clung to him like she was afraid he might disappear.

"Just breathe," he said.

"No, I… my breath…" She pressed her cheek into his palm,

trying to turn away, then gasped in pain and flipped her head the other way. His hand came away slick with blood.

"Don't worry about it. Here, stay still while I…"

He picked up the wet towel, and gently wiped her nose and mouth and cheek, revealing swollen, bright-pink patches of flesh underneath. Fury built inside of him. Someone had struck her, and he knew exactly who that someone was. He fought the urge to hunt Jake down immediately and kill him.

"Breathe."

There was a gash underneath her eyebrow, which explained some of the blood, but certainly not all of it. She stared at his chest while he did his best to clean her face, using every corner of the towel. By the time he was done, the cut in her brow was already dripping again.

"Can I rinse my mouth?" she whispered.

Matt got up and went upstairs to get mouthwash and look for some butterfly bandages. When he came back down, she was standing by the window, looking out, clutching the front of her jeans. There was a fresh streak of blood from the cut under her eye, down the side of her neck.

"You need to sit—"

She met his eyes, and hers were filled with tears. "He broke my phone. And these were my only pants," she said helplessly, releasing them from her grasp. They were soaking wet and slipped low on her hips. The button was missing as if it had been popped, and the zipper—

Matt staggered backward. The air rushed from his lungs like he'd been punched in the gut. Jane's hands trembled as she gathered the waistband of her jeans up again.

"I–I need my phone… Wh–what am I going to do without it? It has all the kids' baby pictures…" she cried quietly. "All the videos of them and Thomas…"

Matt couldn't breathe. As a soldier he had been around plenty of blood, and he had definitely seen his fair share of injuries—the kind that haunted people's dreams. But, in all his years as a *man*, he had never seen anything like what stood before him now.

Jane's eyes pleaded with him as she continued to ramble, oblivious to the swelling of her face, to the crimson patches of blood that painted her like a slasher movie. She wiped her eye, smearing blood into her hair, then hoisted up her pants again, while he stared in disbelief. *How could a man do this to a woman?* His teeth ground together as he imagined how helpless she must have felt at the mercy of that repulsive man. Matt desperately wanted to comfort her, but he didn't know what to do. Should he hold her? Or not touch her? Basic training had not prepared him for—

"So, I k–killed him," she whispered, dragging him from his thoughts.

His brows came together. "What?"

Jane shrugged her shoulders helplessly. "I killed him." She wiped her nose on her sleeve. "I–I killed him, Matt." Her dilated eyes met his, pleading for approval.

Matt dropped his items on the table, crossed the room, and pulled her into his arms, gently pressing her head to his chest as she fell against him. Her knees buckled, and he caught her.

"Oh god. I killed him."

"Shh. It's okay," he said, rubbing circles over her shaking shoulders.

Jane dug her fingers into his back and pressed her forehead into his sternum. "I killed him," she confessed over and over.

"It's okay, Jane. It's okay. You did what you had to. It's okay."

Had she shot him? With the rifle he had given her? Matt stared at the window as lightning flashed. It lit up the field across the street like daylight. It was unlikely that he would have died unless…Had she shot him in the head? Matt winced. *Oh, Jesus.* She continued to sob against him as he ran his palm over her back. This was his fault. He should never have kissed her because then she wouldn't have run, and he would have been there to prevent all of this.

"Shh. It's okay. You're safe now. I've got you." *Don't let her go again.*

He tilted his head back and squeezed his eyes shut. How? How was he supposed to do that? She was a grown woman. He had to respect her wishes. And what did it matter now? Look at her. It was too late. It was like giving a life preserver to someone who had already drowned.

She's not dead. No—thank god. Matt smoothed her hair as she cried. "I'm so sorry, Jane. I shouldn't have let you—"

"It's my fault," she interrupted, stepping back.

"No. None of this is—"

Jane wiped her eyes. "I should have let you help me, but… after Thomas and… I–I was trying to do it on my own, to prove to myself that I'm not… who I've been. That I was st–stronger"—Her voice broke over the last word—"But look at me. I'm not strong," she whispered.

Yes, she is.

"And I was so ashamed of… how I feel about you, I put the kids at risk." She shook her head. "God. What is wrong with me? I am so stupid, I was selfish, and–and—" She buried her head in her hands.

He pulled her back into his embrace, and she slumped against him. "I shouldn't have kissed you," he said against the top of her head. "That is on me. I really wanted to, but I should not have—"

"I wanted you to, too, but that doesn't matter now. All that matters is—" she pulled back and met his eyes. "Oh god. What am I going to do? I have to go home. But what am I going to tell the kids? Look at me!" she touched her cheek. "What are the police going to do when they come for his body? What will happen to the kids if I go to—"

"What you are going to do is sit down so I can close that cut." Matt led her back to the couch and pushed her gently into the cushions. He sat beside her as she reached for the mouthwash, took a swing, and swallowed it.

"I don't care about the cut—"

"But I do," he said. "Now, sit still." With a fresh towel, he cleaned her face again. She closed her eyes and took shaky, minty breaths as he wiped the blood away. "Everything is going to be okay," he said gently. "But I need to know what happened. Can you tell me now?"

She nodded slightly as he peeled the bandage from its wrapper.

"Where were you?"

"I was getting my phone charger out of the van. M–Maddy left it—"

Matt squeezed his eyes closed. She had to be kidding. *This happened because of a fucking phone charger?*

"Did he… hurt you?" he asked, pinching her cut together and smoothing the bandage over it. "Sorry," he apologized as she winced.

"He h–hit me," she said quietly, touching the welt on her cheek again.

Matt peeled the second bandage, swallowing hard. That wasn't what he meant.

"Did he *rape* you, Jane?" He clarified, hating the words even more out loud than he had in his head.

She met his eyes, and he held his breath.

Slowly she shook her head. "No," her voice was almost a whisper.

Matt exhaled in relief. *Thank god.* He pressed the other bandage to her brow. "Did you shoot him?" he asked.

She shook her head again.

"Then how…"

A tear slid down her cheek as she looked down at her right hand clenched in a fist in her lap. "I–I smashed his head in… with a rock."

Matt stared at her. *She did what*?

She rushed on. "He was on top of me–when I f-felt it in the grass… and I—"

That explained the blood, especially if she hit him in the nose.

But she'd have to hit him pretty hard to kill him—The image of that man on top of her made him see red.

"Jesus Christ."

"What am I going to do?" She sounded like a frightened child.

"Are you sure he's dead?"

"Yes. I wouldn't have left the kids if I thought—"

"How do you know—"

"Because I didn't s–stop until…" She paused and closed her eyes. Her hand clenched again. "I *wanted* to kill him…" she growled. She leaned over, and he thought she might throw up again, but she didn't.

"Hey. Take it easy. It's okay."

She opened her eyes, and her voice softened again. "He wasn't breathing… when I… got out from under—"

The tremor in her hands returned as she placed them in her lap.

Matt covered them. "I'll handle it."

Handle what? All of it, getting rid of Jake, the police, whatever she needed. He was going to fix this.

"It's all going to be okay. You don't have to think about it anymore. I'll take it from here."

"But—"

"You're going to take a quick shower, and then I'm taking you home."

She shook her head. "I can't—"

"Your kids can't see you like this, Jane," he said gently.

She looked down at her shirt.

"Come on." He pulled her to her feet. "Let's go upstairs. We will just rinse the blood off, and I'll get you some clean clothes, and then I'll take you home."

Chapter Thirty-Eight

Day 21 // 11:37 p.m

THE NEXT THING JANE KNEW, they were in the van driving back toward the cabin. Her hair was wet, she smelled like Old Spice, and she was shivering in a plaid shirt and a pair of baggy sweatpants. She rubbed the fabric and recognized them as the ones she had tossed to Matt the first day they met. The rain had stopped, and the wipers groaned against the dry windshield as he fumbled with the controls.

"What's going to happen to me?" she whispered.

Matt glanced at her, then brought his eyes back to the dark road. "We'll figure it out," he said, but he sounded worried.

"God. I fucked up," she said, resting her elbow on the windowsill and pushing her hair back. She winced at the fire that ripped across her left eyebrow.

"No, you didn't." Matt shook his head. "How could you possibly think that after what he tried to do to you?"

"I'm a murderer, Matt. I should have just —" she said, not really sure which part she should have done differently.

"What? And let him rape you?" he asked angrily—whether his anger was directed at her or Jake, she couldn't tell.

Jane closed her eyes. It was too painful to hold the left one open any longer, and her head was pounding. "It would have been better than going to prison," she cried.

"You're not going to prison, Jane. It was self-defense. One look at your face and the cops will know that. You didn't do anything wrong."

The van turned, and she felt the familiar bounce as they pulled into the grassy drive.

"Stop feeling bad over that fucking–Wait, where…?" His voice trailed off, and Jane forced her eyes back open.

"I thought you said you left him here?" Matt said, turning to her.

In the headlights, the grass was still slick with rain. Jane made out the tip of the rock, lying beside the flattened grass, but the body that was supposed to be there was gone.

She bolted upright and gripped the door handle. The hair on the back of her neck stood on end. "I did. He was right…" Did she not kill him? But if he wasn't dead, then—

Jane threw the door open and jumped out. Matt jammed the van into the park and charged behind her.

"Maddy!" she called, banging on the door, as he came up behind her. The knob twisted, and she realized she hadn't locked the door when she'd left. *Damn it.* "M—"

She threw the door open and Maddy, hair mussed, and eyes half-closed, stood in the doorway. She raised her finger to her lips. "Shh. You're going to wake—" Her eyes widened as they finally focused on Jane. "What the hell? What happened to you?"

"I'm fine," Jane said, pushing her way in. She spotted Austin and Tommy still asleep on the floor. "Are you guys okay?" she whispered to her niece. "Did—"Jane swallowed hard. "Did you hear anything outside, see… anything?"

Maddy looked from her to Matt, then shook her head. "Anything? Like what? What happ—"

Jane turned and went back to the door and stared into the darkness beyond.

So, he just left? She finally noticed the golf cart was gone.

She crossed the lawn and picked her phone up off the ground, wiping the water from the cracked screen, and willing the memory back.

Matt said something, but she wasn't listening. She heard the door close.

The bloody rock was in the grass, right where she'd left it. Jane closed her eyes. She remembered the tug as he fumbled with her jeans, the weight of it in her palm, the sharp edges… She had aimed for his left temple, but he had turned at the last minute, and she'd hit him in the eye instead. Jake had grabbed his face and cried out, as she connected with the side of his head again. Blood. There was a lot of blood after that. Exactly how many times she hit him was unclear. But she recalled her desire to kill him, mixed with the wild fear of stopping too soon, clearly. She remembered her relief that the kids were safe when he collapsed on top of her, followed by the terror of suffocating under his weight she struggled to crawl out from beneath him.

How could he have survived?

Matt touched her arm. Jane jumped, as a helpless sob burst from her throat. Her heart pounded beneath her ribs, making her feel faint.

"Shh. Okay. Let's get you inside."

"No," she shook her head. Dread planted itself hard in her gut.

Her eye ached, but she held it open as she clutched his arm, scanning the darkness. "We have to find him. Where is—"

"Not tonight, Jane. We'll deal with him tomorrow."

If he wasn't dead, he was going to be angry. What if he came after her again? She gasped. What if he took it out on the kids? What if he came back and tried to burn the cottage down while they were asleep, or… "Oh no." She fell against Matt, and he put his arm around her. How could she protect them like this? She could barely see.

Matt wheeled her around. "Let's go inside, and I'll call the police," he said, heading for the door.

"No—"

He looked down at her. "What do you mean, no?"

Officer Beale didn't like her. He didn't believe her. What would happen if Jake accused her of attacking him first? She had no proof. "No. I don't want you to call the police. Promise me."

Matt searched her eyes for a moment. "Fine. I'll take care of it then."

She pushed away. "You? How?"

"Let's just get you in bed. Okay?"

"But I can't sleep with him out here!"

He put his hand on the screen door. "I'll stay with you."

"But—"

"Jane, look at me."

Her right eye darted between both of his in the porch light.

"Let me help you, okay?"

She stared at him, seriously doubting anyone could help her now.

Matt smiled slightly. "And then, after this is over, you can go back to hating me."

She wiped her good eye. The other was too painful to touch. "I–I don't *hate* you. That's not why—"

He put his arm around her shoulder. "I know. That was just another ill-timed, shitty joke. Come on, let's get you to bed."

"What am I going to tell the kids about my face?" she asked as she followed him inside. He locked the door.

"Let's worry about that tomorrow," he whispered, taking her hand and making his way around the sleeping boys on the floor.

"Aunt Jane?" Maddy whispered from the couch. "Are you okay?"

Jane squinted in the darkness and just made out the shape of her niece's head against the curtain-shrouded window. "Yes. I'm fine. Everything is going to be fine," she whispered. Matt squeezed her hand. "Go to bed," she continued, "and we'll talk in the morning."

"Okay. I love you."

Jane paused, and Matt stopped too, maintaining his grasp on her hand. She glanced back as Maddy settled down on the couch. It had been years since Maddy had uttered those words to her. "I love you too, Maddicakes," Jane said with a soft smile that made her whole face hurt.

Jane followed Matt into the bedroom. He plugged in her broken phone and tucked her in bed—the same way her mother used to when she was little. As her head hit the pillow, she sighed and closed her eyes. She heard Matt squeeze by Bria's playpen. The bed groaned as he sat down on the opposite side. She opened her good eye as he kicked his feet up on the bed, resting his back against the headboard.

"You aren't going to sleep?" she whispered.

"Nope."

"Why not?"

He looked down at her as something she couldn't quite describe flashed in his eyes. "Because if I do, you won't."

"I'm so sorry I dragged you into this."

He crossed his arms. "I'm not."

"But—"

"Go to sleep, Jane."

She closed her eyes for a second, then forced them open again. "What are you going to do all night?" she asked, studying his determined scowl.

"I'm gonna sit here and make sure your kids are safe while you sleep."

She closed her eye in relief, certain no kinder words had ever been uttered to a mother.

Jane reached out and felt for his hand and found it. "Thank you, Matt Patterson."

He squeezed her hand. For the first time, his touch didn't feel sexual. It just felt safe.

Go to sleep, Jane. She took a deep breath—feeling like a weight had been lifted as his warm hand covered her fingers comfortingly.

She was almost asleep when she heard him whisper, "Thank *you*, Jane Moore."

What could he possibly be thanking her for? She was going to ask him, but sleep dragged her into oblivion before the words could come.

Chapter Thirty-Nine

Day 22 // 7:23 a.m

HER BIG BLUE eyes bore into his and dared him to do it.

Matt looked away, unnerved, and unable to believe that he had just lost a staring contest with an infant. He glanced down at the diaper in his hand and seriously regretted the 'take care of the kids' part of the promise he had made to Jane the night before. He had not thought that through.

Bria looked him right in the eye. Then she farted—loudly.

Matt clenched his jaw. *She had nerves of steel, that one.*

Bria smiled ruthlessly and his eyes widened in horror as the smell wafted over.

Matt strained his ears for any hint of sound from the front room, but it was silent.

"Come on, someone wake up," he begged quietly.

Her face turned red in concentration, and she found his eyes again, stared into them and grunted.

His eyes widened in horror. *Oh god.* Could he just leave her until one of the other kids woke up? Would that be child abuse?

Bria made another disgusting sound in her diaper, and Matt almost gagged. *This is adult abuse.*

She shivered, smiled, then clamped her mouth over the side of the crib, and resumed gnawing on it like it was a chicken leg.

"Fuck."

He had never changed a diaper in his life, much less on a little girl… And well, there were a lot of… nooks and crannies down there and—He blanched at the thought.

Matt glanced at Jane again. She was fast asleep beside him. Half of him wished she would wake up so *she* could deal with this literal shit-show. The other half was glad she was still asleep, because—He carefully pushed her hair back off her face—She would be in a lot of pain if she was awake.

The aftermath of the attack was much clearer now, and in the daylight, much more colorful. His blood boiled. Her brow was the worst. A deep cut, framed in gut-wrenching blue, feathered into the purple halo surrounding her eye. Several other bruises marked her face, like misplaced shadows. One on either side of her nose, and one on her chin just below the left side of her mouth. He pulled the cover back. Then there was the gash on her hip he'd seen when he helped her into the shower. Hopefully, it didn't get infected. When he'd asked, she said Jake had kicked her. He still didn't understand why she didn't want to call the police, but he had decided not to push her.

Matt gently peeled the bandage back and inspected it. He was concerned about internal bleeding. He gently pressed his fingers into her abdomen, probing the surrounding area, but she didn't move. Only when he pressed the bandage back down did she moan. You had to be kicked pretty hard to leave a mark like that, and the thought of anyone doing it to Jane, while she lay helplessly on the ground… It made him sick.

So did the smell that was quickly permeating the room. He turned back to Bria and sighed. "You couldn't wait, huh?"

She had the audacity to grin at him.

He narrowed his eyes. "Fuck it," he whispered, pushing himself off the bed. He grabbed a towel off the dresser and laid Bria on it. Then, with eyes averted as much as possible, Matthew Patterson changed his first diaper—and tried not to throw up.

Of course, the kids woke up immediately after he was done.

Maddy told him where to dump the diaper, and he almost threw up again as he dropped it in with the others into the hole Jane had dug at the very back of the yard.

His phone rumbled in his pocket as he walked back inside. He pulled it out and Max's skinny, grinning face lit up the screen. He pushed the green button and lifted the phone to his ear.

"Maximus."

"Hey, man. How you holdin' up?"

Matt looked around the cabin. The boys were eating granola bars and talking. Maddy was on her phone on the couch. Bria was in her little crib thing, they'd dragged into the living room. He peeked in on Jane. She was still asleep. He was doing pretty well—all things considered. "I'm doin' alright. How's Dallas? I saw on the news—"

"Man," Max lowered his voice. "It's fucked up. I've never seen anything like it, it's crazy, all the people dying." His voice lowered further. "And… beginning to think… Prez is… I dunno… I'm not sure I trust him anymore."

That was a pretty strong accusation coming from his very level-headed best friend and a loyal member of the Armed Forces. Matt went into the bedroom so he could hear better, sitting carefully on the bed next to Jane. "Why?"

"Because we came down here on orders from the President to protect the Veil at all cost."

"Well, yeah, they probably don't want another New Yor—."

"But now—They're telling us to pack up—" his voice muffled, and Matt imagined Max's hand over his mouth as he spoke.

"W–what?" That didn't make any sense. "What do you mean?"

"Exactly what it fucking sounds like I mean."

"Why?"

"I don't know. But if we go—Man, the city won't last a day. "

Jane rolled over and Matt turned, but her eyes remained closed.

"And then I overheard my CO on the phone," Max said. "He said he wasn't going to do it again."

"Do what?"

"He said if the President took out another city—"

Matt gasped. "You think *we* took out Atlanta?"

"My CO does. And think about it, there still is no official cause of the explosion. It just—There's got to be a hidden bomb in every city. Otherwise, how do you explain Atlanta? It was like fucking Hiroshima."

"But why—"

"I don't know. Maybe somebody figured out how to deactivate the Veil or something and the President found out and got to them first? Or maybe he's hiding something else? Could this whole thing be a government science experiment gone wrong?"

Could it? Matt pulled his hands through his hair. "Shit."

"I don't know what to do, man. I mean, our orders are to go, but what about all the people on the inside? They are all just sitting ducks for the crazy mother-fuckers on the outside who think the only way to stop the virus is to take out the cities… They are cropping up everywhere. Just yesterday, we arrested a sixty-year-old pastor and half his congregation who were supposedly carrying out 'God's will'."

"Damn."

"I've never questioned orders before, and I trust—I thought I trusted—Command, but what if those conspiracy nuts are right, and he's up to something? Why else would he have us leave?"

Matt rubbed his sore leg. That was a really good question, and one he couldn't answer. "Fuck."

"Yeah."

A wail erupted from the living room and Matt recognized the sound. He looked at his watch, realizing he'd missed Bria's bottle, which Austin had informed him happened every four hours. No wonder she had three chins.

"Shit." He jumped up and headed into the living room, closing the door behind him.

"Was that a *baby*?" Max asked in disbelief.

Matt pressed his hand over the phone. "Maddy, can you hand

me her bottle? It's in the fridge." Then brought it back to his ear. "Sorry—"

"Maddy? Who's Maddy?"

Bria cried harder and Matt set his phone on the table. He lifted her from the crib. Tears and drool glazed her fat cheeks, reminding him of Japanese dumplings he had eaten once in Tokyo.

"Shh… shh…" Matt grabbed his phone and squeezed it between his shoulder and his ear. "Hey—"

"What the fuck is going on over there?" Max demanded.

"I'm… uh… babysitting," Matt admitted as Bria continued to wail. She wiggled in his arms like a little sumo fish and he almost dropped her.

"You're *what*?"

"Hold on. Let me just grab her"—Maddy handed him the bottle—"bottle and…"

Bria grabbed it with her pudgy fingers, shoved it in her mouth, and quieted as he placed her back in her crib.

"There." Matt leaned back and grabbed the phone in his hand.

"Do you even know how to take care of kids?"

Matt peeked in on Jane, who was still asleep. "Nope. But I haven't lost one yet, so…"

"How the fuck many are there?"

"Four."

"Four kids?"

"Yep."

"What the fuck?"

"Yep." Matt pressed his mouth together to keep from smiling. He scratched his head.

There was a long pause, as they both seemed to think that over.

"Anyway, man," Max's voice lowered again. "What am I gonna do?"

Matt took a deep breath and dropped onto the couch beside Maddy. "I think you're going to have to decide if you trust the President or not."

Maddy looked up from her phone, frowned in his direction, then went back to her screen.

"Fuck."

Bria burped in her playpen and Matt sat up to make sure she hadn't puked all over the place.

"But why is he doing this? He's gotta know what will happen if we leave." Max asked.

"I don't know. Maybe he doesn't have a choice."

"How could he not have a choice? He's the goddamned President of the United States."

"I don't know." Matt scratched his stubbly chin. "Well, then maybe the best thing to do then is just trust your gut."

"Fuck. I don't want to do that either."

Chapter Forty

Day 25 // 3:13 p.m

JANE HELD HER HEAD, squeezing her eyes shut against the light coming through the curtain-covered window, and groaned. It took her a minute to remember why she ached. She sat up, pressing her palm gently to her tender eye, and her head swam.

She heard a noise, and the bed sagged beside her. "Hey, Sleeping Beauty. How are you feeling?" A gentle voice asked.

Matt.

She peeled her eyes open, noticing they both worked. She caught her reflection in the mirror and immediately looked away. Her throat felt like it was filled with sand. "I feel like I drank a bottle of tequila then got run over by a bus." she croaked, pushing her legs off the side of the bed.

"So… good then–all things considered?" There was a gentleness in his voice as he joked.

She coughed, then laughed, then grabbed her side. "Ouch. Yes. Good… all things considered."

"Yeah, you got a pretty ugly gash there," Matt said, lifting the corner of her shirt.

His shirt, she realized. When had she put that on? He poked at her belly. "Does this hurt—"

"Hey," she said, pulling the fabric back down.

"At least let me check the bandage."

Bandage?

She lifted the shirt. To her surprise, a rectangle of gauze and tape covered her side.

"Where did you get—"

"Mom!" Tommy said, running into the room and throwing himself into her arms.

Jane reeled as Matt snatched the boy away, tickling his sides.

"Come here, you," Matt said, as Tommy giggled and tried to squirm away. Jane stared at her *normally* very shy son. He was completely at ease as Matt pinned his arms to his sides in a tight bear-hug. "Now, what did I tell you about when your mom woke up?"

"Oh. That I have to be careful?" Tommy looked at Jane and smiled. "Sorry. I just really missed you, Mom!"

Jane frowned. *Missed her? What time was it?*

She looked at the nightstand for her phone, but it wasn't there. She jerked as the image of Jake swatting it from her hand surfaced. Her breath quickened at the memory of the broken screen lying at her feet and what followed.

Matt's hands closed over hers. "Breathe Jane." He turned to Tommy. "Can you go ask Maddy to make some coffee?" he asked.

"Then can I go help Austin?" Tommy asked. Matt nodded, and Tommy ran excitedly from the room, yelling for his cousin.

He turned back to her. "Are you okay?" His voice filled with concern.

"I need to use the restroom."

Every part of her ached as Matt helped her up.

Slowly, he led her to the bathroom. To her surprise, he walked in with her. "Wh–what are you doing?"

"Oh. Are you–you got this?"

Her unbruised brow went up, and she stepped back. "Got what? Peeing? Yeah."

He backed out of the door. "Okay. I'll be right out here if you need me."

She frowned.

What in the hell is he talking about?

"Yeah. Great." She shut the door in his face.

She stared at herself for a good long while. Her face didn't look nearly as swollen as she expected, but the bruising was ugly. Her hair was both matted to her head and sticking out in all directions at the same time. She used the toilet, suddenly realizing that her underclothes were gone. She pulled the bottle of ibuprofen out of the medicine cabinet and took four.

Jane brushed her teeth. She tried to run a brush through her hair but realized quickly that without conditioner; it was hopeless. How had it gotten so tangled? She couldn't remember. She looked at the tub and decided to take a quick shower before facing the kids. Carefully she peeled off the bandage and stepped under the warm water. It hurt and felt wonderful at the same time. She scrubbed her body and washed her hair.

When she was done, she pulled the curtain back. Maddy's concealer was sitting on the sink and fresh clothes, including her underwear and bra. Jane toweled off, got dressed, then dabbed at her face, covering the worst of the bruises. Finally, she put on deodorant and even a spritz of perfume. By the time she opened the door, she almost felt human. *Almost.*

Jane slowly made her way into the kitchen. "What in the *hell*?"

It looked like a tornado had gone through the house, and in the center of it was Matt, stirring something in a pot with Bria strapped to his chest in her baby carrier.

He turned around and smiled–and, damn it if her knees didn't buckle. She dropped into the nearest chair as he sauntered over.

"Wh–What the hell happened in here?" she asked, touching her forehead.

He looked around, and his eyes widened as if noticing the mess for the first time. He scratched his head, while Bria grabbed at the spoon in his hand and shoved it into her mouth.

Matt gave her a serious look. “I don’t know if you’re aware of this…” He bounced up and down as he wrestled the spoon from Bria’s chubby, little hands. “But taking care of kids is really”—He mouthed the word ‘fucking’—“hard.”

Jane tried unsuccessfully not to laugh. It made her head pound.

“And to be fair, I only promised to take *care* of the kids, not clean up after them.” He waved the spoon around. “And as you can see, they are just fi—”

Austin pushed the back door open. “Hey, Matt. Can you help me–Oh, hi, Aunt Jane.” he said, waving a bloody knife at her.

“What the hell?” Jane jumped out of her chair as all the blood rushed from her head.

Matt pushed her back down, then hurried over to the door and shoved the boy out.

“I’ll be right out.” He swung around and Bria shrieked with laughter, grabbing at the spoon he was pointing at her. “Don’t freak out, Jane Moore. I can explain.”

Jane got up, and the whole room moved. She gripped the edge of the table and sat back down, helplessly. “What happened to him? Where did all that blood–What is going on around here?” she demanded.

“Just try to relax. The boys are fine.”

“They’re outside! What if—”

“They’re fine,” he repeated. “I’ve got my eye on them.”

“No. You don’t. You’ve got your eyes on me.” The pounding in her head was so loud she could barely think. “What if–Shit. I sleep for—” She looked at the clock. “Seven hours and—”

“Four days.” Maddy interrupted from the couch.

Jane’s head spun around, and she almost fell out of her chair. “What?”

Maddy glanced over the top of her phone. “You’ve been asleep for four days, Aunt Jane. More or less.”

She turned back to Matt, who had walked back to the stove and turned it off.

"*What*?"

He shrugged. "You were tired. And I thought the rest would—"

"Shit." She hadn't talked to Thomas in four days? She buried her head in her hands. He was going to think they'd all been murdered.

She heard Austin call Matt from the backyard.

"Jane, please. Just relax. Here. Hold Bria, I'll be right back." Matt said, unbuckling the baby and setting Bria in Jane's lap. He went outside. She got up slowly and followed his voice to the window. To her utter surprise, the lawn was mowed. Tommy was laying in the grass playing and Austin was standing over a table… gutting a fish.

A fish? Where in the hell had that come from?

Jane turned back to Maddy. "What is going on around here?" she asked, exasperated.

Maddy sat up. "Did you know Matt was in the Army? That's how he lost his foot. Got blown off by a bomb buried in the road."

Jane just stared at her niece.

"What?" Maddy shrugged. "*I* didn't ask him. Tommy did."

"Wh–What?"

"Also, he taught the boys how to fish. Austin is actually pretty good at it."

"With what?"

Maddy smiled at her smugly.

"What?" Jane said, sounding like a broken record.

"He's been… borrowing things."

"Borrowing?"

She shrugged. "From the cottages."

Jane's eyebrow went up. "You mean stealing?"

"Whatever."

"Is that where that table came from?"

She nodded. "He found a bunch of clothes for Austin, too. Oh, and a broken lawn mower he and the boys fixed."

"What? Really?"

"Yep. He's a regular fucking boy scout."

"Madeline McIntyre!"

"Relax, Aunt Jane," she paused, giving her an approving look. "I actually like him. He's… a cool guy."

Jane's brows went up as Maddy went back to her phone.

Jane dropped Bria in her playpen. Leaning against the counter, she absently began putting dishes in the sink.

Matt had been taking care of her kids for *four* days?

She looked at her daughter, who appeared happy as a clam, then in the pot on the stove. Oatmeal. Her brow went up. Except for the mess… he actually hadn't done too badly.

Her stomach growled, and she picked up her phone, which was plugged in on the counter.

"Matt brought it out here, so it didn't wake you." Maddy said.

"Have you talked to Uncle Tom or your mom?"

"Yeah."

Jane winced as she bunched up the granola bar wrappers that were strewn across the counter. "And what did you say?"

Maddy's alarm went off, and she got up. To Jane's surprise, Maddy took Bria. "She needs her bottle," she said, going to the fridge and pulling one out. "We've been feeding her oatmeal, too. Hope that's okay?"

Jane looked at the clock, thoroughly disoriented, as Maddy sat with Bria and pushed the bottle into her waiting mouth.

Jane dumped the wrappers in the trash. "Did you tell them about…" She hadn't even decided how to explain what had happened yet.

"Your accident?"

Jane looked over her shoulder in surprise. *Accident?*

"Yeah. I told them what Matt told us. How you slipped running in from the van and hit your head on that stupid rock Tommy brought back from the beach, and freaked out. Why are you and mom so afraid of blood? Did you watch a lot of slasher movies when you were kids or something? F.Y.I. It doesn't bother me at all. How are you feeling, by the way?"

Matt had lied? And more importantly, the kids had believed it?

Jane shrugged. "I've been better. So, they know about Matt then?"

"Well, obviously." Maddy rolled her eyes. "Uncle Tom had a heart attack at first, but I explained how cool he's been."

Jane groaned as she met Matt's gaze through the screen door. How long had he been standing there listening?

Maddy continued, unable to see him. "I mean, for having zero experience with kids… he's done pretty good, I think."

"You do?" Jane smiled at him, despite her aching face.

"Yeah. Bria had a blowout yesterday and…" Maddy laughed and shook her head.

Jane looked from Bria back to Matt, who shrugged guiltily.

"Oh, my god–it was *hilarious*," Maddy continued.

Jane's smile widened as he shook his head in embarrassment. But the corner of his mouth turned up in a smile. He ran his fingers through his sunlit hair.

"But man, he owned it. And you should have seen him," Maddy chuckled. "He was so proud of himself."

Matt hung his thumbs through the baby carrier still strapped to him and puffed up his chest.

His brown eyes crinkled at the corners, and his smile turned into a grin under his growing beard. Jane's heart melted in her chest and pooled at her feet, bringing tears to her eyes. Not only was he beautiful on the outside, but he was beautiful on the inside, too.

"Sounds like I owe him a big thank you," she said softly.

"Yeah," Maddy agreed. "Heads up though, he did use like two whole packages of baby wipes… and, obviously, Austin plays with knives now. Tommy too actually."

Jane frowned as she pushed the screen door open, and Matt's smile faded. "Can I talk to you?" she asked quietly, tilting her head toward the side door of the house.

His face fell as he followed her inside, then back out by the van. Jane glanced in the direction of where she'd been assaulted. The grass had been cut, and the rock gone, making it impossible to pinpoint the exact spot. Her eyes filled with tears of relief.

"Listen, I can—" he started.

Jane turned and threw her arms around him and squeezed, cutting off his explanation. "Thank you."

Hesitantly, he put his arms around her. "Um…"

"Thank you for taking such good care of"—her voice broke—"of my kids. Thank you for what you did for me. Thank you for changing Bria, and finding clothes for Austin. Thank you for—"

His arms tightened around her. "Shh. You don't need to—"

"Oh, yes, I do. And I'm so sorry about before," she said, using every ounce of willpower she had to step back. She tucked her wet hair behind her ear. "I never hated you, Matt. On the contrary. I was just…" she shook her head. "Anyway, I am so glad that you are here now."

"Even though you find me irresistibly attractive?" he asked with a cocky grin, pulling her in for a bear hug. The gesture was platonic, but the way it made her feel was not. *Oh well.*

She grabbed the straps of the baby carrier and laughed as she pressed her forehead against his shirt. "God. Why do you have to torment me?" she asked. Jane pushed away a second time, praying he didn't hug her again, because she wouldn't be able to let go a third time.

He shook his head and laughed. "I'm sorry. You just make it so easy. I honestly can't help it." He paused, then his voice softened. "I'm glad I'm here too."

She balled her fists in the sleeves of his shirt she wore and looked at the chipped pink polish on her toes. "Really, Matt. I am so grateful you are here. It's been—"

He gently touched the bandage on the side of her face, and her eyes flew up. "I know how it's been. It will not be like that anymore."

She looked behind him down the road. "Have you seen him at all?"

Matt shook his head. "Not once."

"What do you think that means?"

"I don't know, but it doesn't matter."

She turned and looked at him. "Why not?"

"Because I'm here now, and I'm not going anywhere until that fucking Veil comes down and you and the kids are safe where you belong. Okay?"

Jane broke into a smile that made her jaw hurt. "Okay," she said, as her stomach rumbled.

Matt laughed, and the sound felt like the sunrise after a cold winter night, comforting and breathtaking. "Come on," he said, beckoning her inside. "Let's go get you something to eat. You must be starving."

Jane grabbed his arm. There was more she needed to say. "Matt, wait."

He turned. And if she'd been a younger woman or even a single one, she would have seized that precious moment and kissed him until… She didn't know… the cows came home. But she wasn't young or single. She dropped her hand and frowned, having lost all train of thought.

He threw his head back and laughed, then winked at her.

"What's so funny?" she asked, putting her hands on her hips.

"Stop looking at me like you want to devour me, Jane Moore, and maybe I'll tell you."

"Argh!" she said, throwing her arms up and storming past him. "You are—"

He followed her. "Adorable? Charming?"

She slammed the door in his face—her cheeks burning.

Matt pushed it open and she could hear him chuckling behind her as she got a bowl out of the cabinet. "Look, Bria. Your mommy's cheeks are on fire."

Jane glanced at her niece, and Maddy raised a brow but said nothing.

Jane had the feeling that things were going to be very different from now on.

Chapter Forty-One

Day 26 // 11:22 p.m

SHE THRASHED beside him on the bed. Matt woke with a start, reached for his gun under the pillow, then remembered where he was.

Jane whimpered again and threw her hand into the air—fighting off someone he could not see. He watched her lungs fill with air and—

Matt lunged for her as she started screaming. Her frantic voice vibrated against his palm as he pressed his hand gently over her mouth.

"Jane. Wake up," he whispered in her ear, holding her arm down with his other hand, as she continued to struggle. He didn't like restraining her while she was having the nightmare, but the first time she had fallen out of the bed and woke up the whole fucking house. Tommy had freaked out when he saw Matt on his knees beside the bed, wrestling with his mother—who looked like she had been beaten with a baseball bat. It took Maddy and Austin both, to calm him, and convince him that Matt was helping her, not murdering her. And getting Bria back to sleep had been almost impossible.

Jane wiggled her arm free and threw her fist at his head as he blocked it. He pushed her arm down into the mattress as carefully as he could. She had clocked him hard enough to see stars before he got a hold of her the other night. She was dreaming of Jake again, the same way he dreamed about Tony. Living the same tragedy over and over without the ability to change the outcome.

"Jane, wake—" he said louder.

She sucked in a deep breath and stilled beneath him.

He quickly pulled his hand away from her mouth and backed away, giving her space. "Are you okay?"

She sat up slowly, looking confused.

"You okay?" he repeated.

She nodded as she looked around the room.

"Do you want a glass of water?"

"Sure." Her voice trembled, and his heart broke a little as she tried to collect herself.

"Okay. Try to relax. I'll be right back."

Matt got some water from the kitchen and came back to sit beside her. "Do you want to talk—"

She shook her head as she sipped at the water. "Have-Have we been sleeping together?" she asked quietly, glancing at the mussed blankets behind her on the bed.

"How do you mean?"

"I-in this bed… together?"

"Yes," he said slowly. "There really isn't anywhere else for me to go, and you've been having nightmares."

She met his eyes through the gloom. "I have?"

"Yeah."

"A… lot?" She looked like she might cry.

He took the glass and set it on the dresser. "Yeah."

"I don't remember…"

"That's common," he said gently, knowing all too well. "It's called dissociative amnesia. It happens a lot when people experience trauma."

"Have the kids heard me? Has Tommy…?"

He nodded, and her head fell into her hands.

"Did I scare them?" she whispered.

He paused. "A little. I've been trying to wake you up before—"

She pushed her hair back and sighed heavily as she stared at the floor.

"What are you thinking?" he asked, already knowing the answer.

"I'm thinking I should have known better. I'm thinking I should have done something different."

"What happened to you was not your fault. Sometimes bad things just happen to good people," he said, finally believing the words that had been uttered to him a million times.

"Thanks for waking me up."

"I'm just… trying to return the favor."

It took her a minute, and she scoffed. "What? For barging into your room like a lunatic? You realize I didn't actually do anything except embarrass myself, right? You can relax. If anything, I owe you—"

"I can relax, because I'm sleeping, and I'm sleeping because I haven't had a nightmare since you dashed into my bedroom like Wonder Woman," he whispered.

Jane squinted at him in the darkness. "You haven't?"

He shook his head.

"Why not?"

He shrugged. In the two years since the accident, he had never gone a week without Tony dying in his arms. But now, it seemed Matt's ghosts had been finally laid to rest—and he was pretty sure it had everything to do with Jane. It sounded stupid, but he was beginning to think that maybe she truly had rescued him.

He leaned closer to her. "You're not the first person who has heard me call out in my sleep…" He bumped her with his shoulder. "But you are the first person that actually came to *help*. You brought a stick to a gunfight, and… well, I think you won, Jane."

Jane reached for the cup of water and finished it.

Matt took it from her. "Are you ready to go back to bed?"

She looked behind them at the bed, then her eyes met his, and she nodded.

When he returned from the kitchen, she was laying down.

He frowned. “What is that?” he asked, pointing to the pillow lying lengthwise in the middle of the bed.

“It’s a pillow.”

“Yeah, I see that. Why is it in the middle of the bed?”

“Don’t worry about it.”

“Come on, Jane. You still don’t trust me?” he asked, sitting on his ‘side’ and feeling slightly offended. He was a grown man, not some horny teenager, and he’d been sleeping beside her for close to a week.

She cast him a meaningful glance. “It’s not for you,” she said. Then she turned her back to him, to face the wall.

His frown dissolved into a smile as he laid his head down on the pillow and stared at the ceiling.

Interesting.

Chapter Forty-Two

Day 27 // 4:23 p.m

JANE LOOKED through the cabinets for something to serve with the fish Austin had caught and gutted with Matt that morning. Why had she not thought of fishing?

Because you don't fish.

Thank god Matt did, though. Otherwise, they might have been the first people to die of starvation a block from an endless supply of trout.

It had only been three days, well, for her anyway, but what a difference having him around had already made. They had all spent the morning at the beach catching dinner, and the boys could play outside again.

Grilled baby asparagus spears with a balsamic glaze would have been wonderful with the fish, Jane thought as she stared at the package of instant mashed potatoes. She shook her head slightly, thinking about the holiday dinner party she and Thomas had hosted last year for their friends in the neighborhood. The menu had included roasted turkey, and rosemary-parmesan mashed potatoes, her own concoction. Everyone had raved that she was an excellent cook. She remembered sitting with a glass of wine, telling Maggy from two doors down, she would *never* eat potatoes out of a box. Which was true, she supposed, since these were in a bag. How times had changed. *Oh well.*

Last night before dinner, she had finally gotten through to Thomas and her sister. Well, Thomas had refused to come to the phone, but Jane had relayed the message through Sarah that she was fine—though neither her sister nor her husband seemed too concerned. The conversation had been strained. A few minutes in, and Jane couldn't figure out which one of them was making it so awkward.

Matt's loud laughter drew her attention back to the present.

The boys had clearly taken to him, and she was charmed by how truly smitten he seemed to be with them as well. Jane set the potatoes on the counter beside the can of corn that was to be their dinner and sipped her coffee.

Matt and Tommy sat at the table, heads together. Tommy was describing the three-story treehouse he wanted to build in the tree out back.

"Wait. So, what's this here?" Matt asked, pointing to the corner of the crude drawing. He turned and met her eyes briefly. Jane's insides pulsed. It happened all the time now, that feeling. He didn't even have to be flirting with her. All he had to do was glance at her, or smile, or brush past her, or touch her hand as he passed Bria off to get a diaper change, and her insides ached. It was both wonderful and shameful. She cycled between longing and guilt, knowing it didn't matter either way because she was still married.

True to his word, Matt had not tried to kiss her again, and it was just as well, she supposed—because as much as she wanted to, she could not let him.

"Well, I don't know about this elevator here," he said, rubbing his beard. "Might be kind of hard to get parts." He winked at her, and she smiled. That happened all the time now, too. Despite the soreness of her bruises, Jane had been smiling a lot the past few days. And laughing.

He was such a smart-ass and a tease, but… Jane shook her head. His humor was magical, and it was healing her, inside and out. She was beginning to wonder if instead of Xanax all those years, what she really needed was someone to laugh with.

Jane smiled sadly.

The distance from her life with Thomas made everything so clear. Their whole marriage, not just the last couple miserable years, had taken on a heartbreaking shade of gray. Her phone call with Sarah the night before, when instead of being concerned, Thomas had refused to talk to her, was a perfect example. Except for the kids, there had been very little smiling or laughing, or lightness in their life together, and perhaps the worst part of that was she hadn't even noticed.

She suddenly couldn't remember why she'd begged Thomas to stay when he wanted to move out last year. Why hadn't she let him go when they were both so miserable? *Because you didn't think you could survive without him.* Why did her marriage look so ugly now, when a month ago it still felt worth saving? *Because now you know you can.*

Jane looked at the back of Matt's head as he pulled Tommy's chair out. "I need to talk to your mom for a minute. Can you go take another look at the tree to make sure all this stuff is going to fit up there? I'm not sure the suspension bridge is gonna…" He scratched his beard again.

Jane laughed. No, she wasn't afraid anymore. Not to be without Thomas, anyway.

"I like to hear you laugh," he commented as Tommy pushed the screen open and went outside.

"Well, it's lucky you're funny then."

"So, I've got a proposition for you," he said, coming to stand beside her at the window. Her heart lit up at the sound of his voice beside her. *This is what you need.*

Jane glanced at him and met his deep brown eyes for a moment, then went back watching her son stare up at the tree.

"I was over at Mr. Hamilton–Ed's, and… I think it would be best to move you, the kids"—he paused—"and I… out there."

Jane turned to him and frowned. Yeah, no. Thomas was already pissed off to the point of not speaking to her. He would definitely not go for that. "I don't think—" She shook her head.

Are you listening to yourself? She couldn't move in with Matt. *Why not?*

Matt held up his hand. "Hear me out, Jane. There's room for us, *all* of us out there. Much more room than there is here. The boys could actually sleep in a bed. I'd offer you my parents' place, but it's just too small. Mr. Hamilton's got four bedrooms, just sitting there."

Well, that was true. She did feel bad about the boys having to sleep on the floor.

"And not knowing where Jake is... you would all be safer out there than you are here. We won't have to be on pins and needles every time the kids want to go out..."

Yes, wouldn't that be nice, Jane thought as she watched Tommy consult his paper again, then flipped it upside-down.

"There's more room for them to play, the yard, the barn, the woods. Not to mention, Mr. Hamilton won't be alone."

Jane had been a little worried about that—

"He has a garden, or at least he started one this spring. I checked it out. It's a mess right now, but salvageable. In a few weeks, we'll have produce and eggs."

Jane stared at the bag of mashed potatoes. The thought of a garden full of vegetables made her mouth water. The thought of the kids eating fresh food again filled her with relief.

Matt continued. "It doesn't seem like the Veil is coming down anytime soon, and now with the power outages... If this thing goes into winter..."

Jane blanched. "Do you think that will happen?"

"*If* it goes into winter, do you really want to spend it here? What if the pipes freeze?"

She looked around. The walls of the cabin were not insulated, and without power... she looked at the electric, base-board heat. How would they stay warm? She hadn't even let herself consider the possibility that this might go on until then. She glanced around the room again, trying to picture the five of them riding out a winter snowstorm there. It was a terrifying thought.

"We'll be better off out there. Together."

Together. That word stuck in her head. She thought about the giant fireplace at the Hamilton house. She could see them there together—Ed, her, the kids… Matt. Safe, warm, and happy. They would be like the family she had seen that day when they had been detoured.

He was right; she realized. Staying here simply because she was worried about what Thomas would say was stupid and dangerous. She'd already had enough of both of those to last the rest of her life. She didn't need Thomas's approval to do this. Just like when she ran, she had to do what was best for the kids. *And for you.* They needed a family. And right now, that was Matt and Ed.

"You're—" *right,* she was going to say.

"And there's one more thing," he said, cutting her off.

"What?"

He gave her the playful wink she had come to adore. "He has a…" Matt paused dramatically and leaned closer. Her heart jumped into her throat as his breath tickled her ear. "… wine cellar," he whispered in a sexy voice.

Jane laughed. "Ha ha. Nice try."

Matt stood back and resumed his normal voice. "No. I am dead serious. Turns out Mrs. Hamilton was a famous sommelier."

"You're kidding," Jane said—not sure whether to believe him or not.

He shrugged. "To be honest, I always thought she was a real estate agent. But nope. They have enough wine over there to stay shit-faced for a decade."

"This is not a trick?"

He held up his hands. "I swear. Scout's honor."

"Were you a Boy Scout?"

He shook his head. "Nope."

Jane looked around the tiny cottage, then back at him. "Okay."

"Okay, what?" he asked, looking confused.

"Okay, we move. Together."

His brows came together, and he looked even more confused. "What? Really?"

"Yep," she nodded. "When do we go?"

"Are you serious?"

Jane laughed at his perplexed expression. "Do you *want* me to disagree with you?"

He scratched his beard. "No. I just thought… It would be harder."

"Why?" she asked, tilting her head to the side.

"I don't know," he said. A small smile tugged at the corners of his mouth.

"I'm a reasonable woman."

Matt's smile widened, and his eyes crinkled at the corners. "That you are, Jane Moore. Okay. I'll take the boys up after dinner and let Ed know."

"I wanna go too," Maddy piped up.

Jane had forgotten she was even in the room. And Maddy wanted to go to a *farm*? Really? That was… new.

"How about I gather up the dinner stuff, and we take it over there and cook it? I wanted to take him some food, anyway."

Matt nodded, and his smile turned into a devilish grin. Tommy threw the door open, pulled Matt's wide fingers with his tiny hands, and dragged him back to his table to discuss modifications.

"Out of curiosity, was it the wine that sold you?" Matt asked over his shoulder.

Jane just winked at him and smiled.

"Damn. I should have started with that and saved my breath."

She pulled the second pouch of mashed potatoes out of the cabinet.

The truth was, it was the *together* part that sold her. But she couldn't tell him that—Jane glanced over her shoulder and laughed—it would go straight to his head.

Chapter Forty-Three

Day 37 // 4:47 p.m

MATT SAT at the table with Bria, making sure she didn't fall out of the old highchair Mr. Hamilton had found buried in the garage, while Jane worked on dinner. She had taken over the kitchen as soon as they walked in the door, and never gave it back. Now, every evening between four and six, the entire house smelled like a five-star restaurant.

Over the last ten days, watching her cook had easily grown into one of his favorite things to do. She was a culinary genius, even with the shit food she had to work with, and everything she made was… the best *whatever* it was he had ever had. And she was adorable in an apron. Not that he would ever say that because then he would sound like a sexist prick, but she really was. And she wore one *every* time she cooked.

Bria reached for the plastic measuring cups Jane had given her to play with and gnawed on the smallest one. She had cut a tooth, which explained why she'd been a pain in the ass for the last week, barely allowing either of them a full night's sleep. He didn't blame the kid, though. A sharp tooth ripping through the flesh of your mouth probably didn't feel too good. Luckily, Jane had pain medicine for her. Apparently, letting Bria chew on stuff helped, too.

Ed came in the back door carrying a bunch of greens.

"I thought you might be able to use these," he said, holding out the flowerless bouquet to Jane. All the swelling was gone, and just the yellow bruise and cut on the left side of her face remained. She broke into a breathtaking smile that stretched all the way to her eyes.

"Oh, my god!" She pressed them to her nose. "Yes, this is... perfect."

Ed took off his ball cap and hung it on the hook by the door. The smell of fresh-cut herbs filled Matt's nose. At first, he had been a little worried that they would all be too much for Ed, especially since he and Mrs. Hamilton never had kids. But that old man *loved* having them all there. From the minute they had pulled up in the van, loaded down with four kids and all manner of shit, Ed had been in the thick of things. In the mornings, he took the boys out back to gather eggs. In the afternoons, they went out to inspect the corn that was now about knee high to Tommy, or rummage through the garage. He was always finding things to give to them, his old tools, flowers for Jane, caterpillars for the boys. He gave Maddy a gold pair of earrings that had belonged to his wife. If Matt didn't know any better, he would say Ed had finally gotten the family he had secretly always wanted.

Now, almost two weeks later, they had taken over the house. There were LEGOs everywhere. Maddy's makeup was all over the bathroom. Poor Ed slept in the smallest room off the kitchen, while the rest of them occupied the three bigger rooms upstairs. Yet, every morning, as they converged in the kitchen for a cup of watered-down coffee, their host had a smile on his face.

Jane rinsed the herbs in the sink, then put them on the cutting board.

"Smells mighty fine in here, Jane," Ed said with a smile.

"Thank you." She curtsied slightly, looking more relaxed than Matt had ever seen her. Then she got back to chopping.

Ed turned toward him. "I'm going to see if the kids want to play Mexican Train. Would you like to join us?"

"I'll pass for right now. I've got to keep an eye on..." Matt glanced at Jane's backside, moving as she hummed. "Um... Bria."

Ed laughed, winking at him. "Suit yourself," the old man said.

"Hey, Thomas, you want to get the dominoes out?" he called as he disappeared into the other room.

Matt settled back in his chair as Jane disappeared behind the pantry door. A moment later, she returned clutching a plastic lemon. A shit-eating grin spread across her face. She mumbled something to herself with a smile and kissed the lemon. Matt's insides twisted with jealousy.

So, this is where we're at? Jealous of a plastic lemon? He almost laughed. Yep, apparently.

He shook his head as Bria banged on the highchair with a wooden spoon that was covered in drool.

Jane didn't even notice. She tucked her hair behind her ear as she stared at the lemon.

Matt smiled, then winked at Bria. The best part of watching Jane cook was that he could gawk at her all day, and she didn't even notice.

Chapter Forty-Four

Day 39 // 9:45 a.m

MATT WIPED his brow and looked back toward the door of the barn. He had forgotten how humid the summers were up here, and July was always the worst. His shirt was soaked, but the motorcycle was up and running. Well, technically, it was more of a dirt bike, but it would do. He'd found it half-buried in the barn, and he decided he wanted to take Jane for a ride through the country. It was one of the few things he enjoyed about growing up there, just getting on a bike and flying down the road. It felt like freedom. And when it was hot, it felt like air conditioning. Also, was the only way he could think to get close to her, something he was desperate to do, without breaking the rules.

Ever since the 'incident,' she'd been different. Calmer in general, and less guarded with him—probably because he had promised to be a gentleman, and she trusted him—and he really was trying to respect her wishes and boundaries, but the look but don't touch was *killing* him.

There was an energy between them smoldered just under the surface of their every encounter. The more relaxed and settled into their new life she became, and the more she smiled, the more he wanted her. The more she rolled her eyes and raised her brow at him, the more he wanted her. The more she fucking breathed, the more he wanted her. And she breathed all day, every day. It was driving him crazy.

Just as she was, which, these days, was hair flipped in a ponytail and wearing one of his favorite plaid shirts tied at the waist, he found himself staring at her like a love-struck schoolboy. He didn't know what her life was before exactly, but country life seemed to fit her like a glove, and she damn-near glowed.

He grabbed a rag and wiped the grease from his hands, then pulled his shirt over his head and threw it on the workbench. He looked back toward the door again.

It wasn't all suffering, though.

He smiled.

Sitting next to her on the back porch every morning before the kids woke up was one of his favorite times of day now. Not only because it was the only time they had any peace and quiet, but also because it was the start of another day together. He loved everything about it. The steam rising from her mug as she curled up in a blanket in the chair next to him. The cool air. Jane watched the sunrise, while *he* watched it turn her eyes the color of honey. It was as close to heaven as he had ever been.

He loved mealtimes too, watching Jane cook, the way she tucked her hair behind her ears and tried not to blush as they fought over the last delicious bite of dinner. All of them together, crammed around the kitchen table, talking over each other, filled his heart in a way he could not possibly have imagined before her.

He just wanted more. A *lot* more. He wanted all of her. Heart, soul *and* body. He absently picked up the rag and wiped the fuel tank and vinyl seat of the bike, noticing a tear that needed to be patched.

More importantly, so did she. She tried to hide it, but he caught her all the time when she thought he wasn't looking, staring at him like she had that first day in his bedroom. He could feel it in the air between them whenever they were together.

He wished they could just be together, but he also knew it was not his choice to make. If he pushed her, he'd lose her. He just had to wait and trust in… whatever it was growing between them. When she was ready, she'd come around.

He wiped his forehead again. Damn, it was hot. He remembered his mom used to take him to the lake on days like this, pack a picnic lunch and spend the afternoon at the harbor beach. Maybe they should take the kids? It was the perfect day for a swim.

"Matt!" Jane called from the yard.

That was a good idea. He'd just clean up his mess and—

"Matt!"

Jane in her new swimsuit? He smiled as he put the tools back into Ed's toolbox. He could go for that. *Jane splashing around in the water?* Totally. Maybe seeing him in a similar state of undress would inspire her as it had in his bedroom. Then she would kiss her asshole husband goodbye and they would—

"Matt!"

Live happily ever after and fuck like bunnies until you're a hundred? That made him smile.

"Matt!"

"What?" he yelled back, walking toward her voice. "Jesus," he mumbled. How was he supposed to fantasize about her and plan their future when she interrupted him every two seconds?

They collided at the door. Her head slammed into his chest.

"Oof," he exhaled as her elbow punched his stomach.

She stumbled back, apologizing, and he caught her.

"S'up?" he asked.

Her eyes paused a little too long on his chest, and he couldn't help himself. "Hey," he snapped his fingers. "My eyes are up here."

Her cheeks turned pink, and she scowled. "The power is out."

"What?"

"It just shut off. I don't know—"

He stared into her worried eyes. Power outages were becoming more and more common. It was on the news every time they turned it on. Miami had been without power for two weeks, and he had known it would only be a matter of time before it happened here.

Ed came down the steps with the kids and gave Matt a knowing look. The two of them had talked about it, what they would do when it happened. They had it all planned out. He had brought the generator over from his parents' place. They had also siphoned the gas out of the pickup, and Matt had been collecting emergency supplies on his careful raids of the lakeside cottages.

"I'll go into town, see what the situation is. Maybe it's just a downed line." Ed said, heading toward the Prius.

Matt nodded.

Jane grabbed his arm. "What are we going to do?"

He looked from her to the kids as sweat dripped down the middle of his back, reminding him of his plan. "I say we go to the beach."

The boys cheered their support as Jane frowned. She put her hands on her hips. He had watched her take that stance a hundred times now with Tommy.

"I'm serious. What—"

"In case you haven't noticed, the breeze feels like a blow dryer set on high, Jane. I say we go swimming. We'll worry about the electricity later. You can try out the new swimsuit I got—"

"Matt…" she warned.

He rolled his eyes dramatically. "Ug. Alright. We're gonna do what they used to, before all this fancy e-lec-tricity," he said, adding a little country twang to his voice just to aggravate her.

"Which is what?" she asked, clearly annoyed by his lack of seriousness.

He grinned, and the boys giggled behind her.

"Live off the land, and wipe our asses with leaves, like our forefathers!" Matt waved his arm in the air for dramatic effect.

The boys laughed harder, and Maddy joined in too.

"Language," Jane said through gritted teeth, clearly not amused.

He rolled his eyes again. "Fine," he said, abandoning his accent. "I can see that the Missus has clearly Mis-placed her sense of humor today. Come on," he said, leading the way back to the house.

He winked at Austin, who doubled over with laughter.

"Good one Matt!" shouted Tommy, as they all followed him inside.

Matt went to the hall closet and opened the door. It was filled with boxes.

"Ta-da!" he said, presenting them like a prize on a game show.

Jane peered in the top one. She picked an apple-spice scented candle out of the box and sniffed. "You took these?" she asked, looking at the thirty more that were stacked inside.

He nodded. "When I went hunting for clothes." He pulled out the box then opened the one beneath it. It was filled with flashlights, batteries, and emergency lights.

"We will use these at night, for now. Lucky for us it's July, so no need to worry about heat," he said.

"What about the refrigerator?" Jane asked.

"We don't have anything to put in it, anyway. Whatever we need to keep cool, we'll put in the basement. Ed said there is room down there."

"What about our phones?"

"We have a generator. We'll run it once a day."

"How will we get the news?"

"Watch it when the generator is on."

"What about water?" She lowered her voice. "… The toilets?"

"The well outside has a manual pump, and all you need to flush is a bucket of water."

"How will we…" She seemed to be trying to think of something else, but couldn't.

"How will we what?"

"I–I–" Jane stared at him in amazement—like he had just rescued them all from the sinking Titanic.

"So…" he started, feeling rather pleased with himself.

"So…" Jane repeated.

"Are we going swimming or what?"

Chapter Forty-Five

Day 39 // 12:57 p.m

"IT HAS A SKIRT," Maddy said. The horror in her voice was real as she stared down at the frumpy swimsuit she wore. "I cannot go anywhere in this."

"You think you look ridiculous? Look at me!" Jane said, tugging at the loose fabric that hung around her like an ugly, Hawaiian-painted garbage bag. To be fair, she had told Matt she was a size 12, but as she peered down at her body, it became apparent she had lost quite a bit of weight.

Maddy shook her head. "Nope. I can't do it."

Jane sighed. "We're not going to Metro Beach, Maddy. There will literally be no one else there."

Her niece shook her head again. "I can't —"

"You want to trade?" Jane asked with a raised eyebrow.

Maddy scrunched her nose. "Ugh. No. The only thing uglier than this piece of shit is that piece of shit—"

Jane smacked her in the stomach. "Hey!"

They stared at themselves in the mirror for a moment.

"I can totally picture the old lady that thing belongs to," Maddy said, staring at Jane's chest. "Blond, poofy hair, enormous glasses, and tanned skin that looks like that leather handbag I wanted for my birthday…" Jane laughed as Maddy pulled the belt off the bathrobe hanging behind the door. "Here, maybe this will help."

Jane folded the suit across her stomach and wrapped the belt around her waist twice. It helped a little. "Like this?" she asked hopefully.

Maddy covered her mouth, laughing too hard to answer.

Jane studied herself in the mirror for a moment before she burst out laughing, too. Maddy was right. It was hideous. She leaned closer and inspected her very gray roots, her bruises, her sunburned nose, and the horrific way her eyebrows were growing together. *She* was hideous. "Oh god. You're right. We can't go anywhere. "

Maddy stood up straight beside her, and they stared at themselves again. "I have literally never seen anything more pathetic than the two of us right now."

They erupted in another round of tear-inducing laughter.

"Oh! Ow! My side." Jane leaned against the sink. "Okay no more—" She met Maddy's eyes and the two of them lost it again.

There was a hard rap on the door.

"What's all that giggling in there?" Matt asked from the other side. Jane's cheeks ached as she struggled to answer him. "We can't go. Maddy and I —"

"What? Why?"

"Because we look like we belong in a trailer park in Florida."

"Let me see," he said.

"Oh, hell no," Maddy said.

"Come on," he begged. "I'm sure you guys are just —"

Jane opened the door.

Matt's eyes darted between the two of them. He covered his mouth to hide his smile, and coughed.

Jane crossed her arms self-consciously.

He let out a long, low whistle. "Lookin' excellent ladies!" he gave Maddy a thumbs up. "Maddy, you are the prettiest underwater ballerina I've ever—"

She smacked his arm as she passed. "Ugh. I swear to god if either of you ever tells anyone…" She headed for her shoes and the front door.

Jane tried to scoot by, but Matt caught her around the waist before she could escape. "I mean it," he whispered in her ear. A shiver shot down her spine. "You are beautiful."

Jane looked down at the atrocity she wore and shook her head. She had become a lot of new things lately, but as her inspection in the mirror had proven, beautiful was not one of them.

"Look at me, Jane," Matt said, his voice suddenly rough.

She met his eyes, and—*Holy hell.*

The lightning went straight to her lady bits, and she actually jumped.

His breath came in a rasp as he pushed her back. One hand was still on her waist. The other above her on the door. Matt eased her against it.

She threw her hands against his chest, unable to breathe as his other hand found her cheek. Matt's eyes were wild as he pressed his forehead to hers. He whispered again. "You… are… beautiful."

It was the most wonderful, terrifying sensation of her life.

He stepped back suddenly and frowned, pointing at her waist. "Is that the belt from Ed's bathrobe?"

Jane still couldn't breathe. She nodded absently.

His eyebrow went up. "Weird. But okay. I can try to get into that."

She stared at him, and he winked at her. His playful smile had returned.

"Come on, Jane Moore," he said, turning toward the door. "The kids are already in the car."

Chapter Forty-Six

Day 39 // 1:23 p.m

MATT SAT ON THE TOWEL, watching Jane play with the kids in the lake. This was the best idea he'd had in a long time. He still didn't know what came over him back at the house. One thing was for sure, she was as close to caving as he was. He was sure she would have let him kiss her if he tried.

Why didn't you?

Jane adjusted her swimsuit for the hundredth time. "Are you coming in?" she called.

"Yeah, in a minute."

Because he'd made her a promise, and he wanted to respect her. Because if she did 'cave', what kind of man did that make him? She had enough assholes in her life, she didn't need another one. He desperately wanted to tell her Thomas was a cheater, that she should forget his sorry ass, but… something stopped him. What if he was wrong? What if she still loved that bastard and everything that was happening between them now was just because she was lonely and —Matt had seen pictures of Thomas. He was tall and handsome and… whole.

Matt looked down at his foot.

"Hey! Are you coming or what?" Jane called as the boys laughed like maniacs at something he missed. "This was your idea, you know."

"I'm coming." He brushed the sand from around the edge of his prosthetic. The sun temporarily blinded him as it glinted off the metal footplate.

She didn't care. He knew she didn't, and she had seen him without it before. But it felt different… out in the daylight, in front of the kids. He just—

Jane dropped Bria into his lap, and he howled in surprise as he grabbed her slippery, naked, *freezing* body and held her in the air. She squirmed and slipped back into his lap with a plop.

"Ah! You goddamn little–icicle!"

Jane burst out laughing.

Matt grabbed her arm, pulling her down beside him and dumped the baby back in her lap.

Bria squealed at the game and grabbed a handful of sand. Jane snatched it away just in time.

"You're gonna pay for that," Matt warned.

"What are you going to do?" Jane asked, taking another handful of sand away from her daughter.

"Maddy?" Matt called calmly, never taking his eyes off Jane. "Come here and hold your cousin-sicle, please."

The corner of Jane's mouth turned up as Maddy made her way out of the water.

He pulled his t-shirt over his head, and her gasp was just enough to give him the confidence he needed. Matt unbuckled the strap to his prosthetic and pulled it off.

"That's okay, Maddy," Jane said as her niece reached for the baby.

"Hand over the baby, Aunt Jane," Maddy replied as Matt removed the sock and liner from his calf.

Jane looked from Matt to Maddy, her plan spelled out in her eyes as clearly as everything else was.

As soon as Maddy had a hold of Bria, Jane bolted.

But he was ready.

Matt lunged for her, catching her wet ankle. She squealed and fell into the sand. Quickly, she got to her knees, and he lost his grip. She scrambled toward the water. He was faster though, and his hand closed over her calf again and Jane laughed as she tumbled into a small wave.

"Oh, no you don't," he said, crawling up her body as she tried to squirm away. The cold water pressed against his knees.

He straddled her, careful not to touch her, and put his hands on his hips. "Now where do you think you're—"

The boys assaulted him from the side, rolling him into deeper water as Jane scurried away.

It was like being dropped into a bath of ice water.

"Fuuuck—" he bellowed before he could stop himself.

The boys held him down, screaming with laughter. Matt pressed his hands into the sand and pushed himself back up, flinging them off with a splash. "Shit, shit…" he said, jumping back onto his knees. He grabbed at his crotch, trying to get his balls out of the water.

Jane sat waist high in the water a couple of feet away, laughing so hard she was crying.

The boys assaulted him again, their weight on his back, dipping his man-parts back into the drink. He flung them off, hoping his dick was still somewhere in his shorts. He couldn't feel it.

They hopped back on. "Goddamn little—" he said breathlessly as Tommy threw his arms around his neck and hugged his back like a frozen koala clinging to a tree branch. Austin piled on top and grabbed at Matt's sides like a pair of icy tongs.

Jane laughed harder as he crawled toward her, dragging the boys. "Why do I feel like I was set up?" he growled, narrowing his eyes.

"It was my idea!" Austin confessed proudly from somewhere above him as Jane continued to shake with laughter. *God, she is beautiful.*

She scooted back, trying to wipe her eyes at the same time. "Time out. I can't breathe," she said, holding her hand out.

Matt grabbed her around the waist. "Nope. No time-outs for

you, you *traitor.* You broke the grown-up code. And now you're going to pay."

She wheezed, and he tried not to smile. "What's the grown-up code?" she asked.

"It's like the guy-code, but with girls and different rules, and– You know what? Never mind. And quit trying to change the subject."

Matt threw the boys into the water, then lunged for her. Jane squealed and held onto his neck as he leaned her back slowly. She gasped as her back hit the water and arched against him.

His brow went up. *Well, that's convenient.* He pushed her back more, and she gasped again and shoved her hips into his. Suddenly, the water didn't feel so cold.

"Matt…" she breathed. Her eyes fell to his mouth and his heart took off like a racehorse inside his chest.

One of her hands came around and cupped his jaw as her chest heaved against him. She pulled his head down to hers and pressed her forehead against his. Warmth flooded his body, and he was relieved to discover he did still in fact, have a dick.

"Oh, god…" she whispered hoarsely. *I want you,* her eyes said.

He moved his hand back down her side, wrapping it around her ass, lifting her toward him. She didn't pull away. "I want you too," he confessed with as much restraint as he could muster.

He held his breath as she met his eyes. Yes, his dick was *definitely* still there. Jane pulled his head closer and closed her eyes. Her breath brushed his lips and her heart thumped wildly beneath his. Matt closed his eyes and—

A weight landed on his back, and his arm collapsed. He fell on top of Jane, submerging both of them underwater. Matt roared like a lion as he dragged her, sputtering back up to the surface. The boys shrieked like howler monkeys as he threw them off into the water.

Jane jumped up and ran for shore, leaving him to battle them alone.

They lunged for him again, screaming with laughter.

"Traitor!" he shouted.

She laughed as she fell beside Maddy.

Austin and Tommy threw their arms around his neck and dragged him backward into the water. Matt fell back with a splash as Tommy climbed on his chest. *Fucking kids.* But he was smiling. In fact, his cheeks hurt from the grin plastered on his face.

He had gotten his wish.

He'd had a moment with Jane. More than a moment. An almost-kiss.

Oh yeah, this was definitely a good idea.

Chapter Forty-Seven

Day 39 // 4:44 p.m

JANE WAS SUNBURNT, but it felt good.

After they had gotten home and she had put Bria down for a nap, Matt had informed her he had a surprise for her.

And now she was sitting behind him on a motorcycle, holding on for dear life. She still didn't know what had come over her at the beach. She had just never felt anything like what she felt lying in his arms. But maybe that was what everyone who had affairs said to justify what they had done.

There was no denying she wanted Matt—and god did she want him—but…

Jane pulled a strand of hair out of her mouth. Something was making her hesitate. And it was ridiculous because she knew Thomas didn't even want her, but still. Her dad would have said it was the principle of the thing.

Matt pulled into the driveway of his parent's house and heat rushed to her cheeks as she glanced at his bedroom window. This was her surprise?

He pulled to a stop beside the back door, and she hopped off.

"What are we doing here?" she asked.

"Follow me," was all he said, heading up the steps.

He unlocked the door, then turned the light on in the stairwell leading to the basement.

"Ladies first," he said with a mischievous grin.

Jane frowned as she started down the steps. "You're not going to murder me, are you?" she asked, making her way down the old wooden steps.

"Maybe," he answered deviously as he followed behind her.

"Because if you do, just keep in mind you have to take care of my kids." Jane stepped off the last step and waited, squinting into the dark room beyond.

"Fuck. You're right. Then, no. I guess I'll just give you this instead." He flipped a light switch and lining the three walls were floor to ceiling shelving and hundreds of jars.

Jane stared in amazement.

"Ta-da!" he said. "Welcome to Patterson's grocery store, where everything is canned and everything is free. I made up that slogan myself, just now, by the way."

Jane crossed the room and read the labels. "Apple pie, turkey gravy, peaches in brandy." Tears filled her eyes as she touched Mrs. Patterson's neat handwriting. "Green beans." Jane turned and found Matt through blurry eyes. His mother had canned enough food to get them through the next *year*. "Oh my god, Matt. This is…" She was speechless.

He shrugged. "What can I say? My mom has a *lot* of time on her hands."

Chicken, beef, carrots, beets, pears, cranberries. To Jane's utter amazement, Matt's mom had even canned butter—something none of them had used in months.

"You can *can* butter?"

Matt made a face. "I guess so. Although why you would want to… God, my mom is so weird sometimes."

She laughed and wiped away a tear. "I'm glad she did. This is… this is wonderful. Thank you for sharing it with me. And the kids."

He headed for the stairs. "I'm going to go grab a backpack. Pick out whatever you want to take home today."

Jane turned back to the shelves, totally overwhelmed. She hadn't even realized how *truly* worried about food she had been until that moment. It was like a weight had been lifted from her shoulders and she might float away. She took a jar of butter and a can of chicken.

Matt came back down the stairs and held out a blue backpack. She dropped the cans in and turned to get more, but he caught her wrist. Her entire body began to tingle. He slowly spun her around, placing the bag on the concrete floor.

"What are you—" she began as he stepped closer and slid his hand around her waist. Her hands pressed against his chest, and the feel of him, firm and warm, under her palms, took her breath away.

Jane thought she might faint as his other hand found her cheek. *This is happening.* He leaned in and she felt the tickle of his beard against her lips.

But then something in her reared its head and screamed no.

She turned her head away at the last second. She didn't know why. His lips landed awkwardly on her cheek. "I can't," she said, dropping her forehead to his chest, shaking her head. "I want to, but I—can't."

"Forget about Thomas," he whispered hoarsely, trying to tilt her face back up.

She kept her face turned. "No, I can't. He's my husband."

"He's an asshole."

She stepped back, and the look in his eyes made her pause. "What? No, I told you—"

"And I'm telling you," he said. "He's an asshole, Jane. A first-class, grade A—"

"Stop. Thomas is a good man, and he deserves—"

"Are you really that blind, or are you just playing stupid?" Matt interrupted angrily.

Jane blinked in disbelief at his harsh words. "What are you talking about?"

He clenched his fists at his sides. "Nothing."

No, definitely not nothing.

"You have something to say, say it."

"You don't love him, Jane!"

She stared at him, not understanding the venom in his voice. "No, maybe I don't, but I am his *wife*. I made him a promise, and I am not a cheater, Matt—"

"Yes, you are!"

She stepped back in shock.

"I know you want me. What's the fucking difference—"

She stared at him. "Did you bring me over here to get away from the kids, thinking… we'd have *sex*? Is that why you are so angry?"

It was his turn to look surprised. "What? No. I brought you—"

"Take me home," she said as fresh tears sprang into her eyes.

"Jane—"

She turned and hurried up the stairs.

He pounded up behind her as she pushed open the back door and rushed down the steps.

It was like déjà vu as she rounded the side of his house.

"Jane!" Matt bellowed.

She broke into a run, passed the bike and headed for the road.

She would be damned if any part of her touched him after he'd called her stupid, and practically accused her of being an adulterer. She covered the sob that tore from her mouth as she ran. He might be right, but, damn, it hurt—and she was so tired of being hurt by men she cared about.

"Jane!" Matt called as she sprinted onto the gravel road.

The sun blinded her, and she had to squint through her tears. She should have known. It was all a ruse. All along, he was just trying to get in her pants. A bitter laugh burst from her throat. She probably should feel flattered he wanted to fuck her at all, but…

She heard the bike start and knew she only had a few seconds before he caught up with her.

She looked up at the miles of fields and the empty road. There was nowhere to go. Nowhere to hide. Feeling defeated, she slowed to a walk as the motorcycle roared up behind her.

He pulled in front of her and cut the engine. "Jane, I'm sorry. That came out all wrong."

"That happens to you a lot, doesn't it?" Jane snapped as she skirted past him. She refused to look at him.

"Shit," he swore as his metal foot kicked the frame and he tried to turn the bike around.

"Jane!" he called, coming alongside her again, straddling the bike as he pushed it forward. "I shouldn't have said what I did. I just—"

She kept walking.

"Jane! Don't be—"

She spun around and stormed over to him. "What? *Stupid*? Or a… whore? Save your breath, Matt, because whatever horrible thing you want to call me doesn't even come close to what I already call myself for feeling the way I do about you."

"I didn't mean—" he started. His eyes pleaded with her, but she ignored them. She was tired of not feeling good enough. Tired of being lied to.

She turned back toward Ed's house. "Just leave me alone."

"Jane, come on."

She kept walking. "Stupid. Stupid," she muttered to herself.

"Jane—"

"Just leave me alone!" she screamed, spinning around to face him.

Matt stopped his eyes darted between hers. "Damn it," he said through his clenched jaw.

She lowered her voice. "Leave me the fuck alone."

She turned back around and continued walking toward home.

Chapter Forty-Eight

Day 41 // 2:17 p.m

THINGS WERE CHANGING AGAIN. In the beginning, everything had shut down because of the quarantine, but now, over a month in and with no sign of the virus on the outside, the quarantine had been lifted. The rule was as long as they had a tracking wristband, people could venture out again if they chose, resume what was left of their businesses and lives. So, things were opening up. Not too open because gas was still being hoarded by the government, but services were slowly being reestablished, and small communities were popping up amid the ruins of the sprawling suburbs. A weird, new normal was being shaped and people were once again on the roads.

Still, Matt didn't like the idea of going down to the Veil, even though he would get to see his parents too. The Veil had revealed just how many crazy people there were in the world. There were a lot more than made him comfortable and they also seemed to be drawn to that wall like moths to a flame. He'd heard on the news the night before in London, a man had opened fire on a tower, and was tackled by two other men, then beaten to death. Inside Chicago, a militia group had organized a raid on the Veil, claiming to know how to disarm it. But somehow, one of the homemade bombs they had been transporting detonated a half-mile from their target, killing eighteen people.

Jane and the kids were safer at the farm.

Bria fussed behind him. Matt unbuckled his seatbelt and found her pacifier, popping it back in her mouth, then turned back around.

He couldn't believe he was thinking it, but for the first time in his life, he was *glad* to be out in the middle of nowhere. He was glad to be cut off from… everything. Yes, they had to battle the elements and the land, but those were so much simpler and straightforward than the ignorant, unpredictable masses.

He glanced at Jane. She was still pissed at him about the other day, and he didn't blame her. He had let his utter disgust for Thomas, and his desire for her, get the better of him.

She didn't speak a word to him after she told him to leave her alone, so he had followed her—walking that damn bike all the way back to Ed's. He reached down and rubbed his sore ankle. He had blisters under his prosthetic that burned like hell every time he took a step. Matt looked out the window. The farmland had given way to houses. They were nearing the city.

The good news was, at bedtime, Jane hadn't locked him out of the room. The bad news was all day yesterday she had been both distant and annoyingly polite.

Matt glanced at her out of the corner of his eye. She'd borrowed Maddy's makeup. Her lips were pink. She had lined her eyes in black, making them sultrier than he had ever seen them. That, combined with her hair styled down and the white blouse she had borrowed from the late Mrs. Hamilton, made her almost unrecognizable. He realized she was the woman he'd seen at the harbor that day.

The only traces of the Jane he knew, was the brownish-yellow bruise on the left side of her head, and the scabbed over gash by her eye.

Her knuckles were white as they pulled up to the checkpoint and her mouth pressed into a seam as she put her mask on and rolled down the window.

Once he had his tracking bracelet and they were all scanned, they parked, went through the second checkpoint, and got in line. He recognized his parents, even with masks on, but they hadn't noticed him yet. His eyes moved down the row and stopped when they met the glare of a tall, dark-haired man with blue eyes. Even with his face covered, he was intimidating.

Thomas.

He vaguely recognized the eyes of the woman beside him and knew he was looking at Jane's sister. They waved, confirming his suspicion. He wondered if Sarah knew what a douchebag her brother-in-law was? Then he noticed two little African American girls, about nine years old, standing beside them, holding Sarah's hands, waving to someone behind him.

Matt turned and saw a pretty woman about his age crying and waving back. She must be their mother.

Jane's jaw was tight as she stood behind him. He hated that he was the reason. Tommy waved wildly to his dad as Sarah bent down to one of the girls and pointed.

Maddy pointed out her boyfriend excitedly, which explained the forty minutes in the bathroom before they left. The boy was in line behind Sarah, absorbed with his phone, not even noticing her. It surprised Matt how pissed off it made him. *Fucking prick.* After all the time she spent, he could at least act like he was happy to see her. How he'd even been granted a visit was a mystery. It was supposed to be for immediate family only.

His eyes went back to his parents. His mom had finally spotted him. He waved. She tilted her head to the side and gave him a look he couldn't quite decipher. Matt shifted Bria to his other arm, wondering what he must look like, nestled between all the kids, standing next to Jane. His eyes met Thomas's again. Whatever he looked like, Thomas didn't like it.

Matt looked back at his mom, who was still staring at him. It was crazy. All of them together, but not. Each of them belonged to different puzzles the Veil had mixed up, then doled out randomly. Fate was creating pictures that didn't make sense, assembling mismatched little families that didn't belong together.

Except...

He studied Jane as she watched her husband and sister.

Jane does belong with you.

They fit perfectly together. He knew it in his bones. He looked down at Bria and the kids. They fit too. Like a damn glove. He swallowed hard and looked up at the Veil. If it ever came down…

You will lose them all.

His eyes met Thomas's again. If the Veil came down, it would be him on the other side of their lives.

"I wish the virus was done so dad could be on this side," Tommy complained.

Jane rubbed his hair. "I know. But at least we get to see him, right? And he told me he has something extra special for you."

"My dad buys the best presents," Tommy informed Matt.

Twenty minutes into their wait, Jane offered to take Bria. But he refused. The longer they stood there, the clearer everything became. He didn't want to let the little wiggle-worm go. Matt looked at Austin, then at Maddy trying to catch the eye of her stupid boyfriend, and Tommy, inspecting an ant hill. He didn't want to let *any* of them go.

Finally, the soldier motioned for them to move forward, and they gave their names. He scanned all their bracelets again and radioed the other side. He told Matt to stay with Jane until his parents were up, and then he would move down one station to speak with them.

Jane opened the gate to their little yard, and they all piled in.

Thomas and Sarah stepped up on the other side.

Matt couldn't help but compare himself to what he could see of Jane's husband. He was probably twenty years older than him, handsome. Tall, maybe not in the best shape, but not terrible either. Great dresser. Well-groomed. Matt frowned. And very familiar, now that he was looking at him close up. Where had he seen—

It clicked. He knew exactly what Thomas Moore looked like. "Your husband is Thomas Moore of 'Moore, Arshakian, and Greenwood'?" he whispered. He had seen the billboards all over the city.

"Yeah."

"I'll treat you like family, and in my house, family comes first?" Matt repeated the slogan, the irony not lost on him.

"Yes."

Jesus Christ. He looked at Jane, who was staring at the girls peeking out from behind Sarah. Her outfit made sense now.

Jane Moore is practically a millionaire.

He looked back at her aged Grand Caravan, and his brows came together.

"Then why in the hell are you driving that?"

Jane frowned. "Because I love it. What's wrong with—" her voice trailed off as Thomas crouched down and spoke to the slightly shorter of the girls.

"It's okay, sweetie," he said gently. "That's Mrs. Moore over there." Thomas pointed at Jane and gave Matt a hard look. "That is my son Thomas, but we call him Tommy so we don't get mixed up. And that's Austin and Maddy and baby Bria." He met Matt's eyes again. "And you must be the *infamous* Matt with the missing foot."

Chapter Forty-Nine

Day 41 // 3:00 p.m

BRIA COOED in Matt's arms, and the taller girl stepped from behind Sarah.

"She's so cute!" she said with a shy smile, ending the terribly awkward moment Thomas had created.

Jane automatically smiled back. The girls were adorable. Jane also had no idea who they were.

"This is Alisha and Kyla. They are staying with us until this"—Thomas gestured to the wall—"is resolved."

Thomas looked right at her, and if he noticed the bruises on her face, he wasn't concerned.

Jane smiled at the girls, "Well, you girls are lucky because Mr. —"

"Thomas and Sarah," Sarah interjected, and something about the way she said it made Jane pause.

"Right. Thomas and Sarah have had lots of experience with kiddos. You are in great hands until you're back with your mom."

"We know," the braver little girl said.

"So, they're staying with you?" she asked Thomas, thinking it odd that he would have volunteered —

"With… us," he said.

Jane frowned. "Us?"

"We figured with the girls, it made more sense to stay together at the house," Sarah said, casting Thomas a glance. Jane knew the look well because it was the one her sister always wore when they were fighting. *Or when she wanted you to keep your mouth shut.*

"Is everything okay?" Jane asked, as a weird feeling gnawed at the back of her brain. Sarah and Thomas trying to live together? That couldn't be going well. She imagined the stress of everything, plus two children, was only making it worse.

"Fine," Thomas said. "We're all healthy and that's what's most important."

Jane let out her breath. Of course. For a moment, she thought… She didn't know what she thought.

"Hey, Dad! Guess what?" Tommy chimed in. "I'm gonna build a treehouse…"

Jane stepped back out of the way to stand by Matt and took Bria, who had begun to fuss. She let the kids talk to their parents.

Thomas and Sarah looked genuinely happy to see them, but something was off. Jane watched as they stood side-by-side laughing while Austin regaled them with fishing stories. Jane sensed the strange tension again, coming from Sarah—just like she had on the phone. She didn't understand it. Something about the way her sister kept glancing at her out of the corner of her eye made her feel uneasy. Had something happened that they were not telling her?

Tommy and Austin were dramatically reenacting one of their exploits when Thomas unconsciously slid his hand around Sarah's waist, threw his head back, and laughed. Instead of pushing him away, Sarah leaned into his shoulder. He gave her a comforting squeeze while she shook her head at the boys.

Jane stilled as Bria tugged at her hair. She met her sister's eyes. Sarah froze and quickly pushed Thomas away.

Jane met her husband's eyes, and the guilt—

"… and I helped! Dad?" Tommy piped up. "Dad?"

Thomas dragged his apologetic eyes back to his son, and the boy continued to ramble.

Jane blinked. *What just happened?*

There was no way Sarah would let him touch her like that. There was no way she would lean into him like she was unless…

"Oh, god."

"What's wrong?" Matt whispered beside her. She had forgotten he was there.

She shook her head. "Nothing." She had to be imagining it. There was no way in a matter of a *month* they could have gone from enemies to…

Not a month, Janie.

Her eyes settled on the boys as they laughed. Then she looked at Thomas, who was wearing the *exact* same expression, and her knees buckled. Matt caught her arm as she stumbled into him. He said something, but her ears were full of cotton as she righted herself. How had she not noticed it before? The boys had Thomas's eyes.

Both of them.

Everything slid painfully into place, and Jane thought she might be sick. *That* was why her sister never came around the house. *That* was why Thomas and Sarah avoided each other during the holidays and family events. Jane had assumed they just didn't like each other, but it was because of this. It was because they were having an affair, and they were trying to hide it.

She stared in disbelief. It was like the speedometer on the van. It had been right in front of her for years, but she'd never seen it. Hidden in plain sight this whole time.

Matt said something, but she couldn't hear him.

Thomas and *Sarah*? Jane pressed her hand to her forehead, pushing the hair out of her eyes. How could she have been so blind? Her eyes fell back to Austin, and it was like she was seeing him for the first time. She had always just assumed the similarities between him and Tommy were from her side of the family, but now it was obvious. Painfully so.

Did all their friends know? *Oh god.*

"Jane? Are you okay? I'm up with my parents—" Matt said. "You want Bria's carrier?"

She shook her head, not hearing him, and Matt left to go to the next station over to speak with them.

Did Maggy and all the girls at tennis suspect? Had all the parents at the kids' school been whispering behind her back this whole time?

God. How humiliating would that be? They must all think she was an idiot.

Jane looked from Sarah back to Thomas. They were no longer touching, but the damage was done. The blinds had been lifted. She could see it now. They stood too close. And when she'd called Thomas late that one night, Sarah had been right beside him. It had been two in the morning, but she'd just assumed they were up late, sitting on the couch in the living room, or at the kitchen table. They had been in bed. *Together.* They had been in *her* bed, together.

"Aunt Jane?" Maddy said. "Are you okay?"

She turned and looked at Maddy, scrutinizing her for the first time, searching for any hint of Thomas in her features.

"Aunt Jane?"

No. There were none. Maddy was… not Thomas's. Not that it made her feel any better. Austin was twelve. They had been… together at least over a decade. Or had it been a fling that they just resumed now that the Veil had made it convenient?

"I'm fine."

She wasn't fine. Jane's cheeks burned with humiliation as Austin told his mom and *dad* about helping Ed do chores around the farm, and how he and Tommy had caught a chicken that escaped the pen.

She tugged at the front of her blouse, struggling to breathe. The thought of her sister laying under Thomas the way she had so many times made her want to vomit. She tightened her grip on Bria and tried to ignore the pictures that were forming in her head, of her *sister* and her *husband* and what they must have done to each other beneath the sheets to produce her nephew.

Thomas and Tommy navigated the wagon through the wall again as Jane stared at the ground, feeling like her head was on fire.

The next eleven minutes were some of the longest of her life, as Bria cried in her ear and the kids went on and on, but finally, the bell rang. Jane corralled the boys, grabbed the bags from Thomas and Sarah, and without ever making eye contact, waved a hasty goodbye. She hurried them toward the van.

"But why does Maddy get to stay?" Tommy asked, dragging his feet as Jane pulled him across the thick swatch of pavement toward the parking area. Bria continued to fuss and cry in her mother's exhausted arms.

Jane swayed under the pressure of her rapidly failing composure. Heat rushed up her neck. "She's going to... she's... her boyfriend."

"Are you feeling okay, Aunt Jane?" Austin asked, sounding worried.

The edge of her vision darkened, and she gritted her teeth, willing herself to stay upright. "Fine."

Tommy said something, but all she could hear was Bria screaming and the years of whispers that must have been uttered behind her back. She thought about all the lies between Sarah and Thomas, between everyone who knew them. How long had her friends suspected what she had not?

She had been such a fool. Jane looked at her watch. Damn it, and now she was late for Bria's bottle and medicine.

She pressed the button on her keys and the van door slid open.

"What?" she yelled over the ringing in her ears, as the boys climbed in the back.

"Dad said after the Veil is down, he's gonna take us to Hawaii. Like all of us. Won't that be cool?" Tommy repeated.

That will definitely not be happening.

Jane dropped her screaming baby in her car seat, pressing her hand against her belly to keep her from crawling out. "That will be amazing," she screeched in a voice she didn't recognize.

Her head swam as she dragged the diaper bag around the seat. She fumbled through it, but she couldn't find the bottle. Had they even brought one? She couldn't remember. Bria's face was crimson as she wailed. Jane started pulling everything out of the bag. She couldn't breathe.

Oh god.

A warm palm pressed against her back.

"Jane, what happened?" Matt asked, appearing out of nowhere.

She jerked away, glancing over her shoulder at Thomas, who was talking to the girl's mother. She met Sarah's apologetic eyes. If there had been any doubt, it was gone now. Sarah was sorry? For what? *Sleeping* with her *husband*? Having his *child*?

"Oh god," Jane whispered as she looked up at the sky, and tried to blink her tears back. No wonder Thomas never seemed to be in the mood. She thought it was her. But it was because—

Matt pushed her hand away and picked up Bria, then he reached into the front pocket of the diaper bag and pulled out her bottle. "Hey," he said as the baby hungrily shoved the nipple in her mouth.

"Don't cry," she whispered to herself.

"What's going on?" Matt whispered. "Talk to me."

And tell him what? That she and her sister had both been… fucking her husband for the last decade?

"I–I can't," she said, rifling through the bag. "And I need to find the medicine for Bria, but I can't find a *fucking* thing in this bag!"

"Okay. Take it easy," he said, setting the baby back in her car seat, and buckling her in. "I'll find it, you just—"

"I can take care of my own fucking daughter," she said, wiping the tears from her eyes. She would not cry over this. Not here in front of everyone.

"Jane—" Matt warned.

She looked up. The boys were staring at her.

She wiped the corner of her eye and winced at the still painful bruise. "Sorry. I should not have said—"

Maddy shoved her aside, face red, on the verge of tears herself, and squeezed into the van.

"What happened?" Jane asked.

"Nothing. Can we just go?" The girl asked, plopping beside her brother. She folded her arms across her chest and stared out the window.

Jane turned and spotted Maddy's boyfriend heading back to his car. He didn't look nearly as upset. She looked at Thomas and Sarah and wanted to scream.

Damn it.

"Yeah. Let's get the hell out of here." Jane shoved the diaper bag back between the seats.

"But what about—" Matt started, but he stopped when he saw the look on her face. "I'll find it on the way. Let's go."

THE DRIVE HOME was tense and nearly silent—at least between her and Matt. She hadn't asked him about his parents or how they were doing. She knew she should, but she still didn't trust herself not to break down and cry if she opened her mouth, so she kept it shut.

It was dinnertime by the time they got back home, and Jane had never been so happy to be anywhere in her life.

Matt unbuckled Bria and carried her into the house as the boys rushed in to show Ed the things their parents had given them. Maddy went off to sulk.

Jane lingered, leaning back against the van, staring out over the fields. She looked up at the white cotton clouds as they rolled across the enormous sky. It made her feel small, and she was grateful because that meant her problems were small, too. It meant the shit-show that her life had become couldn't possibly be as big or as all-consuming as it felt.

She closed her eyes as the sun turned her eyelids red and

warmed her cheeks. She inhaled deeply. Unlike the city, there was space here for her to breathe, for her to process her pain, and she had a lot just then.

She knew she needed to let it go—the regret of having wasted so much time trying to love someone who would never love her back, and the sadness over something she could never change. And she was ready. Finally. What she saw today was the last nail in the painfully constructed coffin they'd made for the death of their marriage. She looked out over the ocean of corn as the wind blew over it in waves.

The one thing she could not let go of, though, was her anger. Her sister and Thomas had both betrayed her. The most hurtful part was that they'd done it *together*. She thought about the other day, in the basement with Matt. She hadn't had the guts to kiss him, even though she knew Thomas didn't love her. So, how could Thomas sneak around her back and fuck her sister, when he *knew* she loved him?

How could he sink his dick into Sarah, then come home and sit across from her at the dinner table and pretend he hadn't? How did he not die of guilt when Jane put on a sexy piece of lingerie and tried her best to seduce him? She understood now why it hadn't worked, but how could he let her keep trying like an idiot? How could he humiliate her like that and still face himself in the mirror every morning?

And Sarah? Sarah was her best friend—or so she thought. Jane suddenly had a very good idea why Sarah's yoga studio hadn't known who she was. She shook her head as her teeth ground together. She'd literally watched their *son* while they had their weekly little rendezvous. How could Sarah give her a hug and say 'I love you, sis.' after that? What the *fuck* was wrong with her?

Jane pushed back from the van and pulled her phone out of her pocket.

After a brief, frustrating conversation with the Coast Guard, she hung up and dialed Thomas.

She needed to know why. She needed to know why they kept it a secret for so long instead of coming clean. She needed to know how they could look her in the eye, day after day, and still sleep at night. She needed to know how long it had been going on, and why Thomas had bothered to marry her — when he obviously *never* loved her. Not even in the beginning. She'd been so caught up in everything else, she hadn't really noticed, but now... Now it was painfully obvious. Thomas had never looked at her the way Matt did, never made her feel what Matt did. Not once. Tears stung her eyes. All that time she'd wasted when she could have had something more. Why would he steal that from her?

Jane tucked her hair behind her ear as the phone rang.

"Jan —" Thomas's voice was tense on the other end of the line.

"I tried to make another appointment at the Veil–but they won't let me," she said tersely.

"Jane—"

"I know you know people."

"Jane, listen—"

"I am not doing this over the phone, Thomas. Get us a meeting. I am not bringing the kids. Do not bring my sister. Call me back when you've made the appointment."

"I can't just—"

"Yes, you can. You owe me at least that much." Jane hung up the phone before Thomas could get another word in, then headed into the house to make dinner.

Jane slathered peanut butter on crackers and opened a jar of applesauce, spooning big scoops into bowls for the kids. Maddy wasn't hungry, and the adults were content to eat leftovers from the night before. It was a shitty dinner, but she was in a shitty mood.

She eyed the folder that Thomas had sent. Considering recent events, she had forgotten that she had even asked him to find it. He couldn't send her computer through the Veil, but she was pretty sure she had printed a draft of her thesis at some point, and if she had, it would be in there. She was anxious to open it, but also dreading it at the same time.

Matt was wisely giving her space, but as she sighed and sat down at the table to feed Bria, he came in, limping slightly, and offered to do it.

She handed him the spoon and towel, then took the folder upstairs into the bathroom and locked the door. She took three ibuprofen, then sat down on the toilet, wondering why she was even bothering to dig up more ghosts from her past. Hadn't she suffered enough today?

Her phone buzzed. It was a text from Thomas.

11:00 tomorrow.

She set her phone on the sink.

Jane stared at the folder on her lap. It was red with the words "thesis stuff" written in black marker in the center. She had been a different person, expecting a very different future when she had written those words. She hesitated, touching the letters. Even if her paper was responsible for what was happening, there was nothing she could do about it. It wasn't like she could call the President, or the ICPH and ask them to please stop implementing her strategies, because it was making her feel bad. She heard the kids laugh downstairs.

She sighed and opened it, anyway. Both pockets were crammed full of slightly yellowed papers. She looked through them until she found what she was looking for.

She cringed as she read the note Robert had left in the margin.

It's a solid first draft! Congratulations, Jane, you just saved the world.

She took a deep breath and read.

Twenty minutes later, she was interrupted by a knock on the door.

"You okay?" Matt called from the other side.

She had gone through most of the paper, and it was just as she remembered. She tucked the pages back into the folder before unlocking the door and pulling it open. "Yeah, I'm fine. I'm going to heat up some warm water for a quick rinse, if you don't mind." She scooted past him into the bedroom, put the folder in the dresser drawer, then headed for the stairs.

"Sure. I'll help you haul water," he offered.

Jane looked at his leg and remembered it was bothering him. She knew why. It was because she'd made him walk the other night. She met his eyes and felt like such a jerk.

"No, that's okay. I'm just going to —"

"I'll help you haul water," he repeated. His voice was tight.

She noticed his clenched fists and frowned, but didn't argue. "Okay, thank you," she said, heading for the stairs.

After six buckets of water, four of which were heated to a boil on the stove, Jane retreated into the bathroom and undressed. Her hip was healing nicely, she noted, before climbing into the tub. There was only about three inches of water in it, but it was hot and felt good on the parts of her it reached. She folded her knees and laid against the back of the tub and just sat, staring at the wall of square beige tiles. Between the revelation about Thomas and Sarah, and her fear that she was somehow responsible for the Veil… she was drained.

Let go of thought.

Jane closed her eyes and repeated. "Let go of thought…"

THERE WAS a loud knock on the door, and Jane's eyes flew open. She grabbed the edge of the tub and sat up. The water had turned lukewarm around her, and she shivered.

"Mom?" Tommy called.

She had fallen asleep. "Shit," she said, jumping up and reaching for a towel. She had intended for the kids to bathe after her. Jane dragged a towel across her body, got dressed, then ushered Tommy inside. Maddy brought Bria up and Jane dropped the baby in too, while Matt carried up a couple more pots of hot water.

After the kids were in bed, Jane went back to her room and sat on the edge of the bed and stared at herself in the mirror through the soft candlelight that illuminated the room. It reminded her of her first night home after the accident, and her first night on earth without her parents. Her body felt like it was filled with lead, and she was almost certain she would never be able to move again.

"Care to tell me what's going on?" Matt's voice asked from the doorway.

She continued to stare blankly at the dresser. How could she explain she was upset about her husband having an affair when she was sleeping in the same *bed* with another man? How could she explain she thought she might be responsible for the Veil? He'd think she was crazy. Hell, s*he* thought she was crazy.

He sat beside her on the bed, and her gut twisted. *Do not feel bad.* Why not? Matt was right. She already had cheated, maybe not physically, but in her heart she had. He could have moved downstairs on the couch when they came here, but he hadn't—and she hadn't made him. Didn't that make her just as guilty? *Not the same.*

They weren't having sex, but the truth was, she wanted him there. She really did.

Matt's warm hand slid under hers. Jane was torn between wanting to fling it off and hold on to it forever. She cared about him, and not just because he helped her with the kids and woke her up when she started screaming in her sleep. She cared about him because she had *feelings* for him—Jane flexed her fingers around his—feelings that had confused and tormented her conscience since the day she met him. Even now, when she knew about Thomas and Sarah, she *still* felt guilty. She *still* felt like a horrible person for being attracted to him.

"Jane," he whispered, trying not to wake Bria.

"It's nothing," she lied.

Discovering her body could move after all, she crawled into bed and pulled the covers up around her neck. How could she be angry at Thomas for having an affair when *she* wanted to have one with Matt?

You want much more than an affair. That was true. She wanted what she *thought* she thought she had created with Thomas. A life, a family. A lover to grow old with.

"It's not nothing. You haven't said a word since we left. Are you… should I have stayed back? Did I make things bad between you and Thomas?"

Jane almost laughed. No, things had been bad between her and Thomas for a lot longer than Matt had been around. She just hadn't realized how bad or how long until today.

Matt continued. "Or are you still pissed about the other day? Because I told you—"

She turned. "No. It has nothing to do with you. And I'm not angry. You-you were right."

"Are you —" He stopped. "It? What is *it*, Jane?"

She wasn't ready to tell him how stupid she'd been. "It's nothing."

He laid down on the other side of the bed, propping his head up over the pillow that was still between them. "Are you sure? Because I got the distinct impression that I was making everyone—"

"No. I'm glad you were there. I just…" She swallowed and turned away. "It's just been a long day."

He reached across and put a comforting hand on her shoulder, but she pulled it away. She turned toward the wall as her tears soaked the pillow.

"Good night, Jane."

"Good night, Matt."

Chapter Fifty

Day 42 // 8:47 a.m

THE TV WAS ON, and Matt saw the headline as soon as he came down the stairs. Rome had fallen.

Jane was curled up on the couch, looking pale and writing in a notebook. She scribbled something as she looked at her phone. Ed sat in his chair with his coffee, shaking his head. Tommy was on the floor playing.

He tried to listen to the report over the sound of the generator outside as he went into the kitchen and poured himself a cup of coffee. The Vatican, the Colosseum—it was all gone. Just like New York. Just like Atlanta.

Jane looked like she might be sick as he sat down on the opposite end of the couch.

"How many people?" he asked, sipping his coffee, noticing it looked more like tea. It tasted like water, but it was hot and at least it smelled good. They were running out, and Jane was trying to make it last.

She looked down at her notebook. "Three million, two hundred and fifty thousand."

Was she keeping a news diary? She punched something into the calculator on her phone.

"Ruth and I went to Rome once," Ed said, sounding far away. "Some fancy restaurant had hired her to put together their wine list." He smiled. "We drank so much wine… The good stuff too. Couple hundred dollars a bottle. I don't know about her, but I was drunk for four days straight." He shook his head, as if not believing his own memory. "It was one of the best vacations in my life. Rome was a beautiful city…" His face fell. "It would break her heart to know it was gone."

Matt's stomach rumbled, and he rubbed it.

Jane finally looked up at him. "I made omelets. They're on the stove," she said, licking her pale lips and closing her notebook.

He went to find them, and she followed him into the kitchen.

"I need to go back down to the Veil," she said to his back as he lifted the lid of the pan. Inside were eggs with onions and mushrooms.

He shook his head. "Nope. That is a terrible idea. Is this ham?"

"It's Spam, and I already made the appointment."

He turned, and she was putting her shoes on. "What? When?" The sudden death of the Pope had half the world in a full-blown panic. This was not the day for them to be going down there.

"Yesterday."

"No. It's not safe," he argued, forgetting about the eggs. "The kids—"

"I'm not taking the kids," she interrupted, standing up.

He frowned. "Well, then why in the hell do you need to go down there?"

She opened her mouth, then closed it, either unable to find the words or not wanting to speak them. He suspected it was the latter.

"Jane, what the fuck is going on?" She had been weird since they got back yesterday. Distracted and… tense.

"I just need–there are things that Thomas and I have to discuss that we can't do in front of the kids—"

Matt rolled his eyes. "That's what the damn phone is for. Go outside if you want privacy. You don't have to go down there to do that."

Her eyes flashed. "Yes, I do, and I don't have to explain myself to you," she said in a tone he had not heard before. "You're not my…" She struggled to find the word and couldn't. "… anything." She threw her hands up in the air.

Something was very wrong. He could feel it.

"Oh really? I'm not anything to you?"

"You know that's not what I meant." Jane went for her purse.

"Don't go down there." He stepped in front of her.

"Why not?" she said, putting her hands on her hips.

He met her eyes. "Because I have a bad feeling about it."

He could tell that she did too, which only worried him more.

"I have to go. I have to do this."

"Then I'm going with you."

She shook her head. "I need you to stay with the kids."

"Why?"

"If something happens to me—"

"So, you *do* think something is going to happen." he accused, exasperated by how stubborn she was suddenly being.

"No. I–I don't know!" she whispered. "Look at the world, Matt. An alien invasion wouldn't surprise me at this point. I just need to know if zombies attack before I get back that… that my kids are safe. And I know they will be safe if they are with you." Her eyes softened. "Will you do this for me, please?"

"Do not play the sad kitten card."

"Matt… please."

It was the same look Bria gave him, and his will crumbled beneath it. "Fine."

"Good. Bria's bottle is in the fridge. Tell Maddy if—"

"What? You're leaving now?"

"The appointment is at eleven."

"I don't like this at all."

"I'll see you tonight." Jane grabbed her purse off the table and headed for the back door.

Matt stood in the middle of the kitchen as the screen slammed behind her.

He watched from the window as she backed the van up, turned around, and headed for the road.

You let her go again, moron.

He hit the cabinet, and the door popped open.

"Damn it."

Chapter Fifty-One

Day 42 // 4:30 p.m

MATT PACED THE LIVING ROOM. He hadn't been able to sit down since she left. Every time he did, he was reminded of the last time he had let her go. She'd been beaten half to death and almost gotten raped.

Jane was right. He wasn't her anything—but he wanted to be. Desperately. And while he wouldn't act on it if she didn't want him to, he at least needed to tell her the truth. Get it off his chest. And if anything happened to her before he got a chance to tell her he loved her… His sense of self-preservation writhed in fear. *Are you sure,* it asked? Yes, he was fucking sure. And yes, they were strong words, but they were also the *right* ones. He would not deny it anymore. He loved them. Jane and the kids. They had taken over his goddamn soul and he would die before he let anything happen to them. "Where's Aunt Jane?" Maddy asked, coming down the stairs for the first time all day.

"She went back down to the city," he said tersely.

She stared at him in surprise. "What? Really? What for?"

"I don't know. She wouldn't tell me." He pulled his hands through his hair. "She said she had something important to discuss with your uncle."

"And you're worried?" Maddy observed, her brows knitting together in a frown.

He paced. "Whatever it is, it's bad. I can feel it. She was weird all last night. Something happened, but she won't—"

Maddy's eyes widened in understanding, and he stopped.

"What? Do you know what happened?"

"No." Maddy wheeled around and hurried into the kitchen.

Matt was quick on her heels. "You're almost as bad a liar as your aunt," he called. The girl ignored him. He followed her out the back door. "Maddy!"

"I don't know—" She hurried across the porch, and down the stairs.

"Please," he begged.

She stopped at the bottom of the steps and turned. To his surprise, tears filled her eyes.

His anxiety shot through the roof as he met her at the bottom of the stairs.

"What is it? What's the matter?"

"She knows!" Maddy said helplessly, as she paced back and forth in front of him. "I wasn't sure if she saw, but she must have."

"What? What does she—"

Maddy shook her head, and her eyes overflowed with tears.

"Come on." Matt put a comforting hand on her arm. "Please. If she's in trouble, I want to help. Is it your Uncle Thomas?"

She looked up and nodded.

He knew it. He was afraid of something like—

"And my mom."

He frowned. *Her mom?*

"What does your mom—"

"They're having an affair! They have been for a… a long time, and I think Aunt Jane just figured it out."

Matt stared as his brain tried to process what the teenager was saying. The woman Thomas was having an affair with was Jane's *sister*?

He pulled his hands through his hair. *Holy fucking shit.*

He had not seen that coming, and from the look of things, neither had Jane.

"What? How do you know—"

Maddy turned away in shame. "I caught them together!" she admitted in disgust. "I-I ditched school one day my freshmen year." She wiped her eyes, and her voice shook. "My mom was supposed to be at yoga, and I came in the house and heard—"

Oh, Jesus. Matt pinched the bridge of his nose.

Maddy tucked her hands in the sleeve of her shirt and wiped her eyes again. "They were upstairs, and I was so… shocked. You know?"

Yes, he could imagine.

Maddy's eyes were wide as she whispered. "I was so embarrassed. I didn't know what to do so I-I just… I left, went back… to school."

"Maddy—"

"I didn't tell Aunt Jane, and I know I should have but…"

Well, that was it then. That was a pretty heavy epiphany for Jane to have at their little family reunion yesterday, and it totally explained her behavior. He hadn't noticed anything particularly obvious between Thomas and Sarah, but then but he didn't know them like Jane did, and if they were hiding it…

"It's not your fault, Maddy."

"But I didn't tell her!" she cried. "I thought about it a bunch of times, but then… then she got pregnant with Bria… and—It all just seemed so fucked up."

"It wasn't your place to."

"But—"

Matt wrapped her in a hug. "None of this is your fault." Something clicked, and a little piece of the Maddy puzzle slid into place. "Is that why you're not close to your aunt anymore?"

"Yeah." Maddy hung her head, wiping her eyes with her sleeve again. "I just feel like such a traitor…"

He held her back at arm's length. "Well, first of all, you are not a traitor. Second, you don't have to carry that secret alone anymore. Okay? I know it now, and I've got your back. And I'm telling you, you didn't do anything wrong. That's on your mom and your—"

Maddy burst into tears again. Matt stood still for a moment, totally confused. "What? Is there more?"

"No…" she paused. "Yes."

She wiped her eyes as the boys ran around the side of the garage. Tommy and Austin waved at him simultaneously and another puzzle piece slid in place and his eyes widened in disbelief.

No way.

"I-told Uncle Tom that I thought you liked Aunt Jane…"

If there was one thing that could drag Matt's attention away from the *brothers*, it was that. "What?" he choked.

"I didn't tell him you kissed her, but…"

He sighed. "You saw that, huh?"

"Yeah."

"Did the boys?"

"No, just me."

"I shouldn't have done that. It's not your fault, either. It's mine."

"No. I was just… jealous that she had you, while my boyfriend was… I fucked up. I'm sorry."

He looked down at her and his tear-soaked t-shirt. *Poor kid.*

"Don't worry about it. And don't let your aunt hear you swearing."

Maddy wiped her eyes and gave him a look that said she was plenty old enough to fucking swear.

Matt laughed. "I'm almost afraid to ask, but is there anything else you want to add? May as well get it out while you're on a roll."

She shook her head.

"You sure? I could probably take one more hit if I sit down first."

She smiled at his attempt at a joke. "No. That's it."

"Okay. Thank god."

"We're… good? Me and you?" she asked.

"We're good," he said.

"Are you going to tell Aunt Jane what I told Uncle Tom about you two?"

"Nope." He answered and turned back to the house, praying he made it inside before she changed her mind.

"Matt?"

He released a long sigh.

So close.

"Yeah?" he answered, keeping his back to her, not sure he wanted to turn around.

"*Do* you like Aunt Jane?" There was a pause. "Like for real?" she continued.

He turned slowly.

Maddy's perceptive eyes met his. She definitely was not a child anymore, and definitely old enough to say whatever she wanted.

Should he tell the truth? Or not?

Fuck it.

"I do," he said, watching her closely.

She nodded. "I thought so."

"Why do you ask?"

She studied him a moment before answering. "I think she likes you too, but…"

"But what?"

Maddy shrugged apologetically. "I think she gave up believing anyone could love her a long time ago."

They stared at each other for a moment.

"But if anyone can change her mind—" Maddy nodded at him. "—it'll be you. Oh, and by the way, her birthday is tomorrow."

"It is?"

"Yeah, but don't tell her I told you. She hates celebrating it."

They stared at each other for a moment.

It surprised Matt how much Maddy's vote of confidence meant to him. She had known Jane her whole life and was clearly an observant girl. If anyone would know, she would. And he was grateful for the heads up about her birthday. He had no idea what he could possibly do, but if anyone deserved a happy birthday this year, it was Jane. Especially after… Matt glanced at Austin and Tommy running through the corn, and his heart ached. *Yikes.*

"You are not going to say anything to Aunt Jane… about our conversation?" Maddy asked.

Matt shook his head. "This is between her and her husband. If she wants to talk about it, she'll tell me. If not…" he shrugged.

"Give her time."

It took him a second.

"She's not going to be feeling too good about herself for a while. It's a pretty big shot to your confidence when you find out… you know. I still feel like absolute shit. So go… easy on her. Give her time."

"Noted," he nodded toward the very astute young woman standing before him.

Maddy stuffed her hands in her pockets and headed toward the garden.

Her boyfriend was an idiot, Matt thought. Maddy was a really cool girl.

"Hey!" he called.

Maddy turned, tucking her red hair behind her ears.

"For the record, your ex was a real fucking ass-hat to break up with you."

Her face broke into a smile, and she turned back toward the garden. "I know. Thanks."

Chapter Fifty-Two

Day 42 // 6:23 p.m

MATT GRABBED Bria just as she reached for the step. He put her back in the middle of the living room for the fiftieth time, and tried Max, but his friend didn't answer.

When it beeped, he said, "Hey, call me back when you get this." Then hung up.

Like a twenty-pound suicidal snail, Bria got back on her hands and knees, and crawled through a slimy trail of her own drool back to the stairs.

What was it with babies trying to kill themselves? Every time he turned around, she was trying to off herself. Eat a rock. Climb the damn stairs. Stick her fat little fingers in an electrical socket. He supposed the latter wasn't so bad since there was no electricity but… Matt cocked his head. It looked like Bria had a mole on her chin. He bent down and saw legs attached to it.

"What in the—Gah!" Matt swiped at the dead spider and quickly wiped it on his pants. "Fucking hell—" he muttered, standing back up. "Where did that come from?" he demanded, putting his hands on his hips.

As usual, Bria stared up at him like he was speaking Chinese and happily ignored his question. She resumed her slippery trek to certain death and Matt sighed.

Please get home, he begged silently. His eyes were drawing back to the front windows as a truck drove by.

Home.

They had only been at the Hamiltons for a couple of weeks, but that's what it felt like. It felt like he, Mr. Hamilton—who insisted on being called Ed from now on—Jane, and the kids were a family. This was their home, and damn it, he didn't like it when they weren't *all* there.

Matt checked his watch. She should have been back hours ago, and she wasn't answering her phone.

He pulled Bria off the steps *again*, set her back in the middle of the living room floor *again*, and watched Austin and Tommy doing a puzzle at the kitchen table.

They were brothers. They had to be. He remembered the first time he met them. That's what he had thought. He tried to imagine how that would make Jane feel, but he couldn't.

Matt gave up and put Bria back in her playpen. He thought about what Maddy had said. He knew she was probably right about how Jane would be feeling when she got back.

The thing was, he was pretty sure she was already feeling like that before she knew. It made sense. How much confidence was a woman, whose husband cheated on her, going to have? He glanced at Austin again. It had been a long time since Thomas loved her—if he ever did. Did Jane even know what love was? Matt caught his reflection in the mirror on the wall. Did he? Was he brave enough to figure it out with her?

His phone buzzed in his pocket and he fished it out hastily. He pushed the green button and pressed the phone to his ear. "Hey, mom," he said. "How's it going?"

"Good. We are good. Just wanted to let you know they have widened the quarantine area, to include us, so we won't be able to make any more trips to the Veil to visit you until they lift it."

"Are you okay?" he asked. "Is dad —"

"Oh, we're fine, honey. Just wanted to hear your voice. Nothing has really changed really, and we haven't… you know, seen anyone being taken away. It's very quiet, in fact. Nothing to be worried about, I'm sure."

"How are you holding up?"

It took her a moment to answer. "This time with your father has been very good for us. I only wish—Well, wishes are for fishes, aren't they?"

A brief smile crossed Matt's lips before they sobered again. "Did they say anything? How do you know…"

"The news. They put up barricades and have police monitoring them. We aren't allowed outside, which we weren't doing anyway… Although, your father has been going out on your balcony to feed the birds. Your air conditioning is wonderful. I have been telling your father for years we ought to get one, and he's *finally* convinced." She laughed softly. "Better late than never, I suppose. You should see him lying on your couch in his underwear watching TV. I've never seen him so relaxed. You wouldn't recognize him."

Matt did not want to picture that.

"You're really okay, Mom? You sound kind of down."

"I'm fine. I wish I would have brought my quilting stuff, but… I'm okay. How are you doing, honey?"

"I am… surprisingly good."

His mom paused again. "She suits you better than Katie did."

He was going to deny it, but instead he said, "I think so too."

"I'm so happy for you, Matty."

"Thanks mom. I just wish—"

"How are Jane and the kids, and Mr. Hamilton?"

"Everyone is good. We are all fine."

As if on cue, Bria began to cry. She looked like she missed Jane as much as he did. She held up her fat little arms, indicating she wanted to be picked up.

"Okay, well, I just wanted to let you know what was going on," his mom said.

"Okay, thanks, just stay inside, and… don't… do anything."

"We won't. Your father sends his love. Say hello to everyone for us."

"I will. Love you, Mom."

"Love you too, Matty. We'll talk to you soon."

Bria continued to cry, and Matt sighed, dropping the phone in his pocket. He looked out the front window, over the driveway, and the field of corn, to the empty road. He looked at his watch again.

Matt knew he was going to lose his mind if he sat there any longer waiting for her, and his conversation with his mom had brought him down for some reason. "Anyone want to go explore the woods, maybe pick some boysenberries?" he asked out loud.

Chairs skidded across the vinyl floor in the kitchen as the boys jumped up.

He went to the closet and got Bria's baby carrier and scooped her up.

"Okay. Let's do this."

Chapter Fifty-Three

Day 42 // 6:47 p.m

JANE LEANED against the van door, staring out over the fields, glad to be home. She'd taken a slight detour down to the harbor in Harborview and had spent a few hours staring at the water, trying to wrap her mind around everything that had happened in the last two days. It was hard to believe, but it was over. Seventeen years of marriage, gone in a day.

She had confronted Thomas, and he had explained everything. Jane had listened quietly. To her surprise, by the time he got to the end, most of the anger she had brought with her was gone. She felt incredibly stupid for not noticing he was in love with another woman, and betrayed by the fact it was her own fucked-up sister, but… what could any of them do about it now? She and Sarah would never be close again, but then Jane realized the truth was, they'd never been close to begin with. Sarah was same selfish, manipulative, self-centered drama queen she'd always been. All Jane had really lost was the illusion of a person who never existed.

It had all been a lie, right from the beginning.

Sarah had always been a drama queen, and Jane had thought she had left that behind after college, but apparently, she had not. Sarah had dragged Thomas through it instead. And he put up with it because he loved her. After hearing the truth, what Jane mostly felt was sad. Sad for Thomas. Sad for herself.

The wind tugged at her hair as two hawks circled the field to the west, searching for food.

She had surprised herself and forgiven him, whatever that meant. They clearly hadn't needed her blessing before, but who knew how much time any of them had left?

Jane didn't want to spend it being angry and bitter. If things in Detroit took a turn for the worse… she didn't want her last words to the father of her children to be filled with hate.

It was an accident, at least initially. The whole thing had started the way most tragedies do, with one stupid error in judgment that spiraled out of control faster than any of them could stop it. She wouldn't hold that against Thomas. They had all been young and stupid — including her. They decided to wait until the Veil was down to tell the kids they were over.

Thomas had wished her luck with Matt just before he left. It hurt more than it probably should have, to hear him say those words. She nodded, and then left before he saw the tears in her eyes.

Jane took a deep, cleansing breath, feeling lighter and lonelier than she had in a long time. Then, she squared her shoulders and headed inside the farmhouse.

Ed was sitting at the kitchen table when she pushed the door open. He was twirling an empty wine glass. The house was quiet.

She sat down beside him. "Care if I join you?" she asked, dropping her purse and keys on the table.

He shook his head.

"Where are the kids?"

"Matt took them for a walk in the woods out back."

"How are you doing?" she asked. His melancholy mood seemed to match hers. "I know it's a lot, having all of us here—"

"I love it," he interrupted. "I'd have gone crazy in this big old house by myself." He spun the glass again. "I'm just…"

"You miss Ruth?"

He set the glass down. "Yeah. And most days, I remember that she's gone, and I feel sad, but I'm okay. But then some days… It's like I forget, and it's like she's just died all over again."

Jane covered his hand with hers. "Can I ask you something?"

"Sure."

"How did you know she was the one?"

Ed looked down at the glass in his hand. His mind was somewhere far away as he twirled the stem beneath his fingers. "You drink wine?"

Jane laughed. "I'm a spoiled housewife–or I used to be, anyway. Of course, I do."

He gave her a look. "You've never seemed spoiled to me." Ed hoisted himself from his chair and headed for the basement door. "Follow me then."

Jane followed him down the stairs. She hadn't been down here yet. She gasped when he flipped the switch. A small crystal chandelier hung above a wine barrel table in the center of the room, illuminating hundreds of bottles lying neatly in racks lining the low stone walls.

"Oh, my god," she breathed.

Matt had not been kidding. It was like she had stepped into a Napa Valley dream.

"Ruth was a sommelier. She was world-renowned," he said proudly. "This was her collection."

Jane stepped closer, inspecting the photos that hung on the wall at the bottom of the steps. One showed a picture of Ruth looking like a nineteen-eighties Vogue cover model. She was gorgeous and so full of life. Jane recognized the woman next to her.

"Is that…?"

"Yep. Princess Diana."

"No kidding." Jane walked along the wall, smiling at the next picture of Ruth and Ed in what must have been their early twenties. Ruth was in a tailored suit and heels, and he was in a shirt and pants almost identical to the one he was wearing now.

"She was just as comfortable in a ballgown as a pair of muddy dungarees, and she didn't care that I wasn't. That's the photo from Italy, by the way."

Jane laughed, not quite believing his wife let him get away with that outfit in Rome. "You two were quite the couple."

"That we were. Pick a bottle," he encouraged.

She turned. "Oh no, I couldn't."

"Of course you can. What am I gonna do with all this besides drink it?"

"But—"

"But nothing. Pick one. What do you like? Red? White? Earthy, fruity, buttery, or crisp?"

Jane raised her eyebrow and pulled a chardonnay from the shelf. "Are you sure?" she asked.

"Of course, I'm sure."

She read the label, put it back, and retrieved another bottle, then another. Some of the bottles were thirty years old.

"When she retired four years ago, we started drinking these. Two bottles a week. Tuesdays and Fridays. And when she died, I thought… how am I supposed to enjoy these without her? And I think… You're gonna call me a superstitious old man, but she's always been my guardian angel. I'm convinced she sent me you and the kids, and Matthew."

Jane turned, her eyes filling with tears. "We are the lucky ones."

Ed pulled two glasses out of a rack and set them on the table. "Will you share a drink with me?"

Jane looked down at the Sauvignon Blanc in her hand. The label was written in French. "This one?"

"Perfect." Ed smiled at her, then opened it and poured each of them a glass.

Jane sat at the table, swirling her wine, and remembering the woman she once was. The one who was married to a wealthy lawyer, and lived in a four-thousand square foot house. The woman who got a mani-pedi every week, spent two hundred dollars on a haircut, and thought she was better than country folk like Ed, who chose open spaces over luxury ones. That Jane had slowly begun fading away the moment the Veil went up.

She stopped the glass. *That* Jane had taken her last breath this afternoon as she listened to her husband confess he had been in love with her sister for almost twenty years.

"A toast." Ed held up his glass.

"To the past or the future?"

Ed smiled at her sadly. "Both of those seem a little iffy to me at the moment. How about we make a toast to now instead?"

Now. Yes, that was easier than thinking about everything that had happened. It was certainly easier to think about than what she was going to do now that her marriage was over.

"To now." She touched her glass to his and took a sip. The cool, sweet taste was cut with just the right amount of tartness and acidity. Across from her, Ed, in his worn-out jeans and faded plaid shirt, twirled his wine. Like a true expert, he sniffed it, *then* took a noisy sip, rolling it around in his mouth a couple of times before swallowing.

Jane laughed.

He winked at her. "I learned from the best." He took another, more normal sip. "But to answer your question before… As you can tell from the pictures, Ruth and I weren't all that much alike. So, you might wonder how someone like her could end up with someone like me."

Jane smiled guiltily. "Well…"

"But really, we weren't so different. At least not in things that mattered. We were good, honest people. We were passionate about what we did. And what we did really wasn't as different as one might think. She knew wine, which is a product of the climate and the soil, and I knew crops which were the same. We were passionate about each other. She was my best friend. Everything else, style, age —" Ed's glance was loaded. "… preferences in music or food, none of that mattered."

Jane smiled slightly and took another sip of her wine, tasting pear and honeysuckle.

Ed stared at his glass. "She was smarter than me, and my god, there was not a thing in heaven or earth that woman didn't have an opinion on. Blew my damn mind the things she knew. I could listen to her talk for hours."

He chuckled. "She could talk shop, the impact of rainfall on vines, on crops. Altering the acidity of the soil, harvest, and then turn around and discuss fine art, or the rise of rap music in Detroit. Seems to me most people pick one way to be, and then they shut out everything else. Up or down. Black or white. But Ruth wasn't black or white, she was both, and every color of the rainbow in between. She lived by her own rules. And she didn't care about what anyone thought. She loved sipping mulled wine on Champs-Élysées at Christmas, and the corn farmer from Michigan who was walkin' beside her."

"So that's how you knew then? That she was the one? Because you could talk?"

Ed laughed. "Well, no, not exactly. I also had a friend, Bill Myers, that I could talk to for hours too, but I didn't want to marry him."

Jane laughed. "So, what was it, then?"

"It was so many things, Jane. She saw me. The man I aspired to be, the one I felt like inside. And I saw her. But, if I'm bein' honest, the main thing was…" Ed blushed and took a big sip, leaning back in his chair, remembering. "… when she touched me… It was like goddamn lightning through my veins."

Matt.

"It never happened like that with anyone before her," he said, sounding far away. "And never with anyone else in the fifty-four years we were married."

They sat quietly for a while longer, just sipping their wine. She and Thomas had never talked about anything but the kids and his work. As for what they had in common, well, there wasn't much. Just the accident… and the kids. One sad thing. Two happy ones.

The sound of footsteps upstairs pulled her away from her thoughts. Jane heard the faint sound of voices. She quickly swallowed the last drop of wine in her glass and got up.

"I'm always here for you if you ever want to talk about her. If you want to remember," she said, squeezing his shoulder, but Ed was somewhere else.

She headed up the stairs.

"That's what he feels for you," Ed said.

Jane paused, then retreated a couple of steps, so she could see him below the low ceiling. "What?"

He turned slightly in his seat. "Matthew. I see the way he looks at you."

Jane didn't know what to say. She knew how *she* felt, but… "I don't think—"

"I don't know everything, but I know love when I see it. And Jane"—he turned and met her eyes—"That boy loves you."

Ed's words rang in her head as Jane met Tommy at the top of the stairs. He was holding a white, plastic five-gallon bucket between his hands.

"Look what I got for you, Mom!" he said with a smile.

Jane peered in and immediately jumped back.

"Get that thing out of the house!" she yelled as a little green snake wiggled up the side.

Matt and Austin laughed as Maddy passed her with Bria strapped to her chest and gave her arm an unusually affectionate squeeze.

"Come on, Aunt Janie. It's just an adorable little snake," she said, on her way to the living room.

"Jesus Christ! Get that thing away—" Jane pressed her hand to her chest and backed down the stairs.

"Alright, your plan to terrify your mom worked. Take him back outside." Matt ordered.

Tommy and Austin gave her a devilish grin before retreating out the back door.

Matt and Jane stood near the top of the stairs. She stared at the kind, handsome, incredibly hilarious man who had suddenly become such an anchor in their lives.

"I've gotta say, I'm really digging the way you're looking at me right now, Jane Moore."

That was good, because she was kind of digging the way she felt. A month without alcohol, and she was gloriously buzzed off a single glass of wine.

Matt's eyes fell to the empty wineglass in her hand.

"Did I miss happy hour?"

A blush crossed her cheeks, and she actually enjoyed it. "Ed is still down there if you—"

"How did it go?" Matt interrupted. "Did you accomplish... whatever it was you needed to?" His question felt more loaded than it should have, and Jane frowned. "I'm sorry I kind of disappeared on you. And yes, I did."

"And how are you feeling?" he asked carefully.

The wine took over, and she broke into a smile. There were parts of her that would hurt for a while. But most of her was... "Fine." She had her kids, all four of them, and she was there with him, and Ed. They had food, shelter, clothes, and room to breathe.

He studied her for a moment. "Good."

Jane set the glass in the sink and turned back toward Matt. Ed's words echoed in her head.

I see the way he looks at you.

He was doing it right now.

But this wasn't the same as what Ed and Ruth had shared. Jane's heart pounded as he shrugged out of his jacket and hung it on the hook, his eyes never leaving hers. No, this was different.

He doesn't even have to touch you for the lightning to strike. He just had to look.

"Jane?" he asked, breaking the spell.

She blinked. "What did you have for dinner?"

"Spaghetti. Want to have a glass of wine with me?"

"Absolutely," she answered far too quickly. "After I put the kids to bed?"

He nodded, and she noticed a cocky smile hiding beneath his beard. "After *we* put the kids to bed."

Handsome Underwear God wants to help you put your children to bed?

Jane broke into a grin. He really was a god. "After *we* put the kids to bed."

Matt grabbed her hand gently pulling her toward the living room. She followed. *Happily.* "You take the drool machine," he nodded toward Bria, who was gnawing on the side of her playpen, "... and I'll take the boys." He held up his hand. "Fair warning, you're going to have to change her before jammies. I don't know what was going on in her diaper on the way in, but it sounded like a bear and a lion mud wrestling. And I want nothing to do with the aftermath of that battle. You're on your own."

Jane burst out laughing and picked up her baby girl.

PUTTING the kids to bed that night was easier than it had been in months. They were truly exhausted from whatever they had done all day.

Matt was standing with his back against the counter when Jane reentered the kitchen. The light from outside was fading quickly. In the candlelight they were now using at night, he looked like a dream. In jeans and a white t-shirt, he was as handsome as they came. The two long-stemmed glasses and the bottle of wine she and Ed had been drinking, sitting next to him on the counter, didn't hurt either. The corners of his eyes crinkled in a smile as she met them.

How had she gotten so lucky?

"Hey." She leaned against the sink. "I wanted to say thanks for today, watching the kids, for helping me put them to bed." She watched the candle jar on the table flicker and cast shadows on the ceiling. "And thanks again for thinking ahead about all the candles and stuff. I don't know what we would have done —"

"Sure." He said, pouring them each a glass and handing her one.

"And I wanted to apologize for the last few days. I get a little caught up in my head sometimes..."

"A little?" he asked with a raised brow, sniffing his wine.

She smiled. "But you gave me space to do what I needed. I am... grateful."

Jane took a deep breath and set her glass down on the counter. *It's now or never*, she told herself. Her arms shook as she timidly wrapped them around him. "I want to know you, Matt," she whispered, squeezing her eyes shut against the terror of being so bold. She was not good at this. She pressed her forehead to his chest, still feeling guilty even though there was no longer a reason for it. He inhaled sharply, and his heart pounded beneath her ear.

Matt set his glass on the counter. His arms closed around her, and Jane thought she might faint.

"I'll tell you anything," he whispered back, stroking her hair. The blood in her veins began to boil.

"I am so glad you're here and I'm not alone," she said against his shirt.

Matt kissed the top of her head. "I am too."

Neither of them moved for a moment, and Jane savored the weird mixture of chemicals spilling into her blood. Then Matt looked at his watch and pushed her back.

"Are you running late for something?" she asked with a frown.

"Yes. But let's finish our wine. Whatever you had to do today with Thomas, it went well?" he asked.

Jane leaned back against the counter beside him. "It went."

"I noticed you dressed up again."

Jane looked down at the blue satin blouse she wore. Yes, she supposed she had.

"May I ask why?"

She sighed. "I don't know. Not to impress Thomas, if that's what you're asking. I am finally done trying to get him to notice me. Today was about... I did it for myself."

"Well, for the record, I think you look really cool with two eyebrows."

She shot him a dirty look and nudged his side with her elbow. She'd plucked her eyebrows herself a couple of days ago. He'd noticed that?

He frowned. "Well, now they look like one again."

She tried not to laugh and covered it with a sip of her wine.

He took a curl of her hair in his hand, then touched the red tips of her fingers. "For the record, you are beautiful either way, but my favorite look… is you in the rain."

"Ha ha," she said as her heart galloped in her chest. *Lightning.* He was doing it again.

"No, I'm serious." For once, she could tell he was.

Jane frowned.

"The day we took Mrs. Hamilton up to Sandusky. You looked at me and—" he touched her cheek. A shiver raced down her spine, and her terror returned. She wanted him, but—

"I'm not going to hurt you, Jane." His eyes searched hers.

"I know. I've just…" How did she explain that she'd never been with anyone but Thomas? It was happening so fast.

She stepped away back and looked out the window. "Do you like it here?" Twilight had slipped into night. She could see the trees behind the barn, and the corn waved in the breeze that seemed to blow straight from the plains all the way across the Midwest. She loved it here. But… Did he?

He frowned. "What do you mean?"

She turned back to face him. "Are you happy here?"

"Here at Ed's?"

"Here with… us."

"Why would you ask that?"

It was one of the things she'd contemplated that afternoon by the lake. She was happy, and the kids were happy, but… Matt's whole life had been down in the city. He hadn't been back home in ten years, and she knew it had to do with his father, but still she wanted to know. "I don't know. I just never asked you and I'm curious—"

"Yeah, I am," he said without hesitation.

She searched his eyes. "Are you sure?"

He swallowed his wine and looked her right in the eye. "Yes, I'm positive. Now finish your wine."

She drained her glass, feeling relieved.

He took her glass, set it on the counter, and pulled a flashlight from the drawer. "Okay, come on. I got you something."

Jane followed him onto the back porch.

"Got me something?"

He flipped on the flashlight. "Sorry, didn't have any wrapping paper," he held out a plastic grocery bag with something heavy in it.

Wrapping paper? "What's going on?" she asked, putting her hands on her hips.

"Tommy's not here," Matt said, jiggling the bag. "And that look doesn't work on me. Come on, open your present."

It only took her a second to put two and two together. She rolled her eyes and groaned. "Who told you?"

"Told me what?" Matt asked, shaking the bag again.

"Was it Maddy?"

"Open your damn birthday present, Jane."

She grabbed the bag, reached inside, and pulled out an empty jar. It looked suspiciously like the one she'd washed this morning. "You got me an old mason jar?" she asked. It had to be Maddy that had sold her out. "Oh Matt, you know me so well," she said dryly.

"Ha. You're hilarious," he said, undeterred. "And I'm offended."

"Why are you offended?"

"Because that is a *magic* mason jar, and it costs twice as much as a regular one, and you didn't even notice."

Jane laughed. "Magic?"

"Come on," he said, flipping off the flashlight, leading the way down the stairs. "And don't forget your magic jar."

She followed him through the dim moonlight, down the steps, past the barn, into the corn, toward the trees. Where the hell were they going? It was so dark she could barely—

"Oh!" she stopped as a little blinking light flew between them. "Wait! Matt…" she whispered.

Another caught her periphery, and she turned.

Then another.

And another.

Jane twirled as hundreds of tiny lights turned on and off all around them.

"Surprise," Matt said, walking back and forth through the grass, coaxing them into the air.

"Oh…"

She had seen some beautiful things in her life, but none came close to the fragile miracle rising into the surrounding air.

"Oh, Matt…"

His warm hand touched hers, as he felt for the jar and took it. He unscrewed the cap, and she watched breathlessly as he crept up on a light and slowly closed the jar around it.

He handed it back to her, and she stared at the tiny little bug inside. "See. I told you. Magic—" he whispered. "Hey, what's the matter?"

She didn't know why she was crying. She shook her head.

"I was going to let it go—" he said, trying to take the jar back.

"No, it's not that. It's just…" she started, then realized she didn't know what she wanted to say. She could feel it all, but…

He wiped the tear from her cheek. "I know. Come on, it's your turn."

He knew? *What does he know?* She looked back down at the jar. "Thank you for this."

"My pleasure."

She unscrewed the lid, then Jane Moore, one-time socialite, and ex-city girl, spent the eve of her forty-first birthday tromping through the woods, in the dark, catching fireflies.

Chapter Fifty-Four

Day 43 // 9:33 p.m

MATT RUBBED his hands together and then pressed his palms toward the flames. Jane sat across from him, looking content. Her eyes glittered in the firelight.

Ed got up from the stump beside him, holding a wine glass. "I'm gonna head on in. Happy birthday, Jane." He held up the empty glass and nodded at her.

"Thanks for the bread and the cheese and the wine," she said sincerely. "Want the flashlight?"

"Nah, the moon is bright enough. I'll be fine. And I don't know what you're thankin' me for. You cook the best food I've ever eaten, you clean the house, manage my laundry… You kids enjoy now."

Matt watched him cross the yard and head up the back steps. "How was your birthday?" he asked, turning back to her.

He had surprised her first thing, with a pound of coffee he'd stolen on one of his raids, and she'd sat at the kitchen table looking as content as he'd ever seen her and drank a whole pot while he and Maddy made pancakes for breakfast.

Then they'd gone for a walk in the woods and the boys had collected her a beautiful bouquet of wildflowers, and before dinner, Ed had surprised her with a fresh-baked loaf of bread and something called butter cheese, both made by the local Amish. Then he had opened a 1968 Cabernet Sauvignon from the Loire Valley, that she mooned over like it was the best thing she'd ever tasted.

Finally, after dinner, and two rousing games of dominoes,

Maddy offered to put the kids to bed, so the adults grabbed another bottle of wine and headed out for a bonfire.

She smiled and looked up at the starry sky. "It was the best birthday I've had in years… maybe even ever. Thank you."

Ed was right. It was he who should be thanking her. For bringing purpose back into his life, for making him feel whole, for turning a box of macaroni and cheese into a goddamned culinary masterpiece.

Jane got up and threw a couple more logs on the fire. "Thomas always did this," she said. "I don't think I ever lit a fire the whole time we were married." She laughed sadly. "Literally or figuratively, it turns out."

That *was* the reason she went down to the Veil then—to confront Thomas.

She sat back down across from him and pulled the blanket back around her shoulders.

Matt poured himself another glass of whatever the hell delicious wine this was—He turned the bottle and read the label again. Pinot Noir—and passed it to her.

"When we first got up here, I tried to do a couple of fires with the kids and… failed miserably. I had been failing miserably at a lot of things for a long time…"

She filled her glass and passed it back. He waited, sensing more.

"I meant what I said last night, Matt. I want to know you. And… I want you to know me. Who–what I really am before…" She took a sip.

"Before?"

She didn't answer, but he could guess. She meant before they became intimate. And it was about goddamn time.

"I already know who you are," he said.

She shook her head. "No. I don't think you do." She laughed. "I don't even know anymore."

He decided not to argue with her. "Well then, ask me anything, Jane Moore. Let's get to know each other."

She took another small sip and stared into the fire a minute before she bcgan. "How about we take turns?"

"Sure."

She met his eyes. "How old are you?"

Why was it always the older person the age bothered? "Twenty-eight."

She inhaled sharply and looked like she was going to cry. "I'm forty-one."

"I don't care how old you are, so that doesn't count as my question."

"Sorry."

"No need to apologize. How did you meet your husband?"

Her smile seemed sad. "My version, or what really happened?"

"Let's start with yours."

"I met Thomas at a… a party. I was with Sarah. She is two years younger than me, and we were always… opposites, even when we were kids. She liked sports. I liked Barbies. She was outgoing and friendly, I was not. She had no desire to go to college. I was in my second year of grad school." Jane stared into the fire as she spoke. "The party was on campus, but the friends were hers, not mine. I didn't have many friends back then, and I definitely didn't party. She was beautiful and confident, and a flirt. As I stood in the corner with my bourbon and coke, she walked right up to the quarterback of the football team—his name was Darren and he ended up playing for Kansas City for a couple of years—and just kissed him. In front of everyone."

"I figured she'd be going home with him, so I decided to call it a night. I sidled my way onto the dance floor where they were… grinding against each other—"

Matt laughed.

"—and told Sarah I was leaving. Just then, Thomas walked up to us. Naturally, I assumed he wanted to talk to her, but his eyes were glued to mine as he approached. I was so flattered. I never caught the eye of guys like him…"

Jane glanced at him, and his insides warmed. *Until now*. That was what she was thinking.

"He asked me to dance and pulled me away from Sarah before I could even answer. The next thing I knew, I was swaying with this incredibly handsome man who couldn't keep his hands off me. It was surreal. He had been on the football team the previous year, a linebacker, and had come with his friends, but he wasn't in school anymore. He had already taken the bar, and was working at an entry-level position at one of the more prestigious firms in the city. I was pretty drunk at that point, but to be honest, I was more in shock. He was the kind of guy that usually went for girls like Sarah. Only he didn't. He walked right past her and… Looking back, I think I was jealous of her. She had a way with men that just…"

Jane leaned forward, resting her elbows on her knees, swirling the glass between her palms. "She was beautiful and carefree. She worried about nothing and no one but herself. I was the opposite. I worried a lot. I analyzed everything before I did anything. *Except* for that night." She tapped her finger on her knee. "*Except* with Thomas. One thing led to another, and we ended up back at his place. I'd messed around a lot in high school, but um… he was my first. And my last."

Matt winced.

She's never slept with anyone but Thomas? That actually explained a lot, particularly why he got mixed signals every time he touched her. "Wait, how old were you?" he asked.

"Twenty-three. And it was… fine. It wasn't quite what I expected, but then, I didn't know what to expect exactly so… I called Sarah the next morning, you know, to brag a little. I gave her all the sordid details…"

Matt waited while she took another sip. She stared into the fire, unblinking.

"Long story short, a month later… I found out I was pregnant. That one-in-a-million risk of pregnancy with a condom… that was me. I saw him put it on. I know he did, but somehow one got through, and I wasn't on birth control at the time because I wasn't having sex, so..."

She shrugged. "It just didn't work. And Thomas was–is a good guy. So, we started dating after that, and the rest is..."

So, he got her pregnant?

But... the math didn't work. If she was twenty-three when she got pregnant, then Tommy would be almost twenty years old.

"My turn," she said, pulling him from his calculations.

"Shoot."

"Why don't you and your dad get along?"

The wind had died down, and the crickets were almost deafening. Matt thought about how best to explain it. He looked back over his shoulder and could just make out the top of the barn and the silo in the darkness.

"My dad is a farmer, through and through. As were my grandpa and his father. Dirt men, I used to call them. I remember the three of them sitting around the kitchen table, dusty and sunburnt, talking for hours about whether to plant soybeans or corn, and..."

Matt looked up at the sky as he had so many times as a boy. "I wanted something different. I wanted to see the world. I wanted to do something meaningful with my life, not spend it in filthy jeans, riding a tractor back and forth across a field."

"What did your dad think of that?"

He laughed. "What do you think? He was pissed. Who was going to take over the farm when he retired? How dare I turn my back on the family legacy?"

"So, what did you—"

"The weekend after graduation, I packed a bag, told him I was going to Cedar Point with friends, and enlisted."

"Oh god, your poor mom."

"Yeah, she wasn't too happy, but my dad was... still is, pissed."

Jane gave him a sad smile from across the fire.

"What?"

"And now you're right back where you started. Stuck here—"

"Don't put words in my mouth, Jane. I'm not stuck. I am exactly where I want to be." Matt thought about his dad. "I get why he did it now, because I feel the same way."

Everything you want is right here.

"But—"

"It's my turn."

She let it go.

"The real version."

Jane drained her glass and set it beside her. "The real version is Thomas and Sarah had actually been casually dating for about a month before that party, and he really liked her. Like a lot. She liked him too, but Sarah liked to make boys jealous. She liked to play hard to get."

Jane took a deep breath.

"She liked them to beg, and they usually did. So, to spice things up, she made a move on his best friend." Jane kicked the ground with her foot. "But instead of begging, Thomas got even… He asked me to dance."

"So, you didn't know about him? Before?"

"No. Sarah and I were in pretty different circles back then. She was more into partying, and I was so busy with grad school. In addition to my classes, I was teaching an intro class for Robert, and working on my thesis."

Matt remembered his previous question. "But if you were pregnant—"

"It's my turn."

"Fine."

"Have you ever been married?"

That was an easy one. "No." He could have left it at that, but he added—just for transparency—"I was engaged once, though."

"For how long?"

"Two years."

"What was her name?"

"Katie."

"Who called it off?"

"Technically? Me, but we were both—"

"Why?"

"That is way too many questions. It's my turn."

Jane got up and walked around to his side to retrieve the bottle of wine.

"Where is your baby, Jane?"

She froze.

The grief on her face almost brought him to tears.

"I lost her."

Matt pulled her on the log next to his and intertwined their fingers. She didn't seem to notice. "How?"

"I was eight months pregnant. Thomas had been out drinking with his friends, and he called me to pick him up. It was December, right before Christmas, and… the roads were icy."

Matt squeezed her hand. "You can stop. I don't need—"

"I want you to know," she said, wiping her eyes. "It was a conversion van. Hit a patch of black ice, and t-boned us in the intersection."

She swiped at her eyes again, and her hand settled on her belly. "She was dead by the time we got to the hospital. But… I still had to deliver her."

"Jane—"

"They asked me if I wanted to wait for labor to start naturally, and I did… because I didn't want to let her go… because I couldn't believe she was really gone." Jane gasped like she couldn't breathe. "But Thomas insisted I be induced, that it was better to get it over with right away."

Tears stung Matt's eyes as he listened. "They offered me pain medication, but I didn't want it. Because that was the only journey we were going to take together, and I didn't want to miss any of it… I was in labor for six—" Her voice broke. "Six and a half hours. Thomas left when I asked to hold her." Jane smiled through her tears. "They wrapped her in a blanket and put a little white cap on her head, and I sang to her, and held her. She was so beautiful. And all I wanted was to be dead too, so I could be with her."

Matt wiped his eyes and stared into the fire. The utter horror she must have felt.

"Jane, I am so…"

She sniffled beside him. "M-my turn," she said, shaking her head and pulling her hand from his.

"Why?" she asked.

"Why what?" he asked, wiping his leaky eyes and pouring the last of the wine into her glass.

"Why did you call off your engagement?"

He handed Jane the glass. "Things just weren't the same after this." Matt extended his left leg and rubbed his thigh.

She hesitantly placed her hand over his again, sliding her fingers through his.

"For her or for you?"

"I was just so angry, and she… couldn't help but feel sorry for me."

Jane was quiet.

"My turn."

She nodded. "Is the baby the one… someone else helped you bury?"

Jane nodded. "My mom did. I just couldn't… Everything was different after that. Everything seemed so… trivial, so pointless. I just wanted my daughter, and she was dead. I felt so… empty. I couldn't even get out of bed. I started having panic attacks. I was a mess. But Thomas saw it as a sign. He wasn't happy we'd lost our baby, but he was still in love with Sarah. He thought it was a second chance, to come clean and start over. According to him, after Sophia was gone, he wanted to tell me the truth, but…"

"Your sister wouldn't let him."

She nodded. "She loved him, but she was also twenty-one and selfish and stupid. Our dad was supporting her while she sowed her wild oats, and she was afraid if he found out, he'd cut her off.

Thomas tried to convince her it was for the best, but she wouldn't listen. She insisted dad would never forgive them. He knew he was losing her, so he threatened to tell me and our parents everything if she didn't. She called his bluff, married the first guy she met, and got pregnant. They lasted less than a year."

"Maddy?"

She nodded. "Thomas was pretty devastated and confused, so he married me like we'd planned and… remained in love with her."

"When did the affair start?"

"He said it was innocent at first. He didn't intend to do it. After Sarah broke up with Nick, he would stop by to check on her and Maddy. Bring her take out. I guess they kind of hung out a lot, but I don't remember much from that time. I was highly medicated for almost three years, and I couldn't bear to see Sarah with Maddy after losing Sophia. It was just too hard." Jane sniffled. "My parents supported Sarah while she went to community college. My mom used to watch Maddy. But after they died and left her the house and pretty much everything, that's when she and Thomas began the affair. He wanted to leave me, but…" Jane shook her head. "Sarah was just starting out in interior design, and most of her clients were old friends of the family. She was worried about her reputation. She was worried about his. When she got pregnant with Austin, they broke it off for a while. But then…"

Jane shook her head, probably wondering how she hadn't seen it.

"He loves her. I can see it now. She begged him to keep it quiet. So, he did for a long time. But after Bria–Thomas said he was just so sick of the lying. He just couldn't do it anymore. To me, or himself. He promised Sarah he would keep their relationship secret, but he just couldn't be with me anymore. He was looking at apartments when the Veil went up."

Matt pulled his hands through his hair. *What a fucking mess.* He actually felt kind of sorry for Thomas, supposing it was all true.

"Your sister is a real piece of work."

Jane huffed a laugh. “Yeah. She is. To tell you the truth, they probably deserve each other.”

“Your turn,” he whispered.

She opened her mouth a couple of times, then closed it.

“Out with it. I told you, I’ll tell you anything.”

She rubbed her thumb absently over the back of his hand. “Who… was dying in your arms when I barged into your bedroom?”

His eyebrow went up. Usually, people asked how he lost his foot—as if that was the only thing that mattered. Not who else was there or if anyone else might have lost more.

“His name was Antonio Ruiz. He was my best friend in high school. We enlisted together. I didn’t tell him to do it, but I know I inspired him to join. Unlike my family, his family was proud. They had a party for him… and everything. He has–had–a wonderful family.”

Matt tried to hold the memories at a distance, but they were closing in fast. “We served together for seven years and went through some harrowing stuff, you know. So, it was pretty fucked up when… We had just gotten off leave. We hadn’t even been in Afghanistan for four fucking hours.”

Jane gasped quietly beside him.

“They buried the IED in the road. We keep a lookout for them. We know what to look for, but… I just missed it. He and I were in the front. It happened so goddamn fast.”

As it always did, the sounds and smells came back. Burned flesh, the odd ringing in his ears as he held onto his friend, whose insides lay sprawled beside them from the hole in his stomach. Looking into Tony’s bloody eyes, screaming for help—

“You can stop,” Jane said, and he could tell she was crying.

He blinked back tears. His jaw was tight as he continued. “I want you to know.”

“It was… obvious that he wasn’t going to make it. But I couldn’t leave him there to die alone. He was my best—I didn’t know where the other guys were, if they were alive, or if we were going to be under fire. I screamed for help, but no one came. I remember laying in the shadow of that damn Jeep and watching my best friend die. Then I looked up and saw my boot. With my foot still in it. It's crazy, but until that point, I hadn't even realized I'd lost it. Things got a little foggy then, and I guess I passed out." He took a shaky sip. "The next thing I knew, I was back in the States. I don't remember a damn thing in between."

Matt finished his wine with a gulp. It was the first time he had told anyone about Tony. It was the first time anyone had asked about him. "In one day, one minute, I lost my best friend. I lost my damn foot, and my career."

"They won't take you back?"

He shook his head. "Nope."

"Would you go if you could?"

Before he would have said 'yes' in a heartbeat, but now… he studied Jane in the firelight. Now he wasn't so sure. Matt shrugged. "Why speculate on what will never be?"

"But—"

"My turn."

"Fine."

He turned his body to face her. "I'm going to collect my raincheck."

She turned slowly. "What rain check? And that's not a question."

He cupped her face in his hand and leaned closer. "At the beach the other day. You were going to kiss me."

"I was?" she asked. Her entire body shook beneath his hands. Or was he the jittery one?

"And my question is"—he tucked her hair behind her ear—"Are you going to"—his lips barely touched her, and a jolt of electricity raced down his spine—"kiss me back"—he brushed her lips again, and she shuddered—"Jane Moore?"

She answered with her mouth, and he almost fell off the log he was perched on. Matt pressed his lips to hers as she leaned into him and gasped softly as her lips moved against his. He could taste her hunger. It matched his own. He pulled her off her seat, and she fell to her knees between his legs. With one hand on his thigh and the other anchored in his hair, Jane pressed her body up into his as his tongue swept into her mouth. He grabbed her ass, lifting her, pulling her against him. *Oh god.*

"Oh god," she moaned.

"I have been wanting to do this for so—"

She cut him off, pulling his mouth back to hers with both hands. Their lips collided again, and every cell in his body lit up until Matt was sure he was glowing. His hands roamed her body, the small of her back, the sides of her breasts, the curve of her neck, giddy after finally being granted access.

"I want you, Matt Patterson," she said in a voice that nearly undid him.

"I want you—"

And then they both froze and turned toward the house.

Another cry pierced the night.

"Bria," Jane said, pulling away, and glancing up at their bedroom window.

Bria cried again, and they stared at each other.

No, no, no…

She wailed again, and Matt imagined her up in her crib, tears running down her fat little cheeks, giving him her sad puppy eyes…

"Fuck."

"I'm sorry," she apologized.

"No, go."

She planted a quick kiss on his lips. Then she pressed her hands against his thighs and stood up.

"Is it just your kids who have terrible timing, or are they all like this?"

Jane laughed, wiping the dirt off the knees of her jeans. "I'm pretty sure all kids."

Matt huffed. "To be continued, Jane Moore."

She nodded with a shy smile and rushed inside.

Matt looked down at his crotch and wondered how in the hell he was supposed to get to sleep tonight after what had just happened. Especially with her sleeping—one *really* annoying pillow-length away—in the same damn bed.

He gathered up their glasses and the empty bottle and kicked dirt over the fire. Shaking his head, Matt headed for the house.

Chapter Fifty-Five

Day 45 // 7:46 a.m

"CAN we do away with the pillow?" he asked as soon as her eyes opened.

Jane blinked, then stared blatantly at his naked chest. He'd been sleeping with a shirt on and sweatpants for propriety's sake, but they had made out the other night… Well, it was July and hotter than shit, and he was much more comfortable this way.

"What do you mean do away with it?" she asked, propping herself up and glancing at Bria, who was playing quietly in her crib.

"I mean, take it to the nearest bridge and drop it over the side. I mean run it over it with a combine, I mean pour a gallon of very expensive gasoline —"

She threw her head back and laughed. "You are heartless."

"No, that damn pillow is heartless, and I am tired of being jealous of a sack full of duck feathers. It's humiliating."

Jane met his eyes. "Can we keep it a little while longer? While we… get to know each other?"

"I thought we got to know each other the other night," he said, taking the pillow and throwing it over his shoulder dramatically.

Jane's eyes widened, not in terror specifically, but something close. He reminded himself that she'd only ever been with Thomas. Matt sighed as he pulled her into the crook of his arm. And it had only been a day. She needed more time, and he could be patient. "Fine, we'll keep the damn pillow, but it goes on the floor during snuggle time."

Jane snorted and covered her mouth. "What in the hell is snuggle time?"

"It's this," he said, squeezing her.

Her shoulders shook with laughter. "Does snuggle time involve kissing?"

He looked down at her and his brows went up hopefully. "Yes?"

She leaped from his arms. "Then I need to go brush my teeth."

Matt groaned and pressed his hands to his face. "If you brush your teeth, then I have to–Damn it."

He propped himself up on his elbows and shook his head at Bria. "Your mother…"

He heard the boys asking Jane for breakfast and knew snuggle time was officially rained out.

Matt put on his prosthetic, scooped up Bria, and headed downstairs and into the kitchen.

Jane was pouring a cup of coffee.

"Sorry," she apologized. "I'm just a little nervous and…"

He got it. He was also getting his damn kiss. Matt cut her off before she made it to the chair and backed her into the refrigerator. "What are you—" she tried to duck away, but he pressed his arms on either side of her, caging her in. Her breath hitched, and her gaze fell to his mouth. Matt smiled. He loved that about her—the inability to hide what was on her mind. He rested his hand on her hip, loving that he finally could. Heat spread through his body.

"Are you just going to stand there or—" she began.

He swept in and claimed her mouth. She thrust her coffee out of the way and he pulled her body into his. He slid his hands under her hair and kissed her as thoroughly as he knew how.

Maddy rushed into the kitchen. "Quick, turn on the–Shit."

Matt jumped up at the sound of her voice. Jane turned away in embarrassment.

Maddy stood there, covering her eyes as if blocking out the sun. "Sorry, but…"

"You can look," Matt said. "What's the—"

"Dallas fell."

The hair on Matt's arms stood on end. "What? When?"

"Early this morning, I think. My mom called. She said..."

Matt was out the back door before Maddy could finish the sentence. He hurried down the steps toward the generator. He pulled the cord, but didn't catch. Ed was on his way in from the chicken coop with a handful of eggs. "What's the matter?" he shouted.

"Maddy says Dallas is gone." Matt pulled the cord again, and the engine roared to life. Matt hurried back into the house and flipped on the TV.

Jane sat on the edge of the couch and Maddy dropped beside her as they stared at the all too familiar fog of ash and smoke that filled the screen. The video looked like it was being taken from several miles away.

"This is the site where, until this morning, the city of Dallas, Texas existed." The scene switched to a home video. ***"Eyewitnesses in Fort Worth recorded this unidentified explosion that has razed the once-glorious city to the ground. The cause of the explosion is..."***

Matt pulled out his phone and dialed Max. It went straight to voicemail. "Shit," he said, pulling his fingers through his hair. He paced the small room as he waited for the beep. "Call me as soon as you get this."

He ended the call and dialed Carlos. *Voicemail.*

"Shit," he said again as the knot in his stomach grew. He caught Jane's eye as he scrolled through his contacts for Bingo's number and dialed.

"What's the matter?" she asked.

"Hey—" Bingo said. Matt sighed in relief, but then the recording continued. "This is Brad. Leave a message and I'll call you back." The knot turned into a wrecking ball as he searched for Gates's number.

Finally, someone picked up.

"Have you heard from them?" Gates asked before he could say anything.

That meant he hadn't. "Damn it. No." Jane got up and stood beside him, her eyes filled with concern.

"Fuck." Gates said.

Jane touched his arm, and he looked down at her as he spoke into the receiver. "When's the last time you—"

"I talked to Max yesterday."

"Was he still in Dallas? He said they were shipping—"

Gates's voice was heavy. "He stayed. A bunch of them did."

Matt stopped. "What? He was still doing patrols in—"

"Yeah."

Matt's eyes flew back to the TV, where they were showing an aerial view of the aftermath. Not only was the city destroyed, everything within a couple mile radius was as well. "Shit."

"Maybe —" An incoming call interrupted Gates's voice. Matt jerked the phone away from his ear. Hope and adrenaline swirled through his veins, making him dizzy. But it wasn't the guys, it was his mom.

"Hey man, it's my mom. I gotta go. Call me if you hear anything."

"Yeah. Likewise."

"What is —" Jane started, but he held up a finger and whispered, 'my mom,' as he turned and headed into the kitchen so he could hear better.

"Matty?" a muffled, masculine voice whispered. Matt stopped at the doorway, pulling the phone away from his ear to confirm he'd read the name right. Mom Cell.

"Hello?" he said, frowning.

"Matty?"

His eyebrows went up in disbelief. "Dad?"

His dad mumbled something.

"What?" Matt asked.

The line was silent.

"Dad?"

Nothing.

"Dad!"

"We got the virus, Matty."

Matt's blood turned to ice. "Wh–what?"

"Your mother is gone," he whispered.

Gone?

"She's gone," his dad repeated.

Matt fell back against the doorjamb as his brain tried to catch up. "What do you mean, gone?"

"Last night. When I woke up this morning—"

"How?"

"She had a fever. It started a couple of days… Oh, my sweet Carol-Ann," his father cried pitifully.

Matt could barely hear him over his pounding heart. His mom couldn't be dead.

"Are you sure? Did you call the paramedics? The pol—"

"They won't come."

"What? Why not?"

"Because we're in the quarantine zone."

Matt braced himself against the wall. *No*. "But I just talked to mom day before yes—"

"She didn't want to worry you."

What the fuck? He knew it when she called. He knew something was wrong, but he'd been so focused on Jane.

"Worry me? Of course, I'm fucking worried! You're my parents–Shit. How? How did you even get it?" Matt raked his hands through his hair.

This cannot be happening.

"I–I don't know. We didn't go anywhere but to see you. I never thought I'd outlive—"

"When did your symptoms start?"

"Day after we got back from the Veil."

Had they picked it up from the meeting station? Matt felt like he was caught in a nightmare. “What? No… Dad.”

“I’m sorry about everything, Matty. Being angry at you. Not buying your mother the fucking air conditioner she always wanted. What–what have I…”

Matt had never heard his dad drop the f-bomb before, and his worry deepened.

“No, dad. I’m sorry. I get it now.” Matt could barely speak past the lump in his throat. “You were happy.”

“I was. And I’m glad your mother went peacefully in her sleep instead of…” He couldn’t finish. “But you’ve got to understand. I can’t breathe without her.” It was the most romantic, heartbreaking thing Matt had ever heard his dad say. It reminded him of Ed and Ruth, and the same agony ripped through his soul.

Matt looked up at Jane, who was standing in the living room, watching him.

He heard a familiar noise that he couldn’t quite place as dad went on. “I can’t–I can’t handle this kind of–Oh god. I can’t—” His voice faltered. “I love you, Matty. I always have. And I’m proud of you for… blazing your own trail and doing what makes you happy.”

Mat wiped his eyes. “I love you too, Dad.”

“You know how much your mother loved you, right? She would want you to know. You were the light of her life.”

“Yeah. I know.” Something wasn’t right about his dad’s tone.

“Okay then. I… love you, my boy.”

My boy? His dad hadn’t called him that since he was eight years old. “Wait, Dad? Hey, what’s going on?”

His old man didn’t answer.

He pulled the phone away from his ear. The call had dropped. *Or he hung up.* He called his mother’s number back.

His dad didn’t answer.

He tried again, and his worry grew.

Nothing.

Matt dropped into one of the chairs around the kitchen table.

Jane was beside him instantly, saying something, but the ringing in his ears made it hard to hear her.

"What?" he asked, trying to focus on her moving lips.

Jane put a hand on his arm. "What happened?"

The sound he heard. He remembered what it was. There was a pistol in his nightstand. That was the sound of the magazine being locked into—Matt's fear exploded. "Oh, god." He frantically dialed his mom again.

The phone just rang.

When he heard his mother's voice on the recording, "No. No… no…."

He tried again.

And again.

"Hello, you've reached Carol and Al, leave a…"

Tears spilled down his cheeks.

"Matt?"

He dropped the phone on the table. "My parents got the virus. My mom… She is dead and I think my dad…"

Don't say it.

He fell against Jane's shoulder. "Oh no," she breathed.

A sob clawed its way up his throat and tore itself from his mouth. She wrapped her arms around him.

Matt sobbed against her shoulder. Small arms gently circled his neck and through his tears, he saw Austin standing beside him. He wrapped an arm around the boy and hugged him.

Jane's voice was soft as she continued to hold him. "Shh."

Matt didn't know how long they sat like that, he, Jane and Austin. When he pulled away, Austin stepped back, looking scared.

"What happened?" the boy asked.

"Can you go check on Tommy?" Jane asked gently. "I need to speak with Matt for a minute."

Austin hesitated, then nodded. "I love you, Matt," he said before turning to go. That brought a fresh round of tears to Matt's eyes. How did kids do it? Love so freely, so quickly?

"I love you too, bud," he choked as Jane took his hands in hers.

"I don't understand. You said they were obeying the quarantine."

"They were."

"Do you know if they went outside at all?"

Matt shook his head. "The only time they were out was when they went to the Veil, and they were masked from the moment they left to the moment they returned." He shook his head again. "They went through the sanitation protocol. I asked my mom specifically. But that must be where…"

Jane's eyes were wide. "Tell me what happened."

"My dad said her symptoms started the day after. He said she had a fever and then last night…"

Jane was shaking her head. "The incubation period is longer than a day. She got it before they went to the Veil."

"That isn't possible." Matt said.

"Maybe the food supply was contaminated? Or it got in the water? But, if that's true, then…"

He followed her train of thought. If it got into the food or water supply, then everyone in the city was as good as dead.

"What about your dad? How is he feeling? What are his symptoms?"

Matt turned to her, and shook his head, praying he was wrong hoping his father hadn't just taken his own life with *his* gun.

Chapter Fifty-Six

Day 46 // 11:11 a.m

SOMEHOW, Matt made it through the next twenty-four hours—although he didn't remember how. One minute, he was at the kitchen table, the next he was sitting on the couch next to Jane and staring at the back of Tommy's head as the boy zoomed a little car across the floor. The next minute, Matt was in bed, staring at the ceiling. Jane had called his mom's phone a million times, but his father hadn't answered.

He was sitting on the couch when his phone finally rang. Matt prayed it was his dad, but Gates's cocky face lit up the screen instead. Shit, he'd totally forgotten about Max.

"Hey," he said.

There was a long pause and then, "They didn't make it."

He must have heard wrong. "I'm sorry, What? Are you—"

Gates's voice was flat. "I'm listed as Bingo's next of kin. They just called."

Max is gone?

"They stayed. A bunch of the guys did. They went out on patrol the night-before last. They never checked back in after the explosion."

Carlos and Bingo are dead?

They had been through *wars* together, how could they…

"Are you sure?"

"Well, fuck, Farm. I mean no. I haven't seen their bodies, but I got the fucking call. You know they would have checked in by now."

Matt's guilt was sharp. He squeezed his eyes closed. He should have been there. They were his men, his friends. While they were dying, he had been lying in bed, happier than he had ever been, watching Jane sleep. He had let them down *again*. First his parents and now this? He couldn't take anymore.

He wanted to say something, but he couldn't find the words through the numbness that had settled over him.

Tommy ran into the room carrying a little brown toad in his hand. "Look what I found!"

Matt held up his hand. "Gates, hold on a—"

Jane hurried in and, seeing him on the phone, quickly sent Tommy back outside.

"Is it your dad?" she asked hopefully.

Matt shook his head, and her face fell. She sat down beside him.

"Is that a kid?" Gates asked, reminding Matt of his last conversation with Max.

"Yeah."

"Whose?"

"Mine–until the Veil comes down."

"You met someone?" Gates sounded surprised.

"Yeah. I did." He felt Jane's hand in his.

"That's great, Farm. I… um… I gotta go. I just…"

"Yeah, thanks."

"I'll let you know if I hear anything else."

Matt hung up, looked at Jane. He couldn't think.

"Who was that?" Jane asked.

"Army buddy. Why is the TV off?"

"They just started repeating themselves, so we turned it off."

Matt pulled his hands through his hair, feeling more helpless than he ever had. Even more helpless than lying on the side of the road, without a foot, holding his dying friend. At least then he could still scream for help. Now, all he could do was sit and stare at his fucking phone, and know that five of the people he cared most about in the world were gone, and he hadn't even tried to help them.

"Do you want to put the TV back on?"

Did he want to see the news? *No.* But he pushed himself off the couch anyway.

"I need fucking answers, Jane." He ground his teeth together. "I need to know why the fuck all of this is happening, and no one is doing a damn thing about it. Because right now, none of this is making any *fucking* sense!" He stormed toward the back door.

Matt threw the door open and stopped short at the view. Rain clouds hung on the horizon to the west, but high above, the sun darted between brilliantly white, puffy clouds. He couldn't believe how beautiful it was. Tommy was in the driveway, totally oblivious to the state of the world, playing with his frog. Matt was jealous. He wished he could go out in the middle of one of the fields and just lay in the dirt, between the rows of corn, and hide. Bad news couldn't hurt him if it couldn't find him. It was cowardly, he knew, but he ached for ignorance. It was so much easier to deal with than the pain.

He looked to the east, toward his parents' farm, and his eyes filled with tears. The phone call from his dad had to be a dream. There was no way his parents were dead. How could they be, when everything out here was the same as ever? His parents were a part of this place. They didn't change. They didn't die.

They are gone.

In his heart, he knew it. Matt could feel the void.

The pressure in his head grew, and his anger returned. He wiped his eyes as he stomped down the stairs. Adjusting the choke, he pulled on the cord. This whole damn thing was someone's fault. The generator came to life, cutting the calm. And whoever it was—He wiped his eyes again. They were going to pay. If it was the last thing he did, Matt was going to get justice for all the people wrongfully murdered by the fucking Veil. And if it was the President, so be it. Then he'd—

The back door opened. "Matt—" Jane's eyes were wide, and worried.

He hurried back inside.

When he saw the TV, he knew why.

There were people in hazmat suits, carrying a body out of a house. The ticker under the video footage read ***Outbreak confirmed in Detroit.*** Matt recognized the roof of his apartment complex behind the house.

"Shit." The field of corn surfaced in his mind as he sat down.

"Twenty-seven cases of the X-virus have been reported in the last twelve hours. Despite rigorous attempts to keep people isolated, the virus has found its way into the quiet neighborhood of Glenhaven. Authorities are urging everyone to stay inside and keep their doors and windows locked. All food preparation depots have been closed until the facilities can be tested—" Matt looked at Jane. She'd guessed the same thing. ***"—and water mains have been shut off. The mayor has scheduled a press conference for twelve noon to discuss the crisis."***

"That's exactly what you said."

Jane nodded. "Is this near your—"

"Yeah. That green roof back there—" Matt pointed. "That's where I lived. But how did this happen? I thought they were being careful with everything."

The segment went on, and they watched more bodies being removed. Finally, the mayor came on. ***"Every distribution center was tested, and water samples were taken from several locations around the city. All tests came back negative. That is the good news. The bad news is we still don't know the source of the outbreak. But whatever it was, it did not come from contaminated food or water supply. Water mains are being turned back on as I speak, and food distribution will resume this afternoon. The best***

guess right not is that residents of Glenhaven did not follow the quarantine and—"

"That is a lie!" Matt shouted at the TV. "My parents did exactly what they were supposed to, Jane. They didn't go anywhere. They haven't been outside… I don't…" His anger erupted. "This–this is bullshit! They shouldn't even be in there. They didn't bring the goddamn virus to the city! My dad's a fucking farmer, for Christ's sake! They had nothing to do with…"

"There are always margins of error with these kinds of things," Jane said quietly.

Matt gave her an incredulous look. Margins of error? They were talking about his parents. "What the fuck does that mean?"

"Austin, why don't you take your book out on the back porch?"

Matt turned. He hadn't even noticed Austin sitting in Ed's chair. The boy got up and headed for the kitchen.

"I'm sorry." Matt apologized.

"No. I'm sorry. I didn't mean to sound insensitive. It's just… you said you wanted answers."

"Oh, and you think you understand all of this?" Matt said, waving at the TV.

Jane turned the volume down and met his eyes nervously. "I–I think I do."

"What? How?"

She got up and headed for the stairs. "I'll be right back."

A minute later, she reappeared.

Jane turned off the TV and set the paper on his lap.

"What is this?"

She gnawed on her lip. "It's a paper I wrote in college."

"A paper on what?"

"Read it. I'll be back in a second."

It was the draft of a paper, titled *Limited Solutions to the Release of Super Contagions on Biological Organisms through Analytics and Mathematical Modeling*. Beneath the rather confusing title were the names Jane McIntyre and Robert Fullton.

Matt looked up as the engine of the generator died, then went back to the paper. In the margin, written in red ink, were the words "*It's a solid first draft! Congratulations, Jane, you just saved the world.*"

He flipped through the forty pages. There were a lot of equations—Matt recalled Jane and her notebook this morning as she watched the news—and at least a dozen charts. Time vs. Number of deaths, variables… Where 'x' was the incubation period, and 'y' was the infection rate, and 'a' was—His eyes landed on the words margin of error, and he read the paragraph that enclosed it. It was something about the models requiring at least a twenty-two percent margin of error to contain the virus, but he had no idea what that meant. What virus?

Matt gave up, went back to the beginning, and read the abstract.

He wasn't positive he understood, but the gist of it seemed to be that she had written a paper predicting the spread of a super virus, and then through a bunch of equations, had figured out how to stop it. Matt's brows went up as he read the last three sentences that spelled out Jane's rather simple, but horrifying, solution.

Jane returned with two cups of coffee and sat down beside him.

"You wrote this?"

"Yeah."

"There's a lot of… math in here."

She took a tentative sip. "Yeah."

Matt glanced back at the paper. "And a pretty extreme solution to the problem."

"Yeah."

He took the mug she handed him. "So…"

"So… you don't notice anything?"

He frowned. "Like what?"

"Like a similarity between what's happening and…" Her eyes fell to the paper.

"Well, yeah, I guess. You did write it about a super virus, so…"

Jane shook her head. "So that's it. You don't think…?"

"I'll be honest with you. I have no idea what the fuck any of this says. Can you just explain it to me? I'm sorry. I'm just not in the mood to…"

Jane tucked her hair behind her ear. "Um, sure." She took a deep breath.

"When I was in college, I studied biology and math, statistics specifically, as an undergrad. When I went on to grad school, I started working with Robert, and I combined the two subjects. For my thesis, I invented a hypothetical super-virus, defined as 99.9% infection rate, and 99.9% mortality rate—"

"Why not a hundred?"

"Robert wanted me to assume a small population was immune. And the subject of my paper was to find a way to stop it if it got into the population."

Matt looked down at the title again, not really sure where she was heading with this, or why she chose now of all times to share it.

"So, what I did was compile a database of all major infectious diseases—from the plague and up through HIV. I analyzed all the variables that played an important role in the dissemination of the viruses. Everything from rate of infection, to time of year, method of transmissibility, to proximity to clean water. There were hundreds of—"

Matt was trying to listen, but he just couldn't. He held up his hand. "I'm sorry, Jane. I'm just not…"

"I know. But you said you wanted to understand."

"I meant understand what's happening now. What does any of this have to do with a paper you wrote… years ago?"

"Please?"

Matt sighed. "Okay, go on."

Jane turned to face him and tucked her leg under her. "Basically, what I did was take all those variables and run them through a series of simulations that predicted the numbers of survivors after the period of a year. I weeded out the ones that had little impact on the final numbers and ended up with six critical variables. And one of those, time, was by far the most important."

Matt set his coffee on the table and rubbed his eyes. "Okay."

"Um, and what that means is that hours, translated into not tens of lives, but millions. The relationship between time and number of deaths was—bear with me, exponential, meaning a minute could mean the difference between an entire city being wiped out or just a single person. The longer it took to isolate and destroy the virus, the more dramatic the numbers became."

Matt stared at her. He'd never seen this side of Jane, and he felt like he was listening to his high school science teacher.

"So, I ran the sims, hundreds of them, trying to find a solution that resulted in the survival of the species. The shocking thing was, with the infection and dissemination rates that Robert gave me… none of them worked. They were all too slow in stopping the virus because we could not wait for the sample size to get big enough to accurately predict anything. Infected individuals were constantly cropping up through probability equations, and the only way to eliminate them was to increase the margin of error."

"Jane…"

"Twenty-two percent. That was the margin. Anything lower and the virus got out."

"So, what does this…" he was trying to be patient. He really was, but his world was crashing down around him and—

"That's why your parents are there. Because they didn't have time to separate the high-risk group from everyone else. Because if they took the time to weed them out, and didn't meet the twenty-two percent margin requirement, the virus would escape. The math proves it."

"They? Who is they?"

"The ICPH."

"So, what are you saying, Jane? That your paper predicted all of this?"

"No," she met his eyes. "I'm saying all of this is *based* on my research."

Matt laughed. "What? You can't seriously think—"

"I can prove it."

Matt studied her. Her claim was absurd, but he could see she believed it. "How?"

She pulled her notebook off the coffee table.

"As I said, in the case of a super-virus, the thing that matters most is time. Every second wasted on mapping, researching, screening, testing, quarantining, whatever, dramatically lowers the chance of survival for everyone. An hour could be the difference between a million deaths and a *billion*. In order to save humanity, I had to destroy the virus faster than any of the traditional methods allowed. And each scenario had an 'expiration date' that was based primarily on incubation period. A point at which the solution no longer worked."

Jesus, Matt thought, stretching his leg. He did not have the patience for this right now.

Jane continued, "When I ran numbers, I had between a two and eleven-day 'expiration date' window in which to contain the virus otherwise…" Her voice trailed off, and she paused for a moment. "Anyway, we know the incubation period of the X-virus. Luckily it is between two and three days."

"Luckily?"

"The longer the incubation period, the shorter the expiration date, and harder it is to track. We also know it's airborne."

Matt shook his head. "So?"

"So, when I fed that into my equation, the output was six days."

She showed him the page in her notebook, and it looked like her paper—confusing and full of numbers.

"Matt, the CDC was informed of the virus on May twenty-ninth. Backtrack two days for the initial infection, and you have May twenty-seventh. Six days later is June second. But depending on when they received the reports on the twenty-ninth, it could be pushed back to the third." Jane pointed to the number on the page. "And *that* is the day the Veil was activated."

"Well, that's a weird coinci—"

"That's not all." She licked her lips nervously. "You read what my solution was, right?"

Matt looked down at the page and read. "*The only viable solution based on extensive analysis is to completely isolate every city where the virus is suspected to have spread, within the designated expiration window.*"

"At the time, there was only one way to do that. Raze them to the ground. As long as the incubation period was less than five days, the solution worked. It was fast. It was thorough. But now the Veil… that's basically what it's doing. It has completely isolated the virus."

"Yeah…" Matt shook his head. "I think you're reading a little too much—"

Jane rushed on. "I think the Veil was created to give people a chance, Matt. It was built to buy time. It meets the margin of error by isolation and it provides time… *infinite* time to track it. Where it is, but more importantly, where it isn't." She placed her hand on his arm. "The Veil is a genius solution to an impossible problem. It's giving them a chance, no matter how small, to survive. Look at Detroit, how long they've hung on. They have a chance. L.A. it wasn't looking good, but the news reports are that it's slowing down there. They might make it after all. Some people will still die, but maybe, hopefully, not all of them. But if they don't follow the mandates like they didn't in Atlanta and Dallas… Like in Phoenix and Istanbul now… then when the virus gets to critical mass—"

"Meaning?"

"When it's reached the point in the population where it becomes self-sustaining, and the survival rate of the group essentially falls to zero."

Matt pinched his nose.

"I think the President is allowing the cities to be destroyed once they cross *this* threshold and I can predict when it's going to happen."

Matt's last conversation with Max surfaced. Was his commanding officer, right? Was the President not being honest with the American people about what was happening? Did he *want* the cities to be destroyed?

"Why? Why would the President do that if they were already behind the Veil?" he asked.

"I don't know. Out of mercy, maybe? If they were all going to die anyway, get it over quickly rather than…"

"Are you serious?" Matt couldn't believe President Rodriguez would do that.

"Or… maybe at that point it's not worth the risk?"

"Risk of what?"

"Of someone on the inside figuring out how to deactivate the Veil, and letting the virus out? Of something happening and the Veil failing somehow?"

Matt stared at her, his jaw hanging open. *Is that what the President is up to?* Pulling the plug on millions of lives once a city gets a little too risky?

"Look, here are the numbers from Atlanta." She pointed. "According to the news, this was the population of Atlanta, inside the Veil." She pointed to the number beside it. "This is the official tally of infected individuals before the explosion. If you work it out, it comes to fifty-two percent of the population. Here are the numbers for Rome." She pointed again. "It's the same. Fifty-two percent."

The hair on the back of Matt's neck stood on end as her finger moved to the next equation. Above it was the word 'Dallas.'

"This is Dal—"

"When did you do this?" he asked, as a rage he could not even begin to describe began to boil in his stomach.

"Do what?" Jane asked, confused.

"When did you work this out? This problem, right there." He jabbed at the paper. His head was suddenly on fire.

"A couple of days—"

You could have warned them. A blast went off in Matt's head, equal to the one that killed his best friend. He stared at Jane, finally believing what she was telling him.

"No," It couldn't be. He looked at the page in disbelief. *You could have saved them?*

"Matt?"

"You *knew*?" he whispered through his clenched jaw. The edge of his vision reddened.

"I… suspected."

"Suspected?" Oh god. He couldn't breathe. *Max, Bingo, and Carlos are dead.* He tugged at the collar of his t-shirt. *Because of her.*

"Well, I—"

"You knew Dallas was going to fall, and you didn't say *anything*." Matt spit, his voice thick with anger.

She looked down sharply. "No—"

"Yes, you did, Jane. You said it yourself. It's right there in your paper," he shouted, jumping off the couch. "Fuck!"

Jane got up quickly. "Matt, I didn't *know*. I mean… It seemed so preposterous."

He threw his hands into the air. "Then why are you fucking telling me all of this?"

"I don't understand. Why are you so angry?"

Matt pulled his hands through his hair as he paced. *Max would be alive now if only*—"Fuck! How in the hell did the ICPH get your fucking paper?"

"I don't know. I never finished it. It-it was never published. But… I think it was Robert."

He looked down at the couch, at the note on the front of her paper.

Robert Fulton.

"Why?"

"Because he knew about the Veil before it went up," she whispered.

"What?" Matt whipped around. "How do *you* know that?"

She met his eyes. "Because he warned me."

"He *what*?"

Jane waited guiltily for him to figure it out. He racked his brain, then finally found it. "You took the kids…" he whispered, in disbelief. "And you ran."

She nodded.

He gasped. "You *knew*."

She nodded again. "Yes," she whispered.

He stared at her incredulously as everything she was telling him sorted itself out in his head. "How long?" He choked on the question as he stepped toward her.

Jane backed away from him. "Wh–what?"

"How long did you know?" Matt clenched his fingers into fists, trying to keep his anger and grief in check.

"How long did I know about the Veil?"

"Yes," he seethed.

"About f-forty-five min—"

Matt didn't wait for her to finish. "So let me get this straight. You wrote a paper basically telling the President to kill a bunch of innocent people. People like my parents, who were just in the wrong place at the wrong time. People like my fucking friends who have given their lives to protect you. But *then* when the time comes to implement all this shit, you fucking run away and save *yourself*, *your* family, and leave everyone else to fucking hang?" He shouted the last part in her face. "What the *fuck,* Jane?" His anger took over, and he shook with it.

You wanted someone to blame. Here she is.

She turned her head away like she thought he might hit her. "No, Matt, I didn't know—"

"Look at me," he spat. She raised her eyes, and the guilt in them made him sick. She was lying.

He jabbed a finger at her. "You. Ran."

"It was not like—" Tears filled her eyes.

"My best friend was killed in Dallas, Jane," he seethed. "He and two of our guys were–they were on patrol outside the Veil when it exploded."

Jane squeezed her eyes shut again. "I am so sorry—"

Matt held up his hand, and she cowered again. "No! Don't you fucking apologize. You knew all of this and you didn't tell anyone? People deserve to know, Jane! They deserve to know that if they don't get their shit together, the government is going to *murder* them all!" Matt's voice boomed off the walls.

"It's not that simple. Then people would panic."

He laughed bitterly. "What, like you? When you ran like a fucking coward and left everyone else to die?"

"Matt—"

"They deserve to know they've been assigned a death sentence." He pointed a finger at her. "My parents deserved to know. Maybe they would have been more careful. Maybe they could have done something… different, and my mom wouldn't have died. Maybe my dad wouldn't have killed himself with my own fucking gun!" She touched his arm, and he jerked it away. "Don't fucking touch me," he warned.

Jane stared at him with her terrified puppy-dog eyes, like she didn't understand why he was angry, which only infuriated him more. *Oh god.* He had to get out of there before he hurt her. He spun around and headed for the stairs.

"Matt? Where are you going?" Jane called in a wobbly voice as he pounded up the steps.

His dad was probably lying dead in a pool of his own blood. *Because of her.*

"Matt?"

He rushed into the bedroom and dragged his bag from the

closet. How could she do it? Save herself and leave everyone else to die? What kind of—

"Matt, please," she begged from the doorway. "You don't under—"

He pulled the drawer and began shoving clothes in. He thought he knew her, but apparently not. God, why did he do this to himself? He was such an idiot. She was just like Katie. One thing on the surface, someone totally different underneath. "You are a goddamn sociopath."

"I wrote that paper twenty years ago! I didn't know…"

Jane stopped at whatever she saw in his eyes. He ripped the phone charger from the wall and stopped in front of her.

"You ran." He seethed, then pushed past her.

Matt threw the back door open and blinked in the bright sunlight as he headed for Ed's truck.

The old man looked up from the garden, where he was picking something with the kids.

"Everything okay there, Matthew?"

Matt dumped his bag into the bed of the truck. "I need to borrow your truck."

"Yeah, sure," Ed said.

"Matt! Look at this tomato!" Tommy said, holding up a bright-red sphere the size of a softball. "That's great, buddy," Matt said, yanking the door open and climbing inside. It took a couple of tries to get the engine to turn over, and when it finally did, Matt roared past Jane as she ran down the steps and onto the driveway. "Wait!" she shouted.

He slid onto the road and gunned the engine.

Matt looked at the fuel indicator. He needed gas, and then he needed to find Diggs before anything happened to him. He needed to call Gates back and tell him—

His phone buzzed in his pocket. He looked at the number, not recognizing it. It was probably Jane. *But it could be the police.* He answered it, holding the phone to his ear. "Hello?"

"Is this Matthew Patterson?" an unfamiliar voice asked.

"Yes," he said tersely.

"We are calling to inform you that police responded to shots fired at your address on Lincoln Boulevard and discovered two bodies. The deceased, one Carol Ann Patterson, and one Albert—"

Matt hung up his phone and threw it on the seat.

Chapter Fifty-Seven

Day 65 // 8:19 a.m

MATT SPRAYED SHAVING cream onto his palm, then dabbed it on his cheeks.

It had taken three days, but he had found Diggs stationed in Chicago.

He spread the foam on his chin, and upper lip.

They had been sitting across from each other, eating shitty oatmeal, when the news broke. In the bleak breakfast area of the hotel-turned-barracks on the south side of Chicago, they had watched with the other soldiers as President Rodriguez was finally exposed as a liar.

Up until then, everyone thought that he and the vice President were trapped inside the Veil. But when reports surfaced of an explosion at the White House, while the President sat comfortably in his chair addressing the nation, the truth was revealed. As soon as the video of the small explosion aired, the President's feed was cut, leaving everyone staring at their TV with their jaws hanging open, wondering what the fuck had just happened.

Matt took the razor and dragged it across his right cheek. That had been almost two weeks ago.

Almost immediately after, riots broke out on both sides of the Veil putting an enormous strain on both local law enforcement and the military. To make matters worse, it seemed the President's charade had cost him this trust of a large contingency of the Armed

Forces because they had gone AWOL in droves. So many abandoned their posts that the President had been forced to lift almost all restrictions on enlistment. He was leaving it up to company commanders to recruit as they saw fit. And if Matt was anything, he was fit.

He ran the razor under the running water in the sink and tapped it on the porcelain bowl.

Chicago and Vancouver were still without a single case of the virus. But instead of counting their blessings, Chicagoans were angry, making it one of the most restless cities. There was a rumor circulating that a group on the inside had come up with a means to disarm the Veil. In response, people on the outside were threatening to take down the whole city. Because of that, and half the company going AWOL, Diggs's commanding officer had offered Matt immediate reinstatement.

He dragged the razor across his cheek again.

And of course, he had accepted. His only condition was that they reinstated him at his previous rank. He wasn't about to start over again, and he didn't want a desk job. He wanted to be out there, wherever Diggs and the guys were, and he wanted the freedom to protect them.

He tapped the razor against the sink again.

A mere three hours after he'd signed the papers, and he was back in fatigues with a company of men, heading out to assist local law enforcement inside the Veil subdue a mob that had gathered near the west side of the city.

Matt started on his left cheek. Swipe. Tap. Rise.

Since then, they had sent him out on more than a dozen missions. Sometimes the orders were to shoot anyone who got too close to any of the towers. Other times, they had provided security for meeting stations, similar to the ones in Detroit.

He pulled the razor across his chin. Water dripped onto his chest as stared at his clipped hair. It had been a long time since he looked like this. He met his haunted, bloodshot eyes. *Well, not exactly like this*. It was harder than he remembered. But his men trusted him. That was the most important thing.

He pulled the razor across his jaw again, pushing thoughts of Jane and the kids aside. And Matt needed the control that commanding provided. He needed something to channel his twisted emotions into because his grief tortured him night and day and made it impossible to sleep, and there was no other way to get it out besides hitting something.

He finished shaving, then wiped his face with a towel.

No one knew why the President had lied about being an Insider, only that he had, and for most, that was enough to confirm that he'd been in on it from the start, that there was some sort of conspiracy playing out under everyone's noses. If he hadn't known about Jane's paper, Matt would have thought so too. But everything she'd predicted had come to pass.

Daily he'd been calculating the numbers from the news reports, checking the infection rates. When Moscow hit fifty-two percent and went boom, Matt knew she was right. President Rodriguez must have known Dallas was going to go, which is why he tried to pull the men out, but he didn't pull the trigger. Someone else was doing that. And they were doing it everywhere.

In London, Insiders were demanding to see the queen and members of parliament in person for whatever reason. If not, they threatened to riot themselves. The whole thing was a fucking disaster.

Diggs appeared in the door, pulling a shirt over his smooth, brown head. "Mount up, Farm. We got another call. A bunch of rednecks with assault weapons headed our way."

That had been happening a lot lately. Luckily, the groups were small—anywhere from one to about ten people. Matt realized that was probably why the President had shut down the internet. The way it connected people and spread information was powerful. He couldn't even imagine where they'd be if it was still up and running.

Despite that, he knew it was only a matter of time before those numbers went up.

Matt nodded and hurried into the room he shared with Diggs. He pulled on his shirt, then checked to make sure his prosthetic was secure.

Diggs's brown eyes met Matt's as he pulled his cap over his head. "I'm gonna grab grub for the road. Want anything?" he asked.

"No." He hadn't had an appetite since he left Jane and the kids. He knew he needed to eat, but almost every time he tried, his stomach betrayed him. Like it was trying to convince him he'd made a mistake by coming back.

"I'll meet you downstairs," Diggs said, before closing the door behind him.

Matt holstered his gun, then took one more glance at himself in the mirror as he placed his own hat on his head. He certainly looked like a soldier.

Then why don't you feel like one anymore?

Jane's big, brown eyes popped into his mind, followed by Bria's fat cheeks and the boys' infectious laughter. Matt pushed the images away for the hundredth time. Damn it, he even missed Maddy. *Then why are you still here?* His jaw tightened. He was there because his country needed him. *Your family needs you more.*

He met his own eyes in the mirror. He no longer had a family.

Then why are you thinking about them?

Because he didn't know how to stop.

Chapter Fifty-Eight

Day 67 // 11:10 a. m

JANE STARED out the kitchen window as the breeze rustled the corn. It was now taller than Austin. It blew past her in a rush, carrying with it the scent of wet dirt.

It had been three weeks since Matt left, and she hadn't heard a word. She had left him a dozen messages, apologizing for everything. She had tried to explain that she didn't know what she was running from, that she had written that paper a lifetime ago and thought it was buried on the hard drive of her old computer. But if he listened to them, her explanation was not enough to change his mind.

She replayed the scene over relentlessly. Why did she insist on telling him everything right then?

You were trying to help.

Her heart throbbed with regret. By explaining that his parents were… margins of error?

Jane buried her head in her hands. It all happened so quickly. For one precious moment, they had been good, and then… she went and fucked it all up.

Every time she closed her eyes, she saw the betrayal in his—and he was right. She was responsible for the death of his parents and his friends. She ran and left everyone else to die. Maybe she couldn't have warned the entire city, but every person she knew… every child sitting in any of the classrooms she had passed on her way to get her own kids, if *they* died, that was specifically on her.

Especially now that the virus seemed to be taking hold of the city. The ICPH had expanded the quarantine area to include the whole northwest section of the city, running barbed wire fencing along I-75 and I-696 to contain it. She had done the math this morning. They were at a twenty-three percent infection rate.

She glanced out at the gray sky. Self-hatred was a vicious beast, inescapable, and it was devouring her.

Matt was right about something else. Everyone deserved to know. So, why wasn't the President telling them? He had to realize they would be more likely to respond to the mandates if they thought they were going to die. Jane couldn't help but think there was a good reason. She just couldn't imagine what it was. But, then again, maybe not. Since he had been exposed, no one trusted him, and she still couldn't imagine what would be worth paying that price.

Jane looked down. Carrots that Maddy had gathered that morning filled the sink. There were bowls of peppers, radishes, beets, tomatoes, and green beans on the table. It was August already, and the produce was coming in all at once—which was both a blessing and a curse.

Jane had cried last week when she found a tomato rotting on the vine before they could eat it. It had prompted Ed to get in touch with a local Amish family who had agreed to come out today and teach Jane how to can.

Yesterday, Ed had taken her to the blueberry patch at the back of his property. She and Maddy had picked three huge bowls of berries that she planned to make into jam. Only two remained because the boys had devoured one the night before for dessert.

She went to the back door and pushed it open. Maddy was on the back porch, tying bundles of herbs to hang and dry. The air was a kaleidoscope of smells, with the mint and rosemary vying for first place, as Jane watched her.

"Save some of the basil. I have a soup recipe I want to try with the tomatoes and butternut squash tonight."

Maddy scrunched her nose. "I hate—"

Jane held up her hand. "It's gonna be fall soon, and then winter. We need to be grateful and appreciative —"

"Ugh. I know. Sorry."

Jane smiled. Ever since she came back from her visit with Thomas, Maddy had been different. For a while, she had even been cheerful, but after Matt left… Well, they were all a little down. *Just a little? You cried over a tomato.* She sighed. "The Amish people should be here any minute."

"Have you ever met any Amish people before?" Maddy asked nervously.

"At a flea market once. I bought a beautiful quilt from them," Jane said, remembering the intricate needlework of the quilt that lay spread across the bed in the guest room back home. "But otherwise, no. It was very thoughtful of Ed to ask them to help us, and very generous of them to come—"

Jane heard the faint sound of the doorbell and turned. "That must be them." She hurried through the house to the front door, hoping the sound wouldn't wake Bria.

Her smile fell at the sight of Officer Beale in the doorway.

Matt.

"Mrs. Moore." He nodded. "I have a message from the Coast Guard…" He cast a quick glance at her empty ring finger.

Relief and worry sloshed in her stomach as she stepped out onto the porch. "The mayor of Detroit is requesting your presence Tuesday, August third at"—He stopped and glanced at the paper in his hand—"11:30."

"The mayor of Detroit?" she repeated. She'd never even met him before. What could he possibly want from her? Did he know about her paper?

Jane's stomach sank as Beale continued to read. "Report to 3288 Marshall Drive. It's the exit before Anderson Air Force Base. No firearms or weapons of any kind are allowed. Mandatory body cavity search of all adults over the age of sixteen and all vehicles will be inspected at the initial checkpoint. Masks and wristbands are required in order to enter the base. Do you understand?"

"Do you know what he wants?" she asked nervously. Were they going to arrest her?

"It says to bring your kids."

"My kids? Why?" Jane's unease grew.

"No idea. Do you know where the base is, how to get there?"

Jane nodded. She had seen the signs a million times on her way up north.

"Alright then. August third, at eleven-thirty. You have a good day."

Jane stared after him, wondering how she was supposed to do that when she was probably going to be arrested before the week was over?

Chapter Fifty-Nine

Day 70 // 11:27 a.m

MARSHALL DRIVE WAS about a mile north of the actual base. As she exited the freeway, a news van sat off on the side of the road. A bored-looking reporter leaning against the hood eyed her as she passed. A little further down, the road was blocked by two large camouflage-painted transport trucks. Jane slowed as a man dressed in army fatigues appeared with a clipboard. She showed her ID, and he inspected the contents of the van. They searched her, Maddy, and Ed, and issued Ed a wrist band, before sending them to what looked like an industrial park surrounded by barbed-wire fencing.

Their bracelets were scanned again, and the guard directed Jane to a non-descript, brick building. The Veil was about a mile away. It transected one of the two air force-base runways. Jane saw the barracks and hangars on the other side and gasped. The base was inside the Veil. One of the towers was visible to the west.

When they approached the parking area, Jane noticed the sign that said **Johnson Steel Works**. They must have taken over an industrial park. There were armed soldiers waiting for them. Maddy cast Jane a worried glance in the rearview.

"Aunt Jane?" Austin said from beside his sister. "I'm—"

Jane cut him off. "It will be fine." He and Maddy both knew what might happen. She had pulled them and Ed aside after Tommy went to bed last night and explained everything. "Whatever happens, you guys are safe here. And you have Ed." She put the car into park and cast Ed a grateful smile. He nodded, looking just as nervous as she felt.

She opened the door and got out. One man, his jacket said Wallace, approached her. "Jane Moore?" he asked.

Jane nodded, wondering if that was what Matt was doing. Matt had called and spoken to Ed briefly a couple of nights ago, to tell him he had re-enlisted. If she wasn't convinced before, she was now. Matt was not coming back.

She had put the kids to bed, then cried herself to sleep in the spot that used to be his. She understood, and she wasn't angry at him, but she was heartbroken. But that was love, wasn't it? Bound to the joy of holding it in your hands was the risk of it slipping through your fingers. She had taken a chance, and for the briefest moment, she *had* held him. Then she lost the bet. It hurt but, if given the chance, she'd do it again. So, what was the point of regretting it?

Wallace asked Ed to wait in the van while the rest of them climbed into a jeep. Bria sat on Jane's lap. They passed back through the check-in gate, and then headed down the road, toward the Veil.

Jane noticed Wallace's wedding ring as he clutched the steering wheel.

This facility is too close to the Veil.

If Detroit went, everyone here would die. She thought of Matt again as she studied Wallace's tight jaw. He deserved to know. They all did. She wouldn't make the same mistake twice. Jane was about to tell him when she spotted a very familiar vehicle parked on the other side of the Veil, where it angled sharply to the south to a tower about a mile away. It was Thomas's white Land Rover.

Jane clamped her mouth shut as they pulled to a stop. Frowning, she got out.

"I don't understand," she said.

"That makes two of us," Wallace said angrily, as she unbuckled Tommy's seatbelt.

Despite the fact that everyone on the other side of the Veil wore masks, she recognized Thomas and Sarah immediately. They had the two little girls with them. The only other person there was a man dressed in fatigues. The mayor was suspiciously absent.

"What—"

"You have fifteen minutes, not a damn second longer," Wallace said.

Jane approached the Veil cautiously. With Bria in one hand and a vice-like grip on Tommy with the other, they came to a stop in front of the barbed-wire fencing.

Bria stared in fascination at the Veil, waving her chubby little hands at it.

"Dad!" Tommy shouted happily, finally recognizing his father.

Thomas smiled from behind his mask. "Hey, bud! I've missed you."

"Can you come over here with us yet?" Tommy asked.

Thomas shook his head. "Not yet. But maybe soon." He met Jane's eyes.

"What are you doing here?" she began.

"I called in a favor. I needed to see the kids before—" Thomas let the sentence hang, and Jane finally understood. He had used his money, or power, or both, and arranged an illegal meeting for them. Jane looked back at Wallace. No wonder he was pissed.

Thomas looked thinner and grayer than the last time she had seen him. Jane fingered her hair and glanced at her own body. He was probably thinking the same thing about her. She had forgone makeup and dressing up and stood in a pair of jeans and Matt's flannel shirt that she desperately wished still smelled like him. Jane looked at her sister. Sarah looked frail somehow, and Jane wondered if she was sick.

"Hey," Jane said, meeting her sister's eye. It was the first time they had talked since Thomas confessed.

"Hey, sis," Sarah said with a soft smile. "You look more like mom every day."

That was a high compliment, because their mother had been a beautiful woman, but it was also untrue. Jane shook her head.

"No, I mean it. Country life… suits you. All of you. I'm glad—"

"How are you holding up?" Jane asked.

"We're doing okay. We planted a garden in the backyard." She pointed to the girls. "These two have quite the green thumb."

Jane smiled. "We have one too. Maddy is our head gardener."

Sarah's brows raised as Maddy laughed and shrugged. "Yeah, I know how to can vegetables now too, and how to make jam," she said, holding up her blueberry-stained fingers. "I actually have Amish friends now, Mom," she said seriously.

Sarah laughed at that. "You all look good. The kids look…" Her eyes filled with tears and Jane's did too.

"Where is Matt?" Thomas asked. For once, he sounded concerned instead of accusing.

"He's gone. He went to the Army." Tommy piped in.

Thomas met Jane's eyes. "When is he coming back? I owe him an apology."

She shook her head slightly and gave Thomas a look she hoped he understood. She hadn't told the kids yet that he wasn't coming back. "Don't worry about it."

Whether or not Thomas understood, Sarah did. "Oh, Jane…" she began.

"What's in those bags, Daddy?" Tommy interrupted.

Thomas turned. "Ah, yes! Stand back," he said. He picked up the first one and tossed it over the fence and through the Veil. "Let Austin or Maddy get them." He told Tommy as he tossed the other one over. "And then no peeking until mom has looked through them."

Austin and Maddy each picked up a backpack and put them on their backs.

Tommy nodded. "I drew you a picture at home, but I didn't bring it. It's one with me and you and mom and Maddy and Aunt Sarah and Mr. Ed and Austin and Matt and the chickens having a bonfire! Bria's not there cause she always goes to bed before we do fires. I'll bring it next time."

"I'm sure I'll love it, bud—" Thomas's voice wavered.

More tears filled her eyes and then—Jane heard a weird, popping sound that reminded her of the Fourth of July. A loud boom brought everyone's head around as one of the buildings they had just come from exploded in a ball of fire.

"Ed." Jane breathed. Had there been an accident or—

Wallace pulled his gun from its holster. "Get down!" he shouted over his shoulder as he peeked around the side of the jeep back up the road.

Jane looked frantically around for somewhere to hide. It was all just fields. There was nowhere to go.

"Quick!" she shouted to the kids, all but dragging them to the grass. "Lay down!" She covered Bria with her body and pushed Tommy's head into the dirt. "Don't—" The surreal staccato of gunfire cut her off. She pushed Tommy's head down harder and lifted hers just enough to make sure Austin and Maddy had done the same. Bria squirmed and cried beneath her. Jane squeezed her eyes shut in terror. They were trapped between the gunfire and the Veil.

A weird whizzing sound forced her eyes open, and she watched in horror as the road around them and the Jeep exploded in a cloud of dust.

She turned and looked through the Veil. Thomas and Sarah were laying on the asphalt runway thirty feet away, shielding the girls.

Jane turned her head in the direction of the gunfire. She could see them now. Three pickup trucks barreling down the highway. There was a pop and something sailed over their heads through the Veil, and erupted on the other side, like a small bomb.

Wallace opened fire on the trucks as machine-gun fire erupted around them. One truck veered wildly, flew off the road into a field, and overturned. The man in the back screamed as he flew out and was crushed by the rolling vehicle. The two other trucks continued toward them. More shots were fired, and Jane watched in horror as

Wallace's head exploded in a pink mist. He dropped lifelessly to the ground.

She looked down at the kids, grateful that their faces were hidden and none of them had seen it, trying to figure out what to do, how to protect them. Everything was happening so fast. Jane struggled to unbuckle Bria from her chest, then thrust her in Maddy's arms. "Stay down. Do not let her go."

"Aunt Jane?" Maddy cried.

"Stay down!" Jane yelled as she pushed herself to her knees and jumped to her feet. Keeping her head low, she made a run for the jeep. She spotted the rifle propped between the seats and yanked the gun out. She flipped the safety, set it against the hood of the jeep, aimed and fired and missed. The trucks barreled past her.

Stunned, Jane turned as one of the men in the back shouted, "We're almost there, boys!"

Her relief was short-lived, as her eyes focused on the metal spike rising from the ground in the distance. *They are going to take out the tower.*

Jane's head whipped around to the fleet of vehicles approaching the Veil from both sides. They were too far away. They would never make it in time. Thousands of innocent people would die.

She looked at Thomas and Sarah, and the two little girls laying helplessly on the ground. They would certainly be killed. And while there was no love lost between them, she did not want her kids to lose their parents, to witness them die. And those little girls—

Jane pressed her lips together and gripped the gun in her hands. She couldn't do anything about the people she'd failed to warn when she'd fled the city, but she could do something about this. She had to at least try.

Gritting her teeth, she ran as fast as she could down the road after the trucks.

"Jane!" Thomas shouted, but she didn't look back. There wasn't time.

She ran until she was out of breath, then stopped in the middle of the road as they made the turn onto the adjacent road that led to the tower. They were about a half-mile away. Jane didn't know if the bullets would even go that far, but it was now or never.

Images of Matt flashed before her eyes as she aimed. She felt his hand on her arm, his breath in her ear. Jane held the gun just as he had taught her. *Breathe in.* She exhaled and pulled the trigger. The gun bucked painfully against her shoulder as the shots fired. One, two, three, four. BANG. Five, six—She kept her finger pressed until no more shots came.

The truck on the right fishtailed briefly, tossing the gunman onto the road before colliding with the one beside it. The gut-wrenching sound of crumpling metal filled the air. A split-second later, the trucks flew apart. One crashed into the barbed wire fence and went through the Veil. The other went headfirst into a water-filled ditch that lined the other side of the road.

"Jane!"

She turned around and saw it. Another pickup racing down the road toward her, followed by a slew of military vehicles. She started back toward the kids.

Half the jeeps and trucks on Thomas's side skidded to a stop next to his SUV, while the other half continued on along the Veil toward the truck that had crashed. Armed men jumped out, training their weapons on the truck as it flew toward her. Shots erupted from Thomas's side of the Veil, trapping her and the kids in the middle of the gunfire.

"Mommy!" Tommy cried.

He had lifted his head and was looking around.

She dropped the gun. It clattered to the ground. "Stay down!" she yelled, racing toward them.

More shots rang out, and she covered her head as she ran past Wallace's body. She slid down into the grass beside the kids as the pickup truck hit the corner of the parked Jeep. She lifted her head as it tore through the gravel, then spun out in the middle of the road fifty feet away.

"Are you guys—" The staccato of gunfire resumed coming at them from both sides and she dropped her head back to the ground. She heard the screeching of tires, and men yelling, then the pop of more gunfire. "Keep your heads down!"

"Aunt Jane!" Austin cried.

"Keep your head down!"

She heard more shouting. It took all of her willpower to do the same. Another shot fired.

The repeated honking of a horn finally drew her head up. She recognized her Grand Caravan as Ed barreled toward them. She looked at the wall of vehicles now parked between her and the kids and the gunfire.

Jane jumped to her feet, dragging Austin and Tommy up with her. "Get up! Quick! The van!" She grabbed Bria from Maddy. "Go!" she ordered. Jane glanced back at Sarah and her husband.

"Go!" Thomas shouted as he dragged Sarah and the girls toward his car. "Go!" he yelled again.

Jane covered her baby's head and ran toward Ed as more shots rang out.

Chapter Sixty

Day 73 // 8:10 a.m

MATT STOOD in front of the TV, blocking the view of the other soldiers who were just finishing up breakfast.

Diggs was saying something to him, but Matt couldn't hear anything above the thumping in his chest.

He held up his hand, trying to focus on the news anchor's words. "***Stunning footage from Detroit yesterday, where a group of gunmen bombed a temporary joint Airforce and Coast Guard facility north of the city. They were part of a larger operation that was trying to attack several key towers and destroy the city. An unknown civilian woman, single-handedly thwarted an attempt to destroy a tower on the north side of the city. Dubbed G.I. Jane by the media, it is estimated that her heroic deeds saved over twenty-thousand people yesterday, including all the men and women stationed at Anderson Airforce Base, who would have been lost to the Veil had the terrorists succeeded in destroying the tower. Only the attack on the west side of the city was successful, where an estimated ninety thousand people, forty-thousand of which were already infected with the X-Virus, lost their lives.***

"The gunmen were later identified as Marcus Wilson, Adrien Brockman, and Adam Langley…"

The news called her G-I-Jane. He called her Jane Moore, and the moment he saw her running for her life with the kids, Matt's anger over his parents and Max dissolved into gut-wrenching regret, and he knew he'd made a terrible mistake.

Diggs said something else, but Matt held up his hand as they replayed the video. The news crew that had been there at the scene had caught the whole thing—or most of it, anyway. He stared in horror at Bria's fat little cheeks as Jane pressed her head to her shoulder. Matt stumbled into the nearest chair.

"Farm? What's wrong?" Digg asked.

Matt recognized his favorite shirt and Maddy's red hair. He also recognized the two brothers holding hands as they ran for their lives.

You should have been there.

"Farmer? What's…" Diggs looked up at the TV and then back. "What's going on?"

The report moved on to death tolls before he could tell if they made it or not. He sat up and shouted at the TV.

"Wait. No, no, no… go back!"

Matt stared blindly at the escalating numbers in Baltimore, San Diego, and Jakarta for a moment, then pulled his phone out of his pocket. His head swam as he found Jane's number and dialed it.

"Hey man," Diggs said. "We gotta go."

Matt held his breath and squeezed his eyes shut, dropping his head into his hand. If anything happened to her or the kids… He should have never left.

She answered on the fifth ring.

"Hello?"

Tears sprang to his eyes. "Are you okay?"

"Matt?" she said, sounding confused.

"Are you okay?" he repeated. "Where are you?"

"Home. Why?"

Matt heaved a sigh of relief. "You are all over the news."

"I am?"

"Damn it, Jane. Why did you go down there?"

"I—"

He didn't hear the rest of what she said because Sergeant-Major Jones stormed in, yelling at him to get off his ass and join his squad.

Matt pulled himself up from the chair as Diggs hurried out the door.

“Can I call you tonight?” he asked, meeting Jones’s eye. His commanding officer didn’t look happy.

“Um, sure,” she said.

Matt ended the call, and not having time to take it back upstairs, dropped his phone into his CO’s hand. Then he hurried to join his men.

Chapter Sixty-One

Day 74 // 2:44 p.m

JANE SAT on the back porch snapping green beans because she didn't know what else to do with herself. Matt hadn't called her back last night like he promised, and she didn't know what that meant. She had tried calling him, but it went straight to voicemail. So now she was waiting and wondering if he had just changed his mind or if he was dead. Neither of those was very appealing, but if she had to pick one, she'd take the former. A world without Matthew Patterson was not one she wanted to live in, even if he didn't want to be with her.

It was excruciating, because things were getting worse everywhere and she didn't even know where he was stationed. There were more and more reports of Insiders having found ways to disable Veil, and whether or not they were true, the rumors had many of the Outsiders worried about a breach. Detroit was not the only city attacked from the outside. Miami and Boston had also been hit. A military base outside of D.C. had been targeted and thirteen soldiers were wounded, one in critical condition.

She had also finally seen herself on the news last night. They were calling her 'G.I. Jane', which was laughable.

Thomas had called after seeing the broadcast and for the first time, maybe ever, she heard true admiration in his voice when he said, "That was a hell of a thing you did, Janie. I… I didn't recognize you." The truth was, she didn't recognize herself either.

"Is Matt coming home soon?" Tommy asked, playing with Bria on the floor.

"I don't think so, Bud."

"Can we go see Dad and Aunt Sarah?"

"Nope. They are not allowing visitations right now."

"Because of the virus?"

"Yep."

"I wish it was done," he said wistfully.

Bria grabbed Jane's leg and pulled herself to her feet. Her tiny arms tried to reach for a handful of beans. Jane smiled as she pulled the bowl away. Her baby girl would be walking in no time. It made her sad that Thomas would miss it. If nothing else, he had been a good father to the kids.

She squinted out over the fields, then looked at her phone again.

Where is Matt?

She checked her phone at least fifty more times before Ed announced the van was loaded.

They all piled in and made the short drive into Mariette.

They parked on a side street, and Austin helped Jane carry the folding table the short distance to where they were setting up shop. Jane stared in amazement as she waited for Ed and the boys to bring the boxes. The main street of downtown Mariette had been transformed into a small flea market. Dozens of tables lined either side of the road, and people were setting up their wares. She recognized the bra-less woman from the grocery, who had a bunch of toys and children's clothes folded neatly beside them. There was an old man setting up a table with various sized jars of honey. There was an empty table with a small sign that announced fresh cuts of beef would be available in the morning. There were household items, dishes, blankets, and the most incredible thing about all of it was that it was free.

The community had decided to come together and help each other. People were to come and take whatever they needed.

Ed and Austin hauled items from the trunk as Jane laid them out on the table. It was mostly old tools, but there was Ruth's extensive costume jewelry collection, too. Ed had also decided it was time to let her clothes go. Except for a few pieces either he or Jane kept, it was all in boxes ready to be shared with the community.

Jane was bouncing Bria and walking as the boys inspected the other tables for treasures. Austin shouted, "Aunt Jane, look!" He pointed to a tackle box full of colorful lures and bobbers. "Matt would love this!"

He and Tommy went to inspect the box, and a pretty dark-haired woman, about ten years younger than Jane, warned the boys about the hooks that lay inside. Then she turned and smiled at Jane. "Your daughter is adorable," she said.

Jane smiled back. "Thanks."

"Unfortunately, I only have boy's clothes," she pointed to Tommy. "But I've got tons in your son's size."

Jane smiled, noticing the pile of sweaters, sweatshirts, and coats. Those would be handy for fall.

"You don't remember me, do you?" the woman asked.

Jane frowned and studied her. "I–I'm sorry. Do we know each other?"

"I saw you at the store right after the Veil went up. I think I scared you by talking to your son." She nodded toward Tommy again, and Jane remembered.

"You were wearing a T-shirt that said—"

The woman laughed. "Yep. It's a stupid shirt, but my late husband bought it for me and I… I wear it sometimes. I was only talking to your—"

"Tommy." Jane supplied.

"—Tommy, because I knew you guys weren't local, and I had all of my boys' old summer stuff and beach toys that I thought you might be able to use."

Jane's cheek turned pink, as she looked down the street at all the people, families, that had come to support each other. They might be a little rough around the edges—Jane spied a camo-happy family pulling coolers out of the back of a truck, and setting cartons of eggs on a table—but they were kind. And they worked hard—Jane looked at Ed—and most of them were pretty decent.

She had been wrong to judge everyone. "I am so sorry. I think I should have been the one wearing the 'I'm The Bitch' shirt."

The woman laughed. "My name is Danny."

Jane held out her hand. "Jane."

"Can we get this for Matt?" Austin asked hopefully.

Jane shook her head and pulled her phone out. If he'd called, she would have heard it, but she checked anyway.

"Let's wait and see until—"

"He's in the Army," Tommy informed Danny, and she frowned.

"Matt Patterson?" she asked.

Jane's brows went up in surprise. "Do you know him?"

Danny wore the same look. "Do you?"

"Yeah. He was um… helping us out for a while, but then… he had to go," she finished lamely.

"He taught me how to fish," Austin said proudly. "I'm the best fisherm–person in the family."

Danny's brows raised higher. "He did what?"

"You know him?" Jane asked, trying to remember Matt's ex-fiancé's name. Was this her? *No, that was Katie.*

"Yeah, we grew up together. I've known Matt since kindergarten."

Jane smiled, unable to imagine what he must have been like then.

"He was back?" Danny asked. "*Here*?"

Jane frowned. "Yeah, is that—"

"Huh. That's weird."

Jane didn't get it. "Weird?"

"I've never met anyone that hated being a country boy more than Matt Patterson."

Jane frowned. That didn't sound like Matt at all. "Really?"

Danny laughed. "Oh my god. He couldn't wait to get out of

here, and as far as I knew, he hadn't been back." She studied Jane. "You don't believe me?"

It wasn't that she didn't believe her; it was just… she thought he had left because of his father.

Danny pulled out her phone and scrolled through it. "Look." She handed it to Jane.

Jane barely recognized Matt with his shaved head and clean jaw in his white polo and flip-flops. The photo must have been taken before he lost his leg. He was standing next to a shorter man with black, clipped hair and a darker complexion.

"Keep scrolling," Danny said.

The next picture showed Matt in a suit, looking like a runway model. "That was for our friend Gates's wedding."

Jane recognized Danny and the man from the previous picture and…

"Who is that?" Jane asked, pointing to the woman beside Matt. She was tall and thin. Her long, dark, wavy hair was punctuated with expensive auburn highlights. She had pouty red lips and huge breasts that spilled out of the sexy, skin-tight silver dress she wore.

"Oh, that is Katie," Danny said, rolling her eyes.

Jane's heart stopped beating in her chest.

That is Katie?

Jane's eyes fell back to the phone as she studied every perfect detail of the woman's body. Then she studied Matt. He looked so relaxed and… happy. And there was no denying they made a gorgeous pair.

Bria made a grab for the phone, and Jane pulled it away just in time to hand it back to Danny.

"Are you okay?" Danny asked.

Jane plastered a smile on her face. "Yeah. I'm… I—" The boys took off toward the next table. "It was nice to meet you."

"Likewise," Danny called. "If you talk to Matt, tell him I said hi."

Jane nodded and hurried away.

Matt had told her he'd been engaged, but what he hadn't said was Katie looked like a supermodel.

Jane looked down at herself, picturing the body she knew lay underneath her clothes. She'd changed a lot over the last couple months, inside and out—but she would never look like that woman. Maybe that was why he was staying away.

They made the walk down the street and back, and then it was time to pile in the van and head home.

Jane stared at the fields as they drove back to the farm. The crops were getting close to harvest. The problem for the farmers was how they were going to bring it all in without gasoline for their tractors.

She stared at the rows of sugar beets as they sailed past, and then the green fields of soybeans. She loved it here, and she thought Matt had too, but the picture Danny painted, the ones she actually showed her, was not the man she knew.

As they pulled into the driveway, Jane couldn't help but wonder. *Which man was the real one?*

Chapter Sixty-Two

Day 75 // 10:55 a.m

BRIA HAD BEEN up all night, so Jane sent the kids with Ed to the swap while she stayed behind. After a dose of Tylenol and a half-hour of rocking in Ed's recliner, she had finally gotten the baby down.

Taking the last sip of her cold, watery coffee, Jane put her mug in the sink and started the dishes. The doorbell rang. She grabbed a towel, wiped her hands, and hurried to the door. *Please don't wake up Bria.*

She quickly unlocked it and pulled it open. Her smile fell.

Standing on the other side of the screen was Jake.

He held a gun, aimed at her head, and looked way too pleased with himself.

Jane met his eyes, or eye rather, as his left one was white and cloudy. The skin on that side of his face was red and patchy.

A spine-chilling smile appeared on the corner of his lips. "Saw you in town yesterday."

Jane winced. She had been a fool to think he would forget about her after what she'd done to him. "Get your ass out here or I'll shoot you through the fucking door," he said.

Jane quickly weighed her options, and she would have tried at least one of them if it had just been her at the house, but—*Bria is upstairs.*

Jane prayed her baby stayed asleep. Slowly, she opened the door and stepped out onto the porch.

He waved the gun toward a black sedan that was parked in the driveway. "Get in."

Jane looked down at her bare feet, then at the car. She willed herself not to turn and look up at Bria's window as she made her way down the steps and across the gravel drive to the car.

"You drive," he said.

Jane hesitated, then went around the other side, and got in. Her hands shook as she reached for the unfamiliar seat belt and tried to remember how to breathe. Bria would be fine in her playpen until Ed and the kids returned—still, it went against every instinct she had to leave her baby girl all alone. Maybe she could drive them into a telephone pole and escape? She'd seen that on TV once.

Jake kept the gun pointed at her as he got in. He had to turn his whole head to see her with his good eye. As if reading her mind, he said, "Take off your seat belt."

Jane undid hers as he buckled his across his giant stomach. "Now fucking drive, bitch," he snarled.

They went down the dirt road, onto the highway, past the cottage, then south about four miles. "There." He indicated a short driveway that led to a big brick house on the water.

Jane shielded herself as his arm came toward her, but he was only pressing the button to the garage door opener that was clipped onto the visor above her head. Jake laughed. "Soon."

To her surprise, the garage opened. *They have power here?* She pulled in, then it closed. She saw his golf cart parked in the corner.

He told her to get out, then open the door into the house.

It was a beautiful lake home, with a wall of windows that looked out over the water. It was also Jake's current home. The soiled white carpet in the living room and the clothes and trash everywhere indicated it had been for quite some time. *Probably since the night—*

"Upstairs," he grunted. "And just in case you're thinking of doing anything stupid."

A gunshot rang out behind her and she ducked as a bullet shattered a picture hanging on the wall.

She slowly made her way up the curved staircase. Jake shoved her down the hall to the master bedroom. It was at the end. Nausea filled her stomach at the sight of the mussed bed, and her heart pounded in her chest.

But then he indicated she should go into the bathroom. It was floor to ceiling white marble, and the stone was cool against her bare feet. There was a huge walk-in shower, a gorgeous clawfoot tub, and a massive vanity with double sinks. There were two windows, one between the tub and shower that faced that main road, and one above the toilet facing the neighboring house to the north.

"Put this on your right wrist."

Jane turned and stared at the pair of handcuffs he held out for her. Fear slithered down her spine as she took them and clamped one side around her wrist. The metal was cold and heavy against her skin.

She looked back out at the bed, wondering what it was Jake had planned for her.

He laughed, then shook his head. "Now get down on the floor and hook the other side around the foot of the tub."

Jane didn't move.

He lifted the gun and pointed it right at her nose. "Get on the fucking floor."

She got on her knees, and then awkwardly hooked the other side of the handcuffs around the tub.

Jake set the gun on the sink, and her eyes went to the bed again. He bent closer to check her bonds, and she scooted back between the tub and the toilet. "Want to know something funny? You're not even my type. I prefer young and firm over old and saggy. Your daughter is more my speed, actually." He grabbed her chin. "But I am still going to enjoy this because by the time I am done with you, you will be *begging* me to fuck you."

He got up abruptly to leave and then stopped.

He pulled a key out of his pocket and held it up. "This is the key to the cuffs." He opened the window above the toilet and punched the screen. She heard it clatter onto the roof. Jake gave her a deadly look then threw the key out the window. "You messed with the wrong man, Jane." Her name on his lips made her want to vomit. "All you had to do was shake my hand. I really am a nice guy. But you didn't." He jabbed a finger at her. "Now, you are going to die alone and humiliated in this room," he said before disappearing around the corner. He'd left the gun.

Jane listened to Jake's heavy footsteps as he made his way down the stairs and lunged for it. She was short by several feet. She laid on her back and tried to knock it off with her toes, but it was no use. She was still too far away. She tried to lift the tub. It didn't budge.

Jane tugged at her wrist, spit on her hand and tried to pull her hand free, but the cuff was too tight.

She crawled back into her hiding spot between the toilet and pulled her feet up to her chest, staring at the sink and the gun. Maybe she should have just killed the both of them in the car.

Chapter Sixty-Three

Day 75 // 9:18 p.m

IT WAS LATE when they finally got back to the hotel, and Matt was exhausted, but he needed to call Jane. He'd had all day and all last night to think about what he needed to say, and he was ready. When he got back to his room, he saw that someone had thoughtfully plugged his phone in.

He grabbed it off the nightstand and winced at the twelve missed calls from Jane. There was one from Ed, too. They were all probably worried.

He tried her phone, but she didn't answer. That was weird. She always had it on her. He tried again, wondering if the screen they had covered with packing tape had finally given out. He decided to try Ed instead. He picked up on the first ring.

"Matthew," he said.

"Hey, Ed, is Jane's phone—"

"Did you get my message?" Ed asked anxiously.

"What? No. I didn't have my phone. I just got back from a raid on—"

"Jane is missing." Ed rushed, not waiting for him to finish.

"What do you mean—"

"We came home from town and she was gone."

"Well, maybe she went for a walk?"

"I don't think so. Her shoes are here by the door and…"

Fear crept up Matt's spine

Ed lowered his voice. "She left Bria, Matthew. In the house alone."

Matt's blood ran cold. *Jane would never leave her baby.* It was like Max and his parents all over again. Something terrible had happened, and he was just standing there, with a stupid fucking phone in his hand.

"Poor thing was screamin' her head off in her crib when we got back. The kids are scared and askin' for her. I don't know what—what to do."

Jake.

"Did you call the police?"

"Yeah, Don Beale came out. But he said we can't do anything until—"

Matt rolled his eyes. Jane would probably be dead in twenty-four-hours. "It's got to be her neighbor, Jake. I don't know his last name. But it's gotta be him. Call Beally back. Ask him if he ever found that asshole's body. He'll know who I'm talking about. If not, tell him to go to his house, and search it from top to bottom."

Diggs walked into the room and dropped his hat on the dresser.

"But what do I tell the kids?" Ed asked.

"You tell them I'm on my way."

Diggs's brows went up as Matt jumped to his feet and started shoving things in his duffle.

"How long has she been gone?" he asked into the phone.

"I don't know. We got home around twelve-thirty."

Matt looked at his watch. "Call Beally, Ed. Then call me back."

Matt hung up the phone and dropped it on the bed.

"Shit, shit, shit!" He grabbed the lamp off the dresser, ripping the cord from the socket, and threw it against the wall.

"Hey, what the fuck?" Diggs asked. "What's the matter?"

"I need to go home."

"Why? What happened?"

Matt met his friend's eyes for a second. "Jane is missing." He grabbed his bag and went to find the commander.

Fifteen minutes later, Matt sat staring at his commanding officer in disbelief. What part did he not understand?

"But I *have* to go, sir," he insisted.

"And I'm telling you, you can't."

"But—"

"You know the rules, Farmer. My hands are tied."

Matt couldn't believe what he was hearing. "But—"

"She is not immediate family. Hell, she's not even your girlfriend."

"Well, she's kind of—"

"No. I asked you very specifically when you got here if there was someone waiting for you back home. You told me—"

Matt winced. He did not need to be reminded of what he said. "But she's got kids. They are all alone."

"Well, no. You just told me there was a guy named Ed there."

This cannot be happening. "He's an old man, and—I have to go. They need me." He could only imagine how terrified the kids were. "And every second we waste—"

"We need you." Master Sergeant Jones said. He took his glasses off and pinched his nose. "Look, I feel for you, but I can't. Without her being next of kin and without a Red Cross verification that anything is even wrong… my hands are tied. No one is getting leave, Farm. You know how things are right now. We are under attack. Yesterday it was a garage full of rednecks and guns, tomorrow… Things are escalating. Millions of lives are at stake."

There was no way he was staying. "Sir, I have to go. I have to try—"

Jones put his glasses back on. "Get some rest, Farmer. You look like hell, and who knows, maybe she just needed a break. This whole thing is stressful on everyone."

"They found her one-year-old daughter alone in the house." Matt seethed.

Jones gave him a look that he couldn't quite read, then shook his head. "Some mothers can't handle the—"

"She's the best mother I know. I have to—"

"I am done arguing with you." Jones interrupted.

"But—"

"Dismissed."

Matt stormed out of the office, grabbed his bag out of the lobby, and headed for the doors. His metal plate echoed off the tile floor. Before he could reach it, two young recruits, Molena and Weir, stepped in front of his path.

"Farmer," he heard Diggs call from behind him. Matt turned. His friend hurried over and said in a hushed voice, "Don't do this man. They are not messing around."

Matt shook his head. "I have to go, Diggs. I have to try…" His heart ached, remembering what Jane looked like the first time she was assaulted by Jake. If he was being honest with himself, he'd realize she was probably already dead. But he wasn't. He couldn't. His heart wouldn't let him. "I have to try."

He turned and headed for the door.

"Return to your post," Molena warned. The kid was cocky and fearless, reminding him of someone he once knew—*You are not him anymore*.

Clearly. Matt shoved him out of the way. That was why he needed to leave.

Weir grabbed his arm, and he threw it off. That's why he was leaving. "Get the fuck off of me," he growled.

"Farmer!" Diggs called.

Matt pushed the door open, then made a run for it. Even before the accident, he wouldn't have made it. But he had to try.

He hadn't even made it halfway across the parking lot when the men caught up with him and wrestled him to the ground.

"Let me go!" he bellowed.

Weir confiscated his gun while Molena handcuffed him, then pulled him awkwardly to his feet. "I need to go home!" Matt yelled again as they dragged him back inside.

Jones and a bunch of other guys were in the lobby. Jones shook his head in disappointment, then turned and went back to his office.

"You've got to help her, Benny," Matt said to Diggs as they pushed him back towards Jones's office. "Wait." He dragged them to a stop in front of his friend. "Take my phone. Call Ed back. Help her. Please."

Diggs's mouth was pressed into a seam, but he nodded imperceptibly as he pulled Matt's phone from his pocket.

"I'll call Ed," he said as they pulled Matt away.

Chapter Sixty-Four

Day 76 // 10:20 p.m

JANE WOKE UP, not knowing where she was. It was dark, but the moon from outside made the white marble glow. It took much longer than it should, but she finally remembered. Her body felt heavy as she pressed herself up from the floor and turned toward the grunting noise in the bedroom. Her head swam, and she could barely swallow. She stared for a minute, not understanding what she was seeing, then turned away when she realized Jake was sitting on the edge of the bed, watching her and rubbing himself.

She scooted back in the corner, her bloody wrist on fire. Her throat ached for water. She was pretty sure it had only been a day… or two, but she hadn't had a single thing to eat or drink. Despite being in a bathroom, there was no water. The only liquid in the room was the toilet filled with Jake's piss.

She licked her lips with a dry tongue and felt them crack. She did it again and tasted blood.

Jake's noises came quicker, and then he groaned.

A moment later, he walked in naked and stood over her. "You ready for a piece of this?" he asked. Her heart erupted in her chest, making her feel faint as she threw her gaze to the floor.

He set a bottle of water down on the floor, just out of reach. "Come on, one little taste, for one little taste? That's fair, isn't it? What do you say?"

Never. Jane stared at the bottle. She shook her head.

He laughed. “Suit yourself. I’ll leave that there in case you change your mind. You know where to find me.”

Chapter Sixty-Five

Day 77 // 1:20 p.m

"PATTERSON!" the guard called. Matt turned. They had tried to put him on restriction, but when he refused to stay put, they had placed a guard at his door.

"You got a phone call."

Matt hurried across the room toward the door. The guard opened it and led him to a hall and a phone. Matt grabbed the receiver.

"Hello?

"Hey man. I'm here."

Thank god.

"Did you find her?"

There was a pause, and Matt's heart sank.

"Not… yet," Diggs said. He didn't sound hopeful.

"Did you find Jake? Did Ed ask—"

"No one has seen him."

"Diggs. It is him. I know it."

"I talked to Officer Beal. He went to Jake's house, but his wife hasn't seen him in weeks. We filed a missing person…"

Matt buried his face in his hands.

"We looked in all the surrounding cabins… by their old house. I don't know what else… Hold on."

Matt heard Maddy's excited voice in the background. "Wait, slow down, what?" Diggs said, away from the receiver. "Shit."

"What?" Matt asked.

"Maddy's got an idea. We'll call you back."

"Thanks, Benny."

"I always got your back, Farm."

Chapter Sixty-Six

Day 78 // 12:10 p.m

THE SUN WAS BLINDING as she pried her eyes open. She no longer had the energy to move, and strangely, it was like her throat was forgetting how to swallow. Jake came in and pissed all over the toilet, spraying some on her pants. He laughed while she just laid there next to it. Everything in her head was blurry. Except for the kids' faces. And Matt's.

Her heart skipped a beat as she tried to pull her lips apart. They were stuck.

"You ready to make amends?" Jake asked.

She turned her head and looked up at him towering over her, then back at the bottle of water that was still on the floor.

He picked it up, and she heard the cracking of the seal as he unscrewed the cap. He took a big sip and then poured a puddle of water on the floor in front of her.

She lifted her head as the pool spread, then glanced up at him. Was it a trick? She decided to take her chances. Forcing her lips apart, she leaned over and began to lap it up off the marble. It was cool and almost sweet on her swollen tongue.

Jake laughed and ruffled her hair. "Good dog. I'll be back in a bit. Just need to grab a bite to eat. Don't go anywhere." He laughed again as he left the room.

Blood mixed with the few precious remaining drops of water as she pressed her lips to the floor. A few moments later, Jane heard the garage door open, then close.

She pushed herself up and then closed the lid of the toilet to curb the smell. Then she rested her head on it. Her heart pounded like she'd run a marathon. She looked at the window. It was daytime, but she had lost sense of time.

You can't stay here. The kids need you.

Jane lifted her head. She had searched the room a million times. There was nothing—

There is always hope, a voice whispered.

She licked her bloody lip.

"He threw away the key," she choked.

Then make a new one, the voice said.

Jane's head swam as she looked around, trying to figure out where it was coming from.

She slumped back down on the floor and rolled onto her back. "With what?" she whispered to the ceiling.

Her eyes traversed the room for the thousandth time. She couldn't reach anything but the tub. *And the toilet.*

Jane's head turned, and she stared at it.

Slowly, she sat up. Blinking back dizziness, she got to her knees. With difficulty, she lifted the top of the tank. It felt like it was made out of lead. Her arms shook and her heart felt like it was going to explode. She slid it to the side. She couldn't stand and see what was inside, but she could reach her hand in it. She felt around until her fingers closed over metal. She pulled it, and the handle of the toilet moved.

She jerked on it.

Again. The voice said.

She did it again, but her strength was gone.

Again. It demanded.

"I can't."

Again, Jane. The voice changed, and it sounded like Matt's.

She took a shallow breath.

Don't stop until it's free Mommy, Tommy's sweet voice called.

With a weird, raspy cry, Jane did what she was told.

Finally, it broke free on one side. She bent the metal back and forth until it detached from the back of the handle. She slid the top back on before falling back onto the floor on the verge of passing out.

Jane turned the little six-inch metal rod over in her hand. She rolled over and scooted up to the foot of the tub. She tried to shove the end in the keyhole, but it was too big. Next, she tried to bust the actual cuff, by wedging it against the foot, but she wasn't strong enough, or the rod wasn't long enough.

She cried, but strangely, no tears came. Her arms, tired from holding her body up, buckled. Her cheek hit the cool floor, causing her vision to go black for a moment. She blinked and tried to focus on the rod in her hand.

There's always hope. The voice sounded like hers again.

Jane stabbed it into the grout joint and dragged it along the rough surface. Maybe if she could grind it down, it would fit into the keyhole. She did it over and over until there was no sand left between the tiles. Then she moved to the next row and did it again.

Jane heard the garage door and froze. Her 'key' was still too big to fit in the lock. Panic welled up in her chest as she tried to think through the delirium. Should she hide it? If she passed out again and he found it—this was her only chance.

She blew the debris from the grout joints under the tub with shallow breaths. She heard Jake… and shoved it under her left thigh, then fell on her back, winded.

Jake appeared in the doorway. "I'm back."

She turned her head and looked at him upside down, as Plan B quickly formed in her head.

He waved a bottle of water at her. "Thirsty?"

It was a terrible plan. She knew it. But she also realized she had no choice. In order to work though, she needed him to be on the other side of her, near her feet, at the other end of the tub.

Then lead him.

Jane glanced at the window, the one between the shower and the tub, then back at him.

Her heart sounded like a drum in her ears.

That's it. Again. Matt's voice said.

She glanced at it out of the corner of her eye again. Jake's eyes followed hers.

He frowned. "What are you looking at?"

Jane took one more quick look toward the window, then shook her head. "Nothing," she croaked, turning her head toward the wall.

She caught movement out of the corner of her eye and almost smiled.

There's always hope. Maddy said.

He walked past her toward the window. Jane grabbed the little shiv from under her butt. This wasn't hope, she thought darkly, clutching the cool piece of metal in her left hand.

"It's revenge," she whispered.

As soon as he was past her, she drew her legs to her chest and threw her feet into the back of his knees. She rolled out of the way as he fell backward. His head cracked against the floor beside her as the water bottle he'd been holding rolled under the tub. Jane scrambled to her knees and quickly positioned herself over him. The strain on her raw wrist almost drew her under as she raised her left hand above his stunned face.

If she was going to die in this bathroom—She plunged the rod into his neck, then jerked it toward her—

So is he.

Chapter Sixty-Seven

Day 80 // 4:44 p.m

MATT WAS LOSING HIS MIND. He hadn't heard from Diggs in three days, which meant they had not found Jane. Which meant…

He ran his hands over his clipped hair, then dragged them across his face.

He replayed their fight over and over. *Your fight,* since he was the one who had done all the yelling, while she just sat there looking devastated and confused. He had also played her messages, all twelve of them, and finally understood what an utter fool he'd been. Jane had nothing to do with the dissemination of her paper, if that really was what was driving the Veil and the deaths. And when she ran with the kids, she wasn't being a coward. She was being a mother. She was trying to protect—

"Damn it," Matt hit the wall, and the guard looked up from his desk on the other side of the plexiglass window that separated the common room from the office.

Master Sergeant Jones had moved him here after he tried to escape the third time, and now he was stuck at a rather comfortable low-security detainment center at the Navy base north of the city. He looked out the barred windows. It was more like a dormitory, than a prison. He was free to roam around, he just couldn't do the one thing he wanted to, which was leave.

He had tried appealing to Jones's commanding officer, and that hadn't gone well. Basically, he was fucked. His nightmares had returned too, only instead of Tony dying in his arms, it was Jane.

Every time he closed his eyes, she was there, her bloody face, and terrified eyes, clutching her torn jeans as she begged over and over, "Help me."

The sun was bright, and he squinted, remembering the day at the beach with her and the kids. It had been one of the best days of his life. He could not believe how much he ached to be near them again, to hear them laugh, to be drooled on and jumped on. He remembered Jane's face as she—

"Patterson!" his voice came over the speaker. Matt whipped around.

The guard waved at him through the window and held up the phone.

With his heart in his throat, Matt hurried across the room. The guard buzzed the door, and he flung it open. He snatched the phone out of the waiting man's hand.

"Hello?"

Diggs's voice was flat. "We found her."

"Where? What—"

"Farm, man…"

The blood drained from his head and Matt fell onto the desk as Diggs explained.

"No… no… no…"

Chapter Sixty-Eight

Day 100 // 6:00 p.m

PRESIDENT RODRIGUEZ STARED at the camera. Then, with a slight nod, began to speak.

"In light of the hostility toward the Armed Forces both here in the United States and abroad, and due to the escalating violence, I have decided to be utterly transparent with you about the crisis we face. And in light of that, I have no choice but to share with you some very… sobering news."

He paused.

"The virus, previously called the X-Virus, is now known to be a mutated airborne form of rabies encephalitis called REV1. It is responsible for the death of over twenty-three million people, some 12 million Americans, and it is not done."

He paused again.

"Rabies encephalitis has been known for years in the medical community to be quite lethal. Under normal conditions, it is spread through animal bites." He set his hands, palm down, on his brilliantly polished desk.

"Sadly, I am here to inform you that this is no longer the case. After extensive investigation, it is believed that one of the people present at the taping of Mornin' Manhattan was in proximity to an animal with the REV1 virus, triggering the pandemic."

President Rodriguez sighed, and his eyes were sad.

"While identifying this disease is a step in the right direction, unfortunately, at present there is no cure for REV1, nor is there

for its more familiar counterpart. Once the symptoms appear, and they do much more quickly with REV1, death is imminent. There is, however, good news. There are hundreds of men and women, right now, working on a vaccine. Until it becomes available, we must work together to prevent further outbreaks. As is the case with rabies encephalitis, prevention is key. I cannot state this enough. For those of you on the inside, please, please, please obey the quarantine. For those of you on the outside, stop attacking our military and law enforcement. They are following orders, and they are there to help you. We must work together. It is the only way we survive. I don't want to live through another New York, or Atlanta, or Dallas. I don't want to live through another San Diego. I don't want the world to suffer another Rome, Moscow, or Delhi.

"What you cannot do is attack the Veil around your city. This goes for Insiders and Outsiders alike. Do not try to deactivate them. Do not try to go under them. Do not try to destroy them out of fear, as some have tried in cities like Detroit.

"I have promised you honesty and now you will have it. We cannot let the Insiders out until we have a vaccine. If you try to escape, you jeopardize the lives of everyone. You will be dealt with swiftly and forcibly and be charged with treason. Any Outsider that tries to destroy the Veil will suffer a similar fate."

President Rodriguez paused, and his shoulders sagged.

"That being said, if the cities reach a critical mass, that is, if the number of infected climbs to such a degree that containment within the population is impossible…" he paused. ***"The city will be brought down. That is the agreement all of us in the ICPH made when we activated the Veil. But until that moment, I will do everything in my power to protect the walls from Outsider attack.***

"In this dark hour, every single one of us has a responsibility to the rest of humanity, and if we can hang on for just a little while longer until we find a cure for this virus, we can make it."

He pulled his glasses off and his voice grew impassioned.

"I truly believe we can. I truly believe in the good in all of your

hearts, and I truly believe in the love you have for your children, your families, and your country."

The President continued, ***"And so, while it is with great sadness that I come to you saying the storm is not passed, it is with great joy and hope that I inform you all, that as soon as a vaccine is made, tested, and verified, those living in the cities will be inoculated. And once it is confirmed that everyone is virus free, the Veil will be deactivated."***

He smiled for the first time.

"There truly is hope. But it is up to the citizens of each city to make sure you make it long enough to see that day. It is in your hands whether you survive or not. It is in your hands whether or not your children grow up and have families of their own. You can do it. I believe in my heart, every city can."

The President leaned back, and the feed was cut.

Chapter Sixty-Nine

Day 106 // 1:32 p.m

MATT STARED out the window of the jeep, not even noticing the countryside as it flew by. All he could think about was what he was going to say to them, how he was going to face the kids after abandoning them.

When he heard the news about Jane, a part of him died. And the truth was, he dreaded the idea of going back now. But he had to. He had to at least try, didn't he? He owed them all that much.

It had taken this horrible tragedy to make him see, but he saw it clearly now. Matt saw what he needed, who he was. And what he needed was them. Bria's sweet face with Jane's puppy-dog eyes, Austin with his freckled nose, and Maddy with her snarky jabs, Tommy with his adorable too-big-for-his-mouth teeth, and—

"You don't seem very happy for someone who's been just let out of the guardhouse and granted immediate leave," his seatmate said, gnawing on a piece of gum.

The other man was headed up to Bay City, and they were both being given a lift by a fellow crewman from Anderson Airforce Base.

Matt ignored him. That asshole had no idea what was—*Or isn't* —he winced, and his heart contracted, waiting for him.

He continued to stare out the window. They passed the street that led to Jane's cottage.

A few minutes later, they turned onto his road. The sugar beets in his dad's field were full and green. His parent's house looked abandoned in the tall grass that surrounded it. They passed the spot where Jane had yelled at him as he dragged the motorcycle after her, then a couple minutes after that, they were making their way down Ed's driveway.

Maddy rushed down the steps, and he saw Diggs up on the front porch with Ed.

Matt turned and pulled his duffle out of the back, then sighed.

"You look like you're going to a funeral, man," the other man said as Matt pushed open the door.

"I am," he said, before slamming it behind him.

As soon as Matt turned around, Maddy threw her arms around him.

Tears filled his eyes as she stepped back. "I'm so glad you're back. We—" She gave Diggs an affectionate look. "We really missed you."

Slowly, Matt climbed the steps.

"Ed."

Ed gave him a fatherly hug, and Matt almost lost his composure. "Welcome home, my boy. It's good to have you back." His face clouded over. "I'm so sorry about—"

"Where are the boys?" he asked, wiping his eyes.

"They're out playin' in the corn. We're trying to harvest as much as we can, but…"

Diggs held up his scratched hands.

Matt knew he couldn't prolong the inevitable. He took a deep breath and readied himself to face the firing squad. The funeral he was going to was his.

"Where is Jane?"

Chapter Seventy

Day 106 // 1:35 p.m

ED WAS out looking for gas, while she, Maddy, and Diggs did their best to harvest the corn. Actually, it was only her. She stood up and stretched her back. Where everyone else went, she didn't know. Not that it mattered. She looked over the giant field. It was hopeless. There was no way they'd make it down the first row, much less the entire field that stretched a half-mile in either direction.

But she kept at it because doing something was better than doing nothing. Because hurting in body was so much easier than hurting in her soul, where she ached for a man with cider-colored eyes. Jane shook her head. She was doing it again. Thinking of Matt when—

She took a sip from her water jug. Since the incident with Jake, she couldn't get enough to drink. Her kidnapping still felt like a dream, probably because after her first couple of days in captivity, she didn't remember much. In the hospital, she'd been unable to answer most Officer Beale's strange questions. All she remembered was being incredibly thirsty and the smell of blood. Officer Beale assured her Jake was dead, and when she asked how he died, the old police officer had given her a funny look. She hadn't inquired further, realizing she didn't care.

Latte Jane would have died back there, or at the very least, needed years of therapy and pills to cope. But lucky for her, she was someone else now. Stronger. A survivor. And she was fine. If she was being honest—Jane stared at her bandaged wrist—she felt more than fine. After all *she* was the one still standing, while Jake was rotting in the ground.

She reached for another stalk and began to saw. Blisters covered her hands and bled onto the stalks as she worked, but the distraction felt good.

She heard Ed returning from town and looked back at her progress. A half row. He had been gone for over two hours and she had only managed a half row. It was embarrassing. She shook her head, scooping up the stalks and dragging them back to the tepee she and Maddy had carefully arranged.

She laid two against the pile, but as she laid the third one out, the whole thing began to lean.

"No, no, no!" she shouted, grabbing at the stalks. The coarse leaves cut at her arms and cheek, and she lost her balance. The entire thing collapsed, and she fell on top of it.

"Damn it!" she cursed, thumping the stalks and cutting the side of her hand, yet again. "Ow—"

"Need some help?" a voice asked.

Jane's head whipped around and she stared at his perfect silhouette against the sun—wondering if she had developed heatstroke and was hallucinating. She still got fuzzy sometimes, even though she had been home from the hospital for two weeks. She blinked to clear her head, but he was still there. He took another step, and she saw his face. His hair was clipped close to his head and his jaw was tight, but otherwise he looked just as he had before. Handsome and—

"Matt?" she whispered.

He crossed the remaining steps between them, lips were pressed into a narrow seam as he held out his hand. He looked miserable. Had something happened?

Slowly, she reached up, afraid maybe it was another dream. Her fingers stopped against his warm palm. His hand closed over hers, and a jolt raced up her arm.

"Matt?" she asked again. "What are you—" She searched his eyes, totally confused by what she saw in them.

"I love you, Jane." His voice broke.

She stared at him in shock. How many times had he said those beautiful words in her dreams? How many times had she woken up and thought she might die of heartbreak, knowing he was never coming—Why was he saying them now?

"I'm so sorry." His voice was filled with regret. "I should have been here. For you. For the kids. I am so—"

He came back.

Jane's hand closed around his, and she pulled his arm. He lost his balance and tumbled forward.

"What the—" he said, catching himself just before he crushed her.

She didn't remember much from her ordeal with Jake, but she did remember some things. And lying on that bathroom floor, chained to the bathtub, she realized her only *real* regret was Matt. It was ignoring her feelings for him, not kissing him back that first day on the porch, when she'd wanted to so desperately and every day thereafter. She loved him. Since the day she had stumbled out of her bedroom and found out he'd been taking care of her kids, she had loved him. And life was too short. In her delirium, as she lay, waiting to die, she swore to herself that if she lived, and Matt ever gave her another chance, she would not waste it.

Jane rolled him over onto his back and straddled him.

A smile spread across her face as she met his surprised eyes. Then, with every ounce of energy she had, she bent down and kissed him.

His hands hesitated for a moment before grabbing her ass. They roamed hungrily up her sides, under her sweaty shirt, cupping her breasts through her bra. It sent a jolt straight between her legs, and she pulsed—

"Oh god," she moaned into his mouth. He did love her. She could feel it. She loved him, too.

She ran her fingers through his spiky hair and along the rough stubble of his cheek, wondering how the hell she had resisted him for so long when he felt so right. She pressed her hips into his, and a familiar part of him pressed back.

"I love you, too," she panted against his lips.

His free hand fumbled with the strap of her bra, slipping it down as far as it would go over her shoulder as he swept his tongue into her mouth. She met him with her own and—

"Aunt Jane?"

"Shit!" Matt bolted upright, shoving her off his lap and into the dirt. Jane looked up at Austin, who appeared out of nowhere, then back at Matt. Happy tears filled her eyes, as her chest heaved and her heart pounded in her ears. *He's back, and he loves you.*

"Matt? You're back?" the boy cried, throwing his arms around him.

Jane smiled at the horror-stricken confusion on Matt's face as he covered his crotch and returned the hug. "Hey, Bud. Yeah… I'm back."

"What are you guys doing out here?" Austin asked with a frown, as Tommy emerged from the corn.

"Maaaatt!" the smaller boy screamed.

"Regular Children of the Corn around here," Matt commented dryly, as Tommy rushed him with a hug and Jane burst out laughing. Matt was back.

She got up, dusted herself off, and offered him her hand. Austin reached for his other one and they pulled him to his feet. She smiled again at his dazed expression.

"Come on! Did you see Maddy yet?" Austin asked, running ahead.

Jane went to follow the boys, but Matt pulled her to a stop.

"Jane… I need to apolog—"

She grabbed his face in her hands. "Accepted."

Then she hungrily found his mouth again. She boldly tugged his t-shirt from his pants and slid her hands underneath it, touching him for the first time. She couldn't believe herself, or the way his abs felt beneath her palms. "Jesus Christ," she breathed.

"Jane," he whispered against her mouth, and she almost lost her mind. "You're killing me."

"Mom!" Tommy shouted from the porch.

Matt groaned and pressed his forehead to hers.

"Mom!"

Jane broke away. Shielding her eyes from the sun, she headed toward the house. "Coming!"

Matt quickly caught up to her. He grabbed her ass, and she jumped as he growled in her ear. "We are finishing that as soon as humanly possible. Do you understand me?"

She turned and saluted him. "Yes, sir."

He gave her a hard look, which she countered with a wink. His stoic expression faltered, and he burst out laughing. "Who the hell are you, and what have you done with Jane Moore?"

"I'm a woman who finally knows what she wants."

His eyes crinkled at the corners. "Oh really? And what is it that you want?"

She lifted herself on her tiptoes. Leaning against his shoulder, she bit his ear and whispered, "You."

He grabbed her, slid one hand around her back and the other behind her neck, under her hair. "Don't start something you can't—"

"Mom!" Tommy called again. Matt rolled his eyes with a frustrated sigh. "Cock blocked again by a six-year-old."

"You'd better get used to it," she said breathlessly.

"The very, very sad truth is I already am."

Jane laughed and kissed him, then wiggled out of his arms, heading toward the house.

"I should leave more often," he said.

Jane stopped, and her smile fell. Did that mean he was going back?

"I have to go back," he said, reading her mind. "But I have

almost four days now. And when I go back, it will only be for a little while. I talked to the chaplain. He is going to help me. I'm going to petition for discharge."

Petition for discharge? She didn't have any idea what that meant.

He looked worried. "I want to stay, but I can't."

"Why not?"

"I did some things I shouldn't have, and now there are consequences—"

"What do you mean?" Jane asked, worried. What did he do? What were the consequences?

"It means I shouldn't have reenlisted. It means…" he touched her cheek, and his eyes were more serious than she'd ever seen them. "I'm not a soldier anymore."

"You're not?" she asked, tears of relief stinging her eyes.

He shook his head. "No."

"Wh-what are you then?"

"I am a man desperately in love with you. And I know where I belong now, Jane." He pulled at the wispy strands of hair that hung across her eyes. "And it's right here with you and the kids."

He bent to kiss her, and she closed her eyes as a voice rang out. "Farmer! Come on, man. Either get a damn hotel room or cut it out. There are children—"

Matt laughed as Jane wheeled around and saw Diggs, Maddy, and Ed on the porch.

Matt bent toward her. "What do you think of Diggs?"

Jane laced her fingers through his as they made their way to the porch. "I think he's already a part of the family. Just ask Maddy."

Chapter Seventy-One

Day 106 // 6:19 p.m

THE FAMILY HAD WELCOMED Diggs with open arms, just like he expected—just like they had welcomed him—and it filled his heart. Diggs was fresh out of high school when he joined Matt's unit in Afghanistan, and he was as close to a little brother as Matt had ever had. His family had been killed when Atlanta fell, which was why he'd been so determined to stay and help in Chicago. He'd also gone AWOL for Matt, which he still had to thank him for. That was no small ask.

Matt watched Jane as she sat across from him, laughing and sipping her wine. Her hair was longer, grayer at the top, and her wrist was still bandaged, but despite her ordeal, her eyes sparkled and she looked… happy.

When Diggs had told him they found her unconscious, chained to a bathtub, next to Jake's rotting corpse, his knees had buckled beneath him. When Diggs told him she had practically severed his head with a makeshift shiv, had almost died from dehydration, and was in a coma at the hospital, he had almost fainted.

Matt looked at Maddy, not so inconspicuously holding Diggs's hand under the table. For some reason, the girl looked more like a woman than she had only a couple of months ago. Thank god she had turned eighteen last month. They made a cute couple.

It was Maddy who had realized that Jake must have come in a car that he didn't own, that hadn't been reported as missing. So instead of cottages, they'd started looking at the empty lake houses with attached *garages*. Beale had gotten lucky when he had talked to one of the few full-time lake owners and they mentioned seeing the neighbor's garage door open briefly one day when they were out walking. When Beale approached the house and saw the open window upstairs and smelled the body—*It's over.* Thank god for that.

Their time apart had transformed her, inside and out. He could see it in her sunburnt face, in the blisters on her hands, in the way she'd straddled him like a goddamn bull rider and practically fucked him on a pile of corn.

The thought brought a smile to his lips, and electricity to his groin. *Soon, big buddy*, he thought. *Soon.* Diggs glanced at him, then leaned over and whispered something in her ear, to which she burst out laughing. Matt frowned. How was it that she was over there with Diggs while he was over here with—

Bria pulled on his sleeve.

Matt grinned down at her. "You remember me? I'm Matt. Maaaattt."

Bria gave him a questioning look. "Maaa."

He laughed and rubbed her dark, wispy hair. "Man, I missed you, and your chubby little…" She grabbed his hand and chomped on his finger. He yanked it back. "Ow. Hey!" Bending to inspect her mouth, he pushed her bottom lip down and saw two tiny white teeth. She looked even more like a bulldog than before. "Look! The pup has teeth!" Bria tried to chomp him again. "No. No biting. But you are adorable."

Jane smiled at him across the table and got up.

Matt followed her, sliding his hand around her waist as she grabbed a bowl off the counter.

He still couldn't believe she had forgiven him. He thought after what happened she would never speak to him again—that was why he made Ed, Diggs, and Maddy swear to secrecy. He wanted to at least make his plea in person. Jane smiled up at him, and he kissed her nose. He still needed to apologize, and he would, but as long as she was okay, it could wait.

And she definitely seemed to be okay.

Jane squeezed by, heading for the door. "Where are you going?" he asked, grabbing her again. She smelled like soap and lilies, and it made him dizzy. Now that he was free to touch her again, he couldn't keep his hands off her. "I wasn't done…"

Jane spun in his arms and her eyes widened as she glanced at the table shyly. "I'm going to feed the chickens."

He frowned and looked at the bowl in her hands, filled with greens and herbs and sunflower seeds. "You made them a salad?"

"Yep."

Matt threw his head back and laughed. "Why?"

"Well, they give us eggs, the least I could do—"

"Is cook for them?"

Matt continued to laugh as a gentle hand pulled on his pant leg. "Matt, I want to show you my best LEGO race car ever! Come on!"

Matt planted a quick kiss on Jane's lips and leaned close to her ear. "You have way too much time on your hands," he whispered. "But I plan to remedy that very soon. Like as soon as we get the kids to bed." He cast her his most lustful glance, then followed Tommy to the living room.

TWO HOURS LATER, Matt stared at the ceiling of the darkened bedroom contentedly. He shoved his arms under his head. "I have waited so long for this," he whispered.

Jane giggled. "Are you satisfied?" she whispered back.

He propped himself up and looked at her. "Um. In general, yes." Then his eyes dropped to the two boys sleeping soundly between them while Bria snored like a lumberjack in her crib at the foot of the bed. "However…"

She giggled again.

He kept his voice low, trying not to wake the boys, and laid back down. "I've got to be honest. I kinda prefer the pillow."

The bed shook with her laughter.

A smile tugged at his mouth, too. "This is not how I expected tonight to go."

It really wasn't. It was *much* better because every time he had played out his return and apology, she had slapped him in the face, told him she'd never forgive him, and made him sleep in the barn before sending back to base the next morning.

"How did you expect it to go?" she asked.

But none of it happened. Instead—*She forgave you.* He still couldn't believe it. *And she loves you.*

He grinned. "Well, fewer people, for sure." He scratched his chin. "There were definitely no kids in my original scenario."

Bria continued to snore loudly, something he didn't remember from before. "We're gonna have to get that one her own room pretty soon. Maybe in the basement… or out in the barn."

The bed shook again.

Matt's smile widened. "No, really, this is great. I've always wondered what it would be like to sleep in the middle of a colony of baboons, and now I know."

Jane snorted with laughter. "They're just so happy to see you."

"The baboons?"

Jane propped herself up on her elbow. "Hey, these are my kids—"

Matt propped himself up and met her eyes. "They're *our* kids until… well, the time comes." He said slowly, wanting to be clear that he was all in, without making her worry about after, if the Veil came down. "Okay?"

She nodded, and he wondered if now was the time to apologize, because he had made that same promise before, at the cabin. Then he left and broke it.

"Jane, I—" Tommy shifted beside him, then the loudest fart he ever heard ripped through the silence. Matt fell back into the pillow and dragged his hands over his face. *Maybe not.*

Jane tried unsuccessfully not to laugh.

Matt shook his head and covered his nose, trying not to gag. “Jesus Christ. I can’t breathe.”

Tommy shifted and Matt braced himself for round two, but thankfully nothing happened.

“Baboons,” he said solemnly, waving the smell away.

Jane laughed harder, and Matt’s heart, which had been empty for so long, overflowed with joy.

Chapter Seventy-Two

Day 107 // 4:30 p.m

JANE WIPED the sweat from her eyes. The good news was Matt was back. The bad news was, between the kids and the twenty acres of corn they were trying to harvest, there was no time to *be* with him. It was almost like before, except a lot more second base… or was it third? She shook her head. Whatever it was, it wasn't enough and Jane was sure she'd spontaneously combust if her *vaginey-winey*, as Maddy used to call it when she was little, didn't get some satisfaction soon. She'd never felt anything like it when she was with Thomas, and it was driving her insane.

She looked up from the row they had just finished and wiped the dirt from her face.

With two extra strong pairs of hands, they were actually making good time. It was shocking to see the dozens of teepees of corn that dotted the mostly empty field and know it was all done by hand. Jane smiled and wiped her hands on the back of her jeans. Her transformation into a pioneer woman was complete. She was not the only one.

Jane watched as Diggs helped Maddy tie the latest bundle of corn. He said something and her niece blushed and laughed. Maddy looked more like a woman than Jane had ever seen her. She looked like Sarah at that age. The Veil had changed them all. Gone was the bitchy girl Jane had rescued months ago. Diggs's hand lingered on Maddy's arm, and Jane felt a pang of jealousy. Not for Diggs, although he was an incredibly handsome man, but because her niece seemed to be getting more action than she was.

Danny finally arrived with the boys, wearing her "I'm the Bitch" shirt again, and Jane thought Matt might faint when he saw her.

"Danny?" he choked. His eyes immediately filled with tears.

Jane frowned. Were they old high school sweethearts or…?

Danny wrapped him in a very familiar embrace. "It's been too long, Matt."

Matt stepped back and looked over her shoulder. "Alejandro looks just like Tony," he whispered as he squeezed the other woman. Jane's eyes widened as everything fell into place. *Danny is Tony's wife.*

The boys took off together as if they had known each other for years, and Jane wondered if she'd made a mistake by not telling Matt first.

"Um, I invited Danny and the boys over to surprise you."

Matt brushed his hands over his hair and chuckled. "I am very surprised." He cast Jane a soft smile that she couldn't decipher. "Very surprised. You guys head into the house. We'll finish up out here." He turned to Danny. "Are you guys staying for the bonfire too?"

Danny nodded.

"Excellent."

Matt headed back out to the field, and Jane led Danny to the house.

"What's the deal with your shirt?" Jane asked as she rinsed her torn hands in a bucket of water on the back porch.

Danny looked down and smiled. "Tony bought them at the Harley store in the city. We were gonna get a bike after he retired. His shirt said, 'If you can read this, the bitch fell off,' and mine says…"

"Ah."

"We made a stupid pact. He always wore his on Tuesdays, wherever he was stationed, and I always wear mine…" Danny shrugged. "It's Tuesday."

Jane pulled out the cutting board and started chopping vegetables.

"Here, this is a picture of us before he deployed last time." Danny held her phone out, and Jane smiled. Sure enough—matching t-shirts. Then her smile faded as she recognized Matt looking drop-dead gorgeous in jeans and a white polo, with his arm around Katie. God, did that woman ever cover up? She had some kind of stringy tank top on that showed more of her perfect breasts than not, and the shortest jean shorts Jane had ever seen.

Danny must have noticed her face. She snatched the phone away. "Ugh. Katie," she said. "I am so glad he found you instead."

A terrible thought occurred to Jane. "Has Matt dated anyone since he's been back?"

"I don't think so," Danny said. "But I don't know for sure."

Jane leaned against the sink, feeling light-headed. *Katie* was the last person Matt had slept with? Dear god, no. She closed her eyes. To her dismay, Katie's perfect, perky breasts had been seared into the back of her eyelids.

Danny's voice dragged her from her bitter thoughts. "Matt was different when he came back. I think we all were. You don't have anything to worry about, Jane. He *never* looked at Katie the way he looks at you."

Jane shook her head in embarrassment, then changed the subject. "I didn't realize you were Tony's wife."

Danny smiled. "I know. I haven't seen Matt since the funeral. Although he always sends the boys presents for their birthdays and Christmas. I think he felt guilty or something. Like it was his fault."

Jane heard the buzz of a phone and followed it to the top of the fridge. She pulled it down. It was Matt's.

Danny continued, "I wasn't sure how he was going to react today, but… He's different again. Happy, like before."

Jane wasn't listening, because, in a very odd twist of fate,

Katie's name and photo, in yet another revealing tank-top and aviator sunglasses, lit up the screen. She stared. Were they still talking? She hadn't thought so, but… Had he seen her while he was away? Jane could imagine how wonderful Katie must have been in bed. She looked like the kind of woman who could seduce a man with only a glance. Jane recalled all the times she'd tried and failed with Thomas, how pathetic and humiliated she felt when he rolled over and told her he was tired. Jane suddenly realized she didn't know if she was any good in bed. If she went by Thomas's reaction —*Oh god.* Her confidence dissolved. Why had she not thought of this until now? "I need a glass of wine. Do you want one?

Danny's brows went up. "You have wine?"

Jane laughed as the sinking feeling in her belly grew. "A couple of bottles."

Chapter Seventy-Three

Day 107 // 8:52 p.m

MATT TWISTED the corkscrew into the bottle. It was their last night before he and Diggs had to go back and face the music, and he wanted to make the most of it. So, after a dinner of ratatouille, which sounded disgusting, but was actually quite delicious, they had all gone out to sit around the campfire, enjoy the last day of summer, and a couple glasses of wine.

Matt popped the cork on another bottle and held it in the air. "To Ruth!" he shouted, and everyone raised their glasses.

The problem was, something was wrong with Jane.

"To Ruth!" they exclaimed.

Every time he touched her this afternoon, she had resisted him, and looked like she was going to cry. He didn't know if it was something he'd said or…

Ed chuckled and shook his head, wiping a tear from his eye. "She'd get such a kick out of this. Oh man, would she ever."

Matt slid his hand into Jane's and smiled. She froze and looked at him like a deer about to be shot between the eyes.

He had definitely done something. *But what?*

She jumped up. "I've got to go check on Bria. Anyone need anything?"

He pulled her down for a quick kiss, but her lips were drawn so tightly he couldn't find them. She backed up, smiled awkwardly, then practically ran for the house.

Matt leaned toward Diggs, who was seated beside him. "Hey

man, did I do something—" he looked over at the boys, who were lighting sticks on fire"—f'ed up that you noticed. With Jane?"

Diggs followed his eyes toward the house. "Not that I saw. Why?"

He shook his head. "I don't know. Something is wrong."

Danny spoke up. "You keep in touch with Katie?" she asked.

Matt frowned. "Not really."

Her brows went up, and she gave him what Tony used to call her "come-on-stupid-you-can-do-it" look.

Matt looked from Danny back to the house. He pulled his phone out of his pocket, and saw the missed calls from Katie, and remembered he'd left his phone in the house. The lightbulb went on.

He glanced back at Danny, and she nodded.

Matt got up. "I'll be right back."

He went inside, but to his surprise, Jane wasn't there. He checked the front porch. She wasn't there either. Fear grew in his belly. He knew Jake was dead, but—Matt hurried out back again.

He glanced at the bonfire to see if he'd somehow missed her as he ran to the only other place she could be. The barn. He threw the door open. "Jane?" He listened. *Where could she have—*

He heard a sob and heaved a sigh of relief. She hadn't been kidnapped again. Thank god. But what was she doing, crying in the barn?

Matt followed her voice through the darkness and tripped.

"Shit." He slid his hands over the bike, trying to find his way around it. He couldn't see a damn thing.

He heard Jane drag the back door open, and the moonlight illuminated the floor enough for him to see. "Jane, wait, I can explain," he said, following her out the door. She made it through a couple rows of corn before he caught her arm and dragged her to a stop. "It is not what it looks like."

She shook her head and pushed him away frantically. "It's okay. You don't need to explain. I'm just… It's okay. Please, let me go."

Nope. That was definitely not happening. Not after he had just gotten her back.

He slid his hand from her arm to her fingers and squeezed them gently. "Let's get this straight right now. If I have my way, I am never letting you go again."

She tried to step away.

He pulled her into his chest and held her. "Do you hear me, Jane Moore? I love you and I—"

"I saw her!" she accused, cutting him off.

"Who?" He pushed her back just enough to see her face.

"Your fiancé?"

"Ex-fiancé. How?"

"Danny showed me! I-I saw a picture of you two together!"

Fuck.

"She showed you pictures of me and Katie? Why?"

"Well, she was showing me her and Tony, but…"

"But?"

"I saw she called you, Matt."

"And?"

She didn't answer.

"I'm going to let you go, and you're going to listen to what I have to say, and then this is all going to be resolved. Okay?"

She didn't answer.

He let her go, and she looked up at him through the darkness with tear-filled eyes. "How am I supposed to sleep with you now? Oh god. I can't…" She turned away and buried her face in her hands.

Matt studied her. So, she forgave him for abandoning her and the kids, but she was going to hold a missed call from Katie over his head? His stomach sank. Was this the conversation he'd been expecting all along? The one where she told him what he'd done was unforgivable and ended with her saying she never wanted to see him again?

"Jane… I didn't even answer it. What is this—" he said helplessly.

"It's not about that!" she interrupted. There was a sharp edge to her voice.

"What's it about then?" he asked slowly.

"Don't you get it, I saw her!" Jane yelled, throwing her arm in the direction of the house.

Her? Matt shook his head. "Katie?" Was she in town or something? "Where did you see her?"

Jane cast him an accusing glance, like he hadn't been listening. "Her *picture.* I *knew* it. I knew it would never work," she mumbled, pacing back and forth, sucking at the air like she couldn't breathe.

Matt had no idea what she was talking about. Had they been doing something illicit in the photo she saw?

"God. I'm so stupid."

"You are not stupid. But you are confusing the hell out of me right now."

"Don't," she warned.

"Don't what?"

"Why do you want me?"

He hadn't figured out the first part of their conversation, and now she was jumping tracks on him? "What in the hell is it about? Use your goddamned words, Jane."

"I can't sleep with you after you've slept with her!"

"What? Why not?"

"I've had *babies*." She turned away.

The way she said it made him pause. She said it like it was something disgusting, which didn't make sense, because he knew how much she loved her kids. Was there something about babies—

Matt found the missing piece.

This wasn't about Jane looking for an excuse to leave him or thinking he still wanted Katie. It was about her thinking—His relief turned to anger. "Are you fucking kidding me right now?" he demanded. "The reason you're pushing me away, and scaring me half to death is because you're worried I won't find you attractive when we make love?"

She said nothing as she stared out over the field, but her soft sob confirmed his suspicion.

"Are you out of your goddamn mind?" he yelled.

Jane's head swung around. "Don't act like—"

He stormed over to her. Her face glowed in the light of the moon that had just cleared the horizon, and her wet cheeks shimmered. "Like what?" he growled in her face.

She looked away. "You haven't seen me naked, Matt! I'm—I have stretch marks and I'm not pretty, d-down there," she whispered shamefully. "I don't look anything like her—"

She's lost her damn mind.

Matt held up his hand. "I'm gonna stop you right there because A, I *have* seen you naked, and because B, you know for a fact how much I want you. You've *felt* it, for Christ's sake."

Jane was silent for a moment. "When?" she asked quietly.

"When what?"

"Did you see me naked?"

"When you came to my house covered in blood. You don't remember?" he said, gently lifting her chin. Her eyes glistened with tears.

"No."

"I put you in the shower. There was blood… in your hair, and I didn't think you'd want the kids to see you… and after, the first couple days back at the cottage. You couldn't handle the bathroom on your—"

Jane dropped her head in her hands. "Oh, god."

"I love your body. I want—" he said, sliding his hand around her waist.

She pulled away. "There's no way—"

"There's no way, what?"

"How could you want me when you could have her? My body is—"

"Oh, really? So that's how it works, Jane?" Matt spat back. "That's all sex and intimacy is to you? Fucking a young, *perfect* body?"

Her eyes flew to his, wide with incredulity. *"What?"*

Matt knew he should stop, that she was still probably traumatized by what happened with Thomas and Sarah, but he couldn't. Jane had found his button and pushed it. "So, you'd fuck Diggs if you could instead of me because he's younger? Because he's *complete*?" he accused. He threw his arms in the air. "That's good to know, Jane. Really fucking good to know that you think people have to look perfect to be loved."

"What do you mean 'complete'?" she cried. "And you *are* perfect!" She jabbed her finger at him. "*That* is the problem!"

Matt stared at her, and she stared right back, their breath pooling in an angry cloud between them.

"You know exactly what I fucking mean," he seethed.

There was a long pause, then the lightbulb finally went on in Jane's blessedly honest eyes.

She doesn't care about your fucking—

She looked down. "Your foot?"

"Yes, my goddamned foot."

Her head whipped back up, eyes wide with surprise.

She gasped. "What? No, no, no. That's not the same thing at all. I don't care about—"

"And I don't care about…" He waved his arm in the air. "Whatever the fuck you are so worried about. Your body made two incredible kids that I love more than my own *life*." Matt's voice broke. "I love that about *you*."

She stared at him blankly.

"What did I do to make you think I wouldn't?"

She shook her head. "But—"

Matt threw up his arms, exasperated. "What—what are you talking about, Jane? Who do you think I am?"

She inhaled as if she was about to say something, then stopped.

"I know you are afraid of being hurt again. But damn it, so am I," he confessed.

He could practically hear the wheels grinding under her skull as she stared at him.

"I've never been in love before either," he continued. "Turns out, for as wonderful as it is, it's also fucking terrifying."

She didn't say anything.

"But you know what's worse?"

She shook her head.

He brushed a strand of hair out of her eyes and tucked it behind her ear. "Thinking you've lost it. When I thought you were dead—" Matt swallowed the memory, like he swallowed the ones from Afghanistan. His voice was rough as he continued. "I don't just want your body, Jane. For the first time in my life, I want the woman *inside* of it too. That is what love is. And I—"

Her hand snaked around his neck and her warm lips were desperate and salty with tears, as they pressed against his. She pulled his head against hers, curling her nails into his scalp. Jane deepened the kiss, flicking her tongue against his teeth, and he parted them willingly. Matt's hand slid under her hair and she made the most incredible noises in the back of her throat as his other hand explored her body.

He lifted her off the ground, and she wrapped her legs around his waist, refusing to break the kiss.

Matt's heart raced as he pulled his head back. "We are finishing this right now. I don't care if we have a fucking audience," he growled in her ear.

She nodded, placing hungry kisses down his neck, holding on with one hand while the other went from his jaw to his chest.

Stumbling through the corn, Matt carried her back into the barn. Jane kissed him and her hands continued to explore his body while he tried to find his way through the dark. She tumbled with him into the straw that lay in a big pile in one of the stalls.

He crawled on top of her, pulling his shirt over his head. "I have wanted you since the day you appeared in my bedroom," Matt growled in her ear. He kissed her jaw, turning her head and trailing kisses down her throat. "I have wanted to—" He yanked on her shirt, popping the buttons that held it closed.

She moaned beneath him. "Stop talking and do it," she whispered hoarsely against his hair.

She gasped as his hands found the strap of her bra and slid it down her arm.

They heard laughing, and Jane's head whipped toward the sounds.

"Stay with me," he said, turning her to face him. He claimed her mouth again. Matt slid his hand under her, and she arched her back as he unclasped her bra and pulled it down.

The gasping noise she made grew louder as his lips closed over her breast. He covered her mouth with his hand, worried that she would draw attention to them, and Tommy would come running.

Her mouth closed over his fingers and she sucked—Matt lost his concentration and practically exploded from his pants. He pulled her shirt back off her shoulders, drawing his hands down her sides to her jeans. He found the button, then the zipper. She lifted her hips as he practically tore the denim from her body.

She dragged his mouth back to hers as she fumbled with his pants. "How long have you been wanting to get into these—" he asked, smiling against her mouth.

"My whole life," she snapped, rolling him over and straddling him. "Now, shut up and help me get them off."

She finally managed the button, and her nails raked his hips as she jerked down his pants anxiously. The cool air and sharp spikes of straw against his ass made him gasp.

Matt felt her breath on his thigh. "Do you want me to…" she asked. He looked down and saw her shadow hovering over his groin. *Oh god, yes*. "Not now."

He pulled her up, running his hands over her naked hips. She went to slide over him, but he stopped her.

"Shit. I don't have a condom—" he began, remembering far too late.

She shoved herself down on top of him. As her warmth surrounded him, his eyes rolled back in his head. Matt groaned. She leaned over him and whispered, "I can't get pregnant."

Thank god for—

She began to move against him. The feel of her, the woman he loved, riding him almost sent him over the edge. He pushed the thought back. It was too soon. She wasn't ready yet. But the fire building inside him became an inferno, and he groaned again. It had been so long, so long since he had—*It never felt like this.* No, it hadn't.

Matt pushed himself up to sit, afraid he'd come if he didn't. He removed the rest of her clothes and slid his arms down her sides and over her ass as she wrapped her arms around his neck. *Oh god.* He felt the scar on her hip, as she continued to roll against him. *Oh god.* His hands moved over her warm skin. *Oh god.* His hands circled her waist, pulling her down more fully against him, and he found her breasts again with his mouth. Her movements came quicker. She was getting close. He could feel it. It brought him so much joy he would have cried if he wasn't so damn horny.

She pushed him back, and he fell into the sharp straw. She panted against his ear as she moved faster and faster against him. "I love—" she whispered. He felt himself coming undone and tried to slow her hips—

"Oh god—" she moaned as she contracted around him. Matt wrapped his arms around her and drove with every ounce of energy he had.

A deep, primal groan tore itself from her mouth. He grabbed her ass and drove again. She arched into him, and the sound came again. He felt her come undone, covered her cry with his mouth, then let himself fall over the edge with her.

Matt had always known he wasn't her first, but as he found his own pleasure, he was determined to be her last. Jane deserved love.

And nobody would ever love her more than he did. He gave one final thrust as she throbbed around him. This was love. She was love. And she was his. *Finally.*

She gasped as her hands landed in the straw on either side of his head. Matt pressed his head between her slick breasts and kissed her heaving chest. "God, I love you."

She quickly tried to move off him, but he didn't release her. "No, you don't." He pushed her hips back, and she collapsed against his chest. He could feel her heart thumping against his. He stroked her hair. She was used to a man who didn't love her. But he was not Thomas. "I told you. I love you, Jane." He kissed the top of her head.

"I–I love you too," she whispered.

He held her there until their hearts slowed. Keeping their legs entwined, Matt rolled her to the side.

He touched her cheek and felt like he'd died and gone to heaven as she sighed and nestled against him. He laid back and stared up into the dark. He had not felt this satisfied in a very long time. *Ever.* Ever. He felt her breath on his chest. If he was lucky, this was just the beginning. He didn't know if he could live the rest of his life with his heart being this full, but he was determined to find out. He noticed she was quiet and suddenly wondered if she was smiling contentedly or frowning in disappointment.

It did go a little quicker than...

"Shit." It was so damn dark, he couldn't tell. He turned toward her and brushed her hair back. He found her cheek, then felt for her mouth.

She pushed it away. "Oof. What are you—"

He tried again. "I'm trying to tell if you're smiling or—" His fingers found the corner of her upturned mouth and then her teeth.

"I am smiling, but I will bite you if you continue to poke at my face," Jane said. He could hear it then—the lazy satisfaction in her voice.

Whew. Okay, good. He smiled. "Won't be the first time I was bitten by a Moore woman today," he said, reminding himself to thank Bria tomorrow for staying asleep tonight.

Jane laughed as her fingers hesitantly explored his chest.

His smile widened. "If I would have told you… wait, what month is this?" he asked.

"September."

"If I would have told you four months ago that you'd be fucking the man of your dreams in a *barn* right now, what would you have told me?"

Jane rolled back into the hay beside him and laughed. "Oh god. I would have said–Wait, how do you know you're the man of my dreams?"

He propped himself up, and found her stomach, then hip in the dark, and rolled her back toward him. "Are you kidding me? It's written all over your face."

"You can't see my face," she said, propping herself up on his chest.

"I saw it the first day. When you looked at me like I was an underwear model. I have to admit—"

"God."

What?

"It was underwear god."

It was his turn to laugh. "Jesus, woman, you have to stop feeding my ego."

He shifted slightly and pulled her leg over his as he nuzzled her neck. She smelled like sex and lilies. His new favorite combination.

"Your ego is just fine," she said. "You have to admit what?"

"Huh?"

"You started to say something."

Matt tried to remember as she shivered and snuggled closer to him. He felt around for his shirt and draped it over her. "I felt like when I came back from Afghanistan, I was a different person. As if somehow, the man I'd been before that… died on that road with Tony. And a piece of me did."

He absently stroked her hair and gave a short laugh. "Technically, it was my foot," his voice sobered, "But... When I got back on the other one, everything had changed. I was no longer one of the 'guys' in the unit. The Army wanted to take care of me, but they didn't want me back, and I get it... You're only as strong as the man fighting beside you and I knew I was damaged goods, but..."

Jane hugged him.

"Everyone I knew treated me differently. They either treated me like I was helpless or they looked at me like I was some kind of hero. But I wasn't either of those things. I felt like an imposter in my own skin. And I just—I got lost."

Matt heard Tommy's little voice and then the roar of laughter from around the campfire.

"Then, one morning, I was asleep in my bed and this... crazy woman, *beautiful*"—he touched her cheek, and she laughed—"But really fucking crazy, storms into my room, scares the shit out of me, and then stares at me like..." His voice trailed off. "You didn't see it."

"See what? I don't understand."

"Everything you think is so damn clear in your eyes, Jane. I sometimes wonder if I'm a mind reader. And what you saw when you looked at me was... you made me feel like my old self. For the first time in two years, someone, *you*, looked at me like... Like I was still *me*. Like I was still *all* there. Like I was still that man I had been before that damn IED exploded."

She breathed in.

"No one else in my life, my parents, the guys, Katie, could see that man anymore. My foot made me someone different to them. But *you* saw him." He paused and smiled. "And then the way you practically drooled on the floor..."

She punched his chest. "Hey!"

"You rescued me, and lit me on fire in the same breath, Jane. I swear to god, in the most confusing ten minutes of my life you turned my entire world upside down. You challenged everything I thought I knew… I didn't even have my prosthetic on and I felt so vulnerable and you just–didn't even *notice*."

"You didn't seem vulnerable."

"Well, I was."

"I did see your foot," she confessed. "But…" her hand trailed over his chest.

"Sarah Connor," he said.

"Who?" Jane asked, lifting her head.

"I was your Underwear God, and you were my Sarah Connor."

"What are you talking—"

"Haven't you ever seen Terminator?"

"No."

Matt pressed himself up on his elbows and squinted at her through the darkness. "Seriously?"

"Nope."

"What's the matter with you?" he asked, and she shoved him.

"Nothing. I like Hallmark movies."

"*What?*" He made a gagging noise, and she smacked him again. He grinned. The truth was, he kind of liked Hallmark movies too. He used to watch them with his mom all the time. "Well, as soon as electricity becomes a thing again, we are watching it, so you can see how incredible—"

She made a noise, as if she didn't believe him.

Matt flipped her on her back as his hands roamed her body lustily. "Don't scoff at me, Jane Moore. You are one insanely brave" —He nuzzled her ear, breathing her in—"badass woman."

"Um, no. I—"

"I've played that video of you at the Veil over in my mind a hundred times," he breathed, nipping at her neck as she squirmed beneath him.

"What?"

"The way you went after them. You were incredible."

She pushed him back. "I was?"

He felt for her face and cupped it, propping himself up on his elbows, trying to think with his brain instead of his—

"Yes," he said, kissing her jaw. "You are still a terrible shot"—he trailed kisses down her neck—"but you are"—her breath hitched—"So. Fucking. Hot."

He breathed against her breast as she arched her back.

She moaned, and he slipped his hand between her legs, where she was more than ready for him.

"I had no idea…" she whispered breathlessly.

He paused. "No idea what?"

She pulled his mouth back to hers, and he tasted salt from her tears. "No idea that it could feel like this. It's so different—" she said against his lips.

Matt paused, not following. She had slept with Thomas—clearly. Then he understood. She had *never* been with someone who loved her. Not once. *Jesus Christ.*

He resumed stroking her, but this time he moved much slower.

"Wh-what are you doing? Don't stop," she practically begged as she raised her hips into his hand.

"I'm not stopping. I'm just slowing down."

"What? Why?"

"Because I want to make love to you, Jane Moore."

She bit his ear, and he yelped in surprise. "How about we make a rule—" she whispered, as she moved against his fingers.

"What kind of rule?" he asked against her mouth.

Jane pulled his hand away and rolled him on top of her, between her legs.

"We make love in the house." Her voice was rough. "And we fuck in the barn."

"I can get on board with that," he said with a smile.

Matt obliged her immediately, and they both groaned.

Jane's hands explored his body, and it wasn't long before they were gasping again in the darkness. He matched her pace as everything in the world but her body and his—and the straw that pricked his knees—disappeared.

Chapter Seventy-Four

Day 108 // 9:01 a.m

JANE WOKE up to the sound of laughter coming from downstairs. Sun streamed through the cracks in the curtains, as little motes of dust did cartwheels in the air. She turned and rubbed her eyes, noticing Matt's mussed side of the bed, and Bria's empty playpen.

Jane pulled her hair into a bun as she went to the bathroom to brush her teeth.

There was more laughing, and she heard Bria coo as she hurried down the steps.

Jane stopped in the doorway and stared. It was something straight out of a Norman Rockwell painting. Ed was sitting at the table holding Bria. Maddy was pouring coffee. Matt was wearing an *apron* and cooking eggs, while Diggs wrestled with the two boys in the middle of the floor.

"Good morning, Sunshine." Matt smiled at her as she made her way around the boys toward the thermos. She poured herself a cup of coffee as the boys squealed behind her. Matt spun her around and planted a kiss on her lips, before releasing her and going back to his eggs.

Jane glanced around shyly. She met Ed's smiling eyes. Across the room, Maddy winked at her. *They are happy for you.* She was happy for herself, too.

Matt turned off the stove and stood beside her as Diggs howled and flipped Tommy over his shoulder, dropping him gently to the floor.

"How do you feel?" he asked quietly, leaning toward her.

Jane smiled, taking in everyone in the room, then she turned, set her mug down on the counter, and leaned into him, sliding her arms around his neck. "I am *very* happy."

He smiled smugly, as he picked pieces of straw out of her hair. "And might I have had anything to do with that?"

She reached on her tiptoes and whispered in his ear. "Follow me upstairs and I'll—"

Not even waiting for her to finish, he slung her over his shoulder like a sack of flour and headed for the stairs.

"Hey, Farm! What about breakfast?" Diggs called with a laugh.

"We're switching it to brunch. Keep an eye on the kids," he called.

Jane laughed as he carried her up the stairs.

"Wait!" she shouted as he passed through the doorway. She grabbed the knob and pulled the door closed behind them.

Matt dumped her unceremoniously on the bed, and she fell into the rumpled covers. She stared as he pulled his shirt and the apron over his head. *Good lord.*

"I warned you. Don't start something you can't finish," he crawled on top of her, as she tugged at the waistband of his sweats.

"I'm not. And I was kind of digging the apron," she said with a wicked grin.

"And I'm digging the straw in your hair." Matt sat back, straddling her.

Jane pulled her shirt over her head and wiggled out of it.

"Oh god, you're even hotter the morning after," he breathed, sliding his hands up her sides.

Jane smiled. She couldn't agree more. He was magnificent.

"Talking like that is going to get you everywhere," she confessed, pulling him down on top of her.

"Good, because I want to go everywhere with you."

His lips met hers, and she yanked impatiently at his pants.

"Now hurry up. We've got about three minutes before one of the kids tries to barges in here—"

Matt pulled back with a frown. "You know, your pillow talk could use a little—"

She pressed her lips to his, slipping her tongue between his teeth. He moaned as he lifted her hips to his. "Make love to me now," she whispered against his mouth.

"Better…" he said, gathering her in his arms.

She pushed him back and slid out of her pajama bottoms, and quickly planted her legs on either side of him as she fumbled with the drawstring of his sweats, pulling them down past his hips. *Dear god.* She had most definitely not taken the time yesterday to fully appreciate *all* of Matthew. He was built like a Greek statue—she glanced down—except much more generously endowed. No wonder he was such a good lover.

Matt said something she didn't hear.

"What?" she asked distractedly.

His voice was laced with laughter. "I said, my eyes are up here."

Jane met them and her heart thumped like a hammer beneath her ribs as she laughed. *This* was love. Matt was love. And to think if it wasn't for the Veil—Who could have imagined that the end of the world would bring such a beautiful beginning?

She wrapped her legs around his waist and pulled him on top of her as she fell back onto the bed. "I'm not interested in your eyes right now. I'm only interested in your heart and your—"

He lifted her hips, and she moaned as his target hit her mark.

He pinned her hands on either side of her head and pressed his face between her breasts, kissing her chest. "You have both." He rolled against her. "Oh, god. I love—"

"Mom? Matt?" Tommy called from the hall. "Are you in there?"

Matt froze. "Shit," he whispered, whipping his head toward the door.

"What are you guys doing? Are you snuggling? Can I come—" He banged on the door.

"No!" Matt tried to jump up, but he was tangled in his pants. Jane grabbed his arm before he fell off the bed and pulled him back on top of her.

"Shh," she said, pressing her finger to her lips, trying not to smile.

"But—" Matt cast a worried glance toward the door as he dragged a throw pillow over his ass in an attempt to cover it.

Jane snorted with laughter.

"I hear you," Tommy accused. The doorknob turned.

"Oh, shit." Matt breathed. "What are we—"

Jane ran her palms over his short hair, admiring the terrified profile of her unlikely lover. How did she get so lucky?

"Rule number three of parenting," she said quietly, kissing his neck. "Always lock the door."

"It's locked?" His eyes went from the door to hers and back again, as the knob jiggled back and forth.

"Um-hm." Jane ran her tongue along his collarbone. He was salty and smelled like soap and smoke.

Matt exhaled as Maddy's voice urged Tommy back downstairs.

"What's rule number one?" he whispered.

"Never forget the diaper bag." she whispered back, nipping his shoulder.

Matt shuddered and closed his eyes. "Exactly how many rules—"

Jane shifted until they were aligned again and then pushed her hips into his.

Matt groaned as she cupped his face in her hands and turned his head back to the task at hand. "Stay with me, soldier."

He met her eyes, then slowly leaned down and kissed her. "Forever. I love you, Jane Moore."

Jane smiled and kissed him back.

"I love you too, Matt Patterson."

Afterword

Please Leave a Review
of
The Veil: Book One
DETROIT

If you enjoyed my story and characters, please help spread the word! Independently published authors rely on reviews to help their community of readers grow. If you have a minute, I'd be so grateful if you left a review by following the links below!

Amazon
Goodreads

Join my newsletter for exclusive news, sneak-peeks, and more!
Sign up for my newsletter and receive an exclusive novelette!

The Veil: A Mariette Christmas

After three months, Matt's petition for discharge has finally been approved, just in time for Christmas. Jane is excited for him to return to Mariette and the farm, but nervous too. The weekend he was home was blissful, but now reality was about to set in. Whether the Veil ever came down or not, they were a couple now, starting a new life together. At least that's what he said before he left. But three months is a long time, and now that they've already slept together, Jane is worried. Would the fire between them have faded? Or would it burn even brighter than before?

COMING IN 2022/ 2023
The Veil: Los Angeles
The Veil: Atlanta

ALSO COMING IN 2022-2023

Barn Song

For the first time in her life, Maggie follows her heart. Where it leads her is a place she never expected, with consequences she cannot fathom, and a love worth every ounce of heartache she'll endure.

Maggie Dubois, is a thirty-eight-year-old mother and divorcee living in the suburbs of Detroit. After her son leaves for college, she finds herself on a single's retreat in the country. Instead of finding love, she finds an abandoned, foreclosed farm. On a drunken whim, she buys it. In order to survive the new life she's chosen, and the *haunted* farm she has purchased, Maggie must step out of her comfort zone, out of the shadow of the roles she's spent most of her life hiding behind (mother, business owner, wife), and find the *woman* buried underneath.

Josephine And The Lighthouse Keeper

Josephine is about to forget the only two things she knows for sure, true love doesn't exist and ghosts are not real.

After washing ashore with no memory of her past, Josephine tends to her wounds and awaits rescue in a small abandoned cottage nestled beside a lighthouse. Abandoned until she meets Josh, the confusing, and captivating ghost of the former lighthouse keeper who challenges everything she thinks she knows about reality.

About the Author

J.N. Smith is a scientist, turned mother of two amazing kids, turned writer. She enjoys reading and writing stories that bring people of all walks of life together. Her hobbies include watching her kids play on the shores of the Great Lakes and running. She lives with her husband, kids, and three chickens, in rural Michigan. The Veil: Detroit is her first published novel.

Connect with J.N. Smith Today!

Hi! Thank you so much for reading. If you are interested in connecting with me, I'd love to hear from you. There are several ways you can reach me.

For amazing Great Lakes sunrises, my chickens, and other fun photos from my personal life, you can see what I'm up to on Instagram.

For book release info, and fun stuff like release dates/ book previews/ giveaways, and calls for alpha/beta/ARC readers check out my newsletter, blog, or Facebook Page!

jnsmithcontactme@gmail.com or on Twitter!

Let's connect!

Acknowledgments

I'd like to thank my alpha and beta and ARC readers (Logan, Shawna, Emily, Amanda, Carole, Jeanette, Keri and Melissa to name a few) for their amazing insights and thoughtful critique. All my FB groups: Moms Who Write, Romance Writers Support League, Trauma Fiction, you all are the best! Natalie Dale M.D. and her wonderful book A Writer's Guide to Medicine, your expertise is so appreciated. My formatters Kari Robinson at Fowler Inc. and Maya Monroe at Owlsome Author Services, you rock. My amazing cover designer, Esther van Bokhorst-Beentjes at Meraki Cover Design, it is always a joy working with you. Thanks to my developmental editor Morgan Perryman at Literary Ladies for sticking with me through some very extensive edits, and Maya Monroe for your keen eye and proofread. Last but certainly not least, I want to thank my husband and kids. You all had to give mom a *lot* of time to work to make this happen. I am so grateful, my loves. We did it. Space Needle woohoo! 😊

Made in the USA
Middletown, DE
09 November 2024

64202390R00269